To Jim.
Fortune aids the brave.

Also by Christopher Fowler

THE WATER ROOM
FULL DARK HOUSE

And coming soon from Bantam

TEN SECOND STAIRCASE

Seventy-Seven Clocks

CHRISTOPHER FOWLER

BANTAM BOOKS

SEVENTY-SEVEN CLOCKS
A Bantam Book / December 2005

Published by Bantam Dell
A Division of Random House, Inc.
New York, New York

ISBN-10:0-553-58715-3
ISBN-13:978-0-553-58715-9

Printed in the United States of America
Published simultaneously in Canada

www.bantamdell.com

OPM   10   9   8   7   6   5   4

Each culture produces the delinquency proper to it.
—*Kellow Chesney*

Judgement drunk, and brib'd to lose his way,
Winks hard, and talks of darkness at noon-day.
—*William Cowper*

Acknowledgments

Those with long memories will spot a couple of small anomalies concerning the year 1973. These are Mr Bryant's memories, of course, and are intended to be very slightly imperfect. Recalling the dark days of that miserable English winter, I'd like to thank those who brought this case back from darkness into light: my energetic and charming editor Kate Miciak, my suave U.S. agent Howard Morhaim, and my fearless British agent Mandy Little. Anyone familiar with the origin of my detectives' names will find this tale particularly apposite.

Visit www.christopherfowler.co.uk or email me at www.chris@cfowler.demon.co.uk.

Seventy-Seven Clocks

Prologue

'Talk me through *peculiar*.'

'What do you mean?' asked Arthur Bryant.

'I mean,' said the young biographer, 'why does this special police unit of yours only get the peculiar cases?'

'There, you can speak properly when you try,' said Bryant. 'I don't hold with slang.' He fiddled with his trouser turn-up and extracted the stem of his pipe. 'I've been looking for that all morning. When we were founded as an experimental unit, "peculiar" meant "particular," as in "specialized." But we started to attract certain types of case, ones which were potentially embarrassing for the government, ones nobody else could get to grips with. Before we knew it, we were dealing with goat-bothering bishops and transvestite Conservatives, not that the latter constitutes much of a peculiarity these days. We acquired the cases that proved too obtuse for traditional police methods.'

'Like the business with the Water Room.' The biographer had just finished recording Bryant's thoughts about this case because it had only just concluded, and everyone's memories of it were still fresh, even though they displayed *Rashomon*-style discrepancies. 'I don't suppose you've ever dealt with anything like that before.'

'Actually, you're wrong; there was another case involving water and art, although it was very different. And it happened much earlier, in 1973.' Bryant eyed the young man and wondered if he could get away with lighting his pipe in the small closed room.

'All right, we'll try that. What do you remember about it?' The biographer had given up attempting to keep his subject's recollections in chronological order. He switched on his recording equipment in hope.

'Not a lot,' warned Bryant. 'I wouldn't make a very good elephant.'

'I'm sorry?'

'Memory.' Bryant tapped the side of his bald head with a wrinkled forefinger. 'Or rather, lack of it. Information and experience. I mean, I have them both, but I'm for ever losing the former and forgetting the latter.'

'If you could try to think hard,' the biographer pleaded. His patience had been worn down over the last few weeks of interviews. He was beginning to regret embarking on his project: *Bryant and May: A Life of Peculiar Crime*. No one had written about London Peculiar Crimes Unit's legendary detective team before, and he could see why.

'1973, let's see.' Bryant raised his watery azure eyes to the ceiling and thought for a moment. 'It was the year we joined the Common Market, although I don't think anyone noticed. The Foreign Secretary, Sir Alec Douglas Hume, had drawn up paperwork for the agreement, and I recall it had to be accepted on the fifteenth-floor landing of the Common Market headquarters in Brussels, because there was no one left in the office. Luckily, the building's concierge remembered to run up a Union Jack. An inauspicious start to the year, I thought.' Bryant's memory veered between two points: hopelessly vague and absurdly detailed.

'I meant could you remember the case, not the year.

Do you have any details about the investigation?' asked the biographer.

'We had a terrible heat wave,' said Bryant, providing the answer to an entirely different question. 'President Nixon had started a second term, even though the Watergate investigation was well underway by then. There were still antiwar protests in Trafalgar Square. Spiro Agnew was done for tax evasion, wasn't he? And Gerald Ford started to fall over a lot. I'm pretty sure Elton John released *Goodbye Yellow Brick Road*, which had "Funeral For A Friend" and Princess Diana's memorial song "Candle In The Wind" on it, isn't that strange?' Bryant pursed his lips, thinking. 'Picasso died at ninety-one, a ripe old age. We were involved in the so-called Cod War with Iceland, over fishing rights. It was a dreadful year for haircuts. My partner John had gone in for sideburns, not a good idea at his age. I think the Bahamas got their independence, because I remember laughing when a canopy dropped on Prince Charles's head during the handover ceremony. The ceiling of the Shaftesbury Theatre fell in as well, and *Hair* had to close. Such a shame, I loved that show. "Let The Sun Shine In," what a nice sentiment. There was the IRA bombing campaign, of course, and strikes everywhere. The unions had more power in those days. We had blackouts, and everyone stockpiled candles. There was a fuel crisis. We all had to queue for petrol. Arab terrorists attacked an American jet at Rome airport, didn't they? And I bought some new shoes from Mr Byrite, but the soles came off.'

'Yes,' said the biographer, exasperated, 'but can you remember anything at all about the *crime*?'

'Well, of course. I kept it all here in my notebook.'

'You mean you had it written down all the time?' The biographer was aghast.

'Yes, but I transcribed it in a hieroglyphic code.' Bryant riffled through the pages, puzzled. 'I wrote everything in code back in those days. I don't know why I bothered; my handwriting's illegible. I numbered all the translation keys, and kept them together for safekeeping in my landlady's cow.'

'I'm sorry?'

'She kept a china cow in her kitchen cabinet. An Edwardian milk jug. Hardly an heirloom, but it served its purpose.'

'So you can decipher your notes?'

'No, she threw the cow away when the Queen Mother died, I have no idea why—wait, I do remember something. The newspapers referred to it as the case of the seventy-seven clocks. There was quite a fuss at the time. We got into terrible trouble. But you probably know all about that.'

'No, I don't,' the biographer admitted.

'You don't? Dear fellow, it was one of our most *truly* peculiar cases. Hardly seems possible, looking back. You have to remember that we had no computers in those days, no mobile phones. Most equipment was still mechanical. Typewriters and carbons and telexes—it slowed you down. The whole awful business could have been so easily avoided. Instead, there were frightful deaths, and I had to deal with that appalling family. I remember as if it was yesterday.' This was patently untrue, for Bryant remembered very little about yesterday.

'Why don't you tell me all about it?' the biographer suggested.

1 / Lights Out

She recognized the symptoms immediately.

The stipple of sweat in the small of her back. Ice-heat prickling her forehead. A sense of skittering panic in the pit of her stomach. As she walked faster, she thought: *This is absurd, it can't harm me*. But beneath her mind's voice ran another, dark and urgent. *It's not the night, but what waits in it.*

The sun had barely set, but the road ahead was indistinct in the fading light. She refused to consider what might be out there. *The Prince of Darkness is a gentleman*, hissed the voice, a phrase recalled from her schooldays. She had no intention of meeting the prince this evening, and quickened her pace, not daring to look back. The clouds of night opened like ink blossoming in water, threatening to overtake her. Blackbirds skirted the trees, taking measure of the rising wind.

For as long as she could remember, Jerry Gates had been terrified of the dark. The cause of this nyctophobia was beyond the reach of recollection: some early trauma at the top of the stairs, perhaps. Her mother accused her of having an overactive imagination; she made it sound like a harmful thing. Others would have seen misted fields on either side of the road, bare elm trees blurring in the dusk. Jerry could see demons swarming.

She tried to read her watch, but it was too dark. *Screw Nicholas and his country weekend*, she thought. If he'd shown some warning sign of his intentions, she would never have come in the first place. The man should have been wearing a red toggle, *Pull To Inflate Ego*, like a life jacket. His personality had changed the moment he'd realized that she wasn't going to bed with him.

Now it was almost dark, and she was stuck in the deserted Kent countryside on a Sunday night, without a car, in the freezing cold, with an irrational dread nipping at her, goading her into a trot. She was a town girl, used to city lights and cars and sirens and people. *It's so quiet around here you could hear a cow break wind five miles away. Where the hell is everybody?*

She thought back over the weekend, and the mistake she had made in accepting his invitation. On Saturday morning they had 'motored down to the lodge'—Nicholas's words, as if they were living in the roaring twenties—in the red MG that kept stalling, its roof folded back to admit the freezing country air.

The 'lodge,' a damp Victorian monstrosity situated on the far side of Dettling, had been designed in such a way that the watery warmth of the winter sun was excluded from it through every phase of the earth's rotation. The ground floor was surrounded by tall wet nettles, the brickwork obscured by reeking fungus. The rooms were virtually devoid of furniture. There was no central heating. Nicholas's family might have breeding, but they obviously had no money. The upkeep of such property, he'd explained, was staggering, and his parents preferred to stay in their Knightsbridge flat.

It didn't take her long to realize that Nicholas used the empty house for sex. One look at the bedrooms was all she needed to know. Adult magazines, wine bottles, mirrors, and candles, a lad's pathetic idea of what would please women. The blinds were drawn tight in all the upper rooms, and probably remained so throughout the year.

Her partner's dinner conversation had consisted of college tales laden with sexual innuendo. Nicholas was a different person on his home ground, all smirk and swagger, and she hated it. It was as if she had ceased to be his friend, and had become his quarry. The second time he brushed her breast while reaching for the wine, Jerry had announced that she was going to bed. No amount of persuasion could keep her downstairs.

She'd spent a sleepless night barricaded into her room, wearily listening to his pleas and insults through the door.

She had never looked forward to dawn so much in her life. Rising at the earliest opportunity, she had listened to the farming forecasts of incoming rain while frying herself bacon. Shortly after ten Nicholas had appeared in his dressing gown. The blackness of his mood barely allowed him to acknowledge her presence. The rest of the morning passed in gelid silence. Denied his conquest, Nicholas had regressed to a sullen schoolboy.

Her uppermost concern had been the problem of getting home. Trouble with the car—beneath which he passed most of the afternoon—prevented Nicholas from driving her to the station. Typically, there was no cab service operating in the area. Jerry found herself left alone to wander the rooms of the old farmhouse. As she examined the shelves of discoloured paperbacks, she grew more bored and upset. Finally she had collected her overnight bag and struck out across the field in the direction of the main road.

She would have been happy never to see him again, but he would be there the next morning, at work. They even shared the same damned counter. *Good judgement call, Jerry,* she thought. *You really know how to pick them.*

She studied the dim road, hoping to see a light, but there was nothing. There was no rising moon. The darkness was nearly complete. The thought punched the air from her chest.

She began to run along the narrow lane as a downpour started. The rain added to her deepening panic. Bare branches entwined overhead like the spiny legs of insects. The trees and hedgerows were filled with scampering black imps that dropped with the rain and tried to catch her, but she ran on, hugging the curve in the road.

The dark drew forth stalking men. They lay in wait for her, appearing in clumps of wet leaves, unfolding their fingers like scythes. They could not survive in London, where there was always light even in the darkest hour, but here in the black woods and meadows they could pursue their pleasures without restraint...

Then she saw the light of the telephone box.

A red one, familiar as an old friend, with rectangular windows and directories and a buttery lightbulb that glowed through the torrent. She smothered her crawling fears and concentrated on the sanctuary ahead. Wrenching back the door on its leather straps, she threw herself inside.

Relief, afforded by the single bare lightbulb, washed over her, and she sank to her knees, filling the booth with angry sobs, furious at her own weakness. Everything had gone wrong. She had intended to use the weekend as a protest. Instead of attending some horrible charity dinner at Claridges with her parents, instead of keeping an appointment with her therapist, she had taken off for a weekend with a man she barely knew. She might even have had sex with Nicholas if he'd proved to be a halfway decent human being. She'd only wanted to show everyone that she had a mind of her own, but even carrying out this simple task had been beyond her.

As the rain pounded the roof, she drew the knees of her fringed jeans up beneath her chin and wept, crouching low in the fetid booth, protected from surrounding blackness as hostile as the surface of an alien planet.

She remained trapped in the haven of light, not daring to move, until a passing motorist found her over two hours later.

2 / Seizure

Daily Telegraph, Monday 6 December 1973

MONDAY'S OUTLOOK

The fine sunny spells of the last few days are set to end as we bid farewell to the capital's unseasonably clear skies. Tumbling temperatures and strong northerly winds are on their way, bringing with them moderate to heavy rain. This will affect all parts of the Greater London area by nightfall. No one in London should ever be surprised by the weather, but this year we can expect winter to arrive with a vengeance.

The elderly lawyer dropped his newspaper on to the marble surface of the washroom counter. *Nothing in the business section about the Japanese bid*, he thought. *At least that's something to be thankful for*. Besides, he had something else on his mind. He was still annoyed about his hotel room. But there was no way he could pursue the matter further. He had complained as much as he dared; to say any more would risk drawing attention to himself.

He filled the sink with fiercely heated water and splashed some on his face. What a business; never in all his years of dealing with the family had he heard of such a thing. He stared back at himself from red-rimmed eyes. He needed a good night's sleep. He could do with being ten years younger, too. He was tired of doing the dirty work for others. His profession had once been a noble one.

He dried his hands on a thick cotton towel. A reflected movement in one of the stalls turned him from the basins. One of the cubicles was occupied. As he watched, the toilet door swung half open. The figure behind it remained in shadow, silently watching.

The lawyer stepped to one side, trying to see the face. The door swung slowly wide until it banged against the tiled wall.

He tried to raise the alarm, but the wretched cloth-wrapped creature ran forward and raised his hands, pressing them over the lawyer's face.

After that there was nothing.

Nothing at all.

Then it was a second, a minute, an hour later.

He had no idea how much time had passed, but he was still in the washroom, lying by the basins, feeling dizzy. He checked his ornate gold wristwatch, but had trouble focusing. He had a terrible headache. His neck hurt. The washroom was empty. The cubicles stood with their doors wide, the silence broken only by a dripping tap. He needed to take a short nap. Unable to comprehend what had happened, Maximillian Jacob pulled himself up, picked up his newspaper and weaved his way back to the lobby of the Savoy Hotel. He located a deep armchair in a quiet corner, where he could rest without being disturbed.

Jerry Gates checked her watch again and frowned. Five to six. Another five minutes until the evening receptionist was due to take over. Through the foyer doors she watched the turning taxis' beams fragmenting through needles of rain. The street outside the Savoy was the only one in London where they drove on the other side of the road; everything about the hotel was quirky in some way.

It still hurt to think about last night, but she was determined not to let the pain surface. It had been past midnight when she had finally reached home. She had never seen her parents so angry. Thankfully, Nicholas had ignored her for most of today, except for an acid comment about her tired appearance.

The hotel was unusually quiet for a Monday afternoon, but the lull would not last long. Many of the three hundred rooms above their heads were being readied for Common Market delegates. They were arriving to attend a conference scheduled to start in Downing Street a week from today, on 13 December. Speakers had been invited from throughout the Commonwealth, too. The staff had been briefed on correct modes of address.

For the moment, though, the lobby was a haven of peace. A disoriented Italian family stood with maps folded under their arms like weapons, waiting for the rain to stop before venturing out in new Burberry raincoats. Someone was dozing beneath a newspaper in one of the armchairs near the entrance to the American Bar. Nicholas was dealing with a pair of regular patrons, two querulous Spanish women who had been visiting the hotel together for the past thirty years. For many guests the Savoy was a second home rather than a hotel, idiosyncratic and personalized in its handling of their requests, famed for its attention to detail.

Although she had joined the hotel just a few weeks ago, Jerry had been made to feel like a member of an exclusive, if rather remote, family. Her mother had been upset when she announced her intention of taking the job. Gwen and Jack Gates had long expected her to apply for a position in the family business. For their only daughter to have chosen her own employment—and as a *menial*—was unthinkable. Jerry scowled at the thought as she gathered up her belongings. Let them think whatever they liked. She was enjoying her newfound anonymity.

'You're in a rush,' observed Nicholas. 'Got a hot date?' There was no hint of sarcasm in his voice, but she knew better than to trust him now.

'Chance would be a fine thing.' She threw a book into her backpack and zipped it up. 'I've got a figure-drawing class.'

'Of course, it's none of my business.' Nicholas checked his blond hair in the mottled lobby mirrors. 'If you're really interested in studying art, why are you working here?'

'You're right,' Jerry agreed. 'It's none of your business.' She noticed now that Nicholas had thin hairy wrists, a bony throat, and sprouting nostrils. He was a dim snob who used his public-school accent to ward off undesirables like a vampire hunter with a crucifix. How could she not have seen this before? His habit of joking whenever women were mentioned should have tipped her off to some kind of sexual inadequacy. *Thank God I didn't unlock the bedroom door*, she decided. Hopefully, their weekend encounter would never be mentioned again. Men like Nicholas were concerned about saving face.

'Wait a minute.' Nicholas pointed at the revolving door. The porter was carrying through several pieces of ancient, scuffed luggage. 'Someone's checking in. You may as well make it your last job tonight.'

'Thanks a lot.' She dropped her bag on to a chair and returned to the counter. The man walking across the carpet towards her was tall, broad, and black. His skin seemed an extension of his bronzed leather jacket. Dreadlocks fell in tightly woven strands between his shoulderblades, knotted in complex patterns, like the mane of a lion. She had seen Afros, but nothing like this. Standing amid a jumble of well-traveled bags, he looked like a particularly confrontational piece of modern sculpture. *He's overdoing the rock-opera look*, she thought, vaguely irritated.

'Hullo, I'm checking in—Joseph Herrick.' The voice was softly seasoned with an American accent. As she confirmed the new guest's reservation and assigned him one of the larger suites she averted her eyes, performing the prime Savoy hospitality function of never appearing surprised. She was, though.

The elderly Spanish women stared at the newcomer's heavy motorcycle boots in distaste, lowering their gaze to the ground and up again as if expecting someone to come and remove him.

Jerry felt like coming to Mr Herrick's defence. After accepting his registration form she found herself speaking with rather more volume than necessary. 'Here is your suite key, Sir. If I can do anything to make your stay more comfortable, please don't hesitate to call me.'

'The personal touch, I like that,' he replied with a broad grin. 'Good evening, ladies.' He smiled politely at the disapproving couple and clattered across the lobby in time to pull the first of his cases back from the porter.

'I hate to take your job, man, but you'd better let me have those.' He was loud and friendly as he began hefting the bag straps on to his arms. 'There's stuff in here I don't trust to anyone else, no disrespect to you, Sir.'

His cheerful attitude made her smile. The English crept into smart hotels as if entering cathedrals. They queried their bills in whispers, slinking to their rooms like criminals. Handsome young black men didn't stay at the Savoy. It was a time when England was still running *The Black And White Minstrel Show* on prime-time TV. Liberation remained on album covers and onstage at *Hair*.

'You'd better check the validity of his reservation,' Nicholas told her. 'I mean, this is the Savoy. The other guests don't want to see . . .' he searched for the right phrase '. . . *people like him* . . . hanging around our lobby.'

'I don't see how you can judge someone so quickly.'

'He's probably in that awful rock musical,' Nicholas sniffed. 'Swaggering about in bright clothes just shows a lack of breeding.'

'Funny, I always thought that about the gold-covered white women one sees in Knightsbridge,' she replied. Before the weekend, Nicholas had kept his prejudices hidden. 'I'm running late. I'll see you tomorrow.'

She was returning from the staff room in her Afghan coat when she noticed the sleeping man again. He'd been sprawled in a corner of the lobby with a *Daily Telegraph* over his face for quite a while now. As she passed Nicholas, she pointed at the recumbent figure. 'You'd better wake him up.'

'You're nearer. You do it.'

'I already told you, I'm late.'

Sighing, she crossed to the chair and gently removed the newspaper from their guest. The unveiled face was florid and middle-aged. A flap of grey hair leaned back from the man's head like a raised gull's wing. She recognized the sleeper as a guest who had checked into the hotel on Friday. She tapped him gently on the shoulder. Overhead, the lights in the central chandelier flickered, momentarily dimming the room.

'Mr Jacob, time to wake up...'

Jacob's lips rattled out a furious blast of air and he sat sharply upright.

'What the devil—?' His eyes bulged, his throat distending as he lurched forward in his seat. For a moment Jerry thought she had startled the guest in the middle of a dream. Now she saw that he was choking. Before she could take any action, he jack-knifed forward, spluttering and spraying a fine crimson mist from between his teeth.

She saw Nicholas reaching for a telephone as she tried to hold the agitated guest down in his seat.

'Nicholas, come and give me a hand, he's having some kind of seizure!'

The body beneath her was bucking in the grip of violent convulsions. Jacob's left foot shot out and cracked her painfully on the shin. Together they fell to the floor, landing hard on their knees just as Nicholas arrived at their side.

'What's wrong with him?' he asked, gingerly attempting to grab an arm.

'How should I know? He could be an epileptic. Did you get through?'

'The house doctor's line is busy.'

Jacob's eyes had rolled up in their sockets so that only the whites showed. A glittering knot of blood hung from his chin. Jerry wasn't sure of the procedure in such a situation. With her knees planted on his twisting shoulders, she grabbed his tie and wadded it into his mouth to prevent him from biting his tongue. She felt inside his jacket and pulled out a wallet, flicking it open.

'What are you doing?' yelled Nicholas.

'I'm looking for a card that says he has a medical condition.'

Jacob's limbs suddenly dropped and he became heavy, sliding flat on to the floor, taking Jerry down with him.

There followed a moment of absolute stillness, as if the man's spirit was wrenching free from his body. With a final bark he emptied the contents of his stomach, flooding the intricately patterned carpet.

Jerry looked from the fleshy corpse in her embrace to the benign gold cherubs in the ceiling above. She had felt the man die. As the realization hit her, a wind began to rush in her ears and the room distanced itself, telescoping away as the world fled to darkness.

3 / Vandalism

London hides its secrets well.

Beneath the damp grey veil of a winter's afternoon, the city's interior life unwound as brightly as ever, and the rituals interred within the heavy stone buildings remained as immutable as the bricks themselves. London still bore the stamps of an empire fallen from grace—its trampled grandeur, its obduracy—and, sometimes, its violence.

Having survived another day of rummaging through handbags without discovering a single gun, knife, or IRA bomb, the security guards at the entrance to the National Gallery were about to console themselves with a strong cup of tea.

George Stokes checked his silver pocket watch, a memento of thirty years' loyal service, then turned to his colleague. 'Twenty to six,' he said. 'In another ten minutes you can nip up and ring the bell. There won't be anyone else coming in now.'

'Are you sure, George?' asked the other guard. 'I make it nearly a quarter to.'

Outside, bitter December rain had begun to bluster around an almost deserted Trafalgar Square. Flumes from the great fountains spattered over the base of the towering Norwegian Christmas pine that had been erected in the piazza's centre. The tree stood unlit, its uppermost branches twisting in the wind.

The roiling, bruised sky distended over the gallery, absorbing all reflected light. The gallery was emptying out, its patrons glancing up through the doors with their umbrellas unfurled, preparing to brave the night.

As the two guards compared timepieces, the entrance door was pushed inwards and a figure appeared, carrying in a billow of rain.

'Pelting down out there,' said Mr Stokes, addressing the dripping figure. 'I'm afraid we're closing in a few minutes, Sir.'

'Time enough for what I have in mind.'

The guard shrugged. Office workers sometimes stopped by on their way home to seek solace in a single favourite painting. He took a good look at the man standing before him, and his brow furrowed in suspicion. 'Do you mind if I check inside your bag?' he asked.

There is a mosaic set in the floor of the National Gallery which highlights many emotional concepts: COMPASSION, WONDER, CURIOSITY, COMPROMISE, DEFIANCE, HUMOUR, LUCIDITY and FOLLY are engraved among them. Bill Wentworth was beginning to wonder if these qualities only existed in the flooring. He tugged down the peak of his cap, stepping back to allow a party of Japanese schoolchildren to pass. The excitement of the job lay in the paintings themselves, not in the inquiries of the general public. His fingertips brushed the maroon linen wall of the gallery as he walked. He had entered Room 3 (Germany and the Netherlands). Dark rains drifted against the angled skylights in the corridor beyond.

It was Wentworth's first day as a gallery warden, and he had been looking forward to answering visitors' questions. He'd seen the job as a chance to finally use his art-history training.

'You can forget that,' his superior, Mr Stokes, had warned during their morning tea break together. 'Times have changed. Few people ask about the Raphael or the Titian or the Rembrandt any more. They just want pointing to the toilet or the French Impressionists. They're not interested in the older stuff because it takes more understanding.'

Stokes was a fan of the old Italian schools. He preferred a Tintoretto to a Turner any day of the week, and was happy to tell you so.

Bill Wentworth walked slowly about the room, waiting for the last few members of the public to depart. The only sound was the squeak of his shoes on polished wood and the drumming of the torrent on the glass above. The new warden paused before an arrangement of Vermeers, marveling at the way in which the painter had captured these small, still moments in the lives of ordinary people, peaceful figures in light and shadow, opening letters, sweeping their houses, cool and calm and timeless.

'The public are no problem,' Stokes had informed him. 'Soon you won't even notice them. But the paintings take on a life of their own.' He had gestured at the walls surrounding them. 'You start noticing things you never saw before. Little details in the pictures, always something new to catch the eye. They'll bother and intrigue you, and the subjects will make you care for them. Just as well, because there's bugger-all else to do around here.'

'Surely it can't be that dull,' Wentworth had said, growing despondent.

Stokes had thoughtfully sucked his moustache. 'I know how to say "Don't touch that, Sonny" in seventeen languages. Do you find that exciting?'

Wentworth was still considering their conversation when Stokes himself came puffing in from the main entrance to the gallery, flushed and flustered.

'Mr Wentworth, have you seen him?'

'Who's that, Mr Stokes?'

'The old bloke!'

'Nobody's been through here, as you can see.' Wentworth gestured about him. There was only one exit to the exhibition room, and that led back to the main stairwell.

'But he must have passed this way!'

'What did he look like?'

Stokes paused to regain his breath. 'Tall, overweight, with mutton-chop whiskers. Heavy tweed cape and a funny hat—sort of stovepipe, like an Edwardian gentleman. Carrying a carpetbag.'

For a moment Wentworth wondered if his boss was suffering a side effect of spending so much time surrounded by the past. 'What's he supposed to have done?' he asked.

'I tried to search his bag and he shoved past me,' explained Stokes. 'He ran up the steps and disappeared before I could make after him. My war wound.'

'I'll help you look.'

The guards marched from the room and headed for the circular stone stairs that led to the lower-floor galleries. They had just reached Room 14 (French Painting Before 1800) when a breathless young attendant slid to a stop beside them.

'We've just seen him on the far side of the Sunley Room,' he shouted.

'Going in which direction?'

'Away from us.'

'Then he's heading for the British Rooms,' replied

Stokes. 'We can cut him off by going through forty-four and forty-five.'

Aware of the fragile safety of their treasure house, the three wardens galloped through the empty halls in pursuit. As they raced across a side corridor they mistook a member of the public for their quarry and grabbed his arms from either side, causing him to slide over on the floor. The scruffy, balding man rose indignantly and hauled his trailing sepia scarf about him as his attackers apologized, set him on a bench, and thundered on. At the corner of the next room the guards were met by a startled fourth.

'He's heading for—'

'The new exhibition,' called Stokes. 'We know.'

The British Artists' section was housed in a series of chambers leading from a central octagon. Here the walls were filled with imposing portraits of forgotten English landowners. Tilted to the public eye and ornately framed in gold, they were overlooked by a splendid glass dome through which rain glittered in a shower of dark diamonds. Wentworth had no time to appreciate this pleasing theatrical effect, however. He had just spotted their suspect standing in the room ahead.

The four guards ground to a halt at the entrance to Room 37.

The Edwardian gentleman was standing by the far wall with the carpetbag at his feet, and a cane tucked beneath his arm, looking for all the world as if he had just stepped down from one of the paintings at his back. He ignored them, bobbing his head from side to side as his eyes searched the room. When he found what he was looking for, he reached down into his bag.

'Stop right there!' called Wentworth, throwing out an arm. The other attendants crowded in behind him. They had never thought they might actually have to guard a painting.

For a moment, nobody moved.

The Edwardian gentleman slowly raised his head and turned his attention to his pursuers, as if noticing them for the first time. His eyes glared beneath the brim of his tall hat.

'Leave me be and none of you shall suffer,' he said, low menace sharpening his voice. 'I must warn you that I am armed.'

'Did you press the alarm?' whispered Stokes to one of the others.

'Yes, Sir,' the boy whispered back. 'Soon as he started running.'

'Then we must keep him from harming anything until the police get here.'

Wentworth could hardly see how. The most lethal item he had on him was a plastic comb. He knew none of the others was likely to be packing a pistol. For want of a better course of action, all four stood watching as the old man stooped and reached inside his carpet bag.

As soon as Wentworth realized what he was about to do, he started out across the floor toward the far side of the chamber, but he had not given himself enough time to prevent disaster.

For now the gentleman's arms were free of the bag and rising fast with a jar held firmly in his right hand, the broad rubber stopper being deftly removed by the fingers of the left, and the contents of the glass were flying through the air, the liquid splashing across one of the canvases, searing varnish and paint and filling the air with the stinging smell of acid. As Wentworth dived to the floor and slid hard into a wall, the vandal hurled the emptied jar at him. The glass shattered noisily at his side.

Now the other wardens were running past his head, and further footfalls came from one of the distant halls. Wentworth heard a shout and then a shot, both small and sharp. Stokes fell heavily beside him, blood gushing from his nose. Acid was pooling along the base of the skirting board, crackling with acridity, the fumes burning Wentworth's eyes. He realized that it was no longer safe to lie still, and scrambled to his feet.

The attendants were in disarray. Stokes was unconscious. Another appeared to have been shot. One of the paintings was dripping and smouldering. The police had arrived and were shouting into their handsets. Of the Edwardian gentleman there was no sign at all.

'Excuse me, please.'

The scruffy man they had accidentally assaulted in the side corridor was tapping a policeman on the shoulder.

'I said *excuse me*.'

The constable turned around and began to push the scruffy man back toward the chamber's entrance. 'No members of the public allowed in here,' he said, holding his arms wide.

'I am most certainly not a member of the public,' said the man, hiking his endless scarf about his neck like the coils of a particularly drab snake. 'I'm Detective Inspector Arthur Bryant, and you've just allowed your criminal to escape.'

George Stokes stared unhappily from the tall windows like a man preparing to face the scaffold. He was obviously concerned for the future security of his position.

Arthur Bryant crossed the floor of the gloomy staffroom and stood beside him. 'How's the nose?' he asked.

'A bit bruised,' said Stokes, gingerly touching his tissue-filled nostril. 'The poor lad, though. Fancy being shot at.'

'He'll be fine. The bullet just nicked the top of his arm. Went on to make a nasty little hole in a still life by Peter de Wint.'

'You don't understand, Mr Bryant,' said Stokes, watching the rain sweep across the deserted square below. 'We're the custodians of the treasures of the empire. The paintings housed here form part of the very fabric of our heritage. They are entrusted to us, and we have failed to maintain that trust.'

'Human beings are fallible creatures, Mr Stokes. We never attain the perfection of those exquisite likenesses in the gallery. This sort of vandalism has occurred before, hasn't it?' Bryant shucked off his sepia scarf and draped it over a chair. He turned back to the steaming mugs on the table and withdrew a silver hip flask from his overcoat, pouring a little cherry brandy into each.

The police were clearing away the mess downstairs, and several agitated members of the board were already waiting to speak to their head guard. Bryant wanted to interview Stokes while the guard's memory was fresh, before the recollection of the event had hardened into a much-repeated statement.

'Yes, it has happened before. The da Vinci *Madonna* was damaged. There have been other small acts of violence toward the paintings.' Stokes shook his head in bewilderment. 'The people who do these things must be deranged.'

'And do you think this gentleman was deranged?'

Stokes thought for a moment, turning from the window. 'No, actually I don't.'

'Why not? You say he had an odd manner of speaking.'

'His speech was archaic. He looked and sounded like a proper old gentleman. Turn of the century. Funny sort of an affectation to have in this day and age.'

Bryant pulled out a chair and they sat at the table. The detective made unobtrusive notes while the guard sipped his laced tea. 'Was there something else apart from his speech that made you think of him as Edwardian?'

'You must have glimpsed him yourself, Sir. His clothes were about seventy years out of date. When he first came in, he reminded me of someone.'

'Who?'

'Oh, nobody still alive. He looked like the painter John Ruskin. Because of the whiskers, you see.'

'And he seemed to know his way around the building?'

'He must have been familiar with the floor layout, because there's only one exit from that side of the gallery and he ran towards it immediately after the attack. You just have to go through two rooms, thirty-four and forty-one, before reaching the stairs that lead down to one of the exits.'

'You don't think his act was one of arbitrary vandalism? He couldn't have been equally happy, say, knocking the head from a statue?'

'Oh, no, certainly not. I had the feeling he knew exactly where he was heading.'

'Which was where?'

'Toward the new Pre-Raphaelite exhibition in the British Rooms. He was looking for a specific painting in the exhibition. The acid went all over one picture.'

'Which one?'

'*The Favourites of the Emperor Honorius* by John William Waterhouse. It's quite a large canvas, but he covered the whole thing.'

'I don't know much about restoring,' said Bryant. 'Do you think they'll be able to save it?'

'It depends on the strength and type of acid used, I imagine. From an international point of view, this is very embarrassing for us, Mr Bryant,' said the warden. 'Many of the paintings in the show are on loan from the Commonwealth.'

'Including the one that was attacked?'

Stokes nodded miserably.

'Where had it come from?'

'A gallery in Southern Australia. Adelaide, I believe.'

'The painting is insured, though.'

'That's not the point.' Stokes drained his mug and set it down. 'It's not a particularly important picture, but even so it's quite irreplaceable. If it can't be saved, Mr Bryant, a piece of history has been eradicated for ever.'

4 / Liquefaction

The stalking man halts dead in his tracks, and I rush up behind him at such a terrible speed that I can't stop, and the future turns, and the vile beast is at once both familiar and strange, horrific and inevitable. My mouth stretches wide to scream, but he reaches out and fills the betraying cavity with his hand, and I can't breathe. His fingers reach into my throat, nails tearing at my mouth, reaching deeper and deeper towards my soul, and I know that I will die in a matter of seconds. . . .

Her scream was muffled by the bedclothes knotting themselves around her. Jerry fought her way free and jumped from the sweat-soaked bed. She fell to the floor and lay naked on the carpet, waiting for her heartbeat to return to normal.

She had never seen anyone die before. Was it any surprise she was having nightmares? He was supposed to have suffered a heart attack. But why had there been so much blood? The man was old enough to die, perhaps his time had come—and yet—to be confronted with such sheer, overpowering finality. Her childhood had passed in the quiet frustration of being seen and not heard, in the patient wait for a chance to show the world what she could do—and to be confronted with mortality now, to be gripped by a man in the very act of leaving the world, what could be a more terrible omen for the future?

The dream was an old one in a new guise. As she

angrily thumped the pillows, determined to blot out visions of darkness, she knew that something had awoken inside her.

The therapist would want to know why she had missed her last session; he'd be waiting to report her latest imagined ailment back to Gwen. At least lying to him gave her something to look forward to.

Daily Telegraph, Tuesday 7 December 1973

VANDALIZED PAINTING
SPARKS SECURITY ROW

The National Gallery is at the centre of an escalating international row following an incident yesterday afternoon when a valuable artwork was vandalized beyond repair. The painting, *The Favourites of the Emperor Honorius*, by the Victorian artist John William Waterhouse features seven Roman dignitaries, and was one of several pictures on loan from the Australian government for the largest exhibition of Pre-Raphaelite art assembled in England this century.

The Australian minister for the arts, David Carreras, has lambasted the National Gallery for its 'shoddy and inadequate' security arrangements, and is said to be considering legal action against the British government.

As this year's Commonwealth Congress is expected to examine new European rulings on the movement of national treasures between member countries, Mr Carrera's rebuke could prove to be an ill-timed embarrassment for the government. In the light of the vandalism, the Greek government is expected to renew its campaign for the return of the Elgin marbles.

Leslie Faraday, the newly appointed junior arts

minister, is now likely to head an inquiry into the gallery's security arrangements. Faraday's appointment is a highly controversial one. It is only two weeks since he allowed New York's Museum of Modern Art to purchase Andy Warhol's *Coca-Cola Bottle* from the Tate Gallery, describing the sale as 'good riddance to bad rubbish.'

The offices of North London's Peculiar Crimes Unit had finally been settled directly above the red-tiled arches of Mornington Crescent Tube station. After two months the space was still cramped and overflowing with packing crates, most of which were filled with bulky pieces of technical equipment.

The unit had left its old home in Bow Street (where it had been housed for more than thirty years) to devote more time to its specialized investigations away from the distractions of round-the-clock petty crime. Set up by a far-sighted government during the war, the PCU remained the last resort for unclassifiable and sensitive cases. Police stations like Bow Street and West End Central were occupied by the daily churn of ordinary criminal offences, crowded with colleagues asking for advice and reports waiting to be filed. Too much procedural paperwork, too little room to think. One day, the detectives hoped, the Peculiar Crimes Unit would be freed from the Met's interference in their business, but that time was still a long way off.

Here, above a busy junction pulsing with traffic, it would at least be possible to concentrate on complex cases serially, with less interference and interruption. Only time would tell whether the new system worked or not. Failure would prove costly for police and public alike.

A series of piercing horn blasts caused John May to tip his chair forward and watch from the arched window as, two floors below, another black diplomatic limousine was escorted through a red traffic light by police motorcycles. He'd read that Common Market delegates were gathering in London for next week's conference. That meant the usual abuse of diplomatic immunity privileges, traffic accidents and shoplifting charges quietly folded away. Momentarily distracted, he missed what Oswald Finch was saying.

'Repeat that?' he asked, pressing the receiver closer to his ear.

'. . . Vascular dilation to an extraordinary degree, and tissue lesions you could poke your fingers through . . .'

'Wait, backtrack a minute, Oswald, you're losing me.'

There was a sigh of impatience on the other end of the line. 'Really, John, it would be better if you came and saw this for yourself. He's laid out right in front of me. It's absolutely incredible.'

'Oswald, do I absolutely have to?' John grimly recalled the stench of chemicals and cheap aftershave that always accompanied his meetings with the pathologist. Finch was a brilliant man, but possessed the same graveyard enthusiasm for his job that troubled children had for picking insects apart. His was not just a career chosen by individuals for whom death holds no terror. It was chosen because he really, *really* liked it.

'You know, autopsies usually only take a couple of hours, but so far I've spent over seven on this one. It's playing havoc with my timesheet. You really should see what I'm seeing, John.'

'All right. Give me fifteen minutes.' May replaced the receiver, checked the baleful sky beyond the window, and reached for his raincoat. He needed to find his partner, and he had a good idea where to look.

The strength of John May's surprisingly handsome features, the straightness of his spine, and the clarity of his eyes commanded immediate attention. Those unfamiliar with his profession would have marked him for a corporate head, a natural leader. He continued to dress fashionably, although it was difficult in a London currently enslaved by cheap Lord John suits with foot-wide lapels, and although his immaculately groomed mane showed a few grey flecks he continued to enjoy the fascinations of his youth, those fascinations being, in no particular order: police investigations, gadgets, women, classic cars, television (all three channels), and science fiction. Members of what were once called The Fair Sex still featured in John May's life; he would always turn to appreciate an attractive face or figure, and would be flattered to find his attention still reciprocated. The minefield of modern sexual politics lay waiting in the future.

The girl standing behind the multicoloured counter of the Brasilia Coffee House smiled when she saw him enter. 'If you're looking for Arthur, he's back there,' she told May, pointing to the rear of the steamy café. 'He's very moody this morning. It's about time you did something to cheer him up.'

'All right—I get the hint.' He threaded his way to the back of the room.

May's partner could not have been more unlike himself. Arthur Bryant was three years his senior and considerably more shopworn. Perched on a counter stool, he looked like a jumble sale on a stick. He seemed shrunken within a voluminous ill-fitting raincoat picked out by his landlady; a small balding man with no time for the urgency of the modern world. Bryant was independent to the point of vexation and individual to the level of eccentricity. While his partner embraced the latest police technology, he proudly resisted it. He was a literate and secretive loner, whose mind operated—when it found something worthy of its attention—in tangential leaps that bordered on the surreal.

It should have irritated Bryant that his partner was so gregarious and popular. May was a methodical worker who grounded his cases in thorough research. For all they had in common, their friendship should not have worked at all. They made a rather ridiculous couple, but then, they were little concerned with orthodoxy.

Although they had grown a little more like each other with the passing years, it was the clash of their personalities that remained the key to their success as detectives. Neither man had much regard for the politics of power, and none of their investigations ever followed the official line. They were tolerated because of their success rate in solving serious crimes, and were admired by the younger staffers because they had chosen to remain in the field instead of accepting senior positions. During the part of their week not taken up with teaching, the pair would arrive for work early so that they could filch the most interesting cases from other officers' files. At least, they had been able to do that until two months ago. Now they were out on their own.

'Want another?' May pointed at his partner's empty coffee cup.

'I suppose so,' said Bryant listlessly, unstrangling his scarf. 'There's been no sign of my acid-thrower.'

'Somebody must have seen him leaving the gallery. Sounds as if he was wearing fancy dress. Barking mad, obviously.'

'That's the point. I don't think he was.' Bryant's aqueous blue eyes reflected the café lights. 'He pinpointed a particular painting for destruction. He knew exactly where to find it. The exhibition had only opened the previous week, so he must have visited it earlier to work out his escape route. Perhaps the opportunity didn't arise for him to inflict damage on his first trip. Also, this was sent up from Forensics.' Bryant rummaged around in his overcoat and produced a typed note. His sleeves were so long that they covered the ends of his fingers. 'The acid used was a compound, ethyl chlorocarbonate, chloracetyl chloride, something else they can't identify—it was constructed to do the maximum amount of damage in the shortest possible time. And it did. The painting isn't salvageable.'

'Not at all?'

'A little at the edges. The canvas has been eaten right through. It would mean starting from scratch, and although there are transparencies of the work on file they don't reproduce the exact pigments used. Apparently we can't produce paints in the same manner any more. Their reflective qualities are hard to reconstruct accurately. The original has gone for ever. I dread to think what will happen when the Australian government finds out.'

'Why?'

'Their arts minister is trying to get a number of aboriginal artefacts returned, but we've been refusing to give them up. The Aussies were extremely reluctant to loan us any Pre-Raphaelites at all. This will only prove that their fears were well founded.'

'Do you have anything to go on?'

'Not much,' admitted Bryant, sipping his fresh coffee. 'There were no prints on the acid bottle, and no one in the surrounding streets saw him, despite his extraordinary appearance. The weather was terrible. People tend to keep their heads down in the rain. I'm one of the few reliable witnesses.'

'You were in the gallery?' said May, surprised.

'Purely by chance. I know the concept of looking at pictures is anathema to you, but you should try it some time. The chap who put the exhibition together is an old friend of mine. I'm seeing him tomorrow. Come along if you want.'

'Not me.' May drained his cup. 'I have to go to the Savoy Hotel. Last night one of their guests dropped dead while reading his newspaper in the lobby. The house doctor thought at first that he'd had some kind of a haemorrhage.'

'And he hadn't?'

'Oh, he had all right. With a vengeance. Finch did an autopsy on him last night and found his innards in a state of complete liquefaction. Apparently the ambulance men were lucky to make it out of the foyer without their load falling to bits. I'm told that there's absolutely no known medical condition that could account for such a thing. They wondered if he could have drunk some kind of chemical compound.'

'While sitting in the lobby of the Savoy? I thought their cocktails were supposed to be first rate. Wouldn't the taste have tipped him off? It's very hard to drink a poisonous liquid. The more potent it is, the more pungent it tastes.' Bryant's eyes took on a rare gleam. 'How very odd.' He drained his cup and set it down.

'It would be if it was in your jurisdiction,' said May. 'It could be—if you wanted to join me at Mornington Crescent.'

Bryant pointedly examined his hands. 'I was wondering when you were going to offer me a position.'

'I was waiting to be given full authority from above. Of course, it'll mean sharing an office for a while, until we get everything sorted out.'

Bryant had been holding out at Bow Street, a small stab at independence that was really an excuse to make everyone miss him. 'Are you still smoking those filthy cigars?' he asked.

'I'm afraid so.'

'Have they told you who the acting superintendent will be?'

'Raymond Land. I know you don't get on with him, but he'll only be there until a permanent replacement is decided upon.'

'I'm not sure. I'll be sorry to leave Bow Street.'

'Don't lie to me, Arthur. You know very well they're going to close Bow Street down eventually.'

'The word around town is that you'll be able to choose your own investigations. People are already getting jealous.'

'That's not quite true. It's strictly a high-profile murder squad, no more diamond robberies or gang beatings. It'll include a lot of long-term unsolved stuff. That means research-heavy crimes.' They were Bryant's speciality.

Until now no permanent murder squad had ever been set up in Great Britain. This was partly because the country had a comparatively low per capita murder rate. There was virtually no gun crime. Squads were only formed to solve individual murders, with superintendents drafted in from an Area Major Investigation Pool (AMIP), supported by local detectives from other cases.

Now the system was changing. If the freshly separated PCU worked out successfully, it could affect the structure of the Metropolitan Police. Other specialized units would be formed. John May was aware that quite a few of his colleagues in the AMIPs were happy with the system in its present state, and would be glad to see the new division fail. Consequently, he needed all the friends he could get. More than that, he needed his old partner back.

'This office of yours,' said Bryant, 'does it have decent-sized windows?'

'Huge ones.'

'Good. I need more light these days. Could I have the room painted? I can't think clearly in tasteless surroundings.'

'Choose any colour you like. How's your present caseload?'

'I'll follow through this business with the National Gallery. The rest can be dumped on to someone I hate. I must say your proposal isn't entirely unexpected. You took your time.'

'I had to get the place up and running first. You didn't think I'd leave you behind, did you?' May smiled. He knew how much the daily routine at Bow Street bored his old partner, and hated the thought of Bryant's mind going to waste. As he rose to leave, the afternoon sun threw a lurid glare across the smeary windows of the café. *We finally have a chance to make a real impact on the system*, he thought. He decided not to tell Bryant that they had only a two-month trial period in which to do so.

'I made a standard Y incision from the shoulders to the chest and down to the pubis, as you can see,' Finch began, pointing at the splayed corpse in front of them, 'and I couldn't believe my eyes. The organic damage is quite phenomenal.'

Finch was tall and thin, with spiky hair and bony raw

hands, and his knee joints creaked like desk drawers when he sat down. A suntan gained on a recent holiday was all that prevented him from looking like Stan Laurel. As usual, the sickly smell of cheap splash-on deodorant rose from his skin.

'I don't see anything wrong.' May forced himself to study the body. The whiteness of the skin contrasted shockingly with the crimson hole that had been formed by pinning back the victim's flesh.

'I've seen an awful lot of insides, John, and I know when something isn't kosher,' said Finch, wiping his hands on his lime-green plastic apron. 'Tell me what you know about him.' He moved to the scales and made a note of the calibrations before removing a kidney from the tray.

'Maximillian Jacob, fifty-nine years old, five feet eleven inches, fourteen stone two ounces, partner of the law firm Jacob and Marks, based in Norwich. He checked into the Savoy last Friday. He was visiting London on un-known business—at least, he seems to have given his wife and partner two different stories for leaving town. No history of medical problems, nothing much out of the or-dinary, but we're still searching.' He looked back at the corpse on the table. It seemed that the more cleanly a man lived his life, the harder it was to find anything out about him when he was dead. 'At the moment he's just a statistic, Oswald. I wish he'd been a criminal. At least we'd have somewhere to start.'

'Well, you know that someone hated Mr Jacob enough to want to kill him,' said Finch.

'Nobody mentioned murder.'

'Then let me be the first. Take a look at this.' The pathologist beckoned May to advance on the cadaver. 'Jacob's stomach is a mass of dissolved tissue. Extensive haemorrhaging here, here, and here.' Finch prodded beneath a bloody flap of flesh with the end of his pen. Thick streaks of yellow fat surrounded an abdominal incision. 'And here in the heart, the liver, and lungs.'

'What are you putting down as the actual cause of death?'

'Cardial dysfunction. The heart couldn't pump properly because the vascular bed surrounding it had become riddled with lesions. It had to be some kind of corrosive fluid, but as there were no burn marks in the mouth or trachea I ruled out ingestion and started searching for an injection site. It's not hard to see once you're looking for it. Here.'

He turned Maximillian Jacob's head to one side and pointed to a spot below the corpse's left ear. A swollen patch on his carotid artery was pinpricked with coagulated black fluid.

'If you examine the wound closely, you'll find not one puncture mark but two, like a vampire. Beauties, aren't they?' He twisted Jacob's head and revealed a pair of tiny livid pinpricks.

'And it's become gangrenous. The flesh around it has turned to diseased mush. I carried out the routine toxicology tests, checked for alcohol, cocaine, barbiturates, and so on; nothing much there. I didn't want to run up a bill testing for more exotic stuff, but this had me beaten. I sent blood and tissue samples to the National Poisons Reference Centre for analysis, not expecting to hear back for several days.' Finch absently prodded the end of his nose with his pen. 'Instead, the results were telexed back just over an hour ago. Seems this got them all excited. It's a cottonmouth.'

'Sorry, what?' John had been transfixed by the cadaver on the table. It was hard to believe that poor, putrefying

Jacob would be stitched back together and buried beneath a headstone engraved with a soothing phrase like *Just Resting*. 'Foot and mouth?'

'*Cotton*mouth. That's the common name. Latin, *Agkistrodon piscivorus*, from the family *Crotalidae*.' The pathologist's enthusiasm was always more pronounced when he had just discovered something in an opened body. 'It's called a cottonmouth because it threatens with its mouth wide open, and the inside of the mouth is white.'

'Oswald, what the hell is a cottonmouth?'

'That's the odd part.' He thoughtfully probed his left ear with his pen. 'It's a North American snake.'

'You're telling me this man was bitten by a *snake*?' John threw his hands up helplessly. 'They must have made a mistake.'

'No mistake. They cross-checked their results.' Finch pointed at the corpse. 'You can see the extraordinary effect it's had, even on the minor organs. This is a very particular venom, apparently found only in aquatic pit vipers.'

'God, Oswald—a *water* snake? In the lobby of the Savoy Hotel?'

'I must admit it's a bit of a puzzle,' Finch casually conceded. 'The cottonmouth is more commonly found in marshland.'

'Don't you find that just a little bit strange?'

'Every unnatural death is strange, John.'

'Did they give you an idea of the reaction time between infection and death?'

'Oh, yes. Immediately after the bite, the wound turns itchy, then the victim gets irritable. After this he settles into a quiet aphasic state, and then he suddenly collapses and dies. Ten minutes in total. There's one other thing I wanted to show you.' Finch raised a plastic bag and gently emptied the contents into a bowl. May found himself looking at Max Jacob's brain.

'As you probably know,' said Finch, 'the human brain has the consistency of a well-set blancmange. Fluid protects it from thumping into the skull wall. Look at this.' He touched his pen against a darkened patch on the frontal lobe of the brain. 'When you're hit on the head you get a bruise on the scalp, perhaps a fracture underneath it, and a bruise on the brain below that. All three are on top of each other; that's what we call a *coup* injury. Jacob's brain is marked at the front, but there's no corresponding damage to his scalp.'

'Why?'

'Instead there's a bruise on the back of his head. If someone passes out and the back of their head hits the floor when they collapse, the brain is driven forward and bashes itself on the inside front of the skull. That is a *contra coup*, and that's what Jacob has. It looks like your man took a fall sometime shortly before his death.'

'Thanks, Oswald, you've done a great job.' May hastily made his apologies and left the room. The combined smell of disinfectant and antiperspirant was starting to get to him.

'Let me know how this one turns out,' said Finch with a cheery wave as he turned back to the corpse. 'And John—don't be such a stranger in future. I'm always delighted to see you down here.'

The lobby of the Savoy was in chaos. Commonwealth speakers had begun to arrive in force, and stacks of expensive luggage stood in corners among the arrangement of dried plants arranged to resemble harvested corn bales.

Jerry had spent the morning easing guests into rooms with the aid of encouraging smiles and pidgin English.

'He's no spring chicken, is he?' muttered Nicholas disparagingly. 'They could have sent someone a bit more *with it*.'

'Keep your voice down,' said Jerry, embarrassed. 'He'll hear you.'

'Intelligence is a compensation for the departure of youth, Sonny.' John May set a heavy Dictaphone on the counter. 'As even you may discover one day. I need to talk to this young lady for a few minutes, so perhaps you could busy yourself dealing with the minor grievances of your guests.'

Jerry smiled to herself. There was something instantly appealing about the detective. The old guy looked like a man who had retained much of his own youth by listening to the young. 'There's a room we can use behind here,' she said. 'It'll be quieter.'

Once they were seated in the small cream-painted staffroom, May dragged his own transistorized recorder from his bag and switched it on. 'I trust you've fully recovered, Miss Gates. It must have been a nasty shock for you.'

'I fainted, that's all,' she explained. 'He was spraying blood all over the place.'

'I've read your admirably lucid statement. There are just a few points I need to clear up. You checked Mr Jacob in last Friday, is that correct?'

'I took his filled-in reservation form, gave him the carbon copy, and arranged for his baggage to be sent up. He was booked for a double room even though we had singles available.' She cleared her throat, more nervous than she had realized. 'Nicholas—the other receptionist—made a remark at the time. He handled the actual room allocation because he'd taken the original telephone booking.'

'You think Mr Jacob was planning to meet up with someone? A female companion, perhaps? He'd left his wife and family at home in Norwich. He didn't sign in as Mr Smith, did he?' The detective's friendly smile was designed to relax.

'Mr Jacob didn't look like an adulterer, if that's what you mean,' she replied. 'You can usually recognize them.'

'Oh?' May cocked an eyebrow, obviously intrigued. 'How?'

'Small things. Their clothes are too sharp. You know, dressed up for a date.' She recalled some of the guests she had checked in. 'Often they're not at ease in a smart hotel. They don't tip at the standard rate, usually go over. Mr Jacob wasn't like that. He was old school.'

'How do you know that?'

Jerry shifted in her chair, trying to visualize the man who had walked toward her across the lobby last Friday. 'He had a club tie, done up with a small knot. Very neat. Starch in the shirt. A wet-razor shaver.' She shrugged, hoping she didn't sound foolish. 'Well, it was late afternoon when he arrived, and he didn't have any stubble. Short hair, brilliantined. Expensive shoes, carefully polished. Ex-military, I imagine. He had the look.'

'You don't miss much, do you, Miss Gates?' May smiled again, and reexamined his notes. Jerry wished she could see what he had written down.

'Let's move on to Monday. You say he was sitting in the lobby for about half an hour. Did you see anyone approach him in that time?'

'No one. It was raining heavily, and hardly anyone came in or went out.'

'Before he fell asleep with the paper over him, did

anything happen that was out of the ordinary? Anything at all?'

'I don't think so.'

'You seem like a bright young lady, so I'll let you into a secret.' May beckoned her closer with his fingertips. 'I have reason to believe that your guest did not die a natural death.'

Jerry had not considered the possibility of murder. The concept seemed so alien and theatrical. 'I thought he just had a heart attack,' she explained. 'I didn't know what to do.'

'Try to recall the evening in the light of what I've just told you, and see if you can think of anything else that happened. Mr Jacob came downstairs, sat down in the chair, and died half an hour later. Knowing what we do, something else must have occurred. Take your time about it.'

Jerry thought for a minute, pleased that the detective had clicked off the tape until she was ready to answer.

'There was something wrong with the lights. They kept flickering. Because of the storm, I suppose. It didn't disturb Mr Jacob.'

'Anything else?'

'Wait a minute—I think he went to the washroom,' she said suddenly. 'He wasn't gone for long.' She hadn't mentioned this in her statement to the policewoman who had interviewed her yesterday. 'I guess it's not the sort of thing you really register,' she added lamely.

'I quite understand,' said May. 'Under normal circumstances it's far too commonplace an event to take note of.' He had clicked the tape recorder back on. 'Can you recall any change in Mr Jacob's behaviour when he returned? Try to imagine him sitting back in the armchair...'

'He was scowling,' said Jerry, surprising herself. 'Fidgeting about. I remember looking up from the duty book several times. And he kept scratching his neck.'

'Thank you very much for your time, Miss Gates,' said May, closing his notebook with another twinkling smile and rising.

The abruptness of his leavetaking unsettled her. Having witnessed such a grotesque departure from life, she was anxious to know more, and to see what the police would do next. To them, it was just another unexplained death. To her, it was a window to a world she had no way of understanding.

5 / Malacca

Thursday dawned with an unnatural hazy warmth, steam rising from the soaked streets of East London to form dragons of morning mist. Arthur Bryant paid the cab driver and dug into his jacket for his pocketbook, checking the Hackney address of Peregrine Summerfield. He was thinking that it would help to list his acquaintances in alphabetical order, when the art historian found him.

'Up here, Bryant!' came a booming voice from above.

He looked up to see Summerfield balancing at the top of an extended ladder, his rotund form leaning precariously out to hail the passing detective. The ladder was propped against the end wall of a decrepit terraced house, where Summerfield was supervising the painting of an enormous mural. So far, only the lower third of the picture had been filled, but the full scene was already discernible. Half a dozen schoolchildren armed with brushes and paintpots were working on the lowest portion of the design. Summerfield came thumping down the ladder, causing the surrounding scaffolding to tremble. He pumped Bryant's hand with both of his, transferring a considerable amount of indigo paint in the process.

'This is a pleasant surprise.' He turned to the children. 'That's enough, you lot. Back to the shed for brush-washing. You've done enough damage for one day.' There was a collective moan. 'You'll have to excuse me,' he said, indicating his clothes, which were smothered in every colour imaginable. 'It's a community project. I didn't choose the subject matter.'

The wall showed a thirty-foot-high psychedelic nuclear explosion, around which strikers marched with banners and clenched fists. 'It's the lack of imagination I find depressing, but the council reckons it'll encourage community spirit.' Summerfield lost his hand within his bushy paint-flecked beard and gave his chin a good scratch. 'I suggested a nice abstract, colours reminiscent of lakes and trees, plenty of natural shapes, something to cheer urbanites up a bit. They told me I was being reactionary.'

'Why are the banners blank?' asked Bryant, studying the mural in puzzlement.

'That's so local people can write in their own grievances against the Heath government. Interactive art. Some bright spark in the planning department came up with that one, I suppose. We've already had a few people write things in. *Brian shags dogs, Tracy is a slag*, that sort of thing.'

'Hmm. I think I prefer your idea of the abstract,' agreed Bryant. 'Can we go somewhere to talk?'

'Certainly.' Summerfield examined the paint on his hands. 'Give me five minutes to get the lads cleaned up.' He threw Bryant a set of keys. 'I live over the road, number 54, the one with the sunrise gate. Make yourself a cup of tea.'

Summerfield's house was cramped and cluttered, and surprisingly devoid of paintings. A great number of reference books were stacked in untidy piles throughout the ground floor. The historian's knowledge of Victorian art placed him among the country's top experts, and he was frequently called in to help organize national exhibitions, but Summerfield had eschewed a permanent post in favour of educating young minds at the local primary school. Arthur had always appreciated his directness and lack of pretension when discussing art. He had just located a battered kettle beneath a pile of old newspapers when the historian returned.

'I can't spare much time today, Arthur,' he apologized. 'I've a life class at eleven. Their usual Christ is off sick, so I'm standing in. I've got the beard for it, you see. I don't mind, but it gets a bit tiring on the arms after a while.' He approximated the crucifixion, then searched around for a tea towel. 'Sorry about the mess. I haven't been able to sort myself out much since Lilian left.'

'I had no idea you two were separated,' said Bryant, looking for clean cups. 'My condolences.'

'Oh, none needed. We always had our differences. She was sick of me mixing paint in her Tupperware. I presume this visit concerns the vandalized Waterhouse painting?'

'That's right. You helped put the exhibition together, didn't you?'

'Indeed, and it was a pleasure to do so, just to spite the cynics.'

'How do you mean?' Bryant watched as Summerfield poured mahogany-coloured tea into a pair of mugs and led the way from the kitchen.

'Well, the poor old Pre-Raffs have had a pretty rough ride from the critics over the years. Too medieval, too Gothic, too sentimental, too moralizing; there's never been a school of painting so slagged off. Much Pre-Raphaelite art is narrative, of course, and that's a form which has fallen from fashion. A lot of it is symbolic, and decorative, and they're undesirable qualities, too. Who wants art that looks nice these days? We live in a world of strikes and bombings. It's taken a long time for people to get past the pre-Raff subject matter to the beauty within. Take a look at these.' He selected several volumes from a shelf and lovingly laid them open.

'Artists like Rossetti, Holman Hunt, and Millais revived the poetic and spiritual qualities of fifteenth-century Italian art. Romance and colour for a drab old world. At first everyone made fun of them, but the movement was pretty much legitimized by its popularity. Having lots of tits helped, of course. Victorian nipples were always acceptable in a classical setting. Many a dull parlour wall was brightened up with a nice bit of repro-cheesecake.' He tapped a grimy forefinger on a colour plate entitled *Hylas and the Nymphs*. 'Look at Waterhouse and his horny ladies of the lake. Landscapes were popular, too, beautifully detailed by artists like Brett and Inchbold. And religious art, like Hunt's creepy *The Light of the World*, now hanging in St Paul's. Popular art's a dirty word today. You can pick up Pre-Raffs for a song. The critics prefer stuff only members of their little coterie can appreciate.'

'Tell me about the exhibition.'

'It was a bugger to organize, because the low values have helped to scatter the paintings into private collections. Manchester Art Gallery has a lot of the decent stuff. The rest are all over the place. We still don't know where some of the Waterhouse paintings are. This is a study for the one that was destroyed. The finished work is much more detailed.'

Summerfield tipped the art volume to the light. The picture was of a young man seated on a throne, feeding pigeons from a salver while his councillors waited for an audience. '*The Favourites Of The Emperor Honorius*, an early piece, 1883. Waterhouse's first serious historical painting. Flavius Honorius, one of the forgotten Roman rulers. He was a bit of an ass by all accounts, lazy, greedy, seen here too busy feeding his pet birds to grant his advisors any attention. Even in this crappy reproduction you can sense the genius of the artist. A moment of anticipation captured for ever. The title is ironic, of course. It refers to the birds, not to the seven men in the picture.'

'How did it end up in Australia?'

'At the end of the nineteenth century the big Australian galleries bought quite a few Pre-Raffs. There are two oil studies for this picture, both in private collections. One had been mistitled *The Emperor and Tortoises* for years.'

'Can you think of any reason why someone would want to destroy such a painting?'

Summerfield pulled at the paint-daubed strands of his beard. 'Certainly no one could be offended at the subject matter. It's pretty innocuous stuff. Perhaps your vandal wanted to cause some diplomatic damage. The availability of Commonwealth paintings is a touchy subject at the moment.'

'So I understand. Do we have any other pictures here on loan?'

'Yes, two other Waterhouses, as a matter of fact. *Circe Invidiosa* from Adelaide, and *Diogenes* from Sydney.' He located the prints in his book. 'You think these are in danger, too?'

'We'll have to get them removed from display. I want you to keep thinking for me.'

'That's just it . . .' Summerfield glanced from one print to the next. 'There's something odd which I can't quite—'

'Something about the paintings?'

'Not really. More the act of vandalism. There's a resonance here. Something very familiar. I'll need to think
about it.'

'Well, if you have any ideas at all,' suggested Bryant,
'call me.'

A shrill beep startled them both. 'It's this stupid new
radio-pager gadget May makes me wear,' Arthur explained, rummaging in the folds of his coat. 'Can I use
your telephone?'

'Arthur, I know you're tied up today, but I need your
help,' May told him. 'Oh, and there's a lead on your
vandal.'

'Of course, it wasn't the snake that puzzled me but the
bite,' said May as they crossed Camden Town's hump-
back bridge. A thin layer of mist mooched over the surface of the canal below. Bryant pulled his scarf over his
nose. If he'd known what global warming would do
decades later, he might have enjoyed the vaporous damp.

'If you got bitten by a snake you'd run about shouting,
warning people,' May continued. 'You wouldn't calmly
go back to your seat and resume reading your newspaper.'

'You say he sustained a fall?'

'Backwards, according to Finch.'

'Could be your answer.' Bryant's watery eyes peered
over the scarf like a pair of insufficiently poached eggs.
'Suppose he was chloroformed? Once he'd fallen to the
floor unconscious, his attacker could have induced the
snake to bite his neck.'

'Don't be daft. The only possible reason for using
such a ridiculous murder weapon would be to frighten
the victim first. Why go to all that trouble if your victim
doesn't even get to see it?'

'I've no idea. It's not my case. What have you got on my vandal?'

'Seems he damaged something in his flight,' replied May, savouring his partner's anticipation. 'We did a sweep of the gallery stairs and found this.' He removed a clear plastic sachet and shook out a wooden splinter almost two inches long. Green flecks in the paintwork gave it an iridescent sheen. 'It appears to have come from his cane. The varnish is new.'

May had given the splinter to a colleague who owed him a favour, knowing that this would be quicker than sending it into the system's Bermuda Triangle of evidence examination. 'Stokes remembered seeing a unique cane under your vandal's arm. I popped this over to a cane maker in Burlington Arcade. He agreed that it's a piece from a hand-turned malacca walking stick. The green flecks are malachite, basic copper carbonate. He knows only one company that still makes them.'

'James Smith and Sons,' said Bryant, who had purchased something similar a few Christmases ago.

'Exactly,' agreed May. 'Care to take a stroll down there?'

The brass-paneled store on the corner of Gower Street and New Oxford Street had sold canes and umbrellas for ever. Impervious to the changing times, it survived with unmodernized décor and traditional service, a charming oddity from the past, marooned in a fuming sea of one-way traffic.

The detectives stepped past the freshly polished nameplate and into a room filled with glistening wood. Walking sticks, shooting sticks, canes, and parasols of every size and description hung in racks like forgotten torture instruments. The genial shop assistant required a single glance at the evidence to describe the cane from which it had been broken.

'I think we'll have a record of this particular item, Sir,' he said, turning the splinter over in his palm. 'Canes with graining this rich are expensive, and are only produced as special commissions. The customer usually requires an engraved silver top.' He pinched the wood between thumb and forefinger, and gently sniffed it. 'Less than a year old, I'd say. Won't keep you a moment.'

He summoned an assistant, and they marched to the rear office. Minutes later, they returned bearing a slip of paper. 'We've made only two of these in the past year, one for a Japanese gentleman—'

'Not the person we're seeking,' said May.

'The other we engraved for an elderly gentleman.'

'What was the engraving he required?'

'A small symbol, fire in a goblet, surrounded by a circle of flame. The gentleman was very specific about the design, even drew it out for us. I served him myself.'

'Is there an address on your receipt?'

The assistant checked the slip of paper. 'NW3. Looks like somewhere in Hampstead.'

'You don't recall anything odd about your client, I suppose?' asked Bryant.

'Most certainly,' replied the assistant. 'I remember commenting to the cashier that his clothes were more suited to the previous century. Of course, we could have sold him the same cane back then.'

6 / Mother & Daughter

The uncharacteristic clemency of the day had produced a mist from the Thames which thickened with the passing hours. By six-thirty on Thursday evening, it had obscured much of the South Bank promenade, providing London's few remaining tourists with a Turneresque vision of the city.

After her session with Dr Wayland, her therapist, Jerry caught a cab to Waterloo Bridge. She descended the stone stairway towards the hanging coloured bulbs that decked the National Film Theatre's bar.

At the last minute, her mother had called to change their arrangement. It couldn't be helped, Gwen Gates had explained, as she was due to address a charity trustees' meeting at eight, and would only be able to spare an hour.

Jerry hoped she would be able to survive the full sixty minutes without being backed into another pointless argument. Gwen's unhappiness with the choice of venue was apparent from her expression. Appearing awkwardly out of place in her fawn Dior suit and gold jewellery (the look that would be redefined as 'bling' thirty years later), she was seated at a counter near the window, surrounded by hairy students and film buffs. Although she tried to keep her attention focused on the fog-shrouded river, she could not resist revealing her distaste for her surroundings at every opportunity.

As Jerry pushed open the door, Gwen beaconed her

location with a violent coughing fit, pointedly fanning the smoke from someone's cigarette. As she herself was a smoker, the gesture was redundant. Jerry threaded her way to the table and pecked her lightly on the cheek.

'All those badges are ruining your jacket,' Gwen remarked, carefully shifting an empty coffee cup away from some imagined mark on the Formica. 'I don't know why we had to meet in such a ghastly place. Surely a few linen tablecloths wouldn't compromise their socialist ideals. If you want coffee, you have to serve yourself, apparently."

Jerry bought beverages and returned to the table. 'I'm sorry you don't have time for dinner,' she told her mother. 'There's something I was hoping to discuss with you.'

Gwen's eyebrows rose a fraction. Serious discussions rarely took place between them. 'If it's about the job, you already know my feelings,' she said.

'I like it there, Mother. It's the Savoy, for God's sake, not some flophouse. And it's not as if I'm going to make a career out of it.'

Gwen examined her coffee suspiciously and sighed. 'I suppose you're mixing with the right sort of people.'

'I'm serving them. There's a difference. That isn't what I wanted to talk to you about.'

'Then what is it?' Gwen set down her cup and searched her handbag for a cigarette.

'I want to move out.'

'Don't be absurd, darling, you're not even eighteen yet.' She tapped out a gold-tipped Sobranie.

'There's a flat share going in Maida Vale. I could afford the rent, but there's a down payment to be made . . .'

Gwen's attention crystallized. 'Share? You mean cohabiting? Have you met someone, Geraldine?'

'No, nothing like that. There's a guy at work who shares with two others, and one's moving out.'

'It's simply out of the question.' Gwen spouted a column of blue smoke at the window. 'You must try to understand that I only want what's best for you. There's absolutely no need for you to be stuck in some awful little flat when you have the complete run of the house. It's not as if we hold you back, or stop you from having friends over.'

'I want to be independent for a while, surely you can appreciate that.'

'But why must you be? Why can't young people accept the help of their parents with good grace? Other girls would be grateful for a helping hand, Geraldine.'

'I'm not a girl any more, Mother.' She didn't want to be given a cozy position in the family business. Lately she'd been thinking about taking a course at an art college. It had been a mistake to inform Gwen of her plans. 'Look, I wouldn't need to borrow money after the initial loan. It won't be a large amount.'

'That's not the point, Jerry. You went behind our backs to get this job, and now you want to sever your home ties with us. You know what the doctor said about learning to deal with authority. Interaction with others is difficult for you. Besides, art is not a career for a woman, it's a hobby. I'd be hard-pressed to name a single successful female artist.'

'That says more about the system than the artist, and anyway—'

'So now you're against the system!' Gwen shook her head sadly. 'No, I know these rebellious feelings, and believe me, they only last for a couple of years. I blame all these students marching over Vietnam. Americans are trying to halt the spread of Communism, and they're getting no thanks for it. You'll see, soon you'll want the things we wanted at your age...'

'I'm not like you and Jack. I don't have the same values. Don't you see how much things are changing? I don't even know what I want yet. I'm just trying to figure out what I *don't* want.'

'I suppose you think we're snobs,' replied her mother, stung. 'Well, I really have to put my foot down this time, Geraldine. I couldn't possibly allow you to leave home yet. I hate to bring this up...' Jerry groaned inwardly, knowing what was coming. 'After your illness, your father and I knew we had to do something to help you. That's why we set up the trust in your name. We wanted to help you make a start in life. That trust matures when you are twenty-one, and until then we are empowered to influence your decisions about the future.'

She reached forward and sealed her hands over her daughter's, pink nails ticking on the tabletop. 'You know we love you. Darling, it's for your own good. You'll see one day that I was right. When you come of age, you'll be able to choose for yourself. Until then, carry on in this job, if that's what you want. But think about your father's offer. Eventually you'll meet a nice boy. You'll want to settle down and start thinking about children. It's only natural. And hopefully by that time you'll be ready to assume your responsibilities in the business, just a couple of days a week, nothing taxing. You're lucky that girls are taken seriously in the workforce these days. You can be a mother and still have a nice career.'

'Like you, you mean.'

At the moment nothing seemed less desirable than following in her parents' footsteps. She knew there was no point in trying to explain her confusion to Gwen.

'Anyway, how is the Savoy?' asked her mother, switching subjects to fill the uncomfortable silence.

'Someone dropped dead in the foyer on Monday, and the police think it was murder. Apparently the newspapers are suggesting he was a spy.'

'Why have I not heard about this? Is nowhere safe any more? Did you know there are homeless people sleeping in the Strand? It's dreadful.' Gwen checked her watch and rose to leave. 'I have to go. Stay and finish your coffee, and remember what I said. You can try speaking to your father, but it won't make any difference. I know he feels the same way I do. Can you believe this weather? I haven't seen fog like this since the fifties.'

Jerry watched through the steam-slick glass as her mother paused at the door of the café to snap on her gloves before walking briskly into the haze. She had always been this way, for ever suggesting the path of least resistance. Didn't Geraldine realize how lucky she was, to have been born into a family with social standing and respect in the community? Did she understand how generous her parents had always been to her? And how ungrateful she'd been in return?

The coldness that had arisen between them was the result of her nightmarish fourteenth year—an unendurable sequence of fights and hospitals. After this there had been a reconciliation of sorts, but with it came a realization on both sides that the older Jerry grew, the less like her parents she became.

She was increasingly uncomfortable with her mother's ostentatious displays of wealth, and felt unworthy of her cushioned life. It was as if the three of them shared a secret: that she was a common foundling, a usurper to the throne of commerce and society, whose presence would be tolerated for the benefit of both sides.

For a while Jerry had failed to see how the arrangement could possibly benefit Gwen, who had shown her scant attention in the first fourteen years of her life. Jerry recalled an aimless, bored childhood spent in the old house at Chelsea, sprawled out on the untrodden pile of the midnight-blue carpet in the drawing room, reading for hours on end, minded by a slow-witted nurse, waiting for her parents to return home. She remembered exploring the floors above, creeping about as if any minute now her parents would discover the scruffy cuckoo in their midst and throw her into the street. But of course there had been times when they fussed and fawned over her, Gwen especially—and finally Jerry had come to understand.

Jerry was the final piece in the creation of her mother's image. She was there to help Gwen show a caring side to the world. Gwen's friends gathered to watch in warm indulgence as mother and daughter played happily together. Look at them, they seemed to say, what a perfect, loving mother she is. How does she manage it with all of her charity commitments?

'Hey, fancy meeting you here.'

She turned in her seat and looked up.

'Remember me?' said Joseph Herrick, smiling slyly. 'I mean, how could you forget?'

Jerry was stumped for a reply. She was suddenly thankful that Gwen had left.

'You're the receptionist at the Savoy, right? As I'm staying at your place, so to speak, I just wanted to thank you for your hospitality. Do many guests drop dead in your foyer? Is this some kind of regular occurrence I should know about?' He lowered himself into the opposite seat and set down his coffee cup without waiting to be asked. He seemed to be wearing some kind of leather biker's outfit more suited to a science-fiction convention than the NFT cafeteria. His dreadlocked hair was an odd look, but suited him.

'Actually, that was the first corpse this week.'

'I heard you found him. I'm sorry.'

She smiled uncomfortably, not really wanting to talk about it. The true effect of the death was impossible to share. 'How do you like the Savoy?'

'Well, I'd have chosen something a little closer to the street, if you know what I mean, but it's cool. I can't believe what you charge for a coffee. I'm glad I'm not paying the bill.'

'So you're here on business.' She watched as Joseph emptied four packs of sugar into his coffee. He was a little older than she had first thought, twenty-five or thereabouts.

'I'm preparing to start work on a show, set designing. This is my first big commission. They put me in the Savoy while we're meeting with the backers. You've got a bunch of Japanese guys checking in tomorrow. They're the ones putting up the money. Tasaka Corporation. Their boss is a man called Kaneto Miyagawa. In Japan he's considered to be a great patron of the arts, and now he's coming to London. That's why I'm here tonight.' He pulled a National Theatre brochure from his jacket pocket. 'I'm seeing a production at the Cottesloe. It's supposed to be kinda lousy, but the sets are good. Big dreams on a tight budget. How about you?'

'I was having coffee with an old school friend.' Thanks to her sessions with Wayland, lying came easy.

'Listen, you want to come with me? They sent me loads of spare tickets.'

She laughed nervously. 'I couldn't, not tonight.'

'Why not? If it's that bad we can leave. I'm alone and

friendless in a strange land, many thousands of miles from home.'

'Don't push it. Where are you from, anyway?'

'San Diego. I'm the only black guy ever to take theatre design there. I figured it would get me to Europe, and it did. Ten countries in eight days, package tour. I cannot recommend it. You want to come with me to the play?'

After trying to think of a way to turn him down, she realized that there was no reason at all why she should. She knew she should try to set aside the memory of Nicholas pawing at her.

'So, what's your name? If you don't tell me, I'll have to try and guess, and that'll embarrass both of us.' He studied her face with such an earnest expression that she gave in gracefully.

'Jerry,' she said, holding out her hand.

'Jerry, it's a pleasure to meet you. Is that short for Geraldine?'

'Damn,' she said. 'Just when we were getting off on the right foot.'

'How about I never call you that again?'

'How about that.'

So they went to the theatre.

7 / Detonation

'My foot's gone to sleep,' complained Bryant, stamping experimentally on the pavement. For the past hour they had been standing in the mist-shrouded garden beside their suspect's house. 'Nearly eleven P.M. I wish he'd hurry up. I have to say you're not much company.'

'I needn't have come at all,' May pointed out. 'This isn't my case.'

'Yes, I suppose stakeouts are a bit beneath you these days. I like to keep my hand in. Look at this fog. The damp gets right into your bones. It's doing my chest no good at all. I'll need a vapour bath.' Bryant pulled down his scarf and peered over the sodden hedge. Dew had formed on his bald head and ears. He resembled a minor Tolkien character.

'You're getting old before your time,' warned May. 'I can't imagine what you'll be like in your eighties.'

'I'm ageing gracefully, which means not trying to look like a member of Concrete Blimp.'

'I assume you mean Led Zeppelin. Can you hear someone coming?'

A figure solidified from the surrounding haze. Bryant felt a chill as he recognized the whiskers, cape, and cane. Brass-heeled shoes clipped loudly on the street's sloping pavement. May tapped his partner on the arm and the two detectives stepped in front of the garden gate. Their quarry drew up before them, his eyes staring angrily beneath bushy brows. There was an overwhelming sense of the past about him, from the heavy cut of his clothes to the sharp smell of rolling tobacco that hung over him. It was as if the man had stepped through the fabric of time.

'Mr William Whitstable?'

'Would that it were not.'

May unfolded his wallet and held it aloft. 'We'd like to ask you a few questions about an incident which occurred at the National Gallery...'

'That was indeed my doing, but it remains no damned business of yours, Sir.' Whitstable's hand tightened around the head of his cane.

'The destruction of a painting on loan to the nation is reason enough to make it our business,' said Bryant angrily, 'and to apply the full penalty of the law.'

The figure seemed to fall back a little. When he spoke again his voice was tempered with reason. 'My sympathy lies with Mr Waterhouse and with no other. *Nature has burst the bonds of art.* If I cannot remove the symptom of this sickness I must at least remind them of its root.'

Whitstable was starting to back away, one boot sliding behind the other. May moved forward, wary of the cane. 'Why did you do it?' he asked. 'Why this painting?'

'How would any other do?' cried Whitstable. 'I made it known that our ranks are broken. They think they can get away with behaving as they please, but as God is my witness I'll owe no further allegiance, and be gulled no more.'

Suddenly he raised the cane and struck out, catching Bryant hard on the arm. Then he turned and fled into the fog.

'I'm all right,' gasped Bryant, falling back against the garden wall. 'Go after him, quickly.'

May soon gained on his quarry, but the night and the fog had settled in a concealing shroud across the brow of the hill. For a moment he glimpsed a figure darting beneath sodium lamplight, then it was gone, the click of boot heels lingering in the murky air.

'Are you all right?' asked May, returning to his partner and examining his arm.

'Of course not,' complained Bryant, hauling back his coat sleeve and checking for bruises. 'I've had a nasty shock. I need a cherry brandy.'

'We have to put out a call and bring Whitstable in. He can't get far dressed like that.'

'Or perhaps a large Courvoisier,' continued Bryant. 'He said he had to make it known that their ranks were broken. And what was all that about nature bursting the bonds of art?'

'I don't know. It sounded like a quote. That's your department.'

'It doesn't ring any bells, but my memory isn't what it was.'

'Let's hope your investigative powers are intact. We have our work cut out for us.'

On Friday morning, Bryant moved the last of his possessions to the new unit above Mornington Crescent station. As most of his friends were operating double shifts to cope with the criminal fraternity's run-up to Christmas, there was no time for a farewell drink, party, or presentation from grateful colleagues. Bryant left the office with a parcel of belongings under his arm, feeling more like a prisoner leaving his cell than a transferring officer of the law.

'You've an interview with the junior arts minister at

ten,' said May as his partner entered the new PCU for the first time. 'We'll have to move some of this stuff if you're going to base yourself here.' He clambered between the enormous typewriters that still lined the hallways of the unit.

'Just find me a quiet corner to sit,' said Bryant. 'All I need for the moment is a notepad and a telephone.'

'You'll require your own electric typewriter.' May indicated the IBM on his desk, knowing full well that although Bryant had attended a typing course, he steadfastly refused to operate any technical equipment more complex than a fountain pen.

'I hardly think so, John. I blew up the last one.' Bryant removed his overcoat and began to peel off a variety of woollen layers. 'If I'd known it was electric, I'd have been more careful about where I set my soup. Why is it so cold in here?'

'We haven't managed to connect the central heating yet. I'll get you a bar radiator.'

'How Dickensian. Right, I'll settle here.' Bryant slapped the back of a chair and sat, staring straight ahead, his hands in front of him.

'Wait a minute, this is my office,' began May, alarmed.

'You said we could share. You obviously have the best street view, and you can work various bits of electric gadgetry for me on the rare occasions I require their services.'

'But Arthur, I like to spread things around. You're too tidy for me. You alphabetize your toxicology manuals.'

'I'll have to put up with your vile habits, too. Cleaning your nails while thinking aloud, I know what you're like. It'll be good for you to have someone in here to bounce ideas off.'

May regretted his offer. He knew that after a few

weeks he'd be wanting to bounce more tangible items off his partner. Bryant was searching around for a wall socket. 'I hope you don't object to music?'

'Not the Mendelssohn,' groaned May. 'It must be worn out by now.'

'It helps me to think. Perhaps you could find me a three-pin plug. Do we have anyone assisting us?'

He had obviously acclimatized himself to the office. There was nothing for May to do but accept it. 'An old friend,' he replied. 'Janice Longbright. She's sitting outside.'

'I thought she went off to get married?'

'It fell through again. Ian asked her to choose between a husband and a career. Better not say anything about it.'

Bryant straightened the huge knot in his tie and stuck his head outside the door. 'Janice? What are you doing here? I thought you were going to live in a big country house and have lots of babies.'

'No, I was going to live in a one-bedroom flat with a Labrador and a man who's never home before ten. I thought I'd get more regular meals if I came back to work.' The sergeant gave him a bone-cracking hug which left lipstick on his collar. 'Your ten o'clock appointment is already here. I thought you'd probably want to get settled in, so I told him you were in a meeting. Said you'd be free for just a few minutes.'

Bryant smiled approvingly. Just as her mother had been before her, Janice Longbright was the kind of female officer he loved: strong, decisive, and not easily prone to emotion. Inevitably, her personal life had been subordinated to her work. His admiration for her had grown with the passing years, although he was careful not to show it.

'The arts wallah? Let him in, will you?' He grabbed

May by the sleeve as he attempted to slip out of the office. 'I'd like you to sit in on this, John.'

'We're sharing the room, not individual cases. I'm down for witness interviews on the Max Jacob death this morning.'

'You don't need to be there for that, do you? Just give me twenty minutes. Have you had the pleasure of Mr Faraday before?'

'I don't think so.'

'The government's most pedantic civil servant, which is saying something, a professional junior-status minister, but curiously useful for all that. In a brief and unillustrious career he's been shunted all over Whitehall. First he was minister of snow, and managed to bring the road-gritters out on strike. Then he was appointed minister of sport, and sparked off a race riot by inviting a white South African paramilitary leader to a Brixton Jail cricket match—'

'Then how is he useful?'

'Simple. He never forgets anything.'

A pudgy young man with slicked sandy hair appeared before them. Shaking his hand was like removing wet laundry from a washing machine. His brown suit was expensive but badly cut, so that his trouser bottoms were accordioned over his shoes. It would have been hard to imagine a man less interested in any branch of the arts.

'Leslie Faraday,' announced the minister. 'We met two years ago, didn't we, Mr Bryant? August seventh, I think it was, nice and sunny but it clouded over in the afternoon. I read about you in the paper last year, cracking secret codes in a multiple-murder case. The *Daily Telegraph*, wasn't it? Someone fell out of a window and you were in trouble for hijacking a Porsche. This must be your partner. I wonder if I could possibly have a cup of tea? Brooke Bond will be fine, nice and milky, two sugars if you don't mind.'

Sweat was beading on Faraday's pale forehead despite the chill in the room.

'What can we do for you, Mr Faraday?' asked Bryant, anxious to short-circuit the minister's recollections.

'It's about this vandalized picture, the Watermark thing. I know it was painted by an Englishman but the Aussies seem to own it now and they're bloody furious, and not because it was worth a bob or two. To tell the truth, this is a relatively new field for me. I don't go much for your modern arty-farty types. It's not painting, it's exhibitionism. They're very good at building thirty-foot-high plaster models of their private parts but ask them to paint a decent duck in flight and see where it gets you. The trouble with artists is they're not businessmen. What's so awful about giving the public what they want? We don't all have to like The Beatles.'

May seated himself on a corner of the desk and watched, fascinated, as Faraday dabbed at his leaking brow with a handkerchief.

'The Waterhouse painting,' prompted Bryant, as the tea arrived.

'Yes, it seems that there's rather a lot at stake here,' explained the minister. 'Is that tea mine? Nice and hot, jolly good. As you know, the paintings were loaned against the wishes of the Australian government, whose talks concerning the return of aboriginal artefacts from the Museum of Mankind have stalemated. Her Majesty's Government isn't prepared to negotiate for their return because a precedent would be set, and we already have our hands full with the Greeks. Certain aboriginal items were placed on display years ago as part of what has become a highly disputed permanent exhibition. Just some old mud masks, nothing to get excited about. I remember seeing them on a school field trip. Rained all day, although it brightened in the evening as I recall. This chap Carreras is bellyaching and threatening to boycott the Common Market conference. Now, I understand that the painting can't be restored, but the next best thing is to find the culprit as quickly as possible.'

'We already know who he is,' said May.

'You do?' Faraday grew visibly agitated. 'Then why on earth hasn't he been arrested?'

'I am hopeful that he will be within the next few hours.'

'This is capital news.' Faraday slapped his hands together wetly. 'And you'll tell me as soon as you discover a motive for this malicious act?'

'Of course.'

'Well.' Faraday set down his teacup and rose. 'All in all, a good morning's work. Lunch beckons, I think. Is it me or is it hot in here? I can see myself out.'

'What an exhausting man,' said May, closing the door. 'Why is he so interested in the motive?'

'He's hoping for a face-saver. Ideally his vandal would prove to be an Australian national protesting against the English, but I think there's little chance of that.' Bryant shifted his chair nearer the window and looked out on to the street below. 'It's almost as if Whitstable destroyed the picture because he somehow believes himself to be living within its time frame. His speech was as archaic as his dress. He said he wouldn't be "gulled." It's an obsolete term. He may be mad, but he seemed sincere.'

'Mad people always are. Have you had a chance to think about the phrase that sounded like a quote?'

'You mean "nature and the bonds of art." I'll have to run a check.'

'Whitstable hasn't returned home yet. The house is under surveillance, but so far there's been no report of any activity. He has a brother, Peter, registered as living in the same house, although we've had no sight of him so far. Obviously we'll interview William if and when he returns. I'd better let you get on with your unpacking.'

'Looks as if you have a bit of a backlog to deal with yourself.' Bryant gestured at the unsteady stack of cardboard folders propped up on his partner's desk. It was characteristic of May to take on more work than he could handle.

While Bryant had remained at Bow Street to oversee specific ongoing operations, May had been staffing and organizing the new unit. This was a chance for him to set up a division running on entirely new lines. Their high arrest rate had been acknowledged by their superiors in the Met, but their unorthodox techniques were impossible to incorporate into the Greater London network. A revamped independent unit designed to showcase new methodology was the logical answer; much to his surprise, May had been able to persuade the legendarily slothful Home Office and Her Majesty's Inspectorate of Constabulary that this was so. Now they had to prove their claim.

Bryant was filling the last of his desk drawers with files when the overhead lights began to flicker.

'Does that sort of thing affect the electric typewriter?' he asked, staring at the keyboard as if expecting it to bite him.

'It shouldn't,' replied May. 'The London Electricity Board has been warning everyone about outages all month. The National Grid is about to start rationing power. If Edward Heath is forced to put the nation on a three-day working week, we'll be sitting in the dark writing with pencils. It's a dilemma; either Heath gives in to union demands, or he blacks out Britain.'

Sergeant Longbright entered and handed a single sheet of paper to May.

'Well, here's a turn-up.' May tipped his chair forward. 'Guess who we have listed as the largest clients at Jacob and Marks, and personal friends of Max Jacob?'

'Who?'

'Whitstable, Peter, and Whitstable, William, brothers currently residing together in Hampstead. Max Jacob is their family lawyer.' He thumbed his intercom button and called Longbright back. 'The lads on their way to question Peter Whitstable, tell them they're to observe the house and follow the occupant if necessary, nothing more.' He turned to Bryant. 'Looks like our two investigations just became one.'

'Both events occurred around the same time on Monday evening, within a quarter of a mile of each other. At least it rules out William Whitstable as a murder suspect, unless he could be in two places at once.'

'You mean it rules out one of them. William can't go back to his house. If he tries to meet with his brother, we should be there.'

The call came through at four twenty-five P.M.

'Peter Whitstable returned to the house a few minutes ago, and just left again on foot,' reported Longbright. 'Our car's following. Do you want to speak to them?'

'No,' said May. 'Tell them we're on our way.'

Bryant grabbed his car keys from the table. 'I'll drive,' he said cheerfully. May well remembered their last nightmarish journey together. His colleague was more interested in the drivers around him than the smooth navigation of his own vehicle. Staying in lane, waiting for lights, signaling moves, and remembering to brake were all actions that fell below Bryant's attention level.

'Thanks for the offer, Arthur,' he said, 'but I think I'd rather drive.'

'Really, it's no problem. I find it rather therapeutic.'

'Just give me the keys.'

'The traffic system needs a complete rethink,' mused Bryant as the unit's only allocated vehicle, a powder-blue Vauxhall with a thoroughly thrashed engine, accelerated through Belsize Park. 'Look at these road signs. Ministerial graffiti.'

'It's no use lecturing on the problem, Arthur. That's why your driving examiner failed you thirty-seven times.'

'What makes you such a great driver?'

'I don't hit things.' May circumnavigated the stalled traffic on Haverstock Hill by turning into a back street.

'Did you know that in 1943 the London County Council architects produced a marvelous road map for London that was so visionary it would have ended all modern traffic snarl-ups as we know them?' said Bryant. This was the sort of bright snippet of information he was apt to produce while taking his driving test.

'What happened to it?' asked May, turning into a side road.

'One of their tunnels was routed under St James's Park. It's royal ground. The councillors were scandalized and threw the plans out. Progress toward a better world halted by the threat of displaced ducks, that's postwar England for you. There they are, just ahead.'

The unmarked police vehicle was two cars in front of them, at the traffic-blocked junction of Health Street. A portly middle-aged man was threading his way against the crowds exiting from the corner Tube station.

'They'll meet in the station foyer, out of the way. Pull over here.' Bryant had opened the door and was out before the car had stopped. 'I'll stay close by. You get ahead of them.'

He strolled past his subject and stopped by a magazine rack. It was growing dark, and the lights were on in the tiled ticket hall. Bryant glanced up from the magazines. If Whitstable was meeting his brother from a train, William would have to pass through the ticket barrier to his right.

Just then, Peter Whistable hove into view. He resembled his brother in complexion and corpulence, but was dressed in modern-day clothes. Behind him, Bryant could see May's car stalled in traffic. There was no sign of the unmarked surveillance vehicle. If it had turned the corner it would be caught in a rush-hour stream from several directions. Bryant hoped his partner would be on hand to help. He was in no shape to single-handedly tackle a pair of angry fifteen-stone men.

The ticket hall emptied out. Hampstead was the deepest station in London, and reaching the surface involved waiting for a lift. Bryant stepped back behind the racks as the younger brother approached. He asked the stallkeeper for the time, then took a slow walk to the barrier.

His watch read exactly five o'clock. He could hear one of the elevators rising, its cables tinging in the shaft.

The lift doors parted to reveal a car crowded with commuters. As they began to filter out he caught a glimpse of William Whitstable's black silk hat. Whitstable was checking a fob-watch on an elaborate gold chain. Bryant looked around anxiously. There was no sign of his partner. What could have happened?

Peter had spotted his brother and was moving toward the barrier. Bryant stepped aside to avoid the barrage of passengers, and in doing so revealed himself to both parties. William's eyes locked with his, and he launched himself back to the elevator. Just as the doors were closing, he managed to slip inside.

Bryant looked around. Peter had pushed into May's arms, while the two surveillance men ran past him in the direction of the stairs.

'They'll catch him, Arthur,' called May from the entrance, but Bryant was already boarding the next arriving lift.

Below, home-going commuters filled the northbound platform. The south side was almost empty. Bryant could see his men working their way up through the passengers. A warm soot-haze filled the tunnel as the distant rumbling grew louder.

Moments later a crimson southbound train burst free from the tunnel and roared in. The few waiting passengers stepped back from the platform edge. There was a sudden commotion on the opposite side as William Whitstable was discovered by one of the policemen. Bryant saw arms flailing as people were pushed aside. Suddenly he knew that Whitstable would escape unless he did something to prevent it. He rushed on to the platform, stepped through the open doors of the stationary southbound train, and found his way to a seat, watching from the window as his quarry appeared, running along the empty platform, to jump between the closing doors three carriages further along.

As the train moved off, Bryant rose and moved forward. He had walked through the second carriage when he spied Whitstable standing in the aisle of the third.

The train was already starting to decelerate as it approached the downhill gradient to Belsize Park station. If he managed to alight before Bryant could stop him, Whitstable would be faced with the choice of reaching the surface via the lift or the stairs. Bryant knew that if his quarry took the stairs he might lose him. He reached the door to the third carriage just as the train rattled over points. The carriage lights flickered ominously. He tried to twist the door handle, but it would not budge. Whitstable was turning to face the doors, readying himself to jump through.

The train slowed as Belsize Park's platform appeared. Bryant threw his weight down on the red metal handle, but was unable to shift it. He stared through the glass at William Whitstable. The pair were immobilized, hunter and hunted, unable to fix a course of action.

A muffled explosion slammed the tunnel air against his eardrums. He looked up to find that the window in the connecting door had suddenly become coated with dark liquid. For a moment he thought that Whitstable had thrown paint around the walls, in an act reminiscent of his attack in the gallery. As Bryant stumbled towards the next carriage, he could hear shouts of panic as passengers fought their way free of the wrecked compartment.

A shocked young woman with spatters of blood on her face tipped herself into his arms. Before he could ask what had happened, she turned and pointed back at the smoking detritus which had embedded itself in the walls of the train.

'He exploded,' she screamed at him and kept on screaming. 'He was just standing there and he exploded!'

8 / Horology

The familiarity didn't lessen the fear.

Soles slapped on familiar cobbles, slipping and splashing in shallow puddles. Breath came in ragged gasps as the figure vanished around each corner, tantalizingly out of reach. Once again she was running through high-walled alleyways, the flickering lantern held aloft, illuminating the sweating brickwork.

Again, she found herself stopping dead in her tracks. He was turning now, laughing, wanting to be recognized. His arms were coated with blood, as if they had been plunged into a terrible wound.

And Jerry was awake, the pillow saturated in sweat, the house silent around her. In the corner of the room, a nightlight glowed. The alarm clock beside her bed read four thirty-five A.M. Gwen and Jack were asleep at the end of the corridor. She groped for the light switch, knowing that only brightness could dispel the chill touch of the dream.

She had returned home late to find that Gwen had left a glass of chilled white wine with her plated meal. It was the first time her mother had ever done that. Perhaps it was a gesture to show that she understood her daughter was growing up, even if she refused to allow her to leave home.

Jerry knew she meant well. It was a fact that made Gwen harder to dislike. Angry with her mother's underhand tactics, Jerry had deliberately slammed around in an attempt to waken the house, but no one had appeared to reprimand her. Her mother was contemptuous of her need for a nightlight, and refused to accept the reality of her fears. Her solution was to book extra therapy sessions. Jerry's father would explain his position on the subject by launching into one of his stories that began, 'During the war...' During the war he could turn a Chieftain tank on a threepenny bit in pitch darkness with blackout curtains tied around it. Or something equally boring and stupid.

Back then, he would explain, nobody was afraid of the dark. Men were decent God-fearing chums who kept their chins up and their lips stiff whenever the Hun forced their backs against the wall. Not any more, though, judging by the way Jack instantly obeyed his wife's every command. Gwen ruled the house with an iron fist in a Dior glove.

Jerry sat up and flattened her unruly hair. She wished Joseph was staying at the house. She had enjoyed their evening together. After the play, he had taken her for something to eat, and they had squashed in beside each other in a dingy Spanish restaurant, watching the red wax drip from the chianti bottle while they made loud small talk above thundering guitar music.

Joseph had graduated from college with a portfolio of designs that were about to be realized in the grandest way imaginable. His work had been chosen over hundreds of designs from other young hopefuls. Jerry had talked as little about herself as possible, painting a picture of domestic ease with her parents. She explained that she was temping in the receptionist's job until she could start art college. For a brief moment, as she watched the candle-light leaping in his brown eyes, the thought crossed her mind that he wanted to be with her all night. But the moment passed and they parted awkwardly on the steps of Waterloo Bridge, and she supposed that tomorrow the status quo of guest and employee would be restored. A pity; she liked him because he was everything she wasn't. There was something appealingly insolent about him, in the way he swung his arms as he walked, in the sunny, careless looks he threw at strangers. She was sick of being surrounded by men her mother approved as acceptable role models. It was time to choose her own friends.

The thought of Joseph dissolved her nightmares into harmless light. She knew now that she could find untroubled sleep with such a guardian angel to invigilate her dreams.

'You're in early. Couldn't sleep? Sign of a guilty conscience.'

May hung up his overcoat and took a look around the office. His new roommate had been hard at work. Over a dozen crates of books had been unpacked. The shelves now groaned with forbidding procedural volumes, psychotherapy manuals, and medical texts. There was a particularly nasty-looking plant on the window ledge, possibly the remains of a diseased aspidistra. Bryant looked pale and out of sorts. He was trying to lever open the main window by wedging the tip of a screwdriver beneath the lintel.

'I don't sleep much any more,' he said, cracking a spray of paint chips from the window frame. 'I don't want to waste time by being unconscious. It's not every day a suspect explodes on you. Have you seen today's papers? It's been a godsend to the gutter press. They were all preparing features on Princess Anne's wedding gifts when this landed in their laps. Now they can start running hate columns on the IRA again. If I catch any of those weasels near my witnesses there'll be hell to pay. Give me a hand with this window.'

The press wasn't the cause of Bryant's anger, and May knew it. He had seen this mood too many times before. 'You couldn't have prevented his death, Arthur. Nobody knew he was carrying an incendiary device.' Together they shoved at the window until it burst open in a cloud of dust and dried paint.

'Are you sure it was a bomb?' asked Bryant. 'Four witnesses saw a sudden ball of flame appear at Whitstable's midriff. What kind of explosive can kill a man in a half-full railway carriage without injuring anyone else? First his lawyer, and now him. Tell me it's a coincidence if you dare. What else have you got on Jacob?'

May pulled out a handful of papers. 'Some scuff marks by the sinks in the Savoy toilet that the cleaners managed to miss, looks like Kiwi brand boot polish from Jacob's right shoe. The pattern of marks will most likely confirm that he was attacked there. Some tiny scraps of linen at the site of the scuffle, a standard Indian blend, possibly from a pocket lining. No fibre match with Jacob's clothing. One thing—the cottonmouth venom doesn't have to come from a live snake. It maintains its potency, which means that it could simply have been injected from a syringe into his neck.'

'There were two puncture holes, like snake fangs.'

'Perhaps the murderer tried to get the needle in once, and Jacob struggled so much that he had to jab it in again.'

'But he'd been rendered unconscious before the administration of the poison.'

May raised his hands in exasperation. 'Then maybe

the killer wanted it to look like a snake had attacked his victim.'

'Why would he do that?' asked Bryant doggedly. 'Snakes aren't exactly a common sight in England.'

'As for the rest of the findings, take a look at the headlines. The press seems to know as much as we do. The guard on Peter Whitstable will keep the journalists at bay for the time being.' May frowned in annoyance. 'Why do you want the window open, anyway? It's freezing outside.'

'I didn't want it open,' replied Bryant testily. 'I wanted the option of having it open. There are about twenty layers of paint on the frame. It's like seaside rock.' He pointed at the crate blocking May's path to his desk. 'That's the last one I have to unpack.'

May knew that his partner would not settle to a comfortable work pace until he had made the new office his own in some way. He reached down into the opened crate and pulled up a bony brown object inlaid with silver. Turquoise gems returned sight to its eyeless sockets. 'Where on earth did you get this?' he asked, turning it over in his hand.

'A friend of mine brought it back from Tibet,' explained Bryant. 'It's an engraved human skull. So long as the Chinese government is systematically destroying Tibetan culture, it stays on the shelf to remind me of the evil and injustice in the world.'

'You only have to take a look at the overnight crime figures to be reminded of that,' said May, holding the skull at arm's length. 'It smells terrible.'

'I don't think they emptied out the brain cavity properly.'

May watched his partner as he carefully unwrapped a china figurine, a woman dancing in a delicate green dress, and placed it on his desk. It was strange being part of a team again. Arthur wasn't looking so steady on his feet these days. He seemed to be ageing at a faster rate than everyone else.

'Who's interviewing the brother, you or I?'

'I'll take Peter Whitstable,' said Bryant. 'He's a major, fully decorated and highly respected. Let's hope he's capable of providing an explanation for his sibling's behaviour. They're all inbred, you know. Old families never strayed far from the family seat to marry. You can always tell; their eyes are too close together and they like folk music.'

Sergeant Longbright entered the room with a small plastic bag in one hand. Her shift had finished four hours late, at three A.M. Thick makeup hid the crescents beneath her eyes.

'I'm sorry you were pulled in on your day off, Janice,' said May. 'Raymond Land is worried that this investigation will get too much of a public profile. He's canceled all leave for the foreseeable future.'

'That's okay, I was only sleeping.' If she was annoyed, she had no intention of showing it. She dropped the bag on May's desk and displayed its tag. 'Land came by a few minutes ago and left this for you.' She sniffed the air. 'What's that awful smell?'

'You'll have to talk to Mr Bryant about that. Wasn't there a message with it?' May held the bag to the light. Tiny metal shards glittered within, like crystal formations.

'He said he'd call once you'd had a chance to examine it.'

'Is Land based here full time?' asked Bryant.

'I'm afraid so, old bean. He has the office right at the end of the hall.' Raymond Land was a reasonably talented forensic scientist, but his meticulous manner and air of superiority did little to endear him to his colleagues. He was particularly irritated by Bryant, whose elliptical, unorthodox approach to investigations infuriated him. Land had been chasing promotion for some time, and had been appointed acting head of the PCU, a position he had most definitely not wanted.

May unzipped the plastic bag and carefully shook out its contents. He separated the curving slivers of gold with his forefinger. 'What do you make of this, Arthur?'

Bryant searched in his drawer for a magnifier and approached the metal splinters. 'Looks like old gold. Victorian, I should say. Much purer than the stuff you buy these days. Quite red, and very soft. There are some markings...' He slid one of the pieces beneath the magnifier and turned up the light. 'Roman numerals. Calibrations of some kind? I've seen something like this before.'

'Could be pieces of a pendant,' suggested May.

'No, it's something more technical. One of these fragments isn't gold. Looks like good-quality silver.' He turned the metal over in his hand. 'There's a tiny hinge on one side. It's the lid of an enamel container.' The telephone rang. 'That'll be Land. He's been sitting at his desk timing you.'

'Well, John, what do you think?' asked Land, speaking too loudly into the mouthpiece.

'I'm not sure. Where did you get it?'

'Finch removed the pieces from your man, the exploded Whitstable. They weren't inside his stomach to begin with; the force of the blast drove them in. I assume it's part of the bomb casing.'

'Tell him it's not,' said Bryant in a loud stage whisper. He held one of the gold shards between his thumb and forefinger. 'Give me the phone.'

May passed the receiver over.

'Hello?' Bryant shouted back. 'This is from a small gold clock. The kind made for a presentation.'

'That's ridiculous,' replied Land. 'You don't build a bomb out of precious metals.'

'Why not? Craftsmen of the nineteenth century inlaid everything with elaborate metalwork.'

'It's 1973, Bryant,' snapped Land.

'I'm aware of that. Still, I'd like you to spectrum-test the shards for chemical residue.'

'I really don't see what use—'

'No, but I do,' said Bryant rudely. 'If you would be so kind.' He hung up.

'I won't have many friends left around here by the time you've finished,' said May. 'Let's find out if Peter Whitstable has anything more to say.' They had taken a statement from the Major immediately after his brother's death, but he had been too upset to be of help to them. Now it was time for some answers.

9 / Losing Light

Nearly a week had passed since she had witnessed the murder, but Jerry could still feel death on her hands. She turned them over in the light, trying to remember where the blood had stippled the whorls of her fingertips, attempting to recall the exact spot on the carpet where the old man had taken his final breath.

'I wonder how the police knew it was foul play,' she said aloud, studying the brown leather armchair from her place behind the reception desk.

'It wasn't any such thing,' said Nicholas. Jerry's obsession was beginning to bore him. It was bad enough that he had been forced to take a Saturday shift with her, but with Common Market delegates arriving in force, everyone was working overtime. 'The police don't have any idea what happened. There was an exposé of their incompetence in the *Telegraph* yesterday. They're trying to hush the whole thing up.'

'It wouldn't work though, would it? There's been too much publicity already. The truth will have to come out eventually.' With the fallout from Watergate engulfing the presidency on the other side of the Atlantic, everyone was looking for conspiracies.

'I suppose it will, so long as you're alive to talk about it,' said Nicholas. 'There's another batch of delegates being greeted at twelve-thirty. Leaders of emerging nations. A lot of unusual headgear, the national anthem played on logs, that sort of thing. You'll have to check them in by yourself because I'll be off duty by then.' He smoothed a long curl of blond hair back in place and returned to his bookkeeping.

'If it wasn't murder,' she persisted, 'why haven't they taken the police seal off Jacob's room?'

'They have.' Nicholas looked up from his paperwork, exasperated. 'We're putting someone in there today.' He checked his watch. 'In about fifteen minutes.'

Jerry wasn't sure why, but it suddenly became important for her to see the room. Removing the passkey from the wall compartments behind her, she slipped away from the desk and took the elevator to the fourth floor. The room at the end of the corridor had been sealed along the doorframe to prevent anyone from entering. Now the seals had been removed, and the maids had been allowed to make up the beds.

There was nothing left in the room to reveal anything of its previous occupier. Had she honestly expected there to be? The police would have removed Jacob's belongings and forwarded them to his family. The room would have been searched, but their forensic team would have had no reason to examine it. After all, it wasn't the murder site. Instead they had concentrated their efforts on the ground-floor men's washroom.

Jerry walked into the bathroom and flicked on the light. Her pale reflection stared back at her, auburn hair flopping in cobalt eyes. She drew back the shower curtain and checked the ceramic soap holder. Max Jacob had risen and showered on Monday morning, not knowing that this was to be the last day of his life. Why had he come to London? How had he spent his final hours? Presumably the police already knew the answers to those questions. Could she call the detective and ask him? Wouldn't he think it odd that she wanted to know?

She could hear rain hitting the windows in the bedroom. The morning had begun as dimly as last Monday had ended. She knew there was something wrong with the way she felt; that something had been triggered by witnessing an act as private as dying. It all felt so sudden and unfinished. Jacob could have suspected nothing. He had come to the front desk earlier that day and chatted pleasantly to Nicholas. He had certainly not been in fear of his life then.

Jerry reentered the bedroom and searched through the desk drawers. The hotel stationery had already been replenished, and lay neatly arranged for the next resident. If Jacob had left behind any sign of his occupation, it had since been removed by the police and the maids.

She pulled open the bedside drawer, and was about to close it again when she noticed the Bible. Her eyes traveled down the bookmarked page to find a passage heavily underscored.

John 3.19....and men loved darkness rather than light, because their deeds were evil. For every one that doeth evil hateth the light, neither cometh to the light, lest his deeds should be reproved.

A scrap of notepaper had been folded inside. It bore a number: 216. She flicked back through the pages, noting other marked passages.

Psalms 139.11....Even the night shall be light about me.

John 12.35. Walk while ye have the light, lest darkness come upon you...

Genesis 1.16. And God made two great lights; the greater light to rule the day, and the lesser light to rule the night…

There were dozens of penciled references, all of them offering advice on matters of light and darkness. Presuming Max Jacob had marked the passages himself, he obviously believed in practising his religion. But that made no sense. Surely the name Jacob was Jewish? She was about to check that there was nothing more of interest when she heard the lift arriving. The room's new occupant could well be checking in. She slipped the Bible into her jacket, closed the door behind her, and kept walking to the end of the corridor.

John May rang the doorbell and stepped back.

A constable stood guard beneath the large sycamore at the end of the front garden. Water was running from his jacket, soaking the knees of his trousers. There was no sound save that of the rain falling into the trees in the deserted Hampstead avenue. Bryant trudged through the bushes at the side of the house, pushing aside the wet leaves to peer in through dirt-spattered windows.

Finally there was a sound from within, footsteps thumping and stumbling in the hallway. The gentleman who laboriously unlocked the door was a little younger than his brother, but in every other way the dead man's double. The heavyset face, with bulbous crimson nose and pendulous lower lip, recalled to mind any number of Hogarthian caricatures. Peter Whitstable's heavy winter brown woollens were barely of the present era. He seemed to have trouble opening the door. Finally he managed to pull it wide, whereupon he looked up at May, stumbled on the step, and fell into his arms.

'Good God,' said Bryant, returning to the doorstep, 'he's completely drunk.'

'Help me get him into the kitchen.' May hooked his hands under the Major's arms and hauled him across the hall, enveloped in the sour reek of whisky. 'He's no use to us like this.'

'Give him a coffee, by all means,' said Bryant, 'but let's ask him a few questions. We might get some honest answers while he's in this state.'

The house smelled of lavender polish and old Scotch. None of the furniture could be dated after the late 1900s. Oils and watercolours of every size and description filled the walls, butted frame to frame. It was as if they had stepped into a cluttered Victorian home untouched by passing decades. Heavy green-velvet curtains kept light and time at bay. Bryant's eyes grew brighter as he examined the gilt-framed photographs on the walls lining the kitchen corridor.

'It's like wandering into the past,' he remarked.

'How dare you, Sirr,' slurred the Major suddenly, raising his head and fixing Bryant with a bloodshot eye. 'To gentlemen of enlightenment, this was our time of glory. Let others tear down the past with their caterwauling music and their free love . . . and . . .' He collapsed, unable to summon a third example.

May sat their man on a straight-backed chair while Bryant made strong coffee. Beneath the sink were more than a dozen empty whisky bottles. Major Peter Whitstable had not turned to alcohol to numb the news of his brother's death. He and Johnnie Walker were old friends.

The kitchen was immaculate in the old-fashioned manner of having been scoured to the point of erosion. A vast iron hob dominated the room. Copper saucepans hung in gleaming rows. A Victorian ice-cream drum stood beside a rack of spoons and ladles, and looked as if it was still in use. As Whitstable didn't seem capable of organizing this himself, the brothers most likely had a housekeeper.

'Jus' put a shot in it, there's a good chap,' he mumbled as Bryant passed him a steaming mug. When no such action was forthcoming, the Major removed a silver flask from his jacket, unscrewed the cap, and tipped in an ample measure before either of the detectives could stop him.

'We have no desire to impose on you in a time of grief,' began May, 'but some urgent questions must be addressed.'

Whitstable slumped back in his chair. 'I can't believe he's gone,' he said. 'Or rather, I can.' He promptly fell asleep. Bryant nudged him awake, none too gently, and prised the spilling mug from his hands.

'Th' bastards won't get away with it,' Peter Whitstable cried, swinging his great head from one face to the other. 'We're not the only ones against this, you know.'

'What happened to your brother?' asked May. 'Why should someone want to kill him?'

''S obvious,' said Peter Whitstable, making a half-hearted attempt to sit up. 'Enemies. Anarchists. Sybarites and sodomites. None of us are safe! The country's gone to—where has it gone?'

'We're not going to get any sense from him,' whispered May.

'Let me try.' Bryant dragged a chair close. 'Major Whitstable—Peter—may I call you that? I know you'd like to be left by yourself. If you want we can take the guards from your house and leave you alone, in peace.'

'God, don' do that!' he shouted, terror clearing his

drunken stupor. He sat forward, his eyes widening. 'We're in terr'ble danger, horrible things could happen!'

'Then you think whoever killed your brother will come after you?'

'I do believe that. Yess.' He patted his pockets for the whisky flask. 'And you, too, if you get in the way. Darkness is rising, y'see.'

'Explain what you mean,' challenged May.

'S'plain, yes. Follow me.' Whitstable lurched to his feet, holding a finger to his lips, and beckoned to the detectives. 'Have to come upstairs.'

At the first landing, Bryant had to move fast to stop the Major from falling backwards. A gloomy room opened from the landing. Here the smell of furniture polish and dead air was stronger than ever. The heavy floor-length curtains were parted no more than a foot. Photograph frames and military trophies cluttered the green-baize-covered mantelpiece, and dingy oils of horses filled the walls. The Major weaved his way over to a walnut sideboard and searched among the decanters.

'Take a good look around at this lot,' he said. 'We are a dynastic fam'ly. Aristocratic British stock. Traditional values. We obey the landowners' creed: If it's attractive you shoot it; if it's ugly you marry it. Not many of us left, an' gettin' damn fewer by the day. William and I ... Poor William. I don't s'pose there's enough of him left to bury.'

'We can catch the people who did this if you help us,' said May, but the Major was not listening.

'We knew what was expected of us in those days,' he was saying. 'Have a herd of children, marry the daughters into money, stick the bright sons in business, the dim ones in the Church, and the mad ones in the army. O' course you make enemies. 'S only natural.' He sat down heavily with a decanter between his knees. 'I s'pose you want to know who killed him.'

'Yes,' said May, relieved that their purpose was finally being understood. 'Although you could start by explaining why your brother destroyed the painting.'

'Oh, I don't know why he did that. Our family has a long association with—' he paused for a breath '—the sponsorship of art, so you can imagine my s'prise when I heard what he'd done. I called on him to explain hisself, but he told me I should already understand the reason for his action.' He unsteadily filled a tumbler and lost the decanter to Bryant, who managed to snatch it away. 'But I *didn't* understand. William was so attached to the past— how could he be responsible for destroyin' part of it?' May made a lunge for the filled whisky glass, but Whitstable clasped it to his chest with both hands.

'Poor confused William. Our enemies are laughing at us, but we'll be avenged by our ancestors, you see if we won't.' His cheeks became suffused with an angry scarlet as he began to shout. 'They hate the power of the light because they will be damned by their foul deeds! You should have asked Max Jacob, slimy little weasel, he could have told you. Bit by a snake—a traditional weapon, see, meant to strike fear into—somewhere or other.'

'He's off again,' murmured May. 'Take his glass away, quick.'

But Bryant was not fast enough. Whitstable managed to snatch it up and drain it.

'Was Max Jacob killed by the same person who murdered your brother?' asked May.

The Major stared wildly at the detective. 'Don't be bloody daft, man. My brother was not killed by a 'person,' and neither was the Israelite. It was not a Who that killed them, Mr May, but a What. And a bloody frightening one at that!'

'Then if you know, tell us,' begged Bryant. 'You can avenge William's death.'

'William, William, William.' He shook his head violently. 'There'll be plenty more joining him now.'

'What do you mean?' asked May. 'Are more people going to die?'

'Lots more, lots and lots, blood and bodies everywhere, Armageddon for our entire family, all the way to the end of the light. If you try to do anything, you'll die, too. For without are dogs and sorcerers and whoremongers and murderers.'

Bryant was torn between leaving the man to sleep it off or questioning him further now. He felt sure that the Major would not answer their questions when he was sober. 'We can't understand you,' he said. 'You have to explain what you mean.'

'To know what killed William you must understand us all, and the families of others like us.' He reached out for the decanter and found it missing. 'You have to face the true darkness, if you can find it any more, which is bloody doubtful these days.'

Bryant released a hiss of frustration. The Major was never going to give them a straight answer. 'If you don't help us, Peter,' he warned, 'I'll have the guards removed from your house.'

'Then remove them!' he shouted. 'I'll take my chances. I used to box in the war. After tomorrow I'll be safe.'

'How?'

'Why, my Bella is arriving to take care of me.'

Bryant looked across at his partner and mouthed, *'Who's Bella?'*

The Major tipped his head back and dropped the glass to the floor. 'My beautiful Bella,' he sighed. 'The grace of our Lord Jesus Christ be with you all, Amen and good night.' This time he descended into an unshakeable sleep, and was snoring loudly before the detectives left.

10 / Severance

Jerry turned the Bible over in her hands. She was walking through the garden, exhaling clouds into the frosty air, watching as the last dusk-bound starlings left the sky. The peaceful Chelsea backwater in which her family had lived since her birth was green and damp enough to feel like countryside. Trees provided a susurrance that sounded like an off-air TV channel. It was hard to believe that beyond the darkened beeches lay the electric brilliance of the King's Road.

Behind her, the house was filled with bright, dead light. Gwen and Jack had gone for their usual Sunday night game of bridge, and had turned on every bulb in the house, mistakenly believing that this would deter burglars. Jerry reached the verdigris-covered bench in the small brick arbour and seated herself, turning her attention back to the Bible.

When she had seen it lying there in the drawer she had almost been fooled by it, because of the binding. Although it was much older and in poor condition, the book was similar to the standard Concordance copies kept in the hotel rooms. But it wasn't one of the Savoy editions. One of those had already been placed in the right-hand drawer of Jacob's bedside table. She had found this book to the left of the bed. Now she reexamined the unfamiliar name on the flyleaf, *W. Whitstable, St Peter's, Hampstead*, and turning the dry, semitransparent pages within, saw that the Bible was older than she had at first realized. A particular smell exuded from its pages, of church pews and hushed rooms. The printing mark read 1873. Certain letters—*S*'s and *T*'s—were joined together at the top. Exactly one hundred years old. It felt as if it had been given as a gift, something which Mr Jacob had valued greatly. She knew that she should take it to the police, but felt sure that if she did so, she would never know the meaning of her discovery.

Instead she'd gone to the reception desk and begun her search. The phone book yielded thirty-one Whitstables in central London, eight starting with the initial W, three of them in the Hampstead area. She decided that she would ring each of them in turn.

Pulling the house phone as far as it would reach, she unfolded the notepaper on the knee of her jeans, marked off the first number with her thumb and began to dial.

Her first two calls failed to net a reply. Third on the list was Whitstable, William, of Mayberry Grove, Hampstead. By now the sun had fully set and the garden lay in pale gloom. It was never truly dark in the city. Even in deepest night the sky appeared to be made of tracing paper. She studied the dial and waited for her connection to be completed. Instantly, she was sure she had called the correct number. The elderly male voice at the other end was filled with suspicion, as if in anticipation of her call.

'Why are you ringing here? What do you want?'

'Have I reached the home of Mr W. Whitstable?' she asked in her best Savoy telephone manner.

'William?' There was confusion now. 'There's no one here...'

'I have something to return to him. Something he's lost.'

'Well, what is it?' The speaker was agitated. His

words were sliding into one another, as if he was drunk. She had nothing to gain by holding out. 'I have a Bible belonging to a gentleman named Mr W. Whitstable.'

The single word again. 'William.' And a hushed silence.

Bingo. Jerry smiled in the shadows. 'I was wondering if I could return it to the gentleman.'

'He's no longer here,' said the speaker hastily. 'Send it to me instead.'

'I wouldn't trust the post office with something as delicate as this,' she replied. 'I'll bring it to you, if you like.'

'I don't think—no, not tonight, I can't have visitors at night, not now...'

'Then tomorrow,' she pressed. 'I'll call by in the morning, is that all right?'

The line went dead. Jerry replaced the receiver, puzzled. At least she had located the Bible's owner. She considered informing Mr May, just in case there was any trouble, but decided against it. The voice had belonged to an old man. She could handle it. She rose from the armchair and rubbed warmth into her arms, wondering what on earth she was doing.

Mayberry Grove was a cul-de-sac filled with solid Victorian red-brick houses hidden behind swathes of greenery; miniature castles built by confident men whose minds could not imagine the twilight of the empire. As Jerry approached the house she was surprised to find an unfriendly-looking police constable standing in the front garden.

'I've an appointment to see Mr Whitstable,' she said cheerfully, pushing back the wet gate. Having been given no information to the contrary, she was still guessing that the name was correct.

'Oh, yes? And who are you, then?' The constable was not that much older than she, but had already developed an antagonistic attitude.

'I spoke to Mr Whitstable last night. I'm returning something that belongs to him.'

'He can't have visitors.' The constable rocked back on wide polished boots and gave the top of his walkie-talkie a wipe. 'Give it to me and I'll make sure that he gets it.'

'He told me I should give it to him myself.'

'Not possible, lovey.' He gave a dim smile and shifted his gaze away as if he had sighted something in the middle distance. Jerry was just about to argue when the front door burst open and there stood a florid-faced man in an ill-fitting checked suit and crooked tie. He seemed vaguely familiar, and was arguing with a second constable, who had appeared at his side from somewhere within the hall.

'I don't give a damn what your superior officer says,' shouted Peter Whitstable. 'It's where I've been once a fortnight ever since the end of World War Two, and no blasted low-ranking officer is going to stop me now.'

'Then you must allow someone to accompany you,' reasoned the officer, trying to keep pace as they marched down the garden path. 'It may not be safe for you to go out.'

'I am well aware of that,' snapped the Major, whirling on the young officer. 'D'you think I should change my life for the sake of some cowardly assassin who can't show his face in the light? Is that what my brother went to his death for? Is that the spirit that made this country great? Never, Sir! I shall face up to the foe with a strong heart and a . . .' He forgot what the other thing was, and switched metaphors, '. . . Spring in my step,' he finished vaguely, pushing the second constable from his guard duty at the gate. 'And what's more, I shall be back within the hour.' He slipped the latch and passed into the street.

'For God's sake go after him, Kenworth,' said the first policeman. 'If we lose him there'll be hell to pay.'

'Where is he going?' asked Jerry, looking toward the rapidly retreating figure.

'For a haircut,' the officer replied, throwing his hands up helplessly. 'The Major's a possible murder target, and he has to go to the Strand just for a bloody haircut.'

Jerry caught up with the Major in an alleyway leading into Haverstock Hill. The younger constable was trailing a hundred yards or so behind them, pausing only to listen to the crackle from his handset. Peter Whitstable reached the main road and turned in the direction of Belsize Park. Jerry hung back, dipping into the doorway of a chemist's as the Major looked back at the corner. So the man they were following was being kept under surveillance because his brother had been killed? A second death, separate from Jacob's? This was too bizarre to be ignored. Major Whitstable's life couldn't really be in danger, otherwise the police would have put him in protective custody, wouldn't they? What if the old man wasn't going to his barber at all? What if he was about to give them all the slip? Perhaps the police had deliberately let him out to see where he would head.

Perhaps they were just incompetent.

Because now the Major had sidled between the stalled traffic on the hill and was heading into another of the still-misty alleys on the far side of the road. Jerry glanced back, and saw that the constable had missed the move. It was a good job one of them had been watching. As the traffic lights flicked to amber, universal British driving code for 'pedal to the metal,' she darted between revving engines to the opposite pavement and ran into the alley. All she saw was the usual collection of effete Hampstead stores selling Provence potpourris and patchwork cats. No barbershop.

At the end of the passage she could hear the throb of a taxicab, and she ran forward just in time to see the Major's ample rear disappearing into the vehicle. By the time she had reached the kerb, the cab had pulled away, U-turning past her as it headed down the hill. She passed the befuddled constable, who was shouting into his squawking handset.

Where would someone like the Major still be able to have his hair cut in such a severe military style? She was trying to think of as many places as possible when she remembered the constable's complaint: his charge insisted on visiting the Strand. There was only one place he could possibly be heading for. Jerry flagged down an empty cab and leaned in at the window.

'The Savoy, please. As quickly as possible.'

'Right you are, love.'

In less than ten minutes they were pulling up beneath the shining metal letters of the hotel entrance. The steel canopy on the front of the building always reminded her of a Rolls-Royce grille. The barber shop within was timeless and traditional, just right for a man of the Major's appearance.

Inside, the foyer was already crowded with newly arrived delegates for the Common Market conference, due to start in Whitehall this morning. Jerry made her way through the groups, ignoring Nicholas's puzzled look as she headed upstairs to the barber shop. There, within a gentlemen's world of white-tiled walls, stainless-steel fittings, and chrome-trimmed leather shaving chairs, she knew there was a chance of locating her quarry. And perhaps he could be persuaded to explain the link between a Victorian Bible and a dead lawyer.

One question had occupied Peter Whitstable's mind since the police had informed him that his brother was dead. How could it have happened? *How?* These days, of course, they had many enemies. That was only to be expected. The world was changing so quickly. There was no time left for chivalry or honour. The war had seen to that. What was the point of trying to do the decent thing when your adversaries seized the moment to steal a march on you? He had always loved his brother dearly, but the sad fact was that poor William had lost touch with the modern world.

As the taxi left the Aldwych he saw the homeless wrapped in cartons of corrugated cardboard and thought, *My God, there are people actually sleeping in the streets again.* What had their high ideals done for these people, and the thousands like them who arrived at the stations looking for a city that would somehow work miracles? In a hundred years, nothing had changed. The city's underclass comprised men and women of good intent, people who had been systematically robbed of their ideas and their self-worth as they were forced to the gutter by their masters.

Major Whitstable's eyes were blinded by tears as the cab turned into Savoy Street. He kept his head turned from the driver as he paid the fare. *Bad morale for the servants*, he thought from habit, then remembered; there were no more servants. *We are all equal now. Try telling that to the kids in the shop doorways,* he thought as he walked through the congested foyer of the hotel. The damaged, the disenfranchised, the teen runaways—*the other people*— were just blank faces to the well-heeled guests here. How dare they look in on a world to which they had no claim? *We are all equal now,* he thought bitterly, *if you don't count the judges and landowners and politicians and diplomats. If you don't count families like ours.*

He ascended the curving stairway and opened the glass door at the top. The smell of fresh soap and hot towels restored his humour a little. Surprisingly for a Monday morning there were no other customers, and even Maurice seemed absent. A barber he had never seen before was honing an open razor on an umber leather strap.

'Good morning, Major,' said the man cheerily. On second glance, perhaps he had seen him before. The brilliantined hair combed across the tanned bald patch and the tiny waxed moustache were certainly familiar, but this chap seemed to be wearing makeup. The barber's face was painted an unsubtle shade of chalk, and the colour ended at his brown neck. How odd.

'Good morning,' said Whitstable testily, removing his jacket. 'What's happened to Maurice?' He removed the Victorian watch he kept in his waistcoat and tapped it irritably.

'Believe there's a bit of a bug going around, Sir,' said the barber. 'I'm Eric.' He didn't look like an Eric. To be honest, he looked like an Indian, and a very sickly one at that. The Major decided to let it pass.

'Well, Eric, I suppose we'll have to start from scratch.' He studied his watery eyes in the beveled wall mirror.

'Not at all, Sir,' said Eric genially. 'I had the pleasure of shaving you once long ago, and Mr Maurice informs me that nothing has changed in the way of your personal ablutions. Please take a seat.'

As the barber leaned close he became aware of an odd smell, a forgotten scent. It was vaguely familiar, like lime chutney. Something the fellow had been eating? Indian smell, Indian accent. He frowned.

Eric flapped out a white apron with a crack of fresh linen that sounded like a gunshot, and swirled it over Whitstable's head like a matador preparing to antagonize a bull. The Major closed his eyes and listened to the sounds he had heard all his life. Fresh shaving foam slapping in a ceramic bowl, the rhythmic stropping of an open blade. He felt the stiff bristle of the badger flowering foam across his cheeks, and the years melted away.

'Where did you shave me before? Not here, surely?'

'No, Sir. In India.'

The lights above the mirror dazzled and flared through his half-shut eyes as he felt the first sharp prick of the blade upon his throat. Even in the desert, in Rommel's darkest days, he had never shaved himself, and nor had William. Such times were gone for ever.

'Won't take long now, Major,' said Eric soothingly.

The searing steel cut a swathe of bristles from below his jawline to the base of his ear lobe. The blade was rinsed clean, and returned to his face hotter than ever.

'Whereabouts in India?'

'Calcutta, Sir, about fifteen years ago. 1958, I believe it was.'

'That's right, I was stationed in Calcutta then.'

'And so was I, Sir.'

'Well, I never.'

The blade ran lightly across his chin and bit into the bristles at the top of his trachea—a little too deeply, he thought.

'I say, steady on.'

The edge of the razor lifted, caressing his throat with its edge, then suddenly pushed forward, a streak of flame crossing his throat. He was sure he'd been nicked. It was unforgivable!

'Look here—' he began.

With a sudden application of pressure, the honed steel blade popped the skin like a bayonet and smoothly parted it in one wide sweep. The Major raised his arms as a torrent of blood burst forth over the white-hot wound, flowing around his chin and down his neck. He tried to call out but the blade was sawing back and forth, deeper and deeper, severing his vocal chords as the enraged barber whose name was not Eric worked on, his wild eyes glittering in a livid white face.

'Where do you think you're going?' asked Nicholas, grabbing her sleeve. 'You were supposed to be on duty over an hour ago.'

'Couldn't you cover for me?' Jerry pleaded. 'This is really important.'

'Why should I? This isn't the first time you've been late when we've had a rush on.'

Jerry looked desperately towards the doors of the barber shop. 'You're right,' she said. 'I'm sorry.' Nicholas released his grip. 'I'll be back in just a minute.' She ran off up the stairs, leaving her protesting colleague behind.

The doors were locked. She looked at her watch. Ten-fifteen A.M. The shop should have opened at nine-thirty. Besides, Maurice never kept the entrance locked. She could see no movement through the frosted glass. The room seemed to be empty.

She knelt down and peered under the crack of the

door. There was a large figure slumped in one of the shaving chairs. One arm hung down towards the floor. The white sheet covering the body was splashed with cerise.

Then she was on her feet, hurling herself at the door until the wood splintered and the old glass panels cracked from top to bottom. She shoved aside the shattered door and stepped into the salon. The figure lay back in the chair with its throat untidily slashed into a second grimacing mouth. Its face bore a look of disbelief, the eyes protruding in stark surprise. The mother-of-pearl handle of an open razor jutted up from between the victim's teeth. Only the polished army shoes which poked out beneath the encompassing cape reminded Jerry that she was looking at the brutalized remains of Major Peter Whitstable.

11 / Ancestry

The heavy wooden lid slammed back in a cloud of fibrous dust.

John May raised his head above the lintel and shone the torch inside. The attic ran the entire length of the house. The rafters were clean and cobweb free, and a new wooden floor had been laid across the boarding joists, turning the area into a work-space.

Hauling himself up, May ran his beam over the walls and located a light switch. The single mercury vapour lamp was bright enough to illuminate the centre of the room. He wiped the dirt from his palms and sat back against a packing crate. There were at least twenty sealed tea chests here, unsteady stacks of books, dust-sheeted pieces of furniture, carpentry equipment, an old litho press, plaster statues, an upright harpsichord. The Whitstable brothers had hidden away a large part of their past, and all of it would have to be searched.

He rolled back the dustsheet from an open-topped crate and shone his torch inside. A soot-blackened Victorian dinner service, complete by the look of it, and a number of Staffordshire figurines lying unwrapped and unprotected. He raised a pair and studied them. A soldier mounted upon his steed, his helmet beneath his arm, another beside the barrel of a mobile cannon, probably characters from the Crimean War. Bryant would know who they were. A set of horse paintings that looked to be by Stubbs, a bust of Walpole, numerous leather-bound first editions. He tried to imagine how much the contents of the attic were worth. By the look of it, the brothers had been sitting on a fortune. He wondered who stood to benefit most.

It was the theatricality of the investigation that bothered him more than anything else. The esoteric upper-class murder belonged to the world of Edwardian fiction. Such deaths simply did not occur in the modern world. A busy week in the West End could yield half a dozen killings of official interest, but they all fell into the standard categories. A young Chinese man attacked with a sword in Chinatown in broad daylight, possibly a triad connection, bad gambling debts. A punter leaving a club on Saturday night, found dead in an alley, seen flashing cash by a group of shark-eyed kids who waited for him to leave. An altercation outside a bar that left one dead and one in critical condition, knives and drink and a row over nothing much at all. Bryant was right—the common run of city crime was vicious and pointless, usually fueled by alcohol. From the business end, it was rarely worthy of attention.

In the 1970s, most murders still took place at home. Women were more likely to die there than men, nearly half of them suffering at the hands of a husband or lover. Men were slaughtered by acquaintances and strangers, simply because they got out of the house more often than their partners. Ethnic gang violence was unimaginable. Drug-related crimes were unheard of. East Enders still mentioned the Kray brothers in shocked reverence, but nobody really thought they were gentlemen.

May knew that the statistics of death were inaccurate: doctors were pulling more victims through, more crimes were reported, technological breakthroughs were being made, lawyers were disputing terminology, the boundary lines were shifting. They could be certain of just two facts. Murder was more likely to be committed within the family. And each passing year brought rising figures.

But as for this...

He looked around at the accretions of more than a century, relics of the past, overflowing from every corner. There was a touch of Robert Louis Stevenson here, the sense of a long-standing family feud reaching a flashpoint. Over what? A contested inheritance? A missing will? The idea sounded unnecessarily Gothic but promising, especially as the family lawyer had also been killed. What other possibilities were there? An unrighted wrong? Stolen virtue? A debt of honour? The danger was that they would overlook the answer in a rush to pin the blame.

Senior officials were already pushing for a fast arrest. Raymond Land, the unit's acting head, had already paid a visit to May's office. The Whitstables weren't just anyone, he explained; they were a well-connected family whose opinions still carried political clout. Peter had been a personal friend of Montgomery, for God's sake. He had been with the Eighth Army on the east coast of Italy. He had been decorated for his part in the Normandy invasion. His grandparents had left bequests to Balmoral. Brother William had been introduced to the queen at Sandringham, although Land was unsure of the reason for this.

But if William Whitstable was such an establishment figure, May had asked, why would he have wanted to risk damaging the Common Market conference by attacking a politically sensitive painting? Could it—a long shot here, thought May—could it be that someone in government circles had taken revenge for the act?

The meeting had been adjourned with Land virtually accusing him of treason.

May knew that the political dimension of the case would allow him to limit press damage, but journalists wouldn't be held at bay for long. A speedy resolve was essential; this was the newly independent division's first investigation in the public eye, and everyone was watching for results.

Nothing like a little pressure from above to help a case along, thought May, as he raised the lid of another packing crate. This box was filled with books on heraldry. Wedged along one side was a slim mahogany case with a small brass key in its lock. They had not been granted clearance to search the house, but May was prepared to bend the rules a little until the next of kin arrived.

According to his information, Bella Whitstable, the younger sister, had been abroad on a business trip for the past six weeks. She had left a forwarding address with Peter, and had been informed by him of the tragedy that had occurred to their brother. What she did not know, as a British Airways flight returned her from Calcutta, was that her remaining sibling had also suffered a violent death.

By all accounts the Whitstables were not a close family, but with Christmas approaching Bella had planned to stay with her brothers for a few days. Now she would find herself facing a double funeral. May hoped she was a strong woman. There was nothing so disturbing as coping with death at Christmas.

He turned the key and opened the case, examining its contents. Inside was a robe of thin blue silk bearing a woven shield, guarded by unicorns. Underneath, the words *Justitia Virtutum Regina* had been stitched in dark golden thread. He felt sure that these were the symbols of one of the City of London guilds. It seemed logical that the brothers belonged to such an organization. He gently closed the case and returned it to the crate. The collected contents of the attic would help them build a picture of the Whitstables, although he doubted they would provide a clue to their killer. Like most upper-class families, the Whitstables were closing ranks at this time of crisis. The press had yet to break the bond of silence that kept the more scandalous details of upper-class crime from public attention. Reporters still worked in Fleet Street, their code of behaviour set by the powerful print unions. The competitive free-for-all that would change the face of British journalism was still a decade away, and accurate information about the aristocracy was hard to come by.

May returned downstairs and placed a call to Raymond Land.

'They've just got back to me on your bomb,' said Land. 'Your partner was right. It's a rather unusual mechanical device, extremely effective. Can you call by when you finish up there?'

By late Monday afternoon the barber shop at the Savoy had been examined by forensic experts, cleared, and restored to its former pristine condition, with the exception of a six-foot area ribboned with demarcation tape. Arthur Bryant stepped over a section of freshly dusted floor and stood studying his reflection in the tall beveled mirrors above the sinks. *What a scruffbag*, he thought. *I need some better-fitting dentures and a decent winter coat, one without threads hanging from it.* He needed a haircut, too, but places like this weren't his style. The gleaming chrome and ceramic sinks, the iridescent tiling, and hard white towels all belonged to a prewar world of manservants and valets, and Bryant knew where the class system of the time would have placed him: on the side of those who served.

His own father had begun life in service. He had kept his family well provided for, and had always maintained his dignity. It had never occurred to him that he might be as worthy as those upon whom he waited. In later years it became a constant source of conflict between father and son.

Bryant turned away and examined the black leather barber's chair. Someone had done a good job; after being dusted for fingerprints it had been buffed to a fierce shine. You'd never think that just that morning someone had been murdered in it.

The girl was slouching guiltily by the towel rail, contriving to act suspiciously even when there was nothing to be suspicious about. She had a habit of looking down at the ground as she spoke, so that her auburn hair fell across her face, obscuring her eyes.

'Well?' asked Bryant, settling down in the barber's chair and raising his shoes from the floor. 'You walked in and there was Major Whitstable with the razor sticking out of his mouth. Where was the barber?'

'He wasn't here,' said Jerry. 'He could have attacked me as well, you know.'

'I realize that,' said Bryant.

'There's a tradesmen's entrance to the salon, leading to an alleyway behind the hotel. He had a perfect escape route at hand.'

'So I see. Has someone warned you about not speaking to the press, by the way?'

'I wouldn't want to.'

'And you're absolutely sure you saw no one other than the Major in here or outside?'

Jerry shook her head and stared at the door. Thank

God the young were so resilient, thought Bryant. The child had witnessed two deaths, which should have marked her as a suspect, except that anyone with an ounce of common sense could see that she wasn't. She appeared shaken, but intact. Still, there was a chance that she was holding something back.

'Which brings us to the big question: what were you doing up here at all?'

'I was going to ask Maurice if he would give me a free haircut,' said Jerry. 'What happened to him?'

'It doesn't matter.' The less the girl knew, the better. Apparently someone had rung the barber on Saturday and warned him that they were closing the salon to refit some water pipes. Maurice had been told not to come in until Tuesday. Bryant swiveled the chair around to face the girl. 'I wonder if you know more than you're telling me?'

'Look, I just work here.' Jerry hung her head, picking at a thumbnail.

'If you remember anything else, no matter how insignificant it may seem, will you be sure to inform me or Mr May?' asked Bryant, rising. 'Every sudden death is tragic, but this could also destroy the reputation of a hotel, even one as venerable and respected as this one. You must come to me before speaking to anyone else.'

'Mr Bryant?' She raised her eyes to him.

'Yes?'

'Is this to do with Mr Jacob?'

'Your guess is as good as mine.'

'It must be, mustn't it? I mean, didn't they know each other?'

Bryant was not supposed to discuss the unit's cases with outsiders, but frequently did so. He figured they needed all the help they could get. 'It's too much of a coincidence for it not to be, don't you think? But we deal in hard facts, and those seem to have been carefully removed.'

'I want to help,' she said. 'I'm already involved. I can find things out for you.'

'I'm afraid that's not really allowed.'

'But you're in an experimental unit. It's been in the papers. If you wanted me to do something, nobody would be able to tell you otherwise.'

He patted her on the arm. 'I'll bear that in mind. You'd better get back to work. I'll probably need to speak to you again.'

Making his way back to Mornington Crescent, Bryant tried to connect the events of the past week. The situation was not only unique; it was absurd. Three deaths—by snakebite, by explosion, by razor. What next? Death by hot air balloon? Cannon? Trident? For a moment he wondered if the whole thing might be an elaborate joke designed to discredit the unit.

'Watch this.'

Dr Raymond Land handed the experiment over to a pasty-faced young man in a lab coat, who produced a small test tube of what looked like liquid mercury and a paintbrush. Carefully dipping the brush in the solution, he painted a thin strip of liquid on the side of a child's building block. Bryant withdrew a pair of smeary reading glasses from his top pocket and put them on. May was sitting on the only chair in the room.

'We have to wait a few moments for it to dry,' said the young lab technician. 'It's something we haven't seen for years. A form of silver acetylide. You titrate it through ammonia and it comes out like sludge.' He held up the test tube. 'While it's in liquid form it's fine, but if you let it dry out...' He picked up the child's block and checked the line of paint. Satisfied, he tossed the block on to the desk. There was a loud bang, and the clearing smoke revealed a blackened pit in the desk top.

'...it becomes totally unstable,' concluded the technician, somewhat unnecessarily.

'That's state property,' said Land, examining the damage.

'What would a device designed to house such a chemical reaction look like, do you reckon?' asked May. 'How big would it have to be?'

'Not large at all, just so long as the drying area for the liquid was maximized sufficiently. Here.' He produced a pad from his pocket and began to draw. 'Working from a reconstruction incorporating the slivers of metal we found in William Whitstable's stomach, we get something like this. The liquid is contained in a section here...'

'I wondered why one piece was silvered,' mused Bryant. 'It was part of the liquid chamber.'

'A preset clockwork mechanism releases it into a flat drying chamber that might work from, say, the heat of the body. As soon as it's dry, the device is armed and lethal.' The technician held up the finished drawing to reveal a metal chamber the size and shape of a pocket watch.

'Just the sort of thing that a smart Edwardian gentleman would carry upon his person,' said Bryant. 'Thanks for the demonstration.' He tapped May on the shoulder with the back of his hand. 'Come on, you. We've an appointment to keep.'

By eight-thirty P.M. the concourse at Victoria Station had only a light groundswell of homebound commuters passing between the trains and ticket windows.

Bryant stood at the barrier watching the arriving passengers. 'You realize if she's anything like the rest of the family, she'll be wearing a crinoline and bustle.' He looked across at May, who was checking his watch.

'That must be her.'

Bryant followed his partner's pointing finger. Bella Whitstable was broad and stocky, a woman who looked like she spent her time beekeeping or repairing dry-stone walls. She came at them with a purposeful gait and sensible shoes. The practicality of her winter jacket was lightened with a spring of lapis lazuli, and gold earrings balanced the severity of her haircut. Her handshake was firm and dry, her manner direct.

'I don't want you to mollycoddle me,' she informed the detectives. 'It's no secret that we didn't get along, William, Peter, and I, but of course it horrifies me that they met such terrible ends.'

'So you know about Peter,' said May, surprised.

'It would have been hard to avoid items like this,' replied Bella, holding up a copy of the *Evening Standard*.

DEATH RIDDLE OF SAVOY SHAVE
Dead man was brother of
Tube explosion victim

The press were well and truly on their tails now. As Peter Whitstable's identity had yet to be divulged, May wondered how they had managed to link the two deaths so quickly. The official statement for the Hampstead Tube bombing suggested that a technical fault had occurred in one of the carriages. The subterfuge had been necessary to prevent the public from worrying that the IRA was renewing its Christmas attacks on the city.

'I'm sorry you had to find out in such a manner,' said

May, taking her bag. 'There was no way we could contact you in time.'

'I quite understand,' said Bella, with considerable coolness. 'It will take me a while to fully appreciate what has happened.'

'Under the circumstances I wouldn't advise staying at the house.'

'I'm sure you wouldn't, but that's where I'd like to be. I have family belongings there. I'm not fond of London, and intend to spend as little time here as possible.'

They made their way to a waiting squad car. 'You can ask me anything you like,' said Bella, seating herself. 'I have just returned from a city where sudden death is part of everyday life. I won't get sniffly on you.'

'You say you didn't get along with your brothers?' Bryant reminded her.

'The feuds between us all seem so trivial now. I couldn't bear all that living in the past. It seemed so unhealthy. William didn't approve of my finding a partner so soon after our mother died, and put an end to the relationship. I never forgave him for that. There were other things—certain financial arrangements that caused problems. It's hard to be specific. You'll have to give me some time to think.'

'We will need details of the beneficiaries to the wills. I suppose Peter told you that their lawyer, Max Jacob, is also dead.'

'Yes, it seems so extraordinary. I wonder if any of us are safe. I wish I could throw some light on all of this, but I simply don't know where to begin.'

'There is the question of the funeral,' said Bryant gently. 'Although perhaps you'd like to discuss this later...'

'William and Peter will be interred together. There is a family vault at Highgate,' said Bella, looking out of the window at the retreating station. 'It would seem to be the best thing.'

'We want your permission to maintain a police presence at the service,' said May. It was not uncommon for a murderer to attend the burial of his victim.

'I understand. Do you have any idea of the kind of person you're looking for?'

'We're hoping that you can help us there,' said Bryant. 'Why do you think William lived so much in the past?'

'Oh, we're an old-fashioned bunch. The family's history is the history of England.' Bella rummaged in her bag, produced a vast linen handkerchief, and gave a brisk honk into it. 'I don't think William was even aware of the modern world. The late nineteenth century was our grand time. Our ancestors' fortunes grew with the empire, and so did the family. Sons and daughters in every outpost. Unforgiving Christians and hard-nosed businessmen. It was the same with so many old families. Now they're like us, in sad decline. Although I don't suppose they're disappearing in quite the same lurid manner. I wonder if we have any business rivals at the moment. You should check that, Mr Bryant.'

'We're trying, although it will be more difficult to do so now that Peter has died. Had both of your brothers retired?'

'Apart from a bit of dabbling on the Stock Exchange. I heard about William and the painting. What an appalling thing to do.'

'You have no idea why he might have committed such an act?'

'None at all. I can't imagine that either of them had any real enemies. And who would want to kill them over a painting? It wasn't even of any importance, from what Peter told me.'

'How well did you know Max Jacob?'

'I didn't, I'm afraid. He handled the family estate and all of its financial dealings, but he only ever dealt with William.'

'He lied to his family about coming to London,' said May. 'If he met up with William, we have no evidence of it.'

The car had reached St John's Wood. Bella was momentarily distracted by a passing apartment building. 'Look at that,' she said, pointing to a sign on the wall. 'Tadema House. What a marvelous painter Alma-Tadema was. How we all loved the Pre-Raphaelites, Peter included. Mother owned several, you see. All donated to galleries now, of course.'

'Did she own any paintings by Waterhouse?' asked Bryant.

'No, I don't think so. Is that what my brother destroyed, a Waterhouse?'

Bryant nodded.

'What could he have been thinking of?' Bella blew her nose again. As the car arrived in Hampstead, a light rain began to fall.

'We're keeping a twenty-four-hour guard on the house,' said May as they turned into Mayberry Grove. 'If you're planning to go out, you'd better let me have an itinerary.'

'I have to attend a meeting of my society tomorrow night,' said Bella, alighting from the car. 'I know that William and Peter would have wanted me to keep the appointment. I suppose someone will have to come with me.'

'Who is the meeting with?' asked Bryant.

'The Savoyard Society,' said Bella, closing the door. 'Gilbert and Sullivan. I'm the president. Don't worry, I can see myself in.'

'Well,' said May as he and Bryant drove back to Mornington Crescent, 'what did you make of her?'

'She seems to have an extremely calm attitude to all of this. Either she's genuinely undisturbed by what's going on, or she's lying about how much she knows.' Bryant looked out at the rainswept night. 'I hope she can tell us something.'

'I'm not too sure she wants to,' said May. 'If there's anything the Whitstable family members share in common, it's that none of them knows how to behave like a normal human being. How can we ever expect to establish a motive?'

'More to the point,' said Bryant, 'how can we hope to keep the remaining members alive?'

12 / Savoyards

She was startled to find blood on the pillow.

She had bitten her lower lip in her sleep. The dream had returned again. Now that she was awake, her face turned to the growing stripe of daylight bisecting the ceiling of her room, she felt the dread of those endless alleys dissolving within her.

In the past week Jerry had seen stranger things, and they had not been dreams. For the first time, reality had proved more disturbing than her imagination. She thought of the swathed body in the barber shop and shuddered. She had succeeded in stepping beyond the comfort zone provided by her parents, and into an area of unpredictability. The thought excited her. Dr Wayland had ended their session with a warning about the harm of allowing what he termed 'negative aspects' of her nature to the fore. His main concern was to keep Gwen's monthly cheques rolling in.

She checked the alarm clock and rolled out of bed. At eight o'clock the house was still silent. Neither Jack nor Gwen would be awake for another half hour. Wait until the papers arrived, she thought, they'd be able to read about the latest gruesome discovery at their only child's place of employment. Gwen would probably find a way of implying that she was somehow to blame.

Her parents' friends were all offshoots from the same cultivated tree. The men were higher-echelon professionals; their partners were wives before they were women. In the uppermost branches were the families fortified by generations of old money, trust funds, and minor titles. Below were the rising tendrils of the nouveaux riches. Jack and Gwen were locked into a precise level of British life, sparkling ammonites in their strata of London society. They lived in town, which was becoming too *cosmopolitan* for some of their friends, a euphemism for their perception that it was filling up with foreigners. In mitigation, Chelsea was an enclave of comfortable white families like themselves. They had a small farmhouse in Warwickshire, and an orange-tiled villa on Cap Ferrat. Gwen considered herself a working woman. She was a voting member on her husband's business boards, and a hostess on the many charity nights their friends arranged to promote fashionable causes, preferably ones connected with horses or photogenic children. Here in the upper-middle reaches, the rules for social climbing had to be strictly adhered to. Jack's money was not yet old enough for them to be allowed to behave as they liked.

Further complicating the family's position was the fact that Jerry's difficult personality had encouraged her parents to enrol her at a small private school in Chelsea which enjoyed a fine reputation as a clearinghouse for the problem children of the comfortable classes.

Jerry had never had to tidy her own bedroom; that job was reserved for the Swedish au pair. She was not allowed to put posters on the walls because of the pin marks they left. If she told Gwen how she had talked to the police, her mother would probably faint from sheer embarrassment. Jerry had a sneaking suspicion her parents lived in fear of children developing strong imaginations. In their eyes it encouraged creativity, which prevented young people from becoming productive. It was important to them that she did something useful. As she bathed and dressed, she wondered if they would ever allow her to choose her own course in life. So much could happen in the space of a single week. She had glimpsed death and conspiracy, had spoken to the working-class men and women who dealt with it as part of their daily routine, and now she wanted to know more. She still had the Bible in her possession. She needed to consider her next move very carefully.

As she wiped condensation from the mirror and combed back her wet hair, she thought about Joseph Herrick. He had been busy working on his designs for the theatre, but the next time he came past the reception desk, she decided, she would ask him out on a date.

For the first time, it seemed that anything and everything was possible, so long as she kept her own counsel.

Daily Mail, Tuesday 14 December 1973

Exclusive

NEW LINK IN WHITSTABLE DEATHS 'DENIED BY POLICE'

According to a source close to the police team working in London's most controversial murder investigation division, vital evidence linking three bizarre deaths in the past week is being deliberately ignored.

From its inception, the Peculiar Crimes Unit has drawn charges of elitism, and faces criticism for its working methods, which encourage experimentation over traditional investigative procedure. Now it is being suggested that a vital clue common to all three deaths has been discounted in favour of obscure 'alternative' theories.

William and Peter Whitstable, together with their lawyer Maximillian Jacob, were supposedly murdered in circumstances bearing no links, but the *Daily Mail* has learned that police know of a symbol common to each victim that had deadly connotations.

The sign of the sacred flame is popularly used by members of the Whitstable family and their business associates. But during the Second World War this very symbol had a more sinister meaning. It was a code used by German assassins to mark predetermined British targets.

Between 1941 and 1944 no fewer than thirty-seven English men and women who were perceived to be a threat to the German invasion were coded with the sacred-flame symbol. All were subsequently eliminated in a variety of bizarre scenarios. The sacred flame has a mythological origin connected to German Olympian ideals.

Few now remember the terror that this sign once inspired. The reemergence of the flame's use, timed at the start of a conference which is of great importance to Britain's entry into the Common Market, suggests the return of powerful right-wing German interests.

Experts say that the Whitstable family have exploited profitable export connections with German delegates who are attending the conference. Recently their Hamburg office suffered extensive damage and two members of staff were injured after a firebomb was hurled through a ground-floor window.

Confronted with this fresh evidence, a police spokesperson denied any link with recent German banking offences, suggesting that the connection of the sacred flame was 'spurious at best.'

On the morning of 14 December, Bryant and May began the second week of their investigation by facing up to two major problems in their search for information.

The first was a lack of available manpower. Theirs was the only division ranking above the existing Area Major Investigation Pools in Britain. These pools were divided by areas, and handled the majority of homicide inquiries. Typically, they were overworked and understaffed. In theory, the new unit was supposed to receive help from the pools' senior investigating officers, but in practice it was not possible to free them from their essential 'care-taking' duties within the AMIPs. This left the division with a single acting superintendent, Raymond Land; two sergeants, of whom Janice Longbright was one; and an inadequate foot-force.

Their second problem was one of time. The first seventy-two hours following a homicide were the most vital. At the end of three days, a strong sense was gained of whether the case would be solved quickly or not. This time had elapsed, in the cases of Max Jacob and William Whitstable, without any agreement on motive, opportunity, or circumstantial evidence. Little had been established beyond the fact that these were three cases of unlawful homicide, with malice aforethought. Now the detectives realized that they were in for a long haul. Consequently, they decided to divide chores according to each other's specific talents.

Bryant was to question Bella Whitstable about her brothers, while May spent time with the forensic team appointed to the case. The properties of all three victims were now in the process of being searched and catalogued, and Jacob's family was being questioned for the second time. Witness statements were correlated by Longbright, who added them to the growing paperwork at Mornington Crescent.

Faraday, the junior arts minister, had called twice to find out why no arrests had been made, and an expert from the National Gallery had sent a detailed report on the problems that would beset anyone attempting a restoration of the damaged Waterhouse painting.

Forensic information was starting to arrive on Major Peter Whitstable's death, but no one could spare the time to match it to the rest of the investigation. Their personnel situation was scandalous, May reflected. Worse still, their detractors in the Met might well have arranged for it to become so.

Equally frustrating was the fact that it was impossible to find time to follow up this morning's suggestion by the *Mail* that German business interests were to blame for the deaths. The theory was as plausible as any other, perhaps more so, but Bryant had been forced to dismiss it until a team could be freed to investigate the allegation. And who knew how long that would take?

When he arrived at the morgue, May found Oswald Finch tabling results from his autopsy on William's younger brother into the Grundig tape recorder that sat on his bench. The air in the white-tiled room was chilled and antiseptic, but could not hide the chemical smell that accompanied the clinical study of death.

'I'm glad you came back.' Finch rose to offer a thin, clammy hand. 'How are you getting on with your snake man?'

'Not very well,' admitted May. 'It would help if they could get a few readable fibres from him.' Forensics had searched all three corpses, but had failed to find any common substance matches. Quite the reverse, in fact; they had come up with hairs and skin flakes from several different people. It seemed obvious that the murders were linked, but so far they had found no way of proving it.

'Arthur thinks the methods of death are symbolic,' said May. 'They're intended to have a theatrical effect. Why else would anyone go to so much trouble?'

'Your partner always seems disappointed when he hears of anyone dying a natural death,' said Finch, crossing to the banks of steel drawers set in the far wall. 'In Jacob's case I suppose you could be looking at suicide. It's possible that the wound was self-inflicted. It would explain why he calmly returned to his seat and continued reading the paper. Your bomb man could have been an Accidental. He might conceivably have triggered his own device by mistake. Something has cropped up that I thought you'd be interested in.' He unlocked a drawer and rolled it out, deftly unzipping the plastic bag in which the remains of Peter Whitstable were housed. 'This one was more like an execution than an assault.'

'What do you mean?' May attempted to avoid looking at the dry, broad slashes on the major's throat and the split wounds to his mouth.

'If the attack had resulted from an altercation, that is to say was motivated by sudden anger, I would have expected to find a fair bit of damage to the face, and defence marks. But you say no cries were heard outside the barber shop. His attacker could have armed himself with any number of sharp instruments, but he chose the razor. He was very fast, with powerful strokes through the vocal cords here, across the throat. This chap had no time to struggle. Swift and efficient. And then there's this.'

He thumbed open the inside of the corpse's upper arm and shone his pocket torch on the exposed flesh.

'As we're dealing with a lifelong military man, I wasn't surprised to find that he had a tattoo,' said Finch. 'It's the placing of it that's odd. I've never seen one on the inside of an arm before. It's only a few centimetres below the armpit. No one would ever see it.'

John May found himself looking at a familiar aquamarine smudge. The flickering flame symbol was the same as the one he had found on William Whitstable's cane.

'Did you find this on either of the others?'

'No, only on the Major. Probably has military significance. There must be a way of finding out what it means.'

'Yes,' May agreed, all too aware that he could spare no one for the task. 'If the newspapers are to be believed, we're under attack from modern-day Nazis. The journalists are securing information faster than we are.'

'I don't know where to begin,' said Bella Whitstable, standing in the angled corridor of her brothers' attic. 'I doubt either of them could remember what had been stored up here.' Judging by her neat makeup and smart appearance, she had passed a good night. She certainly hadn't sat up for hours crying.

'There are some ceremonial robes,' said Bryant, removing the mahogany box and unlocking it. 'Perhaps you know what they represent.' He had a good idea himself, but he wanted confirmation.

'Oh, that's easy,' said Bella, removing the blue silk gown and holding it to the light. 'It's William's guild robe. Peter has one as well. Most of the men in our family do.'

'What kind of guild does this represent?' He peered into the box and removed an ermine-trimmed collar. He expected to find a heavy gold chain somewhere, and here it was at the bottom of the box.

'It's part of the Worshipful Company of Goldsmiths. We're a craft guild family. That's originally where the Whitstables made their money. Gold and silver. Our ancestors can be traced back to the foundation of the guild in 1339.'

Bryant knew a little about the ancient network of guilds that still operated a system of patronage, performing charitable works within the city. Their apprenticeship schools had once been open to all, but were about to become private. Kids from backgrounds such as his would no longer be welcome.

'Did William and Peter still keep up their contacts, attend meetings, that sort of thing?'

'I doubt it. Neither of them was particularly sociable. My brothers were always too suspicious of others to make many friends. It wasn't much fun growing up with them.'

'So there's no chance that their deaths might have resulted from some past transgression.' His fingers traced the stitched livery on the robe.

'I don't think that's very likely, Mr Bryant. Our business has always been rather bloodless. We've never had much trouble from competition.'

For a moment he'd had a vision of the ageing guild members quarrelling over a fraudulent deal, a distant betrayal. The arcane circumstances of the deaths somehow seemed to fit.

'I have to leave soon,' said Bella. 'I'm meeting my Savoyards at seven.'

'I should come with you,' said Bryant. 'You say this society is connected with Gilbert and Sullivan?'

'Indeed,' said Bella. 'We're attending the new production of *Princess Ida*. Tonight is the first night.'

How could he have forgotten? Ken Russell's new version of this work had received praise at its previews.

Bryant had promised to buy himself a ticket, but the events of the last week had ended any thoughts of leisure.

'I'm sure we'll be able to find you a spare seat,' Bella told the pleased detective.

Fans were arriving beneath the illuminated globe of the English National Opera, London's largest theatre. The purists still attended the Royal Opera House, but there was a sense of fun about the ENO. It was one of Bryant's guilty pleasures to attend the productions here, although May would have hated finding himself in such a middle-aged audience. His partner welcomed the company of the young, and was always prepared to listen to their opinions.

Bella Whitstable had changed into an alarmingly loose black-beaded gown that had been brought down from her brothers' attic and smelled of mothballs. County women rarely adapted from the field to the foyer. Bryant was in no position to criticize his escort, as he sported his usual battered brown overcoat, topped with another of his landlady's unnecessarily prolonged scarves.

'They should be around here somewhere,' said Bella, searching the crowded vestibule from the steps. 'You can't miss them.'

'Oh, why is that?' asked Bryant, before catching sight of a group that appeared to be in fancy dress. One of them, a short, bespectacled man clad in doublet and hose, came over and pumped Bella's arm.

'Oh, well done,' he cried, examining her gown. 'A perfect revival Lady Blanche!' He indicated his own clothes. 'I've gone for the James Wade 1954 production. The original's too laden down with fur and chain mail, unless you're King Hildebrand. I was supposed to be

Cyril, but the chap taking Florian fell off a tandem this morning and landed on his keys, so I took his place.'

Bryant touched Bella's arm. 'You mean they're all dressed in character?' he asked.

'Certainly,' said Bella. 'The Savoyards differ from other Gilbert and Sullivan groups. They live out the parts of each opera. It's not as foolish as it sounds. Our functions raise money for charity, and pay for the preservation and restoration of related artefacts.'

'I take it your brothers had no connection with the group?' asked Bryant.

'Good heavens, no. In our family, theatre is something for the men to sleep through.'

Noting the size of some of the ladies' headdresses, Bryant tried to imagine how the rest of the audience would feel about this embellishment to the evening's programme, until it was explained to him that the Savoyards had reserved Boxes G and H on the right side of the theatre, where they would be able to enjoy themselves in relative privacy.

As they reached the boxes, Bryant examined the faces of the assembled Savoyards, and found himself searching for possible suspects. With fifteen minutes to go before curtain up, champagne was opened, and several members approached Bella to offer awkward condolences. One of the Savoyards was sitting on the far side of the box in a visored steel helmet that hid his face. Bryant excused himself from Bella's side. It was important to ascertain that there was no danger here, and that began by knowing everyone's identity.

'Hello, there.' He pulled up a small gilt chair. 'Mind if I join you?' The man in the plumed helmet said something Bryant could not understand and pointed helplessly to the side of his head. Bryant loosened a wing nut with his fat fingers and worked the visor free. The face re-vealed was sweaty and russet-coloured.

'Phew, thanks,' said the knight gratefully. 'Damned thing keeps jamming. I should have picked someone else.' He held out a hand. 'Oliver Pettigrew. I'm not nor-mally dressed like this. I'm an estate agent. You're the po-lice chap.'

'That's right,' said Bryant, unwinding his scarf and placing it on the back of the chair. Below them the hub-bub rose as the auditorium filled up.

'What do you make of this business, then? Both her brothers gone in a week, and yet she's here tonight. What a trouper, eh?' Pettigrew shook his head in wonderment.

'How often do you meet?' asked Bryant.

'Once every six weeks for a costume reading, usually in a church hall, every Gilbert and Sullivan revival of course, at charity functions, and at fund-raisers to keep original G and S manuscripts and props in the country. There's a great interest in the operas throughout the Commonwealth, and in America. We even have an offi-cial chapter of the Savoyards in Chicago.'

'I'm a bit of a Gilbert and Sullivan fan,' admitted Bryant, 'but I'd never heard of you before Bella told me.'

'It's fallen out of fashion over here,' said Bella, picking up the conversation. 'There's a reaction against anything popular in this country, don't you think? People forget that Gilbert's satirical targets—the judicial system, the House of Lords, the police, and royalty—made him the bad boy of his age.'

'That's right,' agreed Knight Pettigrew, fiddling with his wing nut. 'He ridiculed affectation, snobbery, and nepotism. Gilbert's rude lyrics kept him from receiving a knighthood until he was nearly dead. The Victorian age died with them, you know. Lewis Carroll, Ruskin,

Gladstone, William Morris, D'Oyly Carte, Oscar Wilde, and Queen Victoria herself—all gone with the end of the century.'

'Mr Sullivan's music is the music of the common people,' said Bella enthusiastically, not that she knew anything about common people. 'It's a direct descendant of the folk songs that once bound our country together.' She refilled their glasses. 'That's why the guild supports it.'

'The guild?' Bryant's ears pricked up. 'You mean money from the Goldsmiths helps to run the Savoyards?'

'Sometimes,' said Bella. 'It works both ways. There are many charities involved.' She twisted her gold wristwatch and checked the time. 'I think it's about to start.'

Bryant was reasonably familiar with the plot of *Princess Ida*, a heavy-handed satire on women's rights, but he had never seen it performed. Its tiresome recitative was the reason why it was rarely produced these days. A pity, for it contained what was known as 'Sullivan's String of Pearls' in the second act, a sequence containing some of the composer's finest work.

The opera consisted of three acts, with two intermissions of fifteen minutes each. At the first of these, the Savoyards turned to each other with the falling of the curtain and argued excitedly. The production had obviously found favour with them. The setting had been updated to seventies London with reasonable success. The new version allowed for a variety of jokes surrounding the women's liberation movement, but it was the singing that elicited the group's enthusiasm. Bryant caught Bella Whitstable heading for the door of the box and called her back. 'If you want to go to the lavatory,' he suggested, 'please take someone with you.'

'I was only going to powder my nose,' she replied somewhat archly.

'Then kindly do it here,' said Bryant. 'I don't want you out of my sight.'

Knight Pettigrew had removed his helmet and was refilling his champagne glass. Several more Savoyards had entered from the other box. The bejewelled outfits of the women and the polished silver gilt of the men's armour glittered in the soft red gloom, although someone dressed as a ragged beggar in a floppy hat seemed to have got a raw deal. Bryant had to admit that it was a dottily pleasant sight.

Pettigrew tapped him on the arm. 'You know, people don't realize how much of Gilbert and Sullivan is buried in the national consciousness,' he said. 'Take *Princess Ida*. The lyrics owe a considerable debt to Tennyson, did you know that? The BBC was playing the first act on September the third, just before Neville Chamberlain announced that we were at war with Germany. And you know the last lines that were heard that fateful day before they faded out the music? *"Order comes to fight, ha, ha, order is obeyed."*'

Bryant glanced at his new friend's eager face and knew that he possessed hundreds of similar anecdotes. People like Pettigrew were harmless enough, but it was usually dangerous to show too much of an interest. As the estate agent rattled on, Bryant wondered how many of the others had told their colleagues about their odd hobby.

The house lights flickered and dimmed for a moment, presumably to notify the audience that it was time for them to return to their seats.

He became aware of a commotion on the other side of the box. Several women were bent over someone in a chair. He rose, crossing to find one of them fanning Bella with a programme.

'She feels faint,' she explained. 'It's very warm in here. Do you think we should take her outside?'

'I'll be fine, really,' said Bella. 'I just feel a little strange.'

'She was complaining that her limbs were stiff,' said her friend. 'I wondered if—' She got no further, because Bella suddenly fell forward, her muscles contracting violently. Everyone jumped back in shock as her limbs began to spasm.

'She's having a fit!' Pettigrew was pushing into the knot of horrified onlookers.

Bryant grabbed the two largest men he could see. 'Hold her down,' he ordered, snatching up the walkie-talkie handset attached to his belt. It was the one piece of equipment he had not managed to lose.

'Put something soft between her teeth that she can bite on,' said Pettigrew. 'Something she can't swallow.'

'Does anyone have any Valium?' asked Bryant, kneeling beside her. Several women immediately opened their handbags.

Bryant called for an ambulance and watched Bella's back arching in agony as she thrashed on the floor of the box. The men were fighting to hold her arms and legs, but the power of her involuntary flexing was kicking their hands away. Someone was hammering on the door behind them.

'Get them to stop banging,' shouted Bryant as one of the women scurried to the door. He had a good idea what had happened, and knew that sudden light or noise would only increase the intensity of her spasms. Bella's face, twisted in an agonized muscular rictus, was beginning to turn blue. He administered the Valium as the St John's ambulance men entered the box.

Bella's convulsions began to lessen, but the protuberance of her startled eyes and the frozen grimace of her mouth suggested that her time was running out. As he helped to fasten the stretcher's restraining straps, Bryant caught a brief glimpse of the audience reseating itself below, oblivious of the real-life drama unfolding above their heads. He could only wait and pray that the medics had arrived in time.

13 / Pandemonium

'Hey, you're late,' said Nicholas. 'You should have been here, helping me out. More delegates left this morning.'

Jerry stowed her bag and took her place behind the reception desk. Half a dozen security officers were standing in the reception area awaiting the departure of another Common Market dignitary.

'With the amount of security we have, you'd think they'd feel safer staying here than anywhere else.'

'Suppose this whole thing turns out to have a political cause? According to the *Telegraph*, the chap who got his throat cut was some kind of government spy.'

'You shouldn't believe everything you read,' said Jerry.

'I suppose you know better.' Nicholas swept his hair back disapprovingly and turned his attention to the billing system. Jerry was about to answer a guest's inquiry when she saw Joseph Herrick descending the main staircase. He smiled shortsightedly in her direction and headed towards the breakfast room.

'Be a pal and deal with this gentleman for me, Nicholas.' Jerry slid off her stool, running her fingers through her hair. It was now or never. 'I won't be long.'

'Look here,' complained Nicholas, 'you've only just arrived. Where do you think you're going?'

'I fancy a spot of breakfast.' She knew she could take liberties with him, so long as he continued to study her breasts from the corner of his eye when he thought she wasn't looking. His recent humiliation at his parents' house was obviously beginning to wear off.

Joseph had seated himself against the tall glass wall overlooking the Embankment, and was staring out at the grey expanse of the rain-pocked river. The smile of recognition he gave her suggested he would enjoy her company.

'Mind if I join you?'

'Not at all,' said Joseph, indicating the chair opposite. 'Do you normally take breakfast with your guests?'

'All the time. It's part of the service.' She seated herself and unfolded a napkin in her lap. 'I'm surprised you're still here. Most of the delegates are checking out. They're being moved to a high-security residence.'

'Well, two deaths in the same hotel—it's not exactly an advertisement for healthy living, is it?'

'It's hardly our fault. It's not the usual sort of thing that happens in a hotel. They were, you know—proper murders.'

'I see. You can be killed in a robbery and that wouldn't be a *proper* murder, is that it?'

Jerry waited while one of the waiters brought their breakfast. 'I mean a murder with a motive,' she explained. 'Everything carefully planned out.'

Joseph took a bite of buttered toast and chewed it slowly, regarding his companion with an indulgent smile. 'You mean like Sherlock Holmes. "Red-headed League," "Sign of the Four," stuff like that.'

'If you like, yes.'

'Forget it, Jerry, it doesn't happen. I come from a port city where death is sordid and simple. Guys get drunk and rape women, or they beat on each other when they're pissed. I don't believe there's any such thing as a carefully planned crime.'

'You're wrong. Girls go for nonexistent job interviews and vanish. They get chopped up and left in railway carriages. Murderers are men, and men are devious.'

'And you think the Savoy has a devious murderer? Maybe he's even staying here?'

'I don't know.' She looked down at her plate, embarrassed. 'Maybe.'

'What did you tell the police?'

'Just what I saw.' She needed to change the subject. 'How's your show coming along?'

'Good,' he replied, pouring tea. 'The theatre is a mess. The refurbishment is running behind schedule. It's taking longer than anyone expected.'

'Which theatre are you working in?'

'I thought I told you.' He passed her a cup. 'I'm right next door, at the Savoy. That's why I'm staying here. The Japanese are paying for the renovation work, and they've appointed me as the set designer for their first production. We're opening with a new Gilbert and Sullivan staging, very modern and irreverent. Actually, it's not exactly new. It's been touring the country for a while, but the production is getting a face-lift for its London debut, and that's where my designs come in. I can get you tickets for the first night if you like.'

'Perhaps I could see you before then.'

'Sure. I'm here right through to the opening.' He checked his watch. 'I'd better get going. I promised to call my girlfriend.'

Her stomach dropped. Of course he had a girlfriend. She was probably slender and beautiful. And sadly, still alive.

'Where is she?' she asked, drawing back slightly.

'She used to live in the US, but now she's studying at Oxford. She's gone to visit relatives in Edinburgh for Christmas. Listen, it doesn't stop you and me from being friends. I'd still like that.'

Her instinctive reaction was to withdraw her offer, but she knew that would be childish. 'All right,' she agreed reluctantly. 'Friends, then.'

Joseph seemed genuinely pleased. 'Now we've defused that particular time bomb, you can tell me more about your murder theories.'

'If you like…'

He laid a slim finger against his lips. 'When you get off this evening,' he said with a smile.

John May had woken to the sound of rain pounding against the bedroom skylight, and studied the dark turmoil beyond the glass. He had just taken his raincoat to the dry cleaners. Coffee was called for, but a routine check for messages pushed the thought of breakfast from his mind.

As he ran from his car to the entrance of Gower Street's University College Hospital, the shoulders of his jacket became soaked. At five past six on Wednesday morning the hospital foyer was populated only by an elderly floor polisher. A word with the duty nurse sent him along the corridor to the overnight admissions rooms.

He found Bryant bundled up on a green leather bench, asleep. Arthur had sunk down into his voluminous coat like a tortoise vanishing into its shell for the winter. May's shoes squeaked on the polished linoleum as he approached, and Bryant's bald head slowly emerged at the sound.

'What happened, Arthur?' asked May. 'Why on earth didn't you let them page me?'

'There was nothing you could have done to help,' said the detective wearily. 'There were quite enough people here. You would only have been in the way. She died at three o'clock this morning. Due to the unusual nature of the death, I asked the doctor if she would put down her findings in some kind of preliminary report. Raymond's going to go crazy when he finds out what happened, and I'll need all the information I can get.'

May sat down beside his old friend. Bryant looked done in. 'What happened?' he asked.

'She suffered some kind of seizure. Violent convulsions, uncontrollable muscle contractions consistent with poisoning. It was terrible to watch.' He looked along the deserted corridor, listened to the distant clatter of the awakening hospital. 'She seemed like a good woman,' he said sadly.

The administering doctor was about to go off duty, and stopped by to see them. 'I wouldn't want these notes to be used as a basis for any kind of evidential document, Arthur,' she explained, holding the file against her bosom, 'but you'd better have them.' Bryant imagined that the last thing she had wanted to do after a long shift was fill in paperwork as a favour to the police, but the young Irishwoman had helped him a number of times in the past, and always did so without complaint.

'It's very kind of you, Betty. I'll leave you something in my will.'

'You'd better leave your friend your overcoat,' said Betty, glancing at May. 'He's going to catch his death dressed like that.'

As they walked back along the corridors, Bryant thumbed through the neat handwritten pages. 'At first they thought it was tetanus, but it looks like strychnine poisoning,' he said. 'I thought it would have to be. She died of asphyxiation and exhaustion. There's only so long the body can stave off a total attack on the central nervous system before it gives in. The reaction time of the poison is normally ten to twenty minutes, but it was slowed because she'd eaten earlier, and because I was able to administer Valium to reduce the spasms. There was no point in pumping her stomach because the symptoms had already begun. Instead they intravenously administered succinylcholine to slow down the convulsions and take the strain off her heart. I suppose it didn't work.' He closed the folder.

'What did she eat?' asked May. 'Did you see?'

'She ate from the salad bar everyone else used. And she sat through the whole of the first act without showing any symptoms. She was just a few feet away from me.'

'Did she consume anything during the performance? Chocolates?'

'No. There was champagne, both before and during the intermission.'

'Did you see any of it being opened?'

'There were quite a few bottles, but as far as I know they were all sealed. I kept an eye on the one Bella drank from. She uncorked it herself and we all had a glass. John, we need to get everyone back to that box and re-create this thing while it's still fresh in their minds. And I want the press kept out. They'll catch wind of it soon enough.'

They ran through the rain to the waiting car.

Dr Raymond Land, the acting chief, was not a man who enjoyed life, and today he was liking it even less than usual. His narrow shoulders rose and fell as he fidgeted with frustration behind his empty desk. His hand frequently rose to pat the greying hair combed in thin bands across his head. He did not want to be here at all, but if he had to be, he wanted his tenure to be a quiet one. This new unit was too experimental, too chaotic, too unregulated for his taste. Hopefully someone else would arrive to take responsibility for the division. All he had expected to do was keep his head down and stop his wayward detectives from embarrassing everyone, but now they had been landed with this ridiculous case, and he could see shame and public humiliation looming.

Land did not look up when Arthur Bryant entered the room. 'I know that you and your partner have evolved your own odd methods of working,' he began, attempting to keep a quiver from his voice, 'but this investigation will destroy the unit. Four people, Bryant!' he exploded. 'This latest death managed to make the late-morning editions. The press are having a bloody field day. The *Sun* is running a "Solve It Yourself, Win A Ford Cortina" competition. It's pandemonium. I don't think you need me to tell you that we've never seen anything like this before.' He stood by the window with his index fingers pressed into the bridge of his nose. 'We live in a fractured time. People are becoming uprooted, unemployed. Strikes up and down the country. Heath is the most hopeless PM we've had since the war. Men are losing their wives, their families, their jobs, and their homes at an unprecedented rate. Reasons for murder are becoming as absurd as the times.'

Bryant was well aware of this. Indeed, he had attended Land's recent lecture on the subject at Hendon Police College.

'Statistically, we're catching fewer criminals. You know as well as I do that a murder file can only stay open while we receive help from the public. We can't be expected to search for eternity. And we're marking more and more homicides unsolved. Now we have three blood relatives in the same family dead in six days, and so far no forensic indications, no decent witnesses, no outside information. These aren't random acts of violence, for God's sake. Someone is playing a deliberate, arrogant game with us. What I want to know is, how can so much happen with so little result from this department?'

'Our problem lies in the evidence,' explained Bryant, 'or rather the extraordinary surfeit of it. It's as if there was a team of people involved in each act, altering everything that might be turned to our use. We have plenty of fingerprints but none of them match. Then there's the problem of motive.'

'What about this German business the *Mail's* been talking about, tying the deaths to the Common Market conference?'

'The design of the Whitstables' sacred flame is admittedly similar to the wartime assassination symbol, but I'm positive it's just a coincidence. There are no other corroborating factors.'

'You're positive, are you? How did you manage to protect Bella Whitstable so well that she died while she was in your care?'

'As we have yet to discover how she died, I consider that an unfair remark,' replied Bryant, stung. 'And I'd like to point out that in a murder investigation of this sort I would normally have expected as many as sixty men to be drafted on to the case. May and I are working with barely half a dozen staff. It's essential that we talk to the surviving partner at Jacob and Marks, but because their office is in Norwich neither of us has had time to go there yet.'

'I know,' said Land angrily, 'and at the moment there's

not a damned thing I can do about it. It's this place you've built for yourselves. How can you expect organization without structure? It's all very well wanting to conduct your investigations creatively, but you need to cover the groundwork, just as the Met have to. There's no hierarchy here—'

'That was intentional.'

'And assuming your information is fully collated, which I doubt, there's nothing you can do with it because your system doesn't cross-reference every piece of information received by the police.'

'We have many lines of inquiry that need to be followed,' said Bryant wearily. 'What we need is greater manpower.'

'I'll see what I can do,' said Land, picking up a folder and removing its contents. 'But I don't need to tell you that there's a lot of resentment about this unit. Quite a few lads in the Met think you're being elitist, that the old system isn't good enough for you any more. They're waiting for you to hang yourselves. But unless I receive positive proof that someone is physically trying to hinder the investigation, there's nothing I can do. At least I've had a chance to go over your report,' said Land, brandishing a sheaf of paper. Bryant was pleased that he had found the time to do so; he'd been up most of the weekend assembling it.

As little as he cared for the superintendent, Bryant knew that Land was a reasonable man, and at the moment represented their only path to increased resources. It was important to have him on their side.

'Before you go through it, I need to explain something to you,' said Bryant. 'It's something I haven't put in that document. Little more than a feeling, really. We're looking for more than just a clever murderer. This is about revenge.'

'Don't start, Bryant. I have a limit.'

'The methods rely on a knowledge of the victims,' Arthur continued, 'and the approach is theatrical, as though each death is intended to act as some kind of warning. The standard investigation procedures can't apply, because these are cold executions, cutting off branches of the family tree. I'm not sure there's even any malice. It's more a matter of—pruning. Something quite unprecedented in my experience.'

'Do you have any information on the Whitstable woman's cause of death yet?'

'I'm afraid not.'

Land was clearly dissatisfied with his own powerless role in the proceedings. He stood at the window picking a flake of paint from the peeling ledge. 'I want our backs covered with this one,' he said carefully. 'There are rumours that the Australian Commonwealth delegates have been sent death threats. Their arts minister, Carreras, has scheduled another press conference complaining about the lack of security he's experienced, in order to embarrass our government into official action.'

'We haven't established a positive connection between—'

'Did you know that, until this morning at least, the minister was staying at the Savoy?'

'Yes, I was aware of that.'

'Were you also aware that he attended the theatre last night?'

Bryant felt a crawling sensation in his gut. 'At the Coliseum?'

'The very same. Box L.'

The box exactly facing the one in which Bella

Whitstable was taken ill. Anger rose within him. There was a pattern here. Why could he not see it?

'We'll step up our inquiries,' he promised, knowing that it would now be necessary to call a press conference. He would schedule it for late this afternoon. But first, there was a murder to reconstruct.

On his way out of the office, he walked into Jerry Gates. She had come up to the Mornington Crescent unit in her lunch break, and was still wearing her hotel uniform.

'What are you doing here?' He frowned at her in displeasure.

'You said you might need to talk to me again.'

'I said I'd call you when I was ready. How did you get in?'

'Sergeant Longbright admitted me. I want to help. I know there's been another one. If you'd just listen to me for a minute—'

'Miss Gates, neither I nor my partner has a moment to spare right now. Please, go back to work and leave it to us to take the appropriate steps.'

The police aren't making any progress, she thought. *I can do better on my own. And if anything bad happens, they'll only have themselves to blame for not listening to me.*

They met in the foyer of the Coliseum, a forlorn, dripping crowd in suits and raincoats, like a party of tourists gathered for a particularly unpopular sightseeing tour. Bereft of their finery they seemed smaller and less significant. They awkwardly offered their condolences to Bryant as if attending the wake before the funeral.

'I'm afraid I must ask you all to come back to the box, and it will be necessary for you to don your outfits once more. It seems morbid, I know, but it's necessary to re-create the exact circumstances under which Bella Whit-stable died. It may help us to understand what happened.'

Below them, rehearsals continued as the Savoyards struggled back into armour and hose. Bryant stood patiently at the rear of the box with a smirking police photographer while the group dressed. Then he directed them to their places, marking the seat in which Bella collapsed.

'All right,' he said, raising his hands for silence. 'How many members do we have here?'

'There are twenty-two of us,' said Oliver Pettigrew. 'There are more in the society, but we vary in number according to each production. Principal cast members can't be duplicated, and the main cast of *Ida* is fifteen.'

'So what does that make the rest of you?'

'Courtiers, Soldiers and Daughters of the Plough.'

'I want everyone to take the positions they held last night, at the time when it was first noticed that Mrs Whitstable was feeling unwell,' Bryant requested. There followed much shuffling and pulling free of snagged cloaks.

'Wait,' said Bryant, 'there's somebody missing.' The Savoyards looked at one another, then back at the elderly detective. 'There was a little beggar in a hat standing against the wall.'

'Are you sure?' asked Pettigrew. 'There aren't any beggars listed in the cast of *Ida*.'

'I distinctly remember seeing him there,' said Bryant. 'A tattered man. Surely someone else must have noticed him.' He searched the surrounding faces, positive that the assassin had been discovered, but the Savoyards rubbed their chins and shook their heads. He looked back at the empty chair where Bella had collapsed, and the spot beside it where she had put down her handbag. What could the beggar have done to cause her death?

As he moved toward the door of the box he turned back to the assembled group, who were still watching him and waiting for guidance.

'Thank you for coming,' he told the semicircle of baffled faces. 'Please check that the constable here has your personal details written down correctly, and we'll get back to you if there are any further developments.'

And with that he hastily left the theatre.

'They found no trace of strychnine in the champagne?'

'None whatsoever,' said Raymond Land. 'What's on your mind?' Bryant had blasted into his office like a rainy night and was proceeding to soak everything with his umbrella and overcoat.

'I was thinking about strychnine,' he explained. 'Such an old-fashioned poison. It's fairly fast-acting, so it would have to have been administered within the theatre box. Why would the murderer make things so difficult for himself? Why pick a drug with such a startling effect, and risk capture by still being on the premises when she began to convulse?'

He dumped a large opaque plastic bag on Land's desk. 'You'd have to be very sure of your method of administration, wouldn't you?'

He carefully opened the evidence envelope and withdrew Bella Whitstable's handbag, still covered in fingerprint dust. 'When I saw her initial symptoms,' he continued, 'I knew that something was paralysing her muscles. Strychnine poisoning starts in the face and neck.' He fished about in the bag and withdrew an object in a bony fist. 'How does it look if you buy it in the form of, say, rat poison?'

'It's a powder,' said Land. 'Crystalline and colourless.'

'And it can kill on contact with the skin or the eyes.' He opened his hand to reveal a powder compact. 'She applied it herself when she freshened her makeup in the intermission. We'll run print matches, but it's likely our beggarman dipped into her bag and doctored the compact while we were watching the first act.'

Land took the compact from Bryant's outstretched hand and carefully opened it. Beneath the face pad lay a pool of granules which appeared slightly more crystalline than the fine pink powder below it. 'Well, I'll be damned. Someone's been reading Agatha bleeding Christie.' He looked up at Bryant in amazement.

14 / Occultation

Joseph shone the torch across a paint-streaked brick wall, then up into a network of distant blackened rafters. 'Come on. It's safe.'

'I have a problem with the dark,' she said, peering ahead. 'It's a stupid phobia. If there's a light somewhere I'm okay.'

'There's a junction box here that controls the lights.' The torch beam picked up a grey steel cabinet with electrical warning stickers pasted to the doors. 'All the structural repair work has been completed, but I'm still not supposed to bring anyone else in here. If you fall through the floor you're not covered by the insurance.'

They had entered the site of the Savoy Theatre through the wooden surround that encased the redbrick and Portland stone of the building's ground floor. Joseph wrenched open a door of the cabinet and flicked a row of switches. A handful of dim emergency bulbs threw amber pools of light across the auditorium. Jerry tried to relax her breathing, not daring to think about the surrounding darkness.

Part of the interior of the theatre was still blackened and fire-ravaged, but the proscenium arch and the stage beyond it had been fully restored, and waited under sheets of heavy plastic to be unveiled once more before an audience.

'You wouldn't think we were just two weeks away

from opening, would you?' Joseph said. 'Nobody thought it would ever open again after the fire. It doesn't look as if the paintwork's going to be dry by the time they admit the paying public. Theatres and restaurants—I've worked in both, and you're always busy up to the last minute.'

Many of the surrounding seats had been newly installed, and were covered in cloths. As Jerry followed him down the side aisle, she could hear distant rain falling on glass far above them.

'Richard D'Oyly Carte was ahead of his time,' he called back. 'His theatre was designed for all-round visibility, no matter what you'd paid for your ticket. He abolished tipping the attendants and gave them decent wages instead. Best of all, he ditched all the dingy dark walls and heavy velvets favoured by the Victorians. This whole place was a blaze of yellow satin, white and gold paintwork. The seats were bright blue and the boxes were red. And the vestibule floor was paved in black-and-white marble. It was a monument to light and cool style. The medieval palace of the Princes of Savoy used to stand on this site. I think Carte was trying to recapture that spirit.' He pulled himself up on the stage and beckoned for her to join him.

'The Tasaka Corporation are paying for most of the restoration,' he explained, walking to the rear of the stage. 'They'll also help to decide management policy.'

'It doesn't look like you're even half ready to open,' she said, clambering up on to the front of the stage.

'But we will be open, in the New Year. It will be a Japanese-British co-production, and they'll have touring rights for the East. Mr Miyagawa is hoping that the Savoy will become a forum for world theatre. I keep thinking my luck will run out.'

Jerry watched as he strode back and forth across the stage, a tall figure dressed in black with an extraordinary knotted tumble of hair. She wanted to run up and press her fingers over his heart, to feel the life pulsing inside him.

Somewhere in the rear of the penumbral auditorium there was a yielding sound, like a roll of rope uncoiling. Jerry paused on the stair and listened. The slithering was lost in a renewed stress of rain on the roof. Ahead, metal drums and tangles of wiring blocked the way.

'Where are you?' she called. 'Be careful you don't fall over.'

'It's okay,' he replied, his voice muffled by the curtain hanging at one side of the proscenium arch. 'I know my way around.'

The sound which reached her ears this time was much nearer. A metallic rasping, as if steel cables were dropping past one another.

'Joseph,' she called, 'are we the only people in here?'

There was no reply. The hanging lights strung across the stage flickered momentarily, causing patchwork light to jigsaw between the pipework and the walls.

'Joseph?' Jerry squeezed through the gap between a pair of steel stanchions and walked deeper into the stage area. The wings were dark with equipment and debris. Above, boards creaked as if a weight had been gently laid across them.

She glanced up, but could see nothing.

Surely he wouldn't just have left her here? She walked slowly toward the orchestra pit, moving between deep pools of shade. The chill air pricked at the flesh on her arms, ghosts of the theatre passing by. It felt as if someone was watching her. She smiled at the thought; after all, she was standing on a stage.

There was a ping of metal, and a small steel bolt bounced on the floorboards beside her. She looked up at a gantry half covered in dust sheets. She sensed the figure before seeing it. A small man, wrapped in a brown cloth like some period stage character, was crouched between the bars like a motionless insect, staring silently down at her.

Jerry cried out in horror as the figure jumped to its feet and kicked away from the wall.

With a creak and a groan the gantry began moving toward her. Planks cascaded to the floor in a series of timed explosions. As she turned to run, she knew that the steel stack had been shoved free of its moorings, and would land on top of her. Ahead lay the orchestra pit, its depth impossible to calculate, its floor lost in shadow.

As the gantry dropped, she flung herself out into the darkness, her deepest fears made real.

The pit was shallower than she had expected. As she hit the ground, the gantry slammed on to the floor of the stage and broke into singing steel sections. Above her lay a twisted network of galvanized pipes. One of the fallen emergency lights was shining across her eyes. She raised herself on a bruised elbow as the sheeted figure scampered on to the scaffolding to peer down at her.

Jerry rolled to one side and thrust herself through the gap at the side of the pit, scrambling back into the aisle as the figure darted ahead. The door marked with an emergency exit symbol clanged shut behind him.

She gave chase and found herself in a red-painted passageway leading to the rear of the theatre. The bar of the external door slammed up with a hard echo, and she turned the corner to find it closing on her. Kicking it wide, she ran out into the downpour and caught sight of the ragged figure lurching away towards the Thames.

The rain-slick street impeded her progress as she slid on to the Embankment just yards behind the draped man. She could hear her attacker wheezing as he tried to stay ahead. They crossed to the river, where aureoles of light sparkled around the illuminated globes lining the Embankment, marking the causeway to the sea.

The road in front of her was deserted. There was nowhere for the fleeing beggar to escape or hide. Rain flapped rhythmically from his robes as he loped ahead, his head concealed beneath a dirty brown hat.

For a moment Jerry was reminded of her dream. The enclosing brick walls were absent, but the beggar was as deformed as her nightmare creatures. The image was too close for comfort, and her pace momentarily faltered.

A crippling stitch in her side caused her to drop further back. Her quarry veered out into the road, darting through the traffic, nimbly vaulting the fence into the park. Jerry doubled over in pain, her breath coming in hot gasps. There was no point in going on. She couldn't believe that she had been outrun by what appeared to be a tramp. Pulling her shirttails above her belt, she examined her stomach and found the cause of the trouble. A long red welt was already darkening across the lower part of her ribcage. She had landed badly in the orchestra pit.

I disturbed the killer in his hiding place, she thought. *He knew the police were looking for him. Perhaps he had nowhere else to go.* Anxious to find Joseph, she reversed her direction and made a painful journey back to the theatre. She arrived to find him waiting outside for her. He was covered in dirt and dust.

'What happened to you?' she asked, slapping his shoulder angrily. 'Why didn't you answer me when I called?'

'I couldn't. Someone shoved me into one of the bloody property cupboards.'

'What do you mean? Who?'

'How the hell should I know? I just felt his hands in the middle of my back. The next thing I knew, I was in complete darkness.'

'You're big enough to take care of yourself. Why didn't you do anything?'

'Because I was caught by surprise, that's why.'

'Then why didn't you call out?'

'I did, but the damned thing was filled with dust sheets. I nearly choked to death. There was an enormous bang, clanging metal, God knows what. I managed to get the door open, but I couldn't find you anywhere. He'd turned all the lights off.'

'Then there must have been two of them. There was someone on the scaffolding. He tried to kill me.'

'Oh, come on...'

'You didn't see him, but I did. He tipped the gantry over, nearly squashed me flat.'

'It couldn't have been intentional.' Joseph looked back at the silent theatre. 'What did he look like?'

'A tramp, I guess. No, more like an actor in a play, someone's idea of what a tramp should look like.'

'That's it, then,' said Joseph. He brushed at his sweater, but only succeeded in matting the dust into wet wool. 'We disturbed a couple of tramps, probably scared the hell out of them.'

'This was no ordinary dosser, Joseph.'

'There are plenty of homeless kids in the Strand looking for somewhere to sleep. Maybe they managed to break into the theatre.'

'No, this was deliberate. He cut the gantry loose. And

there was more than one—you were locked up to be kept out of the way.'

'Listen to yourself. You're saying that someone tried to murder you.'

'Why not?' Jerry shouted. 'They're dropping like flies around this place, or did you forget? I'm already a witness to two deaths.'

'If you were a real witness you'd have seen who did it,' retorted Joseph calmly. 'And you didn't, did you?'

'That's not the point. If other people can be attacked, why not me? The management's called a security meeting for all hotel staff. They think we're in danger. Maybe someone deliberately followed me into the theatre.'

'You're a hotel clerk, you're not selling state secrets to the Soviet Union. Why would someone pick on you?'

She felt a knot of rage in her stomach, the anger of not being taken seriously, of being dismissed as insignificant. It was the feeling that had dogged her ever since she was a child.

'Why wouldn't they?' she cried. 'What's so different about me?'

'You make it sound like you want to be part of it, like you've got some kind of victim complex.'

'I just want—'

'Jerry, I've a really big day tomorrow, and I have to get some sleep. Can we talk about it some other time?'

'Well, I'm pleased that you've got your career,' she shouted pointlessly, desperately. 'I'm glad everything's so damned perfect in your life. You're not the only one who's going to do great things, Mr Ego. You'd be amazed at what I could do!'

'Probably,' he called wearily. 'It's been a weird evening and I'm going to bed. Good night, Jerry. Get some rest.'

She kicked out against the wooden casement surrounding the theatre, kicking again and again until stinging tears of fury were forced from her eyes. Above the darkened theatre, the rain stippled the city in glittering sheets.

15 / Oubliette

The offices of Jacob & Marks smelled of age and affluence, oak and mahogany. John May, newly arrived in Norwich on a windy, ragged Thursday morning, found himself surrounded by the burnished parquet and marquetry of fine old wood, and smart young employees who hurried past sporting fashionably conservative suits. No wide lapels and patch pockets here. Legal firms of this calibre dealt only with large companies and old families. Shopkeepers, he had no doubt, were encouraged to go elsewhere.

May had been kept waiting in the law office for half an hour, and as the train's buffet car had been missing due to the ongoing rail strike, he had so far made up for his lack of breakfast by consuming two cups of tea and a plate of biscuits.

Outside the sky was deep and turbulent, the colour of a summer sea, and leaf-churning eddies sucked at the windows, rattling the panes. May had forgotten the glory of the English countryside. Even in December, the verdant contours of low green hills appeared to offer a welcome.

But there was little call for the detective to visit the country. Much of May's family had gone, and the few friends with whom he bothered to keep in touch were citybound. He took the odd trip to the south coast to visit his sister, but this pleasure was mitigated by the fact that she had three outrageously spoiled children to whom Uncle John represented a combination of cash register and climbing frame.

Bryant, of course, reacted to the idea of visiting any area beyond Finchley with a kind of theatrical horror. Whenever May suggested a trip to the countryside, his partner would convulse in a series of Kabuki-style grimaces meant to convey revulsion at the thought of so much fresh air and so many trees. The farthest Arthur ever traveled these days was Battersea Park, which his apartment overlooked. Bryant had been happy to leave this particular visit to his partner.

At five past ten, Leo Marks blew through the doors exhaling apologies, ushering May into his office while simultaneously firing off complex instructions to a pair of tough-looking secretaries.

The detective had expected to meet a much older man. Leo Marks appeared to be in his late twenties, although his excessive weight and dour dress had added years to his appearance. Seated opposite him, May found himself disconcerted by the fact that the grey pupils of the young lawyer's eyes turned slightly outwards, so that it was hard to tell if he was looking directly ahead. After asking his secretaries to redirect his calls, he adopted a look of professional grief and turned his full attention to his visitor.

'We were terribly upset to hear of Max's death,' he began in a measured tone. 'It's been awfully hard on Anne—'

'His wife.'

'All this speculation in the papers has been having a terrible effect on her. There was talk of a snake attacking him—'

'Somebody injected Max Jacob with a lethal amount

of poison, a rare venom. One of our men found a hypodermic needle in the corridor beyond the washroom.'

'Someone should have told us, Mr May.'

'I'm afraid it only just turned up. It had been trodden into the carpet and missed in the earlier searches. Am I right in thinking that Max and your father were partners?'

'Actually, it was my great-grandfather who set up the firm with Max's grandfather.'

'So your families have been close for a very long time.'

'We still are. There are loyalties here which go back well over a hundred years.'

'Does your father still work here?'

'Only part-time since his heart attack, although he hasn't come in at all since Max died. It's been a terrible blow for him. The worst thing is not knowing.'

'Not knowing who killed Max, or not knowing what he was doing in London?'

Leo Marks swiveled a look encompassing May. 'I think I can tell you why he was visiting the city,' he said. May sat forward, waiting. 'He had arranged to see Peter Whitstable.'

'Why would he do that? Peter's sister told me that all financial arrangements were conducted through William. Surely Max would have informed his wife where he was going.'

'Well, it wouldn't necessarily have been official business. Max and Peter were old friends, you see. They were all at Oxford together.'

'Was Max Jacob in the habit of taking off for London to visit the brothers without telling anyone?'

'Not really, but he had mentioned the idea of making the journey.'

'When was this?'

Leo turned back the pages of his diary. 'The previous Thursday. That would have been on December second. He spoke to Peter several times during the course of that week. The brothers were having another argument.'

'You have no idea what they argued about?'

'No. But it wasn't over money, I can tell you that.'

'How do you know?'

'Their finances are tied up from here. We acted as their stipendiaries, allowing each a set annual amount, the revenue from certain investments and so on. They were quite happy with the arrangement.'

'Who stands to benefit financially from their deaths?'

'No one, immediately. You have to understand that the Whitstable financial empire is so absurdly complex that half of the family beneficiaries won't see a penny for years to come. I sometimes wonder if Dickens didn't model the court case from *Bleak House* on them.'

In which case, we could blame the lawyers who set up the system in the first place, thought May. 'What about Max Jacob?'

'That's straightforward enough. His will appoints his wife Anne as his trustee.'

May checked through his notes, feeling as if his questions were leading him around in a circle. 'I'll be honest with you, Mr Marks...'

'Please, call me Leo.'

'The more I find out about the Whitstables, the less I understand them. The brothers were financially comfortable, established, settled in the most old-fashioned ways. I'm informed that they did nothing more adventurous than read the *Daily Telegraph* and listen to the radio. They bothered no one. They had once wielded influence in the City, but were no longer powerful men. Then one day, for no apparent reason, William commits an act of vandalism and subsequently explodes, while Peter gets an open razor across his throat. Concurrent with the first act, their family lawyer is injected with the venom of a watersnake, and finally their sister is paralysed with strychnine. Bombs and knives, poison and snakes. And all this Grand Guignol somehow leaves us without suspects.'

May leaned forward, carefully watching the young lawyer. 'What on earth were these people hiding? They weren't random victims; their deaths were carefully arranged, and must therefore serve a purpose. The killer can't have been looking for some physical object. He's shown no desire to search their homes. My partner thinks they're acts of revenge, but I disagree. I think the goal is knowledge of some kind, knowledge that was also intimated to your father's partner. Something so important and so secret that Max Jacob went down to London without even telling his wife where he was going.'

'I see your problem,' said Leo, not looking as if he could see much at all. 'Could someone be trying to humiliate them by associating the family with scandal?'

There must be an easier way of humiliating people than blowing them all over the Northern Line, thought May, but sensibly kept the thought to himself.

'Tell me more about the Whitstables.'

Leo Marks massaged his florid jowls with the tips of his fingers. 'They trace themselves back to the founding members of one of London's finest craft guilds, as I'm sure you know.'

'The Goldsmiths, isn't it?'

'Actually a subdivision, the Watchmakers' Guild in Blackfriars Lane, although obviously there are strong affiliations with the Goldsmiths. There are still many such companies in existence, the Cordwainers, the Coopers, the Haberdashers, and so on, many of whom have their own boards, schools, trusts, and benevolent funds scattered throughout the capital. Inevitably, there are strong Masonic ties. Peter and William were both Masons. So was Max.'

'Is that common? Are there other Masons in the family?'

'Quite a few, I believe. The Whitstables made and lost fortunes through the decades, but I understand that the bulk of their present income derives from alliances forged in Victorian times...'

May shifted in his chair. His hopes of returning by a mid-morning train were fast disappearing. 'I need to know much more about the family itself,' he explained. 'Their businesses are presumably still active. Surely there are some younger members around?'

'A few, perhaps, but like so many old dynasties in today's climate, the Whitstables are dying out. There was an unhealthy amount of intermarriage in earlier centuries, but I imagine the partial breakdown of the class system did the most damage. We do have a rather incomplete family tree for them, and some of their current addresses. I could let you have a photocopy.'

'That would be a great help.'

'You'll have your work cut out if you're planning to contact them all. Their last big population boom was a hundred years ago. Most of the grandchildren have long since married, divorced, or departed the country.'

'I still need to speak to as many of them as I can,' said May. With three members of the same family murdered there was no telling how many other lives were in danger.

'I understand.' Leo rose and summoned one of his sturdy young secretaries. 'There was one other thing.' He pushed a red-leather appointment book across his desk. 'On the day Max went down to London there were no engagements marked in his diary, but there was this.' He tapped his finger at the top of the page, where a number had been written: 216. 'Does it help in any way?'

'Not that I can think of,' said May, who had already noted the doodle which encased the number. A burning flame, drawn in the exact same style of Peter Whitstable's tattoo.

'I never said they deserved to die,' exclaimed Arthur Bryant indignantly. 'How dare you put such words into my mouth.'

'You more or less suggested as much,' said May, unrolling the Whitstable family tree and pinning it to the notice board beside his desk. Back in London the winter sky was the colour of gutter water, the clouds marshalling themselves around the damp buildings in preparation for another stormy assault.

'I merely said that I disapproved of the way the Whitstables made their money. The British upper crust exploited their colonies and destroyed the lives of their workers to preserve a status quo not worth clinging to. They deserve everything they get.'

'Including murder? I might remind you of your humanitarian oath at this point.' As he spoke, the two workmen who had entered the already overcrowded room a few minutes ago began to fire up an ancient blowtorch.

'What the hell are they doing?' May shouted above the din.

'I'm having the room returned to its original colours,' said Bryant brightly. 'You saw the paint on the sill.'

'Do they have to do it right now?'

'If we don't do it now, squire, we won't be able to start

until after Christmas,' said one of the workmen, shifting a crate to reach the window.

'We need to contact all the surviving relatives listed on the chart,' said May, attempting to concentrate on the business at hand.

'I've requested a source list for the strychnine,' said Bryant. 'According to Land, the granular fineness is very unusual. That's not the way it's usually made commercially available.'

'Good. Janice has found a two-man team willing to check out the visiting members of the Australian Art Commission, and I'm afraid we need to make another appointment with Mr Faraday. It's essential to pinpoint a connection between the deaths and the destruction of the painting, if there is one.'

Bryant walked over to the unfurled family tree. 'Why did Max Jacob come here?' he wondered aloud. 'What did Peter Whitstable tell him that was so important he had to drop everything and come to London? There's some terrible principle at work, John. I can feel it. Everything's out of alignment. There's the cause and effect of each murder to consider.'

'What do you mean?'

'Well, you can usually see who a murder affects the most. But these crimes are free of motive and, more important, *they have no real effect*. They don't change anything. How does Max Jacob's murder benefit anyone? How on earth does Bella's? Unnatural death is usually linked to sex and money. Why not in these cases? Take a look at this.' He tapped a name on the family tree. 'Bella Whitstable never married. She's the end of the line.'

'How many remaining family members are still living in this country?'

'There are certainly more than fifteen, possibly as

many as thirty. Peter Whitstable had a wife who divorced him in the late sixties, so she's not represented on the tree. There are two sons from the marriage, but they're living abroad with an uncle. There's also a Charles Whitstable living somewhere overseas. The rest are up here.'

'If Jacob looked after the fortunes of the whole family, it shouldn't be hard finding a motive for his death.'

'*Cherchez la femme,*' said one of the workmen, wiping his hands on his blue overalls and relighting the blow-torch. 'You can bet there's always a woman involved.'

'Thank you very much,' said Bryant icily. 'If we need your help, we'll ask for it.'

'I reckon you could do with a hand, judging by what the papers are saying about you lot,' said the other work-man.

'Perhaps you'd like to handle the investigation while we do the window frames.' Bryant turned to face the door, where Jerry waited awkwardly. The girl had wet shoulders and a pale, anxious face. She looked much younger than her seventeen years. 'Could you possibly stop appearing like this?' he cried. 'You nearly gave me a heart attack. Well, come in then,' he said, exasperated. 'Have you got anyone else out there you'd like to bring in?'

'I brought you some evidence,' said Jerry, embarrassed to be speaking in front of the workmen, who had stopped tackling the paintwork and were watching the proceedings with fascination.

'What sort of evidence?' asked May.

Jerry withdrew the Bible from her jacket and set it on the desk.

May carefully opened the book and studied the fly-leaf. 'Where did you get this?'

'I found it in Mr Jacob's room. The police missed it.'

'What were you doing in there?' Bryant asked.

'Just having a look around.'

'And why do you think it's of any interest to us?'

'There are some passages underlined,' she said. 'They might mean something.'

'You mean you've been withholding evidence?'

'No,' she said indignantly, 'I was looking around the room and—'

'Suppose his murderer had been looking for this?' said Bryant. 'You could have put your own life in danger. Did you stop to think of that?'

'No,' said Jerry, bowing her face. Suddenly Bryant saw how much of a toll her recent experiences had taken. She had knotted her pale hands over each other to keep them still. Death had unforeseen effects on the living. He wondered about the nature of the discovery it had brought to her.

'She keeps turning up like some kind of awful wraith,' said Bryant as the squad car turned into another water-logged avenue lined with sycamores. 'She obviously has some kind of morbid fascination with this case. She's starting to give me the creeps. I wish she'd smile occasionally.'

'You can't blame her for wanting to be part of the investigation,' replied May. 'The hand of Death has given her a good old shaking.'

'It can't hurt, can it? You taking her around with you?'

'She's bright enough, and I could do with the help. So long as we don't let anyone else know.' May braked to a halt and killed the engine. The sound of rain continued to drum above their heads.

'If you need anything, you can call me on this

number.' He handed his partner a slip of paper. 'Or use your walkie-talkie.' Bryant reluctantly accepted the note and made a show of pocketing it as May watched him with suspicion.

'You haven't got it, have you?' he said finally.

Bryant gave him a wide-eyed innocent look, and saw that it wasn't going to work. 'Er, no,' he admitted.

'What is the point of me providing you with a walkie-talkie if you don't remember to bring it with you?'

'I put it in my jacket this morning,' Bryant explained earnestly, 'but it, er, ruined the cut of the pocket.'

'What are you talking about?' May studied his partner, who had owned four secondhand suits in the last twenty years, all of them brown and shapeless. 'You've lost it again, haven't you?'

'Not lost, John, mislaid. Anyway, they don't work properly.'

'Not the way you use them, filling them up with soup and fluff and bits of dinner.' May unclipped his own and passed it to his partner. 'Take mine, I'll get another. If you lose this one, you're a dead man.'

Bryant climbed out of the car and watched as May drove away. Then he walked in the shadow of the dripping sycamores to the front door of Bella Whitstable's house.

The property was situated in a pleasant part of suburban West London where only the company cars gave any hint of the area's invasion by young professionals. Bella had rarely visited here in the past few years, preferring the peace of the country. Until recently she had allowed a lodger to stay rent-free in return for looking after the property.

Bryant pushed open a wrought-iron gate and crossed the overgrown garden. The sun, invisible during the course of the day, was making a faint embarrassed flourish through the fluctuating rain before dropping dismally behind the encroaching cloud of night.

When he had managed to fit a key to the front door lock, he entered the hall and tried the lights, but nothing happened. The electricity had already been turned off. He dug out a pocket torch and switched it on.

Bella's house proved to be the opposite of her brothers', decorated in a gloomy, spartan manner which suggested that the owner was little interested in comfort or the vagaries of fashion. These rooms were uncluttered by all but the simplest furniture, the walls adorned by a handful of sporting prints. Only the graceful decor of the bedroom upstairs gave any hint of warmth.

Wardrobes and cupboards proved mostly empty. A single unlabeled key lay beneath the lining paper in the empty chest of drawers. The belongings Bella Whitstable required for daily use were presumably stored at her house in the country.

Bryant shone his torch to the landing and up at the ceiling. There was no sign of a loft. He carefully descended to the ground floor again, pausing at the landing window to listen. Incredibly, it had begun to rain again. The sound suggested a long, dank winter filled with harsh saffron sunsets and flooded footpaths, the season of murder and suicide.

Bryant pulled his scarf tighter to his throat and shone the torch across a set of ugly Victorian hunting prints. For a brief second, his reflected face flared back at him. Perhaps there was a basement. Upon reaching the kitchen, he cast the torch beam across the walls, searching for a door.

He soon found it—a narrow wooden panel painted

gloss white—but it was locked, and no key on his ring fitted the lock. Digging into his coat pocket he withdrew the unlabeled key from the bedroom and inserted it, turning the handle. The damp wood had swollen in its frame. Jerking it hard, he unstuck the door and peered inside.

Below him, a flight of stone steps led off into blackness. Beneath ground level, the temperature of the cellar was several degrees lower than in the rest of the house. There was an unhealthy, mushroomy smell.

As he descended, Bryant could see his breath condensing in the beam of the torch. Gardening equipment stood at one side of the steps. Behind the rakes and shovels were fence posts and bales of wire, presumably for use on Bella's country property. Somewhere in front of him, water dripped steadily onto sodden wood. There was no such thing as a completely dry Victorian house in London.

The torch beam revealed the side of a large packing crate. Here were stacks of forgotten games that touched off childhood memories of his own: Lotto, Escalado, Flounders, Tell Me, Magic Robot. Setting down the torch, he reached in among ruptured teddy bears, grotesque china dolls with missing limbs and eyes, pandas and golliwogs with their stuffing protruding, and withdrew a sepia photograph in a mildewed frame of grey cardboard.

Three children stood arm in arm on a manicured lawn, tentatively smiling, as if they had been instructed to do so by an impatient parent. The girl, pale and heavyset, wore a lumpy linen frock decorated with large, unflattering bows. The two boys were older, and were dressed formally in suits and gaiters, adults in miniature. There was an air of melancholia about all three, as though the photograph had been taken during a brief moment of sunlight. Behind them, the ground floor of an imposing country residence could be glimpsed.

On the flyleaf of the frame was handwritten in violet ink: *Will Whitstable, aged 11. Bella Whitstable, aged 8. Peter Whitstable, aged 13. Summer, 1928.*

The portrait exhibited a lack of warmth that Bryant had so often found in photographs of the upper-middle classes. He pushed the picture into his pocket, aware that it might be of some future use.

Behind the crate was an identical box, filled to overflowing but harder to reach. The beam of his torch was dimming.

It was then that he heard the sound of shallow breathing in the dark beside him.

Someone, or something, had just woken up.

He must have disturbed a sleeping tramp. That was it, a tramp had gained entry to the house and had fallen asleep in the cellar. He swung the torch around and tried to trap the nearby figure in its barely visible beam, only to hear a rapid shift of movement to the far side of the room.

As the torch beam fluctuated once more, darkness pressed in. Bryant inched his way across the cellar floor. There was an odd, perfumed smell in this part of the room, a scent he associated with the hippies of the sixties. As he reached the stairs, he sensed the change in air pressure rather than hearing any movement; it was all that saved him from being knocked unconscious.

Armed with a wooden club of some kind, his assailant only succeeded in grazing his shoulder and thudding the weapon against the wall. His hand grabbed the detective's coat, trying to pull him over. Bryant held tightly to the torch, shining its pulsing beam in his attacker's face.

Wide brown eyes stared back as the figure released a frightened cry. Bryant swung the torch hard and connected with flesh. The hand clutching his coat suddenly released its grip.

Bryant stumbled to the stairs and was halfway up when he was tackled from behind. This time, strong arms pulled his legs from under him. He felt himself falling, the torch beam flaring and whirling as he crashed over the steps into a pile of boxes. By the time he had righted himself, his attacker had climbed the stairs and slammed the door behind him, turning the key in the lock.

Bryant groaned, more in fury than in pain. He thumped the side of the torch, but the batteries were dead. Somewhere above a door slammed shut, then another. If he ever managed to get out, he would never live this down. No one knew he was here except May, and his partner was used to not hearing from him for days.

He pulled himself from his perch on top of the squashed boxes and felt in his pockets. Although he was a non-smoker, he always kept a light on him because of the name of the match company. Bryant & May were the bearers of illumination; it was an old joke, and one which still brought comfort. He removed the matchbox from his pocket and struck a light.

In the flare of the burning splinter he found himself sitting opposite a four-foot-high painting in an ornate gilt frame. He must have dislodged it from its packing crate as he had fallen.

Now the painting, in turn, began to topple forward. As it did so, in the moment before the match burned Bryant's fingers, he saw the figure of a Roman emperor feeding his pigeons. *The Favourites of the Emperor Honorius.*

The sulphurous smell of the match filled his nostrils, and he was in darkness again. Bryant fumbled another from the box. Even in the flickering light that was afforded, he could see the signature: it was the mark of John William Waterhouse.

16 / The Coming of Night

John May stood at the foot of the Staircase Hall and carefully refurled his wet umbrella. On either side of him stood pallid marble statues, offering representations of the four seasons. Overhead, a gigantic electrolier hung suspended from the gilded central dome. The supporting spandrels bore the arms of Richard II, by whose charter the Worshipful Company of Goldsmiths had been incorporated in 1393.

The Goldsmiths' Hall stood behind a pair of discreet iron gates in Foster Lane, and nothing outside had prepared him for the dazzling sights within. Golden heraldic mouldings shone down from every wall. Mirrors held an eternity of reflected crystal. Ornamental carvings had been created purely for the delight of the beholder. Displays of ceremonial plate glowed with exuberance, filling the discreet glass cabinets which lined the corridors.

May had called Alison Hatfield, the public-relations officer representing the Worshipful Company of Watchmakers. He was interested in discovering the extent of the Whitstable family's dealings with the Watchmakers' Guild. Her heels ticked across the marble floor as she approached, donning a raincoat as she walked. Miss Hatfield had enormous pale eyes set in a slender face, and all the nervous energy of someone excessively underweight.

'We'll try not to make this too boring for you,' she

said, shaking his hand. 'Do let us know if we rattle on too much. There's a lot of history here.'

'I'm here to learn,' said May.

'Well, where to start?' Miss Hatfield smiled generously. 'The front rooms were badly damaged by bombing in 1941, and of course much of the building isn't open to the public. Mostly that's the part involved with the day-to-day running of an active livery company. The craft guilds still support their own trade, of course.'

'I was admiring the silver plate.' May attempted to keep pace with his guide.

'It's not just for display, you know. It serves a practical purpose. Many of the silver pieces were created to act as a reserve fund in times of need. I'm afraid much of it was sold off in the sixteenth and seventeenth centuries.'

They stepped into the grey, rainswept street. 'It's not very far.' Miss Hatfield marched on, unbothered by the downpour. 'The Watchmakers are a relatively new organization, of course. The first portable timepieces didn't appear until shortly after 1500, when a German locksmith figured out how to replace weights with a mainspring. The guild wasn't formed until 1625, after iron movements had been superseded by brass and steel. Quite late, as craft guilds go. Here we are.' She stopped before another iron gate and rang the bell. A buzzer sounded in reply, and she pushed open the gate.

'I'll hand you over to my opposite number,' she said, leading him briskly along a richly decorated corridor. 'Well, he's actually the Company's general secretary.'

'Would the Watchmakers have a list of members readily available?' asked May.

'The guilds maintain entirely separate identities,' Miss Hatfield explained. 'I'm afraid you'll have to ask Mr Tomlins about that.' She ushered May into a small modern office which contrasted starkly with the elaborate embellishments outside. Seated behind an absurdly large desk, a rotund man in a tight grey suit was speaking softly into his Dictaphone. His hooded eyes made him appear half-asleep.

'He'll be with you shortly,' said Miss Hatfield, clasping her hands together.

'Thank you very much, Miss—'

'Please, call me Alison.' She plainly felt that she was trespassing on alien terrain, and took her leave with a nervous smile. May studied the bare room as Tomlins continued to ignore him. The official finally looked up, but made no attempt to offer his hand.

'I understand you want to know more about the Watchmakers,' he said in an alarmingly high voice. 'Perhaps I may ask why?'

Something about his manner instantly annoyed May, who decided to divulge as little as possible. 'We have an ongoing investigation that could indirectly involve the guild,' he said. 'I'm collecting background information that may throw some light on the matter.'

'If I am to provide that, I need to know the exact nature of the investigation.'

'I'm afraid it's out of the question at the present time,' said May. 'But you could help by showing me around.'

Tomlins was clearly reluctant to provide anything but the most minimal service. This was surprising, considering that he acted as the guild's main contact with the public. As they walked from room to room, each one filled with display cases of ornate gold and silver watches, he spoke only when he was asked a direct question.

'What is your company's link with the Goldsmiths?' asked May, genuinely interested in what had always been, for him, a hidden side of the city.

'The Goldsmiths were founded nearly three centuries before us.' Tomlins's small, highly polished shoes protested as they walked. 'The craft of watchmaking is one of ornamentation as well as mechanics. The Goldsmiths helped our members to become adept in the use of rare and precious metals. Obviously, gold and silver are still the most popular materials for watch cases.' They passed a pair of matching portraits, Queen Victoria and the Prince Consort, unrecognizably youthful.

'There seems to be a lot of symbolism in the decoration of these items,' said May.

'Indeed. Craftsmen have always included certain personal images and signs in their engravings.'

'Have you ever seen one like this?' He produced a piece of paper from his pocket and unfolded it to reveal the circled flame symbol they had first traced from William Whitstable's cane.

'I don't think so, no.' Tomlins shook his head, but May was unconvinced by his hasty rebuttal.

'Do you all meet socially?'

'Who do you mean?'

'The guild members. The old Watchmaker families. You still hold regular meetings?'

'There are certain annual functions to attend, yes. Whether we wish to meet outside of these engagements is entirely up to individual members. Many of our members are also Masons, and naturally some of these gatherings overlap.'

'Then you probably know the Whitstable family?'

There was a brief flicker behind the hooded eyes. 'I believe we have met on occasion.'

'I imagine you've heard about the deaths of William, Peter, and Bella Whitstable?'

'Only what I've read in the papers, Mr May.' He

turned, tapping at one of the display cases. 'This contains some of our finest fob watches. Although two were traditionally worn, one either side of the waistcoat, one of them was usually false.'

'That one would make a nice wristwatch,' observed May. 'When did you last see any of the Whitstables?'

'Wristwatches were not invented until the First World War, Mr May. There was a gala mayoral dinner in June. Members of the Whitstable family would have been in attendance. Perhaps you'd like to see the Court Rooms now.'

'So you haven't spoken with any of them,' pressed May. 'What about their business dealings with the Company? Do they play an active role in your daily financial affairs?'

'That sort of information is restricted to the Company's managers and accountants. I should hardly think it's of any interest to outsiders. It certainly has no bearing on their unfortunate deaths.'

May had the distinct impression that he was being misdirected. Any further pressuring on the subject of the Whitstables would doubtless cause a closure of the ranks. Their Masonic ties had taught them the value of secrecy. He would have to tackle the problem from another angle.

'What I'm trying to establish here, Mr Tomlins, is who profits and who loses by their deaths.'

Tomlins came to a halt and turned to the detective. 'If you're trying to infer that a member of the Watchmakers is somehow responsible—'

'I didn't say that. I need to understand every aspect of the Whitstables' lives, and I'm afraid that doing so means going beyond the usual boundaries of privacy.'

'But they were the victims of violence, not the culprits.

Surely they deserve to be treated with decency. If you're going to go prying into their affairs—'

'Mr Tomlins, I have to know where their money went, who they were involved with romantically and financially, what their hopes and fears were for themselves and for each other. You can make this an easier process for me by asking the other guild members to cooperate. Our inquiries are treated in the strictest confidence. We know that William and Peter had recently argued, and that Bella had virtually severed her ties with the family. Someone here must know why the Whitstables weren't on speaking terms with one another. I need you to set up a meeting for me. There must be guild members who knew the brothers well. You wish to protect your members' interests. Surely the Whitstables deserve to have your help.'

'Very well,' said Tomlins finally, 'I'll see what I can do.'

As May saw himself out, he turned to see Tomlins moving away from him at speed. Something seemed to have urgently summoned him back to his office.

The cellar door was sealed fast. Bryant's eyes were trying to adapt to the dark, and he was finding it hard to draw his breath. His chest felt tight, and he was starting to hyperventilate. He was below ground level in a darkened, sealed house. Normally the darkness did not disturb him; his only psychological weakness was a tendency to suffer from vertigo, but the violence of his earlier encounter had left him feeling suffocated.

Forcing the unease from his mind, he felt his way back to the top of the steps. He swung an experimental kick at the door, but it was made of heavy oak and fitted tightly into its jamb. He tried hard to remember where he had set down May's walkie talkie. He recalled taking it out of his pocket. It was somewhere in the cellar, but the room was completely filled with junk, and he had no more matches left.

He was considering the problem when the distant sound of an opening door reached his ears. Muffled conversation. Someone else was in the house. Bryant began to shout out. He kicked the base of the door until his foot was bruised. He no longer cared whether he would be confronted by friend or foe.

'Is that you, Mr Bryant?' The voice was vaguely familiar.

'Of course it's me!'

'Stand well back from the door.'

An axe head appeared through the splitting wood and the centre panel of the door collapsed. One of their patrol officers stuck his head through the open space.

'Blimey, Sir, this is no time for you to be creeping off for a nap,' said the constable, offering his hand.

Bryant was so pleased to see a friendly face that his customary rudeness deserted him. Remembering his discovery, he returned for the painting and began to haul it up.

'We have to take this,' he explained. 'It's evidence.' As if determined to remain hidden in the shadows, the painting pulled from his grip and fell back down the steps.

The last thing she wanted to do was talk in front of Nicholas, but here was Joseph Herrick striding across the hotel lobby to the desk, his mane bobbing beneath his cowboy hat. Jerry laid down her ballpoint, ready for a fight.

'I should apologize about last night,' said Joseph. 'You have to admit, it was a pretty weird evening.'

Jerry was left defenseless. No man had ever apologized to her before. She was used to arguing with people.

'Want to get something to eat? Goodwill gesture?' He handed his room key to Nicholas with a smile.

'You can't leave yet,' said Nicholas. 'You're on late duty tonight, and there's still half an hour to go.'

Without saying a word, Jerry swung her bag on to her shoulder.

'If you walk out now,' hissed Nicholas, a vein throbbing furiously at his temple, 'I'll see that this is reported. You'll be out of a job when you get back. I won't stand for it any more.'

His words were wasted. Moments later she had passed through the revolving door with Joseph and was out on the street.

The Arizona Bar and Grill had steel-topped tables covered with crescent-shaped dents from a thousand slammed tequilas. A harassed waitress led them to a table in the corner of the room.

'Are you hungry?' Joseph asked.

'I'm always hungry. I maintain a level of hypertension that can burn off a four-course meal in twenty minutes.' Glancing at the menu, they ordered enough food for three.

'Is there any chance that you're going to tell me something about yourself this time?' he asked.

'What do you want to know about me for?' She brought her chair in closer. 'You already have a girlfriend.'

'Things aren't that black and white, Jerry. We can be interested in each other without having to jump into bed.'

'How caring and seventies. Doesn't sound like a good

arrangement to me.' She thought for a moment. 'You want family history or what?'

'That'll do for a start.'

'Okay, personal CV: my parents aren't older than their money. We don't have a great home life. Gwen goes to so many committee meetings I've been wondering if she's having an affair. She lives in the hope of rare animals becoming threatened with extinction so that she can chair committees to save them. Jack still thinks it's 1944. Maybe he was happy then. My mother prefers to throw parties rather than cook and I grew up thinking that a meal with the family meant finger food for fifty. We get along fine so long as we don't talk about my future, which is all they ever want to talk about.'

'How come?'

'I wanted to go to art school and they wanted me to enter the family business. But war had been declared between us long before then.'

Joseph dug into a plate of nachos, licking melted cheese from the tips of his fingers. 'What kind of business are they in?'

'Import-export, gold and silver. Shuffling paper, arranging shipments. I don't know the details and I'm really not interested.'

'Why not? Sounds like there's a lot of money to be made.'

'I've seen the kind of people Gwen and Jack mix with. I never wanted to be part of the old-school network.'

'So their attempts to civilize you have failed?'

'I think they've had the opposite effect. And when I was fourteen, I had problems...' The memory of that time was still fresh in her mind. To talk about it was to lower her guard, but perhaps the past wasn't meant to be bottled away, to ferment in the dark.

He was quick to sense her discomfort. 'We can talk about something else if you'd rather.'

She took a swig of her beer. 'Basically, I screwed up my parents' long-term plans by getting expelled from school. Gwen went berserk. Told me I'd let her down. How could she face her friends, all that kind of stuff, so I smashed the house up and accused her of some pretty terrible things. I didn't know what I was saying. It was kind of a breakdown.'

'So what happened?'

'I got sick. They put me in therapy, and the doctor tried to blame my behaviour on all kinds of revolting stuff, so I hit him. The blow ruptured a blood vessel in his nose. Jack had to settle out of court. Gwen had me sent away to a special-care centre. I wouldn't stay there, kept running away. Eventually we reached a truce, Gwen and Jack and me. If I learned to control my behaviour, they'd allow me to follow my own course. There's money held in trust, which I'm supposed to get when I'm twenty-one. I had to agree to be the model daughter. At that point I even promised to go into the family business.'

'So how did you end up as a receptionist?'

'I guess I broke the promise.'

'And they're upset with you for doing so?'

'That's putting it mildly. Now tell me about you.'

'Don't change the subject.'

'Talking about it is depressing. Tell me something.'

'This is my first job after getting my degree. I've been given a chance to put my design ideas into practice. I've already begun the preliminary work on the Tasaka Corporation's next production. They're paying my hotel bills plus a retainer, but I'll rent a place as soon as my first real salary cheque comes through. Believe it or not, I hadn't expected to meet someone involved in a murder case. Have you heard anything more from the police?'

'Well, I'm involved, but it's not as if I'm related to the deceased or anything.'

'Then why are you so interested?'

She faltered. It was not a question she wished to ask herself. 'I think it has to do with the things that scare me.'

'I guess it's a good way of coming to terms with your fears.'

She studied his face as he ate. Joseph was just the kind of person she wanted to be, self-assured and purposeful. 'I'd like to see your designs,' she said.

'The most detailed plans are with the construction team, but I can show you the rough sketches.' He smiled. 'Come and visit; I'm only on the second floor.'

'I don't know, I may be busy. Nobody's been murdered in the hotel for a few days. The management probably want me to be around in case something violent and disgusting happens.' She stopped chewing. 'I thought you were on the fourth floor?' She remembered seeing his room number on the reservation card.

'I was supposed to be, but there was a mix-up with the rooms. I'm in two sixteen.'

'Two sixteen?' The number inscribed on the bookmark in Jacob's Bible, an odd coincidence.

They arrived at the Savoy reception desk after dinner to find Nicholas in a state of panic. The upgraded security arrangements meant that queues of complaining guests were filling the lobby.

'You can help out now,' Nicholas told Jerry, 'but it's no use begging me to keep quiet about your timekeeping. I'll still have to report you.'

'Why did you change Joseph's room, Nick?'

Nicholas looked over his shoulder at the leather-clad

designer. 'You can't complain about that because it wasn't my fault.' He waved his hands ineffectually, as if the idea was stuck to his fingertips. 'It was the telephone booking that threw everything out.'

'What do you mean?'

'The lawyer, you know—Max Jacob.' Nicholas lowered his voice. 'He made a telephone booking two days before he arrived in London, asking specifically for room two sixteen.'

'Then why didn't you give him the room?' she asked.

Nicholas looked shifty. 'I made a mistake when I typed in the request. I had a lot on my mind, and the security guards for the delegates were swarming all over the place. I told Jacob that his room had been allocated to someone else. I promised to have a word with the new occupant and switch the rooms back, but he didn't want to change. What more could I do? Then Jacob died.'

I searched the wrong room, thought Jerry.

'Do you often give guests incorrect reservations?' asked Joseph.

'He has a point,' she agreed. 'A dissatisfied guest. I'm going to have to report you.'

'All right, Jerry, that's enough,' snapped Nicholas. 'I'll forget it this time, but this is your absolute final warning.'

'Let's go to your room,' she told Joseph, heading for the stairs.

'I don't understand what you expected to find in here.' Joseph unlocked the door and switched on the lights.

'I don't know, either. Why would Jacob have insisted on this particular suite?' Jerry looked around. 'It's no better or worse than his other one. They're virtually identical.'

'Perhaps it had some sentimental significance for him.'

'He was a lawyer, Joseph.' She walked into the bathroom and checked under the sink. 'Suppose it was some kind of drop point?'

For the next ten minutes she pulled the bedroom apart while Joseph looked on. By the time he had decided to stop her, she had finished. If Max Jacob had come to London to collect something from room 216, it had to still be in the suite. 'No one else has come into the room except you.'

'What about the maids? The staff have passkeys. Anyone could have—What is it?'

She was on her knees, feeling the white tiles at the rear of the washbasin pedestal, when one came away in her hands. 'It's an access point for the sink trap,' she explained. Beyond it was a square hole six inches across.

Joseph crept forward. 'What's in there?'

She carefully pulled out a beige envelope, noted the jagged tear along the top. 'Looks like we're too late to find out,' she said. She shook the top section of the envelope, and a slim torn segment of Xeroxed photograph fell out.

'Whoever took this stuff was in a hurry to check the contents. I bet it was narcotics. I bet the lawyer was a drug mule.' She checked the envelope for residue, but found none. Instead, when she examined the photograph, she found herself looking at two pairs of bare legs, a bottom, a breast, and part of an unappealing erection.

'*Pornography?*' she said, confounded.

17 / Art Appreciation

H ow are you feeling?' May seated himself on a section of the Moroccan bedspread that wasn't covered in the Saturday-morning newspapers. His partner's eyes were red and swollen, his face the colour of a supermarket chicken.

'Oh, wonderful. That's all I needed right now, on top of everything else, a cold.' Bryant fixed him with a beady, suspicious eye. 'Have you eaten all the grapes?'

May looked around guiltily. It seemed that he had. For someone who wasn't feeling very well, his partner didn't miss much. 'There were only a couple left,' he said. 'You had a nice rest yesterday. You'll be back on your feet by Monday.'

It had disturbed him to find his friend in such a frail state. He wondered if Bryant's cold had appeared as a psychosomatic result of being shut in the cellar. Friday had been a wasted day of paperwork and procedures, without any discernible progress. He needed his partner back in full health.

The rescued Waterhouse painting had been placed against the far wall. His bedroom was a reflection of Bryant's mind, its untidy shelves filled with games and puzzles stacked in ancient boxes, statues and mementoes competing for space with books on every subject imaginable, from *Sensation and Perception in the History of Exper-*

imental Psychology to *Illustrated British Ballads* and *A History of Indian Philosophy.*

'What are you reading at the moment?' asked May.

'*Batman,*' said Bryant. 'The drawings are terribly good.'

'Your landlady said you weren't to be disturbed, you know.'

'Alma's always looking for an excuse to get me alone. She brings me bowls of foul-smelling broth on the hour and perches on the bed like some overweight Florence Nightingale, prodding at my orifices with a thermometer. No wonder her husband died. You realize how close we came to never finding the painting at all?' Bryant sank into the blankets. 'It's the key to this whole business, I'm sure of it. I wanted you here because Summerfield's on his way over to check its authenticity. My trousers got torn. My suit is ruined.'

'I realize the thought of buying new clothes fills you with horror, Arthur, but you should be glad you're still in one piece.' May drained his teacup and set it down. 'Are you thinking of getting up at all? It is only a cold, after all. You'll be pleased to hear that Janice and I have put calls out to every surviving member of the Whitstable family in the country. We're bringing them all together for a meeting tomorrow afternoon.'

'On a Sunday? We won't have enough staff to take care of them.'

'I've agreed to let the girl from the Savoy give us a hand. The Sunday idea is to stop them from using the excuse that they have to be in their offices. I need you there, if you're feeling up to it.'

'I'm not malingering, you know,' said Bryant indignantly. 'Not like you, and that so-called heart attack of yours that turned out to be angina.'

May knew that his partner was thankful for being rescued, but didn't suppose he would ever say so. Finding Bryant's walkie-talkie down the back of his passenger seat, he had radioed a request for one of the patrol officers to keep a discreet check on the house. If the boy hadn't looked in when he did, May wondered if Arthur would have been found at all.

Peregrine Summerfield entered, his bulk filling the narrow door-frame. He waved a bottle of cognac in a meaty fist. Red and yellow gouache still speckled his beard, as if he'd been using his chin to paint with. Perhaps he kept the pigments there as a way of presenting his credentials.

'Where is the old malingerer?' he asked, studying May. 'You must be John. I've heard a lot about you.'

'Oh, good things I hope.'

'Not really, no. There he is!' Summerfield walked into the bedroom and was about to shake his friend's hand when the sight of the painting stopped him in his tracks.

'I thought you'd be interested,' said Bryant, propping himself up. 'Is it the real thing?'

'Oh, *yes*.' Summerfield crouched down and examined the canvas carefully. 'That's the beauty of Waterhouse,' he said softly. 'He went straight from the idea to the paint pot. No endless squared-up sketches or chalk studies for him. He just rolled up his sleeves. It's the real thing, all right. This is the intermediate study for the painting. I knew it was in a private collection but had no idea where. Waterhouse did a small oil sketch to start with, then this.'

'Would you like to tell my colleague here a little about it?' asked Bryant.

'With pleasure,' said Summerfield, unable to remove his eyes from the canvas. 'It's a very dramatic subject. Flavius Honorius was the sole ruler of the Western world at the tender age of ten. With his empire overrun by invading tribes, and Rome captured by the attacking Visigoths, he sat on the throne sodding about with his pet birds. His army took all the shit while he married a couple of bimbos and did bugger-all for the collapsing empire. On the few occasions he did get involved, he cocked it all up. Weakest of all the Roman emperors, and a total wanker. Seen here ignoring the desperate pleas of his statesmen to grant them an audience.'

'Is there much of a difference between this and the finished painting?'

'Indeed. The central character was removed completely for the final version. The attendant in the middle of the canvas was felt to be too dominant, so he came out. Where did you find this?'

'It would seem to have belonged to one of our victims.'

'So Bella Whitstable lied to us,' said May.

'Not necessarily,' Bryant countered, levering himself from the bed and pulling a dressing gown over his pyjamas. 'We have no reason to assume that she knew which Waterhouse painting her brother had vandalized. These are the sort of people who ferret away valuable items and forget all about them.'

'On a world scale, this isn't particularly valuable,' said Summerfield. 'It's an unfinished study of a neglected picture, primarily of academic interest, although it is rather beautiful. Waterhouse's fame rests on later paintings, particularly *The Lady of Shalott*, painted five years after this. The first one, where she's in the boat looking dead miserable, not the second one where she's got a fat arse and looks like she's breaking wind. It's in the Tate, I think.'

'Thank you very much, Peregrine,' said Bryant. 'You have a way of bringing art history colourfully to life.' He turned to his partner. 'Unless I'm mistaken, that will be Alma Sorrowbridge's heavy foot on the stair. Unless you want to be force-fed Bovril for the next half hour, I suggest we head for the West End with all possible dispatch.'

'The other day you mentioned that there was a resonance,' said Bryant to Summerfield. 'The act of vandalism reminded you of something. Did you remember what it was?' They were squeezed into Bryant's rusty sixties Mini Minor. May was driving, although he had barely been able to fold his legs beneath the steering column.

'Yes, sorry, I should have called you. It was Whistler.'

'What, the one with the sour-faced mother?'

'James Abbott McNeill, the very same.' Summerfield was pressed against the roof of the car, trapped like a sardine in a tin. When he turned his head, his beard cleared the condensation from the window. 'You know, the famous lawsuit against Ruskin.'

'I don't remember the details, Peregrine. Explain, please.'

'Whistler sued John Ruskin for saying that his painting *The Falling Rocket* was "flinging a pot of paint in the public's face." It made me wonder if your man was doing the same thing in reverse. You know, a member of the public hurling back an indignant reply, sort of thing. Whistler wrote about London: *When the evening mist clothes the riverside with poetry, the poor buildings lose themselves in the dim sky, and the tall buildings become campanili, and the warehouses are palaces in the night.*'

'Very poetic,' said Bryant, 'and completely unenlightening. What on earth are you talking about?'

'With the study of the painting held by his own family, it's possible your bloke wanted to increase its worth by destroying the finished article.' Summerfield stared absently through the window. 'Perhaps he was performing some kind of symbolic act.'

'Symbolic? Of what, for God's sake?'

'Well, that's what you have to find out, isn't it?' replied the artist with a smile.

18 / Family

The second-floor conference room of the Mornington Crescent Peculiar Crimes Unit had been planned as a site for future press briefings, but on Sunday afternoon it had been filled with folding chairs and reserved for a very different purpose.

Jerry Gates stood in the doorway, pulled her sweater sleeves over her hands, and surveyed the group before her.

The disparate branches of the Whitstable family had been assembled in the narrow, high-windowed room. So many had turned up that some were left standing around the edges. Everyone was talking at once, arguing, complaining, gesticulating—to each other, to the authorities, to anyone who would listen. Gathered together in this fashion, Jerry could see that the Whitstables possessed certain common physical characteristics, including wayward teeth, large earlobes, and the sort of stress-related blotchiness usually found in cornered jellyfish. It wasn't an especially attractive sight.

'If I could have your attention for a few moments,' said Bryant, facing the group with his arms raised. 'The sooner we get started...' He turned back to May, who was seated on an orange stacker chair behind him. 'I don't believe it. They're completely ignoring me.' He could barely be heard above the swell of so many simultaneous conversations.

'You'll have to shout,' said Jerry. 'I don't think they're used to being ordered about.'

'County folk,' Bryant complained. 'They'd pay attention if I was a horse.' He unclipped a microphone from its stand and held it close to one of the wall speakers. The resultant squeal of feedback caused everyone to clap their hands over their ears. Over thirty indignant men, women, and children turned to face the low stage at the front of the room.

'Thank you, ladies and gentlemen,' said Bryant, returning the microphone to its stand. He studied his audience like a teacher confronting an unruly new class. Here they were, he thought, the Family Whitstable, well schooled, well shod, and well connected, the cream of British society. The kind of Hard Tory, High Church, pro-hunt landowners idolized in magazines like *Tatler*. Photographed at weddings or debutantes' balls they appeared affable and elegant, but gathered en masse, they forgot the rest of the world existed.

'I'll try not to keep you here too long,' he promised. 'It will help if we get to know each other.'

'Isn't there anyone more senior available to look after this investigation?' shouted a catarrhal young man on the end of the first row.

'We are the senior officers to whom you may direct your questions.' Bryant introduced himself and May, accompanied by a chorus of derisive snorts. A baby started crying and a woman stood up to leave.

'I expect you to stay seated until the end of the briefing,' Bryant informed her.

'Then I expect you to pay my baby sitter.' The woman glared defiantly at him and remained standing.

'You should have thought of that earlier, Madam. I am not prepared to commence the proceedings until every last one of you is sitting down,' said Bryant. The woman made a noisily dissatisfied show, but lowered herself to her chair.

'Who's she?' shouted someone else, pointing at Jerry. 'She's not one of us.'

'Miss Gates is a witness directly involved in the investigation, and is assisting us,' replied Bryant. 'You should all have been given a typed brief by now. Although many of you already know each other, I understand that some of you have not met face to face before. We thought it better to bring the family together like this so that we could explain more clearly—'

'What do you intend to do about this disgraceful state of affairs?' shouted someone who appeared not to have noticed that the detective was speaking.

'Perhaps you could identify yourself and your relationship within the family when you address the group,' said Bryant. 'I'll be able to place you more easily in the future.'

'Royston Carlyle Whitstable,' came the disgruntled reply. 'Alec and Beattie's son, although what that has to do with—'

'My colleagues and I will endeavour to explain the course of the investigation to you, Mr Whitstable,' interrupted Bryant. 'Or perhaps I should call you Royston, as you all bear the Whitstable name.'

'I hardly think it appropriate we should be on first-name terms,' said Royston. 'After all, you're *staff*.'

'Would you prefer me to give you all nicknames? It wouldn't be difficult.'

A horrified hush fell over the room. The Whitstables were not used to being insulted. Bryant faced his audience squarely, fixing his eye on each member in turn. For someone so shabbily dressed, Jerry thought, he could cut an imposing figure of authority when he wanted to.

'Some of you knew William and his brother Peter. I understand that many of you were fond of Bella Whitstable. We decided it would be of more practical use to bring you together like this, rather than speak to you individually. First of all, I ask you to ignore the speculation that's been printed in the papers. We are in possession of all the known facts, and will release them to you accordingly.' Bryant eased his tie loose and seated himself on the edge of the press table. 'Today's conversation must be a frank one. If anyone would like their children to be absent from the room, we'll be happy to take care of them.'

As arranged, Jerry gestured to the open door. Much head shaking. Nobody moved. It was ominously quiet now.

'We haven't been able to trace everyone yet, but hopefully you'll be able to assist us in that task. I understand that some family members no longer live within the British Isles. They will be contacted in due course.'

'Look here, who's going to pay our travel expenses?' asked a heavily made-up woman in the second row.

'We'll be happy to discuss reimbursement for any inconvenience caused to you,' said May. 'You should all know by now that three members of your family have died in unnatural circumstances. As the culprit has yet to be identified, there's a possibility that others may still be in danger. If you wish to be provided with police protection, we'll try to come to some arrangement. We face the problem of pinpointing a common enemy of the Whitstable family. Peter, William, and Bella encountered a killer whose plans required preparation and careful timing. I think these deaths were more than just premeditated; they were intended to be symbolic. But of what? To discover that, we must understand the true intentions of your enemy.'

'You want us to do your damned job for you,' complained a citrus-faced elderly woman.

Bryant pointed sharply. 'Your name, please?'

'Edith Whitstable. The daughter of Charles and Rachel.' She looked about her for signs of approval and found none.

'What I am trying to do politely, Madam,' said Bryant, 'is remind you that the withholding of information is a grave and punishable offence. While Mr May and I will attempt to respect your privacy, we need personal details that you may not wish to give—details of business feuds as well as family arguments.' He knew that his request ran the risk of encouraging malicious gossip and hearsay, but it could not be helped. There was also a possibility that the Whitstables' business interests would prove politically sensitive, and might be protected from legal access. 'In return for your assistance, we'll undertake to keep the press away from you. At this point, certain questions will be asked. First, does one of you know the murderer personally? Second, might one of you even be the person we're looking for?'

The room quickly filled with indignant clamour. Bryant knew that, from a legal standpoint, he and his partner were treading on very thin ice.

'Now look here.' A tall young man with narrow features tapering to a feral, pointed nose shoved back his chair and stabbed a bony finger at Bryant. 'As I see it you've managed to put up a pretty poor show so far. The papers say you were with Bella when she was killed. You're supposed to be public servants, but I don't see much service. You're not doing anything at all to put this chap away.'

'And who are you?' asked May, mildly.

'Oliver and Peggy's son, Luke Whitstable.' As they quoted their lineage, Bryant tried to mentally locate them on the family tree. They all sounded sure that he would know who they were. Perhaps it was a trait of wealthy old families. He had no idea. He was from the East End; his mother used to clean cinemas.

'Well, Luke, at the moment it's true we have no way of knowing how, when, or why this person strikes. Normally in a murder investigation, progress must be made in the hours immediately following the victim's death. Connections are completed by talking to family members. Suspects are eliminated, other names recur. When a culprit is pinpointed, he is tied into the crime with corroborative forensic evidence. But this hasn't happened in our investigation. Why? Because, despite our endeavours, all the evidence gathered so far has been conflicting, and the crime scenes have yielded no clear forensic signposts. So now we need to interview every one of you, and we expect you to provide us with any documentation we request, including detailed proof of your recent whereabouts. We will also need to fingerprint all of you.'

Uproar and outrage followed.

Bryant held up his hands. 'We have to separate your prints from those found at the crime scenes. We are dealing with a devious, calculating killer who is capable of devising all manner of disguises and escapes. It's no use pretending that we can completely protect you from him; no one is ever one hundred percent safe. That's why we need to know everything you can tell us, no matter how insignificant or how inconsequential it may seem. Think carefully about our questions. I personally witnessed

William's death. I tried to save Bella Whitstable's life, and saw her die in agony instead. This brave young lady was present at Max Jacob's death and saw Peter lying with his throat cut. Both of us have since been physically attacked. I want this ended as much as you do, but if you hinder our investigation in any way, I'll have you charged with obstruction.'

Bryant blew his nose and sat down. The audience sat in stunned silence. Finally, a small girl in the front row ran up and kicked him hard on the shin.

Before everyone began talking at once, May took over from his partner. 'No one is saying that this murderer *will* strike again, but you must be vigilant. Don't let your children talk to outsiders. Don't allow neighbours to become familiar with your daily routine. We want to make sure that you stay alive.'

Instantly, a scrum of furious relatives formed around their desk as questions and insults filled the air.

For the rest of the afternoon the two detectives remained seated in the conference room. The Whitstables were argumentative, imperious, secretive, and, Jerry suspected, naturally misleading in their information, but most of all they were scared. Their bravado was a reflexive action that failed to mask their fear. No one could agree with anyone else, and the more they fought, the more badly they behaved.

Eventually, though, a sense of weary resignation set in. The detectives took prints and distributed questionnaires, in the hope that they would turn up a common suspect. There were still several cousins, uncles, and aunts left to track down, but as none of them were based in London within the present radius of the murders, their safety was of secondary concern.

After nearly five hours of halfhearted promises and

vague accusations, they terminated the session. The log-ging of details would be undertaken by the new night shift, and would then be fed into a central file of infor-mation, to be referenced and annotated by May and Sergeant Longbright.

For now, though, May took Jerry and his partner over to the smoky saloon bar of the Nun and Broken Compass for a desiccated cheese roll and a pint of best bitter.

The small backstreet pub had been overlooked in the area's recent rush toward modernization. Unable to at-tract a younger clientele, the Nun and Broken Compass had given up the ghost so completely that its only ameni-ties were a hairy dartboard obliterated by overuse and a moulting resident dog of especially peculiar breed and odour.

'I've never met anyone like them,' grumbled Bryant, taking a sip from his pint. 'The backbone of England? The arse-end, more like. They're more concerned with losing face than losing each other. Jerry, you're from a posh family. Are they all like that?'

'No, we're merely middle-middle-class, because my father works for a living. The Whitstables are upper-middle and lower-upper because they own rather than work, except there are also a couple of knights, who would be middle-upper.'

'Surely you'd be upper-upper if you were titled?' Bryant asked, intrigued.

'No, only a direct hereditary line is upper-upper. You need the big three: blood, property, and peerage. But there are certain similarities between us all. You should see the people my mother has over for her charity bridge nights.'

'Leo Marks mentioned that the Whitstables sustained a certain amount of inbreeding in the last century,' said

May. 'Life would have been very different for them then. Arranged marriages, inherited land, the protection of name and honour. An attenuated sense of duty—to the nation, to their tenants, and to the family escutcheon. They had a smattering of titled heads, nearly all gone now. Families like the Whitstables need to breed, but they're dying out.'

'I understand that they're frightened, but I hate their condescension,' Bryant complained.

'They can't help it,' replied Jerry. 'They're used to being deferred to.'

'And they have powerful connections,' May reminded them. 'Three family members in the foreign office, four high up in the Department of Trade and Industry, others in the Church and the armed forces. Policy makers. Friends of nobility. They're not a dynasty to be trifled with.'

'Do you think we could be dealing with political assassinations? It seems like they've made their fair share of enemies abroad.'

'It would be tempting to think that,' May conceded, 'but it feels more personal, don't you think? I get the feeling that none of them can imagine why they've been singled out. If they could, they'd probably be too embarrassed to tell us. Still, something should have come to light by now. At the moment we have their cooperation and we should be thankful for it. So let's have none of your customary rudeness when dealing with the upper echelons, Arthur.'

'How dare you,' complained Bryant. 'I was a paragon of civility. Even when that horrible devil-child kicked me.'

'Let's see how you behave when the Whitstables exert pressure on Raymond. Or start demanding action from the Home Office. Because they will, you know.'

'I'm sure you're right,' said Bryant gloomily. 'And they'll get away with it because their social standing will make sure that the right people listen to them. It's not fair. Class has nothing to do with intelligence.'

'Arthur, they're different from the likes of you and me. Jerry, you must agree with me.' May nodded in Jerry's direction.

'They see you as servants rather than actual people. That makes them different.'

'Nonsense,' snapped Bryant. 'Francis Bacon said that new nobility is but the act of power, but ancient nobility is the act of time. The Whitstables know their power is waning, and are trying to hide behind their heritage. We see it all around us these days: England is shedding its skin. It will no longer have to carry the weight of the past upon its shoulders. In all my years, I've found that the only real difference between one person and the next is what hurt them as a child and what kind of biscuit they like. Everyone has a favourite biscuit.'

Some of Bryant's theories left Jerry behind. This was one of them. 'If the Whitstables are victims of a postwar sociological change in the nation, I don't see that it matters what kind of biscuit they like.'

'Childhood attachments,' explained Bryant impatiently. 'Your favourite biscuit remains the same throughout your life, but life requires you to make certain changes if you wish to stay in pace with it. The Whitstables are being stranded in the past, left behind by the receding tide of history, and they can't see it happening.'

'I still don't see—'

'Excuse me a moment,' said Bryant abruptly. 'There's something I really must find out.' He rose and took the empty glasses to the bar, catching the landlord's eye.

'Why is this pub called the Nun and Broken Compass?' he asked.

'It's a long story,' said the landlord, pulling a fresh pint. 'And it's rude. You know. A bit Rabelaisian. I don't want to offend the young lady.'

'Tell us anyway,' demanded Bryant. 'It's been a long day.'

After leaving Mornington Crescent, Jerry called in at the Savoy. She tried ringing Joseph's room, but there was no reply. Just as she was leaving the lobby, he entered through the revolving doors. He looked terrible.

It was nine forty, and the hotel was finally quiet. The remaining Common Market delegates had left to attend a formal dinner at the Palace. Joseph dropped his bags beside the reception counter and rummaged in his leather jacket for his wallet. 'I didn't think you were on duty.'

'I'm not. What's wrong?'

'You'll have to make up my bill,' he replied. 'I'm leaving first thing in the morning.'

'Why, what's happened?' She came around from the counter and lightly held his arm. 'Want to walk for a while?'

The lights on the Embankment swayed like ropes of pearls, reflecting in the empty wet streets that led towards Blackfriars.

'I can't believe it,' Jerry said. 'How could it have happened so suddenly?'

'You tell me. The Japanese just pulled out, without a word of explanation. Miyagawa called me into his office this afternoon and said that the Tasaka Corporation were returning to Japan at the end of the month. They've canceled their plans for the production and all subsequent events, and they're selling the theatre to a British consortium. The deal has already been completed. They've fired the entire production team. Miyagawa was very apologetic.'

'Why couldn't they have told you earlier?' asked Jerry.

'Perhaps they thought we might jeopardize their deal somehow. I'm out of a job.'

'What are you going to do now?' she asked. The thought of his leaving chilled her.

'Head back to San Diego, I suppose.' He looked up at the starless sky, his voice betraying the hurt he felt. 'There'll be other times. Other opportunities. They paid me for next month. It wasn't the money. It was the chance to do something I believed in.'

'I'm so sorry, Joseph.' She thought for a moment. 'Why don't we find out who they've sold it to? The Savoy's a listed building. It can only be used as a theatre. Maybe you can get work with the new company.'

'I was wondering about that.'

'Then it's worth a try. There are loads of cheap bed and breakfasts around Earl's Court. Please, you must stay on.'

The hand he slipped around her waist took her by surprise, but when his lips pressed against hers she yielded.

19 / Lured

Jerry watched the platform posters slide by as the Tube train lurched on towards Chelsea, and thought back to the Friday when Max Jacob had appeared at the Savoy, summoned by one of the Whitstable brothers. Could that summons have somehow concerned the Waterhouse painting?

Suppose Peter had asked his lawyer to collect the package hidden in 216. Why would a respectable professional be skulking around with a pile of obscene photographs? Could it have been why Jacob was murdered?

Removing the envelope from her pocket, she longed to remove the single damaged piece of photograph, but did not wish to shock the stern-faced woman seated next to her. She held the envelope closer and noticed a row of digits. Someone had sealed the pictures in the envelope, then written a telephone number on top in pencil, hastily erasing it afterwards. In a few moments she had worked out the sequence, seven numbers and part of a name, the letters *And*. It could be *Andy* or *Andrew*. As soon as she alighted from the train, Jerry checked the penciled number and rang it from a call box at the corner of Sloane Square.

'Is that Andy?'

'Who's calling?'

'A friend of his.'

'Hang on, I'll get him.'

The receiver was set down and taken up a few moments later.

'Who's this?' The voice had a heavy cockney accent.

'My name is Jerry. I'm a friend of one of your clients.'

'Yeah? Which one?'

She cleared her throat. Time to take a chance. 'I saw the set of photographs you left at the Savoy. Very impressive. Did you take them yourself?'

'I don't know what you're talking about. I didn't take no photos.' Andy was indignant, or at least feigning it. She doubted his reluctance to talk would hold up for long if money was mentioned. Across the capital, the recession was biting deep; jobs were competitive on both sides of the law.

'I have some of them in front of me right now, and one has your telephone number written on it.' She tried to sound as friendly as possible. 'I thought you might be available for another job. I'll make sure you're well paid.'

'What have you got there?'

Jerry turned the piece of photograph over, trying to see it in the dim light of the booth. Two bodies, naked, a full breast, unappetizing buttocks, a sausagelike erection. The man was still wearing black socks. No light in the room apart from the camera flash. Judging by the odd angle of their limbs, the revelers hadn't expected to be captured for posterity.

'Well,' said Jerry casually, 'the first one shows a gentleman enjoying himself with a very young lady in one of the suites, two sixteen, I think. I'll pay you double the amount you were paid before.'

She held her breath and pressed her ear hard to the receiver. For a moment there was only the hiss of the open line.

'What, you want some more done?'

'That's right, with the same couple. Could you do that?'

'I can't get hold of the girl again. It'd have to be a different one.' So he supplied the woman, too. Handy service. 'He's not going to go for it twice, though.'

'Leave that part to me,' said Jerry. 'I want you to get whoever you think he'd like.'

'Well, the Japs love blond girls. I could—'

'Kaneto Miyagawa.' Suddenly it was obvious. Jerry drew a slow breath as the realization dawned.

She quickly replaced the receiver and left the booth. She needed to think. Andy had sent a girl to the Japanese executive at his hotel. She must have been a real professional; the Savoy would never have let her near his room without a valid reason. It meant that Miyagawa had arrived in London earlier than Joseph had realized. The Tokyo executive had been careful, but someone knew of his libidinous nature, and had exploited it.

She tried to reconstruct the order of events. The girl had come to Miyagawa's hotel room, leaving the suite door unlocked, ready for someone to burst in and take compromising pictures. Which meant that someone had paid to have Miyagawa set up. Had the Tasaka Corporation been blackmailed out of the Savoy deal by the lawyer Max Jacob? Could the photographer have been instructed to do so by the Whitstables? She imagined the dishonour: the respected head of the Tasaka Corporation caught red-handed and blackmailed into abandoning his plans for the Savoy. By doing so he would avoid a scandal that would shatter company confidence and slump share prices. But could the Japanese have hit back by taking their revenge on both Jacob and his employers? And if this was true, why go to the trouble of killing the lawyer with a *snake*? Was this really the sort of thing that happened among the city's power elite? It seemed more suited to an episode of *The Avengers*.

She needed to go to the police with the information, but first she would put her theory to the test. It would mean calling Joseph as soon as she reached home.

Elton John's 'Goodbye Yellow Brick Road' came to an end, and Paul McCartney and Wings launched into 'Band On The Run.'

Michelle turned off her transistor radio and listened for a moment, but no sound came from upstairs. From the window overlooking the lawn she could see low clouds shielding the weakening sun, like courtiers protecting a dying monarch. The garden foliage had darkened to the colour of tinned spinach. The bare winter branches of the cherry trees knocked in the rising wind.

'Daisy, what are you doing?' she called.

Small footsteps crossed the ceiling, then stopped. 'Playing.'

'Do you want a glass of milk?'

'No, thank you.' A tiny clipped voice, precise and polite. Michelle shrugged and headed for the kitchen to make some tea. At the age of twenty-three she had retained the plump figure and bad complexion of her late teen years, and was resigned to the fact that unless she lost some weight she would be unlikely ever to find a boyfriend. Not that she particularly cared. The magazines went on about finding a partner, as if it was the only thing in life that mattered.

Michelle preferred the company of small children. The pleasures of tending them had been bred into her by years of baby-sitting her younger sisters. Her responsible attitude reflected the genuine warmth she felt for her young charges. Still, she had never met a child like Daisy. A pretty little thing, thin and blond, with translucent pale skin and large blue eyes that stared flatly and observed everything. At the age of seven, Daisy seemed to have no friends at all. She never returned from school with the other girls in her class, and spent her free time playing alone in her room.

Her brother Tarquin was now eleven and had been packed off to boarding school. Daisy's parents were hardly ever at the house. The father worked for one of the venerable City banks, and the mother was always organizing charity lunches. It seemed to Michelle that Mrs Whitstable was a modern-day Mrs Jellyby, spending so much time worrying about fund-raising for needy children that she failed to notice how introverted her own offspring had become.

She switched on the kitchen lights, momentarily alarmed as they buzzed and dimmed before returning to their full capacity. As the electric kettle clicked off, Michelle opened the caddy and dropped a teabag—a recent innovation she had only just come to grips with—into her mug. She tuned the radio to a phone-in, and failed to hear the wavering song that sounded from the street beyond.

Daisy rose from the floor of the playroom and listened. The tune was different from the usual one they played. Michelle had told her that it was called 'Greensleeves.' The new one was much prettier. And fancy him coming around at Christmas! She looked up at the mantelpiece, at the tiny gold christening clock her grandfather had given her. The money bear sat next to it.

'Michelle, can I have an ice cream?' she called, but quite softly, so that Michelle might not hear her. She knew it was too near teatime for her to be allowed one.

Outside, the lilting melody played on. In the summer the van parked at the end of the street, but today it sounded as if it had stopped right outside the front door, as if it had come especially for her.

Daisy ran to the head of the stairs and looked down. The lights were already aglow on the Christmas tree in the hall, and it was growing dark beyond the frosted glass of the front door. She wasn't allowed out of the front of the house by herself, because of the traffic. But Mummy and Daddy had gone to London, and Michelle was in the kitchen.

It wasn't fair. She could eat an ice cream and still be hungry for dinner. In the street, the song came to an end. Her mind made up, she raced for the money bear and opened his secret door, releasing coins into her palm. Then she returned the bear to its place, tugged her skirt down, and descended the stairs.

She heard the radio fading down, and crockery being moved about in the kitchen. Michelle was probably foraging for something to eat. No wonder she was so fat. Daisy quietly opened the door and slipped the safety latch on, praying that she would not be too late. The van sat silently at the kerb. It was different from the one that visited in the summer, white instead of blue, and there was no man serving at the window. She walked to the edge of the pavement and looked up, puzzled. From within came a delicious smell of chocolate. Just then, the melody began its warped tape-loop again and the van slowly started to roll out into the street.

'Wait, please. Wait!'

Daisy darted forward with the coins clutched tightly in her hand. The van rolled slowly towards the disused railway arches at the end of the road, its distorted tune tinkling on. Daisy looked back at the house, and the opened front door. It was raining lightly, and there were no customers to be seen. The van driver hadn't spotted her. Now that she had looked forward to it, she wanted the ice cream more than ever. She ran after the van as it rolled to a stop beneath the darkness of the railway arch, its red taillights glowing.

Daisy could see the driver moving from his seat to the counter window. Perhaps he had seen her after all. Inside the archway the song echoed eerily. Daisy stood beneath the window, her money hand raised in a pale fist. The interior of the van was in darkness. She wanted a Ninety-Nine ice cream cone. How could the man see to fill it properly?

She was about to ask him when he suddenly moved forward in the gloom and leaned down from the window, scooping her up in one swift motion and clamping his hand across her mouth. The counter panel slammed down, sealing the van shut, and the vehicle rolled swiftly away into the darkness of the tunnel beyond.

20 / Tontine

Joseph rose from the bed and placed his hands against the chill glass. It was late now, but night suited the area, and the streets remained almost as busy as they were during daylight hours. Above the boarding-house, dank underlit clouds glowed like oilskin, brushing across the red brick and slick slate of a hundred rooftop turrets. Joseph's new room was so small that Jerry could sit at one end of the sickly pink candlewick bedspread and see traffic moving through the rain on the Old Brompton Road.

The room was poorly lit, and made Jerry uneasy. 'Can you put another light on?' she asked.

Joseph came to the bed and sat beside her. She could smell shaving soap, and a musky trace of perspiration. 'No, let the dark come in.' He ran a finger along the seam of her jean-clad thigh. 'There's nothing in it that can hurt you, Jerry.'

Everyone thought she could just wish away the fear, but rationalizing it had no effect. 'It's not just in my mind,' she explained. 'When I look into the night I feel every muscle in my body tighten.'

He brought himself nearer, shadow closing over his face. 'Do you feel it now?'

The light on the far wall seemed to be dimming, blurring the pattern of the wallpaper. He kissed her shoulder, her neck, her throat. His body pressed her back against the bed cover, the heat from his chest warming her breasts. She closed her eyes and allowed him to envelop her, his arms sliding around her back, one hand slipping into her tight waistband. They lay on the counterpane with their bodies lightly touching, exploring each others' mouths, their hands establishing the contours of their arms, their thighs, their stomachs. A warmth spread inside her as his fingers crossed the buttons studding the front of her jeans.

The burr of night traffic buzzed like static beyond the windowpanes. He opened her shirt, kissing the tops of her breasts, moistening her flesh with his tongue, and she allowed her mind to drift. But in its eye she saw the stalking figure in the alleyway, the hunching creature of her nightmares. She opened her eyes. The faulty wall light had gone out completely. It was as if she had suddenly been struck blind.

And shoving down on top of her was a man anxious to devour her body, exposing her breasts, pressing his fingers down towards her sex, stifling her mouth with his.

She pushed him aside with such force that he fell to the floor, cracking his head against the skirting board, pulling down the lamp from the bedside table. She could not hear beyond the pounding of her heart, could not breathe the suffocating air, could not see in the tiny, stifling room. Her only thought was to locate the door and open it.

He found her huddled on the landing, wheezing asthmatically, grimacing as she clutched at her chest with both fists, as though she was trying to suck in the light from the neon strips above her.

'It's me, isn't it?' She gave him no answer. 'Maybe you can't handle going out with a black guy.' He should have been angry, but instead he crouched before her, offering his hand. She stared, unable to accept it, knowing that he would only misunderstand. Joseph's comfortable affinity with the night placed him on the wrong side. He was someone to distrust, not someone to love.

She wasn't nervous about sex. She didn't expect the first time to be the best, because her pleasure would be mitigated by apprehension. But as the darkness had deepened, so had her fears. She assumed all lovemaking involved an undertow of dominance and assertion, but inside her nyctophobia she had no authority. In the act itself—of which she had no experience—she had been terrified of losing control. Perhaps Joseph was right, and she had been unnerved by his skin colour. But it was 1973, for God's sake, what difference did it make that he was *black*? Race taboos had been shattered in the sixties. She and her friends had recently marched to stop white kids from killing Vietnamese peasants, so how could she be bothered by the colour of someone's skin? Racism was a grotesque anachronism.

But not to her parents, she thought. Was she subconciously worrying what they might say?

She gathered her coat and left without apology or explanation, unsure of her loyalties—or indeed, of her sanity.

'He's keeping me awake, Mr May, boots tramping back and forth across the ceiling all night. I don't know what's wrong with him. I hope he's not having another one of his brainstorming sessions, smoking that horrible muck in his pipe and listening to his gramophone. He already gave my Hiawatha a nervous breakdown.'

It was true. Every time her tenant opened the front door, the mongrel cat fell over in fright. Alma Sorrow-bridge moved along the hall with theatrical delicacy, her plump hands raised, elbows moving in opposition to her broad hips. As always, she wore red washing-up gloves and an apron dotted with tiny blue cornflowers; May had never seen her attired in any other fashion.

John May had brought the bad weather in with him. His umbrella trailed pools on the polished linoleum floor as the landlady led the way to the stairs. He had been visiting his partner here for many years, and Alma Sorrowbridge had always insisted on seeing him up. He suspected that, knowing she housed a detective, she had decided to cast herself as a bizarre South London version of Mrs Hudson to Bryant's Holmes.

'Arthur was telling me that he doesn't sleep so much these days,' said May as they edged past a stuffed kestrel squatting beneath a glass dome at the corner of the pas-sageway.

'I don't mind that, but he plays his music all the time. Gregorian chants, *The Gondoliers*, Pink Floyd, you name it. And last night, the clattering! Like he was throwing crockery about the room!' She held the landing door open. 'My bed's right underneath. Could you have a word with him?'

'I'll do my best, Mrs S.' May raised the Victorian brass demon head set in Bryant's door and let it fall. Beyond, he heard a muffled curse and the sound of breaking china. A burglar bolt was withdrawn, and Bryant peered around the lintel, a disgruntled tortoise head fringed with short spines of uncombed hair.

'Oh, it's you. You'd better come in. Am I supposed to be somewhere?'

'No, but I wanted to talk to you.' May stepped inside,

looking around at the framed pictures that covered the walls: Winston Churchill, Dracula, Camus, Nietzsche, Anna May Wong, Laurel and Hardy. There was no recognizable pattern to his partner's tastes. Beneath the sheet music and first-night programmes for Offenbach's *Orpheus in the Underworld* stood a particularly horrible plaster bust of the composer William Walton; why it was in Bryant's possession he had no idea, but it had sat there undusted for years.

May ducked before the hall mirror and smoothed his hair into place. His partner was a collector but not a hoarder, and not much of a materialist, either. Everything here was owned for a reason. Often Bryant took something into his apartment simply to preserve it from destruction. He had once told May that he was conforming to the natural traditions of maturity. 'We spend our youth attempting to change the future,' he explained, 'and the rest of our lives trying to preserve the past.'

The rising wail of the kettle sounded in the kitchen and Bryant went to deal with it, pulling a patched green cardigan around his shoulders. 'You're just in time, John. Go into the lounge, but be careful where you tread. I see the weather's still disgusting. We might as well be living in Finland. What brings you here so early?'

'One of the Whitstable children has gone missing.'

Bryant appeared in the doorway with a teapot in his hands. 'Which one?'

'Daisy. She's seven years old. Walked out of her house between three and four yesterday afternoon and hasn't been seen since.'

'Yesterday? Why on earth didn't someone—?'

'We were only just informed. I'd like you to talk to the nanny. Naturally, she's distraught. West London has over a hundred staff and civilian volunteers out searching the area. The call didn't come through to Mornington Crescent because nobody made the connection with our case. Either that, or they deliberately chose to ignore it.'

'Then how did you find out?'

'I was visiting the Bow Street incident room when some of the sweep details turned up on the radio.'

'Someone's obstructing us. I hope to God this isn't part of the Whitstable vendetta. It wouldn't be, would it? Not a child? How are her parents?'

'Mother's under sedation. They're both at home.'

'And her brother, Tarquin?'

'He's only just been . . . How did you know she had—?'

'I told you, look inside.'

When May did so, he found every cup and saucer, plate, vase, and bowl standing arranged across the floor like pieces in a scaled-up chess game. Coloured lengths of string connected them. Every item of crockery had been given a name and dates with a blue or a red felt-tipped pen. The dining-room chairs had been shifted back against the wall, beside a walnut-faced grandfather clock that ticked sharply.

'The Whitstable family tree,' Bryant explained, entering and setting down his tea tray. 'It's the only way I could get it sorted out in my head. I had to see them properly laid out, who was descended from whom.' He pointed to a milk jug. 'Daisy Whitstable is bottom left-hand corner, by the fireguard. Next to her is the egg cup, brother Tarquin. Stepbrother actually, from Isobel's first marriage.'

In the centre of the china maze stood two upturned vases and a *cafetière*—two deceased brothers and a sister, May noted, reading off their dates.

'What are the blue and red tags?' Some pieces had scraps of paper attached to them.

'Family members killed in the First and Second World Wars. I asked myself why these murders seemed out of place in the present day. The obvious answer is that they originated in events of the past.' Bryant seated himself and leaned forward with his elbows on his knees, surveying the mapped floor.

'What do you mean?' asked May, dropping into the opposite chair. Outside, fresh squalls of rain began to batter the glass.

'Doesn't this feel like an old score being settled to you?' asked Bryant. 'William, Bella, and Peter, one after the other, an entire branch of the family tree chopped away for consciously—or unconsciously—committing some ancient offence.'

It had crossed May's mind that his colleague might be allowing his own interest in the past to colour his perception of the case. For the moment he decided not to voice his concern.

'You mean it's some kind of long-term family revenge?'

'Well, it's certainly not for financial gain. This particular branch of the tree was pretty bare. None of them had any heirs, and there wasn't much ready cash about. As far as I can gather, they have little to leave beyond a small lump sum each, some stock portfolios, and some nice furniture in the attic. There are the paintings, of course, but no one has tried to claim them. On the contrary, nobody even seems to have known of the existence of the Waterhouse study. Now, pass me Marion and Alfred Whitstable over there.'

'What's their significance?'

'We need them to drink out of.'

As they sat back with their tea, Bryant produced a sheaf of handwritten notes from behind his chair. It irritated May that his partner had continued working without consulting him, but he knew this to be Bryant's preferred methodology. At least by now he was used to it.

'William, Bella, and Peter Whitstable had no individual or collective power, financial or otherwise,' explained Bryant, donning his spectacles. 'The only thing that could be gained by killing them was personal satisfaction. But is the culprit within the family dynasty or beyond it? It might surprise you to know that every single Whitstable, past and present, is cared for by the Worshipful Watchmakers' Company. That is to say, they would be awarded an annual stipend in the event of personal injury. Relatives to be compensated in the event of bereavement, and so on, although there's no case for compensation here. Murder makes the claim exempt.'

The remark brought something to the fore of May's mind. 'You don't suppose the Whitstables' collective wealth is being stockpiled by these deaths? You know, concentrated, like a tontine?' Tontines were briefly fashionable Victorian insurance policies, but the thinking behind them was flawed. As each tontine member died, their savings accrued so that the holdings eventually fell to the last surviving family member. The temptation to assist fate had proved too much for some policyholders to resist, and led to criminal activity. The system was soon scrapped.

'I wondered about that. If one of them was knocking off his relatives, it would soon become obvious who was doing it.'

'Would it? The lawyer might have been killed because of his awareness of the family's legal structure.'

'The Whitstables' financial arrangements aren't secret. Nor are the dispositions of their wills. Leo Marks has already arranged for me to inspect all documents pertaining to the investigation.'

May was exasperated. 'Why didn't you tell me this?' he asked.

'I only spoke to Marks yesterday. But this business with Daisy Whitstable changes everything. Someone wants to get back at the family very badly if they're prepared to take a child.'

'Perhaps it's all because William damaged a painting. Or because they all belong to the Watchmakers' Guild. If there's a rivalry going on, it certainly isn't in any of their statements. I'm trying another tack. The guild owns a lot of Central London property. There's big money at stake. We need to speak to a member, or better yet, someone who's been thrown out. Unlike the Masons, guild members are allowed to talk to outsiders. Tomlins is the general secretary, but he's not returning my calls. We need a warrant to search the Watchmakers' Hall. It'll take time and a decent reason, and at the moment I don't have either.'

'Then we need to talk to Mr Lugsea.' Bryant drained his cup and returned it to the tree. 'He'll be able to provide us with some information.'

'Who is he?' asked May. 'One of your medieval historian friends?'

'No,' replied Bryant. 'He's my butcher.'

The formica sign read *Reginald Lugsea, Your Friendly Battersea Butcher*, but the hulking bruiser hooking up rabbits in the window looked far from friendly. Glowering beneath a sweaty red brow, his expression changed as soon as Bryant removed his trilby and made himself known.

'Blimey,' Lugsea shouted to his apprentice, an ethereally pale lad who stood disconsolately weighing mince at the rear of the shop. 'We don't often see Arfur in 'ere, do we, Phil? We was beginning to fink he'd gawn vegetarian.' He raised a chicken and pointed with the tip of his knife to an elderly lady who stood nearby. 'This a bit on the big side for you, Missus?'

The old lady looked up from beneath her woolly hat and smiled through Perspex-thick glasses. 'Ooh, no, lovely, ta.'

'So, what can I do for you gents?' Reg smacked one of the chicken's feet off with a thud of his blade. 'A nice leg of mutton?'

'Heraldry of the London craft guilds,' said Bryant. 'What do you know about it?'

Reg looked at the ceiling as he chopped off the other chicken foot. 'The Tudor company halls in general, or did you 'ave a specific trading family in mind?'

'The Worshipful Company of Watchmakers.'

'Late arrivals, first quarter of the seventeenf century. 'Cause yer first halls were fruit and fish, round the docklands. Then yer Dyers, Plumbers, Vintners, Cordwainers, Woodmongers, Girdlers, Plasterers, Wax Chandlers— one for every profession.' He held the chicken up by its neck and shouted at the old lady. 'You want the giblets, love?'

'Ooh, yes, please.'

He laid the bird down and hacked off its neck, then thrust his fingers up its behind. 'Course, they were able to take advantage of the Dissolution of yer Monasteries and the Reformation, 'cause guilds were able to move into the empty nunneries, like the Leathersellers did in St Helen Bishopsgate round about 1542. Not the Watchmakers, though, 'cause they was looked after by the Goldsmiths, and shared part o' their fancy halls.'

'They all had their own heraldic badges, didn't they?' asked Bryant.

'That's right,' said Reg. 'The Skinners had crowns an' feathers on their livery, the Fishmongers had herrings with hats on, no lie. Watchmakers was fobs and gold chains, orange on blue if memory serves.' He yanked at the chicken's interior and produced a handful of innards, which he proceeded to drop into a plastic bag. He reminded May of Oswald Finch, the pathologist.

'What about a radiant flame, red outlined in yellow?' asked Bryant. 'That's not part of the Watchmakers' livery?'

'Don't fink so,' said Reg slowly. 'Although I seem to remember seein' it in their colours somewhere.' He thoughtfully knotted the bag and wiped his blood-covered hands, smearing chicken guts down his striped apron. 'I got a feelin' it's a recent addition to the Watchmakers. By recent I mean maybe only an 'undred years old. Sometimes merchants formed special "inner circles" wiv new symbols to separate them from their parent companies. Yeah, that's prob'ly it. You'll need to talk to someone on the inside, though.'

'Thanks, Reg,' said Bryant, touching the brim of his hat. 'You've been very helpful.'

'Always a pleasure, Mr B. You sure you don't want a nice pig's trotter while you're 'ere?' He picked one up and walked it along the counter. 'Nice an' fresh. Was chargin' round a field last Thursday.'

'Not today, Reg.'

May hiked his thumb back at the butcher as they left the premises. 'How did you ever get to know about him?'

'I talk to local people,' replied Bryant. 'You should try

it sometime, instead of spending your life wedged in behind a desk.'

'Why does he know so much about heraldry?'

'Reg is rather famous.' Bryant gave a knowing smile. 'He won the Brain of Britain competition two years ago, specialist subject Tudor Mercantile History, self-taught. It pays never to underestimate the arcane obsessions of the general public. This flame symbol, is it common to all of the Whitstables, I wonder, or just to some of them?'

'An inner circle within the guild. I don't think I'm going to get any further with Tomlins without scaring him. Not to worry, though.' May unlocked the passenger door of his car and ushered Bryant in. 'I think I may have found a mole.'

'What do you propose to do?'

'Go back to the Watchmakers. Which unfortunately leaves you to deal with Daisy Whitstable's child-minder.'

'Why do you say that?' asked Bryant, fastening his seat belt.

'I just heard that Daisy's parents are planning to sue us for something called protective negligence.'

'A lawsuit?' Bryant was amazed. 'Why would a member of the public try to sue the police? Does no one have faith in the state any more?'

Michelle Baskin was sitting awkwardly on the orange plastic chair in the hallway when Bryant arrived. Sergeant Longbright emerged from her office and drew him aside, handing him a sheaf of papers. 'I've given her some tea,' she said quietly. 'She's been crying, so you'd better go easy. The workmen are still in your office, I'm afraid. And you've an urgent message to call Mrs Armitage. She wouldn't say what about.'

'I'll handle that, thanks.' He turned to the distraught nanny, who sat miserably kneading her hands in her lap. 'Miss Baskin, would you come with me, please?'

Inside his office, the two workmen were clearing paint from the far wall with their blowtorch. Two distinct bands of colour were discernible beneath the top coat: green, and below that brown. The room stank of petrol. Bryant asked them to wait outside, and opened a window.

'We'll soon have the air cleared,' he said, ushering Michelle into a seat with a smile.

The girl pulled the remains of a wet tissue from her cardigan and wiped her nose, head bowed. 'I understand that there's been no news yet.'

Bryant pulled a fresh linen handkerchief from his drawer and passed it to her. 'You know, children have gone missing for much longer periods than this, and have turned up safely again.'

'Mrs Whitstable warned me to be extra careful with Daisy, just before she left,' said Michelle, sniffing hard.

'Why did she say that?'

'Because of what happened to her uncles and her auntie.'

'You mean William, Peter, and Bella?'

Michelle nodded, pushing her lank hair back from her face.

'Did they ever visit their niece? Were they friendly with Mr and Mrs Whitstable?'

'Never, to my knowledge. Luke—Mr Whitstable—hardly knew them at all. Isobel—Daisy's mother—sometimes saw them.'

'How would you describe Daisy?'

Michelle composed herself and sat up, thinking for a moment. 'Very quiet, not an outgoing child. Like her cousins, rather pale, a bit small for her age. Inclined to be moody. She's a direct descendant from the original Whitstables. She shares the same temperament.'

'I'm a little confused. Did Isobel retain the family name upon marriage?'

'It's something most of the Whitstable ladies are allowed to do. So long as they stay in the family business.'

So long as they stay in the guild, thought Bryant.

'I suppose it has its advantages.' Bryant checked the statement in his hand. 'It says here that Daisy was wearing a light summer frock. It was very cold yesterday. Why do you think she'd have gone outside dressed like that?'

'I don't know,' said Michelle. 'It was warm in the house. That's how Mrs Whitstable likes it.'

'The doors and windows, were any of them kept open, just to help cool the rooms down?'

'No, Sir. And Daisy isn't allowed to go out of the front door by herself.'

'But you found it open when you went into the hall.'

'That's right. Someone had put the latch up.'

'You didn't hear her go out?'

'No, Sir.'

'Think back carefully, Michelle. I want to cover everything that happened from the moment you last spoke to Daisy, whether it has any relevance to her disappearance or not.'

Michelle nodded sadly.

'Let's start with the last time you were aware of Daisy's presence in the house. You were standing in the kitchen, making tea...'

It took them an hour to cover the events of the previous afternoon. Michelle cried at several points in her account. In the minutes after she had found the front door open and searched the street, Daisy's parents had arrived home, and an argument had ensued. Later, Mrs

Whitstable had angrily accused her of incompetence and negligence in her duties. Then she had fired her. Michelle explained tearfully that it was more than just a job—that she really loved her charges, even the difficult ones, that she was more worried for Daisy's safety than for her own future.

Bryant tapped her former statement with the end of his pencil. 'There's a point here I don't understand,' he said. 'You boiled the kettle. You turned down the radio. Then you say you heard Daisy run across the floor upstairs. It says here . . .' he squinted at the sheet, readjusting his spectacles, '"*I could hear her footsteps above the music.*" But by this time the radio was off. Or did you leave it on?'

'No, I turned it down very low.'

'Then how could you have heard music?'

Michelle thought hard. 'There was a song playing.'

'Somewhere else in the house?'

'No, not in the house.'

'Coming from next door? Or in the street? What kind of music?'

'Tinkly. I don't really remember.'

'What, a car radio?'

'No, more like an ice-cream van. Only they don't come round at this time of year, do they?'

'Does Daisy like ice cream?'

'Very much, but she's forbidden to eat between meals.'

'Did she have money in her room?'

'Yes, a little bear bank. You don't suppose—'

'You don't happen to know how much money she had in her room exactly?'

'Not right now, but Daisy kept a written note of it. She's a very practical girl.'

Bryant placed a call to Luke Whitstable, then made an internal call to have someone check the area's ice-cream companies and van registrations.

Within the hour he received two return calls. The first from Daisy's father, confirming that his daughter's tally showed a discrepancy of fifty pence from her bear bank. And the second from an officer reporting that the ice-cream van allocated to the road where Luke and Isobel Whitstable lived was not due to return until next April.

With a sinking heart, Bryant was forced to acknowledge that the Whitstable family might well have lost another member, and this time, surely, a blameless one.

21 / Connectivity

It was time for Joseph to start looking for another job. He had decided to stay on in London for a while longer, until the money ran out. To return home now would be to admit defeat. Jerry needed help, although he wasn't sure what kind, or how he could be of use to her. She was already seeing some kind of shrink. She suffered from an overactive imagination, and her insistence on turning everything into a mystery bugged him. The girl seemed drawn to the morbidity of the police investigation. He couldn't figure her out. When she spoke of her parents, or the conspiracy she imagined surrounding them, it was as if she meant something else entirely; as if her true intentions lay just beneath the surface, and he had yet to bring them into the light.

He was about to leave the room, when the telephone rang.

'It's my turn to apologize. About last night.'

'You don't need to.'

'I wanted to . . . but . . .'

'Listen, I think we both have some issues to work out first. Are you at work?'

'Yes. Something just came up on my daily schedule. There's a meeting arranged for this morning in one of the conference rooms. Savoy Theatre Shareholders. Have you ever been a waiter?'

'Yeah, when I was at college.'

'Is it easy? I mean, could I do it? All I have to do is stand beside the coffee pot and serve them when they take their break, right?'

'Jerry, what are you talking about?'

'The refreshment area is just outside the main room. Hopefully I'll be able to hear every word they say.'

'Now, wait a minute,' Joseph protested. 'You're going to pretend to be a waitress just so you can—'

'It's all aboveboard. Why not? I can arrange to switch shifts for the day, although Nicholas is being a real creep. I even get paid. I already checked it out.'

'But what's the point?'

'People are being murdered and blackmailed and you ask me about the point? Things like this go on all the time and nobody stops them.'

'That's conspiracy-theory crap.'

'Watergate isn't crap, it's real. Men in power abuse their positions. It's not until individuals take matters into their own hands—'

'All right,' he interrupted, 'do it, but promise me something. If you don't hear or see anything suspicious, let the police handle it their way.'

'It's a deal.'

As Joseph replaced the receiver, he had to admit he was intrigued. If he had really lost his job because Miyagawa had been set up, he had a strong case for wrongful dismissal.

PC Charlie Bimsley was at the very end of the Metropolitan Police chain of command. When orders filtered down from the top, when reprimands were issued and disagreeable duties were passed on, they were usually dumped in Charlie's ample lap. If restaurant dustbins had to be searched for a discarded weapon, if a decomposed body stuck in a drain had to be dislodged, people in power would turn to each other and say, 'Let's get Bimsley to do it.' At least, that was how it seemed to the young constable. Charlie had no idea that in a few years' time he would father a boy who would become a beat officer, just like his dad. Colin Bimsley would even end up working for the Peculiar Crimes Unit.

Today, though, Bimsley was one of the thirty or so foot soldiers handling door-to-door inquiries in the pouring rain, asking householders about the disappearance of little Daisy Whitstable. So far the response had been poor, the progress slow. It was no surprise, thought Bimsley as he pushed open yet another garden gate. Most of the residents worked during the day, their houses minded by an army of cleaning ladies, nannies, and gardeners, few of whom spoke English.

As Bimsley rang the bell and surveyed the tailored front lawn, he wondered if his dislike of the neighbourhood stemmed from the fact that he would never have the money to live in such an area.

'Can I help you?' The elderly woman who answered the door was staring suspiciously at him, despite the fact that he was wearing a uniform. She demanded to see formal identification before letting him start his questionnaire. Bimsley impatiently ran through the opening paragraph, explaining that he was trying to establish the exact time and whereabouts of a rogue ice-cream van.

'I remember it clearly, you don't have to go on,' she snapped, in a tone she probably reserved for recalcitrant dogs. 'When I heard it passing I went straight to the window and looked out.'

Apart from the hazy recollections of a Scandanavian au pair in the next street, this was the first positive identification Bimsley had received. 'Would it be possible for you to describe the vehicle?' he asked carefully. The rain was falling in heavy sheets now. He could see his breath. 'Perhaps I could come in for a minute...' he ventured.

'You stay where you are. Muddy boots on my Axminster, the very idea. Please be quiet while I think.' She pushed past him on the porch and looked along the street, narrowing her eyes.

'A little girl was abducted in this area yesterday,' he added. 'Possibly by the driver of the van we're seeking.'

'I don't much care for children. Too demanding. I don't have a television and I don't read the papers. Too depressing.' She pointed in the direction of the Whitstable house. 'It stopped up there. I remember thinking at the time that it was odd to hear an ice-cream van at Christmas, especially one like this.'

'What was different about it?'

'It was plain white, more like an ambulance. Then there was the man inside.'

'You saw the driver?' This was too good to be true.

'Only through the windscreen. He didn't have a coat on, you see. The regular man always has a white coat. This one didn't.'

'Is there anything else you recall about him?'

'He was dark.'

'Black?'

'No, more—Indian. He had long hair, most unhygienic where the preparation of food is concerned.'

'You didn't see the girl?'

'I just took one look, then closed the curtains.'

Bimsley thought for a moment. 'Why did you look out in the first place?'

'As I said, it was too late in the year for the van to come around,' she explained, absently twisting her loose wedding ring. 'And then there was the tune. They normally play "Greensleeves." This one was playing something jolly from an opera.'

'Can you remember what the tune was?' asked Bimsley.

'No,' replied the old lady, shaking her head, 'but I can tell you it was something by Gilbert and Sullivan.'

'You're usually on the desk downstairs, aren't you?' whispered the young girl standing beside her. 'My name's Sandra.' She held out her hand. Jerry shook it and smiled back.

'I'm just filling in for today,' Jerry lied guiltily. 'They're a bit short-staffed.'

For the past ten minutes the two girls had been standing between stainless steel tea urns, behind a low table filled with plates of sandwiches. Until now, neither of them had spoken. Sandra was shy and overawed by the guests. Her hair covered cheeks pockmarked by childhood illness. Jerry wanted to say something that would put her at ease, but realized uncomfortably that to do so might be patronizing. A class gap lay between them like a concealed mine. Jerry wasn't in awe of these people. She saw them every day at home.

Ahead of them, across acres of crimson carpet, the shareholders sat beyond oak-paneled doors which had been pulled tightly shut. The only sound that could be discerned from within was a muffled murmuring.

She'd wasted her time. Jerry dragged at the hem of

her ill-fitting waitress outfit, trying to work it below her knees. The least the duty manager could have done was to find her some clothes that fitted properly. It had taken her ages to pin her unruly hair beneath the white cap. She looked over and found Sandra smiling apologetically.

'It's difficult keeping your legs warm in this weather, isn't it?' said Sandra, ducking her head. 'Then you come in here and it's so hot. I've got these heavy wool tights and they're itching like mad. They should be coming to an end about now.' She nodded toward the conference room, referring to the group rather than her underwear arrangements.

'Who are they?' asked Jerry. 'Do you know?'

'Friends of the Savoy, something like that,' said her new friend, her voice barely above a whisper. 'Something to do with the theatre next door.' From within came the sound of chairs being shoved back. The meeting had been concluded, and Jerry was no wiser than she had been before.

As the oak-paneled doors were folded open and the committee members filed out towards the refreshment table, she examined their faces, trying to see them as con-spirators, but it was impossible; a less sinister group of people would have been hard to imagine. They looked like an average English church congregation. Most of the ladies were middle-aged and wore firmly pinned hats. The gentlemen were suited and spectacled, conserva-tively dressed by family tailors.

As she began filling coffee cups and handing them out, Jerry strained to catch exchanges of dialogue. Be-yond the odd phrase referring to investments and healthy rates of return, there seemed to be very little business be-ing discussed. Of the two couples nearest to her, one was airing the problem of waterlogged lawns and the other was complaining about an obscene play at the National Theatre. It was hopeless.

After a further ten minutes the room began to clear, and Sandra started packing away her end of the table.

'I wonder if I have time for another cup?' asked a pink-cheeked old dear in a ratty-looking fur coat.

Smiling wanly, Jerry took her cup and refilled it. 'Thirsty work in there, was it?' she asked.

'Oh, no, not really.' The old lady accepted the cup and began heaping sugar into it. 'But it's all very exciting, nevertheless.' She leaned forward secretively. 'We're buying a theatre,' she confided.

'Really?' Jerry joined her halfway over the table, a fellow conspirator. 'Who's *we*?'

'Cruet,' replied the old lady.

Jerry frowned. Was she looking for the salt? 'I'm sorry?'

'The Committee for the Restoration of West End Theatres,' she replied. 'CROWET.'

'Oh, I see. And you're taking over the theatre next door?'

'That's right. Two years ago I helped save the otters; last year it was typhoid; but this is much more interesting. How did you know which theatre we've purchased? It's supposed to be a secret.'

'Oh,' Jerry replied lightly, 'we had a Japanese gentleman staying here who was going to buy it.' She waited while the old lady stirred her tea. 'But the deal fell through.'

'So I believe. The yen isn't strong at the moment, or something like that.'

'Rachel, dear, we're going via the Brompton Oratory,

do you need a lift?' called one of the remaining men. The old lady smiled vaguely at Jerry and pottered away to join the group.

CROWET, thought Jerry. It had to be registered somewhere, and it could lead her to a murderer.

22 / Lux Aeterna

John May strode along the marble-faced corridor, his dark mane bouncing at his shirt collar. Having had enough of Tomlins's refusal to return his phone calls, he had decided to pay a surprise visit to the Goldsmiths' Hall.

He pushed open the door at the end of the main chamber and entered, sweeping past a pair of startled secretaries. Tomlins was seated at his desk, fountain pen poised above a sheaf of documents. His eyes bulged in his florid face as he recognized the detective.

'Mr May, I told you I'd call you once I had found someone you could talk to,' he said, attempting to preempt May's complaint.

'And when might that be?' asked May. 'As I see it, you're deliberately attempting to obstruct an investigation.'

'It's not as easy as you think.' Tomlins recapped his pen with deliberate care. 'I mentioned the fact that you would like to discuss certain aspects of the Whitstable family's lives with someone who knew them, but I'm afraid I've had very little response. Perhaps people have no wish to speak ill of the dead.'

'Why would anyone speak ill?' May seated himself in the only other chair. 'Weren't they liked? You told me you barely knew them. How many guild members do you have here?'

'Oh,' Tomlins waved his hand airily, 'it would be hard to estimate...'

'Mr Tomlins, let me make things simpler for you.' May was beginning to lose his patience. He had seen such men in every walk of life, 'clubbable' men who used the privilege of membership as a class weapon. 'I want exact figures from you right now, this morning, or I'll have you brought in and your files sequestered as evidence. I want to know how many members of the Worshipful Company of Watchmakers there are, and how many of those belong to this little inner circle of yours, the one which uses the symbol you couldn't recognize, the sacred flame. Then we'll start going through names and if necessary we'll interview every single person on your list.'

Tomlins's smile froze on his face. 'You must understand that this is information we never give out...' His voice climbed even higher than usual.

May waved the objection aside. 'You send your members mailings; every organization does. Your secretary must have the names and addresses. I'll ask her.' He rose.

'All right, I'll get you the list,' said Tomlins hastily. 'But I don't know what you mean by an inner circle.'

'We'll go through the names first, then we'll come back to the sacred flame. I'll have a number of other requests in due course. Until then, I suggest you make yourself busy, because you wouldn't believe some of the things I'm going to ask you to do for me tomorrow.'

Alison Hatfield stood waiting for him at the foot of the main staircase, dwarfed by the white statues of the four seasons. As May approached her through the temple of chalced marble, he wondered if she had come to a decision. Last night he had called her and asked for her help.

As she was employed outside the Watchmakers' Company but within the same system, he figured she would be the ideal person to assist him.

'Thanks for meeting me, Miss Hatfield,' he said, as she led him to the deserted Court Room in the northwest corner of the building. 'I need a guide through all of this.' He tapped his folder.

'Please, call me Alison. We won't be interrupted in here.' She pushed open a pair of heavily carved doors. May's mouth fell open as he gazed upon the elaborate gold and silver cornices of the Court Room.

'Impressive, isn't it? That stone behind the Prime Warden's chair is a Roman altar from the second century. Some workmen discovered it in the building's foundations about a hundred and fifty years ago. The figure on the side is Diana, or Apollo, we're not sure which.'

'Extraordinary,' he agreed. 'It makes you wonder how much more of London is still hidden away from public view.' They seated themselves at the mahogany banjo-shaped table that dominated the room. 'I thought the guilds were created for the benefit of artisans and their families.'

'They still carry out a lot of work for charity, but they've accumulated great wealth.'

May emptied the folder on to the leather surface of the table. 'I'll be honest with you, Alison,' he said with a sigh. 'There are unusual pressures being brought to bear on us, and I'm desperate for some outside help. These murders occurred within a respected family during Common Market fortnight. Could William Whitstable have died when an incendiary device of his own making exploded? I know the whole family belongs to the Watchmakers. Their ancestors were men with mechanical minds. Are they doing this to each other? If so, why would they abduct a small child? Are the Whitstables members of some private club which exists within the Watchmakers? How can I find out if they are?' He sat back in his chair and turned to her. 'You see my problems.'

'What can I do to help?'

'I need you to find me the name of anyone who can tell me the truth about the Whitstables. Either Mr Tomlins is too scared to talk, or he genuinely knows nothing about what's going on, or he is somehow involved. I fear it's the latter. Can you honestly say that no one here has ever seen this sign?' He held up the picture of the sacred flame once more. He didn't want to tell her that the only person to recognize it as a guild symbol was Arthur's butcher.

Alison carefully examined it. 'Actually, I have seen it somewhere,' she told him.

'Where?'

'I think it was on a brochure. We help the Watchmakers send out their mailings. I don't know whether it was to do with them directly; there are many associated companies. I think it was something connected with their charity work.'

'Would you have any brochures left?' asked May.

'There are bound to be some in the basement. We never throw anything away.'

'Can we go and look?'

'It'll be cold and dark. A real mess. No one ever goes down there.'

'It would be easier than trying to find them by myself.'

'All right,' she said finally. 'I'll take you down. But we'll have to get a couple of torches.'

The old trellis lift shook and rattled as they descended into musty darkness. Bare concrete walls rose around them. It was as if they were leaving the guild hall for the ruined Temple of Diana that lay buried far beneath it.

'Why aren't there any lights down here?' asked May, watching his breath turn grey in the chill air.

'I don't know. There are emergency lights, but they must operate on a separate circuit. I think it's a different voltage or something.' Alison pointed to the tiny red bulb set in the ceiling of the lift. Standing in the gloom with her nose tilted and her hair brushed to the back of her long neck, Alison looked like a Pre-Raphaelite heroine. He wanted to touch her skin, to see if it could really be that soft and delicate.

The lift groaned. May remembered his partner's dictum that bad things happened when the lights went out. They stopped with an echoing thump, and Alison pulled open the trellis. She clicked on her torch and shone it along a dim corridor.

'This way,' she said, holding back the gate for him. They passed nearly a dozen darkened doorways before she turned into a tall, windowless storeroom. 'If the brochures are down here at all, they'll be in one of these.'

'Okay, you start at one end and I'll start at the other,' said May.

For the next half hour they tore open the lids of damp-smelling cartons and checked the mildewed contents. May was just resealing one of the boxes when he heard a scuttling noise in the darkness beyond the room, like tacks being scattered across tiles. 'What was that?'

Alison looked up at him, her pale eyes catching the light like some kind of nocturnal animal. 'I think there might be rats,' she said calmly. 'Hardly anyone ever comes down here because of the leak.'

'What leak?' May looked down at the torch. The beam had begun to falter.

'The river drains run right under here. Sometimes, after very heavy rainfall, you can hear a dull rumbling beneath the floor. It's a really creepy sound. There's a leak in one of the corridors below, and the rats get in. They breed in the river. They're supposed to be as big as cats.'

'There's another floor below this?'

'Yes, but they damned it up with cement because of the danger of flooding.'

May found himself listening for the rush of the underground current. The torch flickered again. He tapped the glass with his hand.

On the other side of the room, Alison ripped open a carton and emptied it. 'I think I've found them,' she called.

May clambered over the boxes and joined her just as his torch beam dwindled to nothing. She held one of the brochures high and shone her light on it.

The back page bore the stamp of the golden flame burning in heavenly light. The words *LUX AETERNA* were written in neat Tudor script beneath it, and beneath this were printed the words *Alliance of Eternal Light*. May took the brochure from her. The headline across the front read: *Renovating London's Most Beautiful Theatres: How You Can Help*. Below was a reproduction of a Victorian painting showing an excited first-night audience. May opened the front cover and found himself gazing at a pair of photographs, smartly bordered in gold.

One showed the late William Whitstable. The other was a portrait of James Makepeace Whitstable, a man who had been dead for the best part of a century. A man, thought May, studying the stern face in the photograph, who still exerted such power over his descendants that nothing, not even death, would allow them to share their secrets with the outside world.

23 / Transgression

The Guardian, Tuesday 21 December 1973

POLICE INCOMPETENCE BLAMED
FOR DAISY DELAY

The search for Daisy Whitstable, aged seven, taken from her Chelsea home on Sunday afternoon, got off to a poor start due to a fourteen-hour delay, after Metropolitan Police units failed to communicate vital information. Daisy's disappearance had not been connected to an ongoing investigation of deaths among other family relatives. Because the crucial link had been overlooked, investigative work was set back at a time when it was most needed.

Daily Mail, Tuesday 21 December 1973

NO CHRISTMAS CHEER IN MISSING
DAISY HOUSEHOLD

Christmas stockings hang above a merrily burning log fire, waiting to be filled. A saucer of water stands beneath the sparkling, bauble-covered tree, a child's thoughtful offering for weary reindeer. But unless a miracle occurs, there will be no joyous Christmas laughter in this house, only anguished tears.

For this is the home of little Daisy Whitstable, abducted on Sunday afternoon. Instead of the welcoming sight of a jovial Santa stacking presents at the foot of the bed, there has been an uninvited, grimmer visitor— and instead of emptying his yuletide sack, he has filled it. See our Leader Column: 'Is No One Safe in Their Homes? Why We Should All Be Afraid.'

Letter to the Evening News, Tuesday 21 December 1973

Dear Sir,

Your recent suggestion that the 'sacred flame' symbol associated with the Whitstable murders has a connection with a secret Nazi assassination bureau is utter hogwash.

The symbol that is currently being flaunted in the national press bears no resemblance whatsoever to the one which made a brief appearance towards the end of the Second World War. It is, however, very similar to the sacred flame of certain Victorian occult societies.

Far from harbouring murderous intent, such societies were merely gathering spots for harmless English gentlemen who welcomed the chance to occasionally escape from the wife and summon up Beelzebub in the company of a few like-minded friends.

Yours sincerely,
The Rev. George Bartlett.

'I want to see John May,' Jerry said, trying to regain her breath after having galloped up the broken-down escalator at Mornington Crescent Tube station.

Sergeant Longbright looked up from a stack of reports and regarded her coolly. 'Good morning, Miss Gates. You're starting early today.'

The desk clock read seven forty-three. Jerry had not slept well, but it was the sergeant who looked as if she had been working all night.

'However, Mr May was even earlier. You just missed him.' She smiled. 'He's doing some more interviews. I'm expecting him back at noon. Do you want to leave a message?'

'No—it can wait.'

She was desperate to share her findings about CROWET, but forced herself to hold on until she could speak to the detectives in person.

'Miss Gates.' Longbright was tapping the pencil against the desk and frowning at her.

'What?'

'If you don't have anything specific to do here, can you come back later? We're really busy.'

'Sorry. I thought I could, you know, help or something.' She was about to leave when she noticed the damp-wrinkled theatre brochure on the sergeant's desk. The front cover showed a painting of the interior of the Savoy Theatre. May had obviously been following the same lead. So much for promising to keep her in the picture.

'At least let me buy you a coffee, Sergeant. You look tired.' Jerry smiled encouragingly.

'I'd love one,' said the sergeant absently. 'I can't get away from this desk.'

'I've only got notes. Do you have change?'

'Let me see.' As Longbright turned to the raincoat hanging on the stand behind her and fished through the pockets, Jerry slipped the brochure inside her jacket. She felt she had the right to do so. Joseph had been cheated out of his job, and the police would be unable to help him. It was up to her now.

* * *

'You said to drop it if I didn't find out anything, but I did.' They were seated in the coffee bar opposite the Savoy, where Jerry was supposed to have started her shift ten minutes ago. 'I'll just go to her house and talk to her. What harm can come of that?' She stared into a cup of scalding, foamy tea and sighed. 'I can't get hurt, if that's what you're worried about. The police may never discover the truth. Lots of murders remain unsolved.'

'If you think you can make a difference, fine.' Joseph threw his hands up in defeat. 'You've already stolen evidence from a police station and it's not even nine A.M. Imagine what you can accomplish by lunchtime. Go and see this woman, pretend you're from the press or whatever stupid idea you've come up with. I can't stop you.'

Jerry was determined to see the thing through, and that meant finding out more about CROWET. Peggy Harmsworth, née Whitstable, was William Whitstable's co-director on the theatre committee, and the only other person to be listed by name in the CROWET brochure. Reading the biographies, Jerry had found Mrs Harmsworth to be a Whitstable, grandmother to the abducted Daisy, in what proved to be yet another uncharted branch of this interminable family.

'Do me a favour? Tell Nicholas I have a cold and can't come in to work.' She reached across the counter to touch his hand, but Joseph withdrew it.

'This is the last time,' he warned.

The rain was drifting through the trees like spider threads as Jerry pushed open the gates of North London's exclusive Holly Lodge estate. The 1920s mock-Tudor houses were hidden beyond billiard-table lawns, and reeked of wealth. Jerry had rung Mrs Harmsworth to suggest conducting an interview with her for a new lifestyle magazine. Peggy Harmsworth had agreed to be interviewed because she could talk about her favourite charities, and because she had been offered money.

Jerry smoothed out her skirt and rang the doorbell. Her Savoy uniform was smart, and added an aura of respectability. Unusually for a Whitstable, Peggy had chosen to change her name on marriage, although she had left the family name on the CROWET brochure. Consequently, she had not been contacted for the PCU briefing on Sunday.

Peggy was seated in the drawing room awaiting her visitor. In its sixth decade, her face had developed a timeless look tightened by disillusionment and low body fat. Her sleek dark hair was arranged in a chignon and fixed with a gold clasp. At her feet lay a small, hypertense dog of the kickable variety. Peggy did not look as if she was about to countenance any nonsense. Nor, judging by the tumbler of Scotch at her side, was she entirely sober. After a brief but frank discussion about payment, they settled down to work.

Jerry looked around at the antelope heads peering forlornly from the walls. 'Did you kill these yourself?' she asked.

'One inherits so many ghastly things from one's family.' Peggy ground out her cigarette in an antelope-foot ashtray.

No tea and biscuits here, thought Jerry gloomily. She rose and examined the smouldering ashtray-foot. 'I assume there are three others like this.'

'I thought you came here to ask impertinent questions about my life. It's a little late to give me lessons in ecology.'

She tapped out another Sobranie and lit it. 'For God's sake, sit down; you're making me nervous. Let's get the interrogation over with.' She exhaled a funnel of blue smoke and sat back, like Circe awaiting the effect of a spell.

Jerry cleared her throat. 'Obviously, I'd like to detail your charity work for London's neglected theatres, but naturally our readers would like to know how you're coping with recent tragedies. Do you think the abduction of your granddaughter is connected to these deaths?'

'Of course I bloody do!' Peggy exploded. 'Anyone can see we're being decimated.'

'But who hates you enough to do such a thing?'

She tipped back her head and fired another jet of smoke at the ceiling. 'That's rather the question, isn't it? All international businesses make enemies. When your main aim is to throttle the life from the home competition, you're bound to tread on a few toes. Of course, these days nobody behaves in an openly vicious fashion. Rivals don't get obliterated, they get gently squeezed out, like spots. We're hardly the Krays.'

Peggy fanned smoke away from her face. 'Don't misunderstand me. The financial world is as cruel as it ever was, but subtler. The Whitstables haven't destroyed anyone in years. Our grandfathers behaved like bastards, but then so did everyone else. The East India Company had set a fine example at the start of the last century— exporting opium to China, monopolizing the drug, and fostering the addiction of the Chinese so that Britain could profit from imported tea and silks. They had always had to fight for their trading rights. The British were outraged after the Black Hole of Calcutta, but that was nothing compared to what we did to the poor bloody Indians. Yet despite its independence, India still carries our legacy—look at the hopeless red tape we left behind in their government. I don't suppose they teach you this sort of thing at school any more.' She peered suspiciously through the smoke at Jerry. 'There's always been bad behaviour in the outposts of the business world. But I thought you wanted to talk about my theatre work.'

'Yes, I read your brochure. Where did the CROWET symbol come from?'

'It's the symbol of the Alliance of Eternal Light. It's not as grand as it sounds, merely an organization founded by some of the Watchmakers' Company.'

'Who, specifically? James Makepeace Whitstable— the gentleman on your brochure?'

'Yes, it was James's inspiration. No doubt the name came to him in one of his evangelical moods.'

'What are the alliance's modern-day duties?'

'It's a philanthropic trust involved in charity work, mainly raising money for churches and hospitals, although it originally began as some kind of get-rich-quick scheme. The family coffers were almost empty, and James came up with a plan to fill them. Whatever he did, it worked for a hell of a long time. Much of the Whitstable fortune was created by him. Now it's evolving into a holding trust for organizations like CROWET. We've just taken over the restoration of the Savoy Theatre. A Japanese consortium was handling it, but we managed to buy them off. Rather, the Japs suddenly dropped out, leaving us with a successful bid for the building. It was almost too good to be true.'

'Why do you say that?'

'Because we've always wanted the Savoy. Now, with the alliance's help, we'll be able to ensure that the theatre reopens in the New Year.'

'Who runs the alliance now?'

'The whole family has helped out from time to time. There are no outsiders involved.'

Jerry was disappointed to hear that the guild's inner organization was nothing more than a family charity. But would Peggy tell her if it wasn't? 'Does the alliance keep records of its history?'

'I suppose so,' said Peggy, reaching down to scratch the dog about its ears. 'They're probably tucked away at the guild, but I don't see why you need to look at those.'

'We'd like to tell readers about your good works. By the way, why theatre restoration?'

'What do you mean?'

'Why are theatres of particular interest when you usually support churches and hospitals?'

'The alliance has been connected with the London stage since its inception, don't ask me why. I'm not sure anyone remembers now.'

'I like your brochure.' Jerry removed it from her pocket. 'Do you happen to know who designed it?'

'We have freelance people we call upon for printing and suchlike,' Peggy said, clearly disinterested.

Jerry flipped through the booklet. 'I couldn't help admiring the paintings that illustrate the copy. Holyoake, Sickert, Chapman, Crowe, most of them Royal Academy. Any particular reason for that?'

'Of course. We never do anything without a reason. The Royal Academy had a strong link with the foundation of the alliance, and the connection has been maintained. James Whitstable was an honorary Academy member. I'm not sure why. You'd really have to ask the RA.' She eyed her Scotch tumbler with longing. 'Most of the interesting things that happened to our family occurred for the benefit of God, profit, and civic duty. Until now, that is. You'd think we were being punished for some past transgression. But murder and abduction? What kind of transgression would we have had to commit?'

24 / Closing Ranks

Bryant insisted on driving his battered yellow Mini Minor to their South London appointment. Although his skill in negotiating major intersections had marginally improved in the last few years (the only useful by-product of endless driving tests failed since the late 1950s), he considered a number of traffic signs to be superfluous, including those that involved changing lanes, giving way, or avoiding pedestrians. Weaving through the lunchtime traffic in Victoria proved to be a logistical challenge, but Bryant remained oblivious to the shouts and honks of dumbfounded fellow motorists. Even highway-hardened lorry drivers blanched and braked when faced with Bryant's blithe disrespect for the road.

'Leo Marks has sent down masses of documents pertaining to the financial history of the Whitstable empire,' said May. 'Janice is going through them, but it's a laborious job. There are literally hundreds of holding companies going back across the century. The family has been suffering from declining fortunes for years. Their philanthropy is well established and beyond reproach, although their business practices throughout the last century show plenty of nasty tarnishes. Lawsuits, maltreatment of workforce, exploitation of minors, racial discrimination, restrictive practices, stuff like that.'

'The Victorians became less forgiving as they expanded

their empire.' Bryant peered through the windscreen for an all-clear, then stamped down on the accelerator. 'They felt God was on their side. It's always a mistake mixing religion and business. Look what happened when Christian soldiers moved into the East India Company. In its early days of trading, it prided itself on empathy for other tribes and creeds, but respect fell away as the desire to convert took hold. We need to find somebody who's been harmed by the Whitstables in their financial dealings. We might hear a few home truths then.'

'They've closed ranks against outsiders, Arthur, ever since we began conducting interviews. Their answers sound rehearsed.'

'Then we'll conquer by dividing them up.'

Bryant and his partner walked briskly along the river footpath at Vauxhall, a dismal part of the Embankment barely cheered by sunlight refracting from the leaden waters of the Thames. Daisy Whitstable had been missing for over thirty-six hours. There had been no new developments in the search for the bogus ice-cream van, and now the capital had begun emptying out for the Christmas holidays.

May kicked out at a stone, sending it skittering. He had never felt so helpless in his search for a common enemy, and the strain of the past two weeks was beginning to show. 'I think they've been told not to speak to us by a senior member of the family,' he complained.

'I don't know who. We've interviewed virtually all of them.'

'No family is impregnable, Arthur. There must be a weak link. We can't just wait until someone breaks from the party line.'

On the previous evening, the detectives had attempted to speak to Mina Whitstable, the bedridden mother of William, Peter, and Bella. For the last five years the old lady's grip on reality had been tenuous, and the deaths of her children had provided the final push into mental aphasia. They were now pinning their hopes on Edith Eleanor Whitstable, a contemporary of Mina and something of an outsider, judging by the rest of the family's comments about her.

Edith was an irascible sixty-seven-year-old matriarch who owed little loyalty to those around her. Referring to her earlier interview with Sergeant Longbright, May saw that the woman had often been critical of the Whitstables' business empire, in which she had once taken an active role. Three months earlier she had moved out of the district where she had spent most of her life, choosing to live instead on a small gated estate by the river. May was interested in finding out why. Bryant tapped him on the shoulder and pointed to a number of large redbrick buildings with arched windows.

'I must have written the address down wrong. This is the old Sarson's vinegar factory.'

'Not any more,' said May. 'Looks like it's been converted into town houses.'

'This sort of property is for single professionals, not dowagers. Why on earth would she want to move here?'

'Perhaps her old house was too large for her to manage.'

The detectives found themselves in a mock-Elizabethan courtyard of pale herringbone brick. 'How did she sound on the phone?' asked May as they searched for the old lady's apartment number.

'Nervous. Certainly not the dragon I was expecting. Here we are.'

Edith Whitstable resided in a ground-floor apartment on the far side of the estate. She had a small manicured garden with brass carriage lamps set in the front wall. The setting seemed out of character for a Whitstable. Bryant gave May a puzzled look as he rang the doorbell and loosened a voluminous purple scarf.

The bird-boned woman who answered the door welcomed them with pleasing warmth.

'You found us,' she said, taking their coats. 'I've already made tea, or would you prefer something stronger on a raw day like this?'

'Good idea, it's cold enough to freeze the—' said Bryant before a look from May stopped him. 'Tea will be fine.'

The apartment had the sparse decoration of a newlyweds' home. If Edith Whitstable had brought any of her old furniture with her, it wasn't in evidence. A number of iron crucifixes lined the hallway, and there were several more austere religious icons in the lounge.

'I understand you wish to ask me more questions,' she said, setting down a tea tray and starting to lay out the cups. Her hands sported pale indentations from wearing rings that had now been removed. Her dress was floral, cheap, off the peg. Around her neck was a large silver cross. Bryant supposed that she must have fallen upon hard times. Yet, when they had met at Mornington Crescent, he remembered that she had been wearing a pearl brooch and a mink coat.

'It shouldn't take long.' May checked his notes. 'Your husband Samuel died two years ago, is that right?'

'Yes. Cancer of the spine. He was in pain for a long time. The children were a great help.'

'You have two boys, don't you? Jack and Harry?'

'Hardly boys, Mr May. They're in their early fifties.'

'What relation were you to William, Peter, and Bella Whitstable?'

'They were my cousins. We can all be traced back to James and Rosamunde in the middle of the last century. I suppose you know all about them?'

'No, our investigations don't go back quite that far.'

'Oh, but they should! James was a fascinating man—kind, charming, a devout Christian. He carried out so many wonderful works, as did his children. Alfred, his oldest son, founded several charitable missions in the East End, you know.'

'What about Daisy Whitstable?'

'A terrible business,' said Edith without hesitation. 'Her grandparents are also my cousins. Her paternal grandfather was shot down in the Second World War.'

A clang of metal sounded in the next room, followed by a grunt. Edith chose to ignore it.

'I understand you recently moved house,' said Bryant. 'You must miss the old place, seeing as you grew up there. The recession can't have been favourable to family fortunes.'

'Selling up has had its good and bad sides, Mr Bryant,' Edith said, nervously brushing the fingers of her right hand over her cross. 'It has brought our family closer together. And it has helped me to rediscover my devotion to Our Saviour.'

'I should imagine the money helped, too,' added Bryant.

'It's no secret that we've had financial difficulties since Samuel died. With the house sold I'm solvent once more.'

'Couldn't you have borrowed from someone else in the family?'

'Neither a borrower nor a lender be, Mr May. Besides, none of us are as wealthy as we used to be, so we can't lean on each other for financial support.'

Another clang and grunt sounded from the next room.

'You say you've been brought closer together as a family, Mrs Whitstable. Some cynics have suggested that's because of the recent assaults. Perhaps you all want to keep an eye on each other.'

'You're not suggesting that one of us killed them?'

'You tell me,' said Bryant irritably. He hated having to fight his way through the family's layers of obfuscation and misdirection.

'It's quite impossible,' said Edith, affronted, her hand now clasping the cross at her throat. 'We may be larger and a little more eccentric than the average English family, but at heart we get on very well together. We are not demonstrative in our loyalties and affections. Nor do we believe in hysterics or histrionics. We go about our duties as honest English folk who have worked hard for their homeland and their children. In that respect we're really quite normal.'

Bryant looked doubtful. A clang and a shouted oath boomed through the wall. Edith smiled peacefully. May threw his partner a look. 'Is there somebody in the next room, Mrs Whitstable?' he asked.

'You must forgive the boys,' she explained. 'I'm living with my grandchildren, my Harry's sons. They're doing their exercises.' She turned in her chair and called out. 'Steven, Jeffrey, would you come here please?'

Two musclebound young men entered the lounge. They were identical: both blond, both broad, both narrow-eyed and feral-featured. They had been lifting weights, and were out of breath. Both had silver crosses fastened around broad necks.

One of them lowered a vast arm to his grandmother's shoulder. 'Is everything all right, Edith?' he asked, looking sourly at the detectives. His crystal-cutter accent suggested public schooling.

'Fine, boys. My friends were just leaving,' she said with a nervous smile. The detectives rose awkwardly and were ushered from the lounge. Bryant tried to see into the other rooms as they were being returned to the hall, but one of the twins threw his arm across the corridor, barring the way. 'We'll see them out for you if you like,' he offered.

'That won't be necessary,' said Edith firmly. 'Everything's fine.'

The boy caught his brother's eye and held it, smiling. 'Praise the Lord,' he said.

'Just like any normal family,' snorted Bryant as they marched back along the Embankment path.

'Well, she doesn't look as if she's been abducted,' replied May. 'She's not being held there against her will.'

'Maybe not, but she was minding her words. I'm willing to bet that her grandsons have been installed to keep watch over her.'

'I don't know, Arthur. We have to be able to trust *somebody*. She sounded perfectly innocent.'

'When it comes to the Whitstables,' said Bryant, '*innocent* is not a word that readily springs to mind.' Talking to Edith about James Makepeace Whitstable had confirmed his suspicions. Although the family's allies and enemies had been created in the distant past, their influence reached through to the present. Connections were maintained. Duty was done. That was the common link—the all-pervading Victorian sense of duty.

He was sure that even now the trail was far from cold and the danger far from over. God forbid she was dead, for there would be a public outcry of such proportions that it would threaten the entire investigation. They were expected to produce a culprit, and fast.

Bryant had a hunch that they were seeking no modern-day murderer. The answer might lie buried in the convoluted lineage of the Whitstable family, but he felt sure it was simple—and still waiting to be unearthed.

25 / Sevens

I'm still hungry.'

Daisy Whitstable wiped the chocolate from her mouth. Her dress was filthy and crawling with lice, and even though the tunnel door was shut she was shivering in the bitter winter air. She had eaten nothing but ice cream since her capture. The wet brick arches had taken on a more sinister appearance since the van's dying battery had faded its headlights. A neon tube had been plugged into the wall, and threw just enough light across the floor to keep vermin at bay.

Daisy was resilient, but her confidence was fading. She could no longer tell if it was day or night. Her ankles were loosely tied with a piece of nylon cord, and she was sick of scraping her knees on the rough concrete floor. She had given up crying. Tears only made her captor more upset.

'Can't I have something that isn't ice cream?' She was glad she could not see him. He was there, though. He was always there among the oil cans and coils of rope, crouching in the darkest corner with his head resting on his knees. Whenever he came closer she tried to move away, even though he had shown no desire to hurt her. She had stopped trying to understand why her mother and father had not come to take her home. Perhaps she was being punished. Suppose she never saw them, or her brother, ever again? Against her will, she began to whimper.

In the corner, her captor stirred and rose slowly to his feet. She tried to stifle her tears but it was too late. He was shuffling toward her now, and would push her back into the corner of the bench, as he had done before.

Or so she thought, until she saw that this time he was carrying a hooked knife in one hand.

Maggie Armitage's face had been created specifically for smiling. She beamed reassuringly at her clients, her eyes waning to happy crescents, and massaged their hands consolingly as she provided conviction enough for both of them. This was an important part of her function, for as the Grand Leader of the Camden Town Coven, Maggie was often the harbinger of distressing news.

Every Monday night, she and the six remaining members of her sect met in the gloomy flat above the World's End public house opposite Camden Town Tube station, and attempted to provide some psychic balm for the city's wounds. Evil could not be stopped, merely held at bay, but at least its victims could be aided and, if possible, forewarned.

John will be furious if he finds out I've agreed to this meeting, thought Bryant. May held no belief in the Hereafter, but his partner kept an open mind. In the past, information provided by the cheery white witch had proved to be correct, and had helped to close a number of long-standing police files. This good work went unacknowledged by the Met, who regarded fringe operators with the same distrust doctors reserve for practitioners of alternative medicine. The *News of the World* ran too many exposés on bogus covens. In years to come they would replace them with features on celebrity sex romps, but for now they were content to run photographs of naked women prancing around bonfires.

Bryant surveyed the ground-floor hall of the Victoria and Albert Museum, wondering why Maggie had specifically asked to meet him here, in this shadowy edifice of marble and stone. He turned to find her striding briskly between the glass cases, her spectacles swinging on an amber chain at her bosom. In keeping with the festive season, she had enough dangling plastic ornaments about her person to decorate a small Norwegian pine.

'Dear thing, how well you look!' she cried, causing several members of the public to turn disapprovingly. 'I hope you didn't mind coming here, but I'm with Maureen and daren't let her out of my sight. She's sitting her British Pagan Rites exam next week and I said I'd help with the research, but she's a bit of a klepto and tends to heave open the cases when I'm not looking. She's liable to have Aleister Crowley's soup spoons up her jumper before you know it.'

'So you're in here uncovering forgotten symbolic rituals, eh?' Bryant asked, beaming jovially.

'Actually I was in the gift shop admiring their casserole covers, but I'm on a diet so let's not dwell. Maureen's doing her Fellowship of Isis and Dion Fortune—it always sounds like a fifties singer, don't you think?—and lately she's developed the habit of dropping into trances, so she needs some looking after, especially when we're on her scooter. I think you've met her.'

'I remember meeting a very pretty Jamaican girl a couple of years ago.'

'Oh, Katherine's still with us, but she's called Freya now and won't talk to anyone who doesn't acknowledge her god, Odin. Her husband's not pleased because he's on night work and keeps forgetting.' Maggie paused for a breath and donned her spectacles. Her eyes swam at him from sparkling plastic frames. 'I wanted to talk to you rather urgently, as it happens. The coven has a resident numerologist named Nigel. He's very good at Chaos Theory, which is just as well because his math is terrible, and at the moment he keeps coming up with sevens. Sevens, sevens everywhere, and it all seems connected with you. Or rather, with your investigation. You'd better follow me.'

She led the way back between glass cases of Victorian fans, canes, calling cards, and snuff boxes, as high above them the late-afternoon rain pattered steadily on angled skylights.

'Very few people bother with this part of the museum.' She turned into a corridor that had been partitioned off from the main floor. 'There's something I want you to see.'

Here the overhead lamps were spaced further apart, and the occultist's multicoloured sweater sparkled like the scales of a tropical fish as she moved between pools of light. 'We've been following the case in the papers, of course, and you know how one makes these connections. It was Nigel who remembered reading a Victorian text about the powers of light and darkness.'

At the end of the corridor, a red velvet rope separated them from a dark flight of stairs. Maggie slipped the hook and beckoned Bryant through. She flicked a switch at her side and a dim radiance shone from below. 'The documents kept here are extremely sensitive to light,' she explained as they descended. 'As a special-interest group we're allowed access to them, although I'm not allowed to bring vegetable soup with me, after an unfortunate incident with a Necromicon. Nigel was checking some numerological data when he got to thinking about the sevens. Do you know anything about the power of numbers?' They reached the foot of the stairs and she looked across at him, her eyes lost in shadow, less comical now.

She paused to sign the visitor's book which lay open on an unmanned reception desk, then walked between dimly illuminated cases, checking their contents. 'Seven is a very special number. It traverses history like a latitude, always appearing at times of great upheaval. It's a schizophrenic number, Janus-faced, often representing both good and evil, a grouping together and a tearing apart. There are many bloodstained sevens in history: Robert E. Lee's Seven Days' Battles in the American Civil War, for example; the destruction of the Red River settlement in the Seven Oaks Massacre; and the battle of Seven Pines. There's the Seven Weeks War—that's the Austro-Prussian war of 1866—and of course the Seven Years War which involved just about the whole of Europe in 1756.

'There are everyday sevens, like the seven-note scale, the Seven Hills of Rome, the days of the week, the seven-year itch. Then there are lots of legendary sevens: the seven Greek champions who were killed fighting against Thebes after the fall of Oedipus, the Seven Sages of the Bamboo Grove, the Seven Holy Founders, the Seven Gods of Luck, the Seven Wonders of the World, the Seven Golden Cities of Cibola, the Seven Wise Masters of ancient Arab myth, and the Seven Sleepers of Ephesus, soldiers who were resurrected from the dead—'

'I think I get the idea,' interrupted Bryant. 'What have all these sevens to do with the Whitstable murders?'

'Well, they don't directly—but this does.' Maggie stopped before the end case and wiped dust from the glass with her sleeve. Bryant peered down. Pinned open in the

case were several pages from a Victorian guild booklet
that had been damaged by fire. The sheets were edged
with gold leaf, a tribute to the Goldsmiths to whom they
owed their origin. The watercolour illustrations had
faded badly. Still, the central photograph was clear
enough.

It showed a sour-faced man with bright, menacing
eyes, muttonchop whiskers, and bushy eyebrows, standing in the centre of an ornately carpeted room. On either
side of this commanding presence sat three men. Each
man had a handwritten phrase marked beneath his
person.

A chill draught blew at Bryant's ankles as he read,
from left to right: *Arathron, Bethor, Phaleg, Hagith, Ophiel,
Phul.* The nomenclature beneath the sinister central figure was *Och*.

'The names pertain to the Seven Stewards of
Heaven,' said Maggie, tapping the glass with a painted
nail. 'God governs the world through them. They're also
known as the Olympian Spirits, and can be invoked by
black magicians. Each has a certain day associated with
him, as well as a particular planet in our solar system.
This central figure here, the tall man, is the Master of the
Sun, Bringer of Light, and he governs Sundays. I wondered if you'd come across him yet in your investigation.'

'Oh, Maggie,' said Bryant, wiping his glasses. 'I most
certainly have. I saw his picture only yesterday. What is
he doing here?'

'I'd say these finely dressed Victorians belonged to
some kind of society, wouldn't you?' The occultist smiled
darkly. 'Look at the arcane instruments on the table beside
them. There's no date to the picture but I'd say it was
around 1870, perhaps a little later. There's no way of

identifying who six of the fine gentlemen are, but we know the identity of the seventh.' Her finger moved over the central figure of Och, then to the panel of text below. The name in the box was that of James Makepeace Whitstable.

'The Victorians were up to their ears in strange sects and movements,' she explained, 'but the Stewards of Heaven had an ancient and extremely powerful belief system connected to the secret powers of darkness and light. Night and day, good and evil, held in perfect balance.'

'Presumably this particular sect is no longer in existence?'

'It hasn't been for centuries, but it looks as if your victims' ancestor was trying to revive it. As the Seven Stewards are hardly a familiar topic nowadays, I assume he failed to draw a large number of converts.'

'It may not have completely vanished,' murmured Bryant. 'It could simply have remained dormant until now.'

'That's what I wondered,' said Maggie, turning from the display case. 'As alternative belief systems go, this one operates on a pretty grand scale. Such societies have a habit of reviving themselves when conditions are right. Their growth and decline occurs in a regular cycle.'

'How long would each cycle last?'

'It could be any timespan of up to one hundred years. In fact, century cycles are rather common.'

The image of the Waterhouse painting had sprung into Bryant's mind. *The Favourites of the Emperor Honorius* depicted seven men.

He took another look inside the glass case, mentally superimposing the painting over the watercolour illustration. Seven acolytes in both. Cold draughts now filled the room, and he gave an involuntary shudder. 'One hundred years,' he said. 'That brings James Whitstable right back into the 1970s.'

'This is a very powerful occult force,' said Maggie. 'It looks as if your troubles are only just beginning.'

PC Burridge's lanky body was numb with cold, and the freezing rain was starting to leak through his sou'wester. His late-night beat was dark, dismal, and depressing. It had never felt less like Christmas.

Be observant, they had always told him. *Be ever vigilant.* But there was nothing to observe beneath the arches of the Embankment except the occasional forlorn tramp, and vigilance was a matter of course with so many antiwar demonstrators around. No wonder they call us Plods, he mused, plodding heavily through the tunnel to emerge in a deserted alley at the side of the Mermaid Theatre. His beat was about to get worse: the prime minister was losing his battle with the electrical unions, and the constable would shortly be walking the streets in darkness.

A thin, echoing wail forced him to break from his thoughts. The cry came from the tunnel at his back. Perhaps there was something trapped in one of the recesses of the dripping wall.

The constable stopped and listened. Suddenly the crying began anew, rising in pitch. He screwed up his eyes and stared into the gloom. He could just make out a bedraggled cat, sitting beside a bundle of coloured rags.

As he walked further into the tunnel the cat ran off, and he saw that the bundle was a small body.

PC Burridge placed his arms around the child to pick her up, wondering if his pleas for recognition had been perversely heard and from now on he would be known as the policeman who discovered Daisy Whitstable. He pressed his ear against the child's thin chest and heard a faint heartbeat within. Wrapping her inside his jacket, he radioed for an ambulance, praying it would arrive in time.

26 / Madwoman

All hell had broken loose at Mornington Crescent.

The press were doorstepping the building, and the phones were ringing off their hooks. All the papers wanted the Daisy Whitstable story. The child's parents had been informed, and Isobel Whitstable was being treated for shock. It was eleven A.M., and Bryant had yet to make an appearance, leaving his partner to face the wrath of their acting superior.

'Where the hell was she all this time? Her clothes were bone-dry. Where had this nutcase kept her? She's not been interfered with and seems to be in one piece, but she's suffering from exposure. We won't be allowed to talk to her for at least twenty-four hours.' Raymond Land flopped heavily on to the sofa and lit yet another Player's Special. In the last few minutes the acting chief's face had flowered with red blotches. 'Why was she taken at all? Child kidnap motives are sexual, or for ransom. It makes no bloody sense. Do you realize how useless this makes us all look?'

'We can't assume anything until forensic tests have been carried out on her clothes,' said May.

'Do we have any further information on the ice-cream van?'

'It seems to have vanished off the face of the earth.

We're searching all the contract garages and storage arches in London.'

'You realize this could be an entirely separate attack,' said Land. 'Have you considered that, or are you just shoehorning it into your current investigation?'

'It seems unlikely that the Whitstables are being targeted from more than one direction. Daisy's kidnap must be connected. Her dry clothes suggest she was dropped off under the arch, so that she could be found alive.' May shifted to avoid the fountains of smoke funneling from Land's flaring nostrils.

'I've had nothing from you or your partner in two days,' Land reminded him. 'Instead of constructive reports all I get is a list of complaints, first from the Whitstables about your unhelpful attitude and the non-advancement of the case, and then from that whingeing twerp of an arts minister who just wants us to shove the whole thing in a file marked *Solved*. Now we've really stepped up into the big time.' He pulled so hard on his cigarette that it crackled. 'They're going to throw us to the lions, do you realize that? It's more or less the end of our careers. The Home Office have called twice in the last hour. I'm having to hide from them. Don't you have anything at all for me?'

May had seen the look on Raymond's face before, a look of panic under pressure that could only bring more trouble. He was begging for something to release to the media, but how could they help him? They had nothing so far that would stand up as substantive evidence.

Earlier that morning, Bryant had hesitantly described his discovery at the V&A. May could imagine Land's reaction when he informed him that their only suspect was a man who had been dead for nearly a hundred years.

'Bloody cold out,' said Bryant, suddenly breezing in behind his superior. 'Oh, hello, Raymond, what are the barbarians doing at the gates of Rome?'

'What?' asked Land, momentarily nonplussed.

'Journalists.' Bryant waved his hand at the window. 'They're everywhere, bullying receipts out of taxi drivers, crawling all over the place shouting their heads off.'

'Daisy's been found, Arthur,' said May quietly. 'She's alive, barely. They took her into St Thomas's a few hours ago.' He recounted the preliminary findings of the admitting doctor.

'I need to know if you have anything for me,' said Land. 'Whatever I tell the press can't be worse than what they're capable of making up. I can't afford to alienate them any further.'

'It's a little late to worry about that now,' said Bryant. 'They've been accusing us of incompetence for the past fortnight. I suppose John must have mentioned our new lead.'

'I've been explaining that we're following a new line of inquiry,' said May, signaling silence to his partner, 'but that we're not quite ready to present it.'

'What line of inquiry is this?' asked Land, confused. 'If you're keeping anything back from me—' Just then the office door reopened and the two workmen entered armed with cans and buckets. Land turned to glare at them. 'Christ on a bike, do they have to be here all the time?'

'We do if you want these offices finished,' said the older of the two workmen. 'We pack up on Friday for ten days. It's Christmas, mate. Do you know how many layers of paint we've still got to strip off before we can do your sills?'

'Oh, for God's sake,' said Land, grinding out his cigarette and rising.

'At least we're making good use of our time,' said the younger workman. 'Leave it to the working classes to handle all the shitty jobs. At least we've got a sense of duty.'

'Yeah,' agreed his mate. 'Try catching a few criminals instead of telling taxpayers where they can't park.'

'I can't delay speaking to the Home Office any longer. I'm going to tell them that this whole thing will be wrapped up by the end of the week,' said Land, heedless of the breach in security represented by the listening workmen. 'And I'll say the same thing at the press briefing if I have to.'

'Why not give them a hypothetical sequence of events?' asked May. 'Release plenty of facts and figures, all the exact times and dates we've held back, and let them draw their own conclusions. There can't be any harm in that. They might even be able to help us.'

'That's not a bad idea,' agreed Land, a little mollified. 'You'd better talk to them. If you can't arrest anyone, at least you can come up with a plausible explanation as to how this whole damned mess occurred. We must explain that whatever triggered these attacks is finally over and done with.'

'He's going to try and shove it all under the carpet,' said Bryant after the door had shut. 'Wait and see.' He unwound his ratty scarf and dropped it on to a chair. 'Four deaths and an abduction, and he doesn't care about getting to the truth so long as he keeps himself off the hook.'

'He's panicking because someone's pressuring him to put a lid on the whole business,' said May. Understandably, the kidnapping of a child was a highly emotive issue, and the media would wring every last drop of coverage from it. Until now, the biggest story of December had been how Bourne and Hollingsworth were stocking up on candles and oil lamps, ready for the strike blackouts.

'It's a government cover-up, innit?' said one of the workmen. 'Stands to reason. Just like Jack the Ripper.'

'Thank you, Fabian of the Yard,' said Bryant, surveying the mess beyond his desk. Half of the office was now a sickly hospital green, which the workmen were scraping off to reveal orange lincrusta wallpaper from the 1930s.

'This room is starting to make me feel sick,' said May, tossing his partner's hat over to him. 'Let's go.'

'But I've only just come in,' complained Bryant. 'It's thick fog outside.'

'It's not much better in here,' replied May, noting the filled ashtray that Land had left behind. 'Come on. We'll slip out the back and I'll buy you a pint over the road.'

'It's much too early for me.'

'We have to talk where no one can find us.'

The saloon bar of the Nun and Broken Compass was mercifully deserted. Only the disgusting dog that lay half in the fireplace ceased clawing clumps of hair from its ears to briefly register their arrival.

'Two days to make a breakthrough,' said May, returning from the bar with pints of Bishop's Finger. 'The chances of wrapping the whole thing up in forty-eight hours are pretty slim. The city's already half empty. Have you found out anything more on James Whitstable's group?' Bryant's first appointment of the morning had been to conduct further research on the Alliance of Eternal Light.

'Only that his family denies any knowledge of his activities,' said Bryant, relishing his first sip of beer. 'There was a biography of him written in the twenties but the

British Library has no record of it, so Janice is searching through private collections.'

'Everything about this case is upside-down,' complained May. 'We eliminate all the suspects, only to resort to digging through the past. None of the traditional investigative methods work, and any evidence that turns up seems to appear entirely by accident.'

Just then the door opened and Sergeant Longbright stuck her head into the saloon bar. 'Mr Bryant, there you are. Your friend Mr Summerfield called. He wants to see you urgently. He says he's made some kind of discovery.'

The Triumph 250 sat beneath a dripping plane tree, its engine quickly cooling. Joseph slid from the pillion and massaged his rump as Jerry kicked up the stand. She had managed to borrow the motorcycle from a school friend.

'You haven't given me an answer,' Joseph said, shoving his sweater further into his jeans. 'What are you going to say when she opens the door?'

'I'll figure something out. I could introduce you as the photographer who works with me. She's the only lead I have and she certainly knows more than she's told me so far.'

Jerry checked her watch. Nearly nine-thirty P.M. The street behind them was shrouded and silent. The lights were on in Peggy Harmsworth's house, but they had no proof that she was even home.

'I don't see how you expect to extract any more information from her without arousing suspicion. Nobody makes business calls at this hour.' Joseph pulled the sleeves of his leather jacket over his hands. The freezing fog had turned the overhead branches crystalline. This was no night for them to be standing around outside. Seen through the saffron aureoles of the surrounding streetlamps, the Holly Lodge Estate took on the unreality of a film set.

'Either knock on her door or turn around and go home,' he told Jerry. 'Make a decision. My blood's slowing down.' He watched as she stared across the glittering lawn, grinding her teeth. 'Maybe I should go with you.'

'No, I can handle it by myself.' She made a fist.

'So tough. What are you going to do, fetch her a punch up the bracket when she questions you? Assault and battery. Great.'

She was about to reply when the front door opened. After pausing to examine her gold pocket watch in the hallway, Peggy Harmsworth stepped on to the drive in a full-length mink coat and head scarf. They pressed back against the trees as their quarry set off across the estate on foot.

'Get on the bike,' Joseph hissed. 'We can follow her with the engine off.' He kicked away the stand and they mounted the Triumph, rolling silently into the road. Mrs Harmsworth marched purposefully to the far side of the street, then turned into the thickening fog within the cul-de-sac.

'She can't get out of there,' Joseph whispered over her shoulder.

'Maybe she's visiting a neighbour.'

When she reached the end of the road, Peggy Harmsworth skipped between two tall mock-Tudor apartment buildings and faded from sight.

'Damn, there's an alleyway.' After several hundred yards the path opened out onto a hill. On the other side stood the iron gates of Highgate Cemetery.

'Where the hell is she going?' Joseph rolled the

Triumph to a standstill. Ahead of them, Mrs Harmsworth rattled a padlock in her hands and let it drop, passing through a smaller gate set within the large entrance. 'Jesus, she's got her own keys.'

The padlock was refastened on the other side of the railings, and the figure in the mink coat began to retreat once more into the mist.

'We'll lose her if we're not quick,' warned Jerry, helping to lean the motorcycle against a tree. She stowed her helmet in the rear pannier and pocketed the ignition key. Then she headed for the gates.

'Wait a minute,' said Joseph. He had agreed to go with Jerry to ask this woman a few friendly questions, not follow her into a graveyard. 'We can't get in there, and even if we could—'

Too late. Jerry was already halfway over the gate.

High heels clicked on cement as the mink coat moved through the thickening fog. They followed as closely as they dared, the cemetery gates lost somewhere behind them. The main path was illuminated to deter dope-smoking hippies, but the light barely reached the ground.

Mrs Harmsworth switched from the main route on to a smaller path that led uphill, through a less accessible part of the cemetery. Jerry and Joseph could barely keep pace with her. Here, new graves gave way to the older family vaults.

Despite their general air of neglect, several monuments had fresh wreaths at their feet. As she passed, Jerry glimpsed the half-eroded epitaphs. There were Germanic Victorian names and grim little platitudes carved in stone, children 'Joyously Accepted into the Bosom of the Lord' as if death were a privilege; adults 'Departing This Vale of Tears for Eternal Peace.' She sensed lives of dutiful toil passed in the anticipation of acceptance into a golden kingdom. She saw crumbling monuments to the Victorian conviction of everlasting life. And she watched as Peggy Harmsworth stopped before an ivy-stranded mock-Grecian mausoleum of disproportionate immensity.

Instinctively dropping from sight, Jerry knelt behind a gravestone. Seeing her, Joseph did the same. Mrs Harmsworth descended the few stone steps and produced another key, inserting it into the portal. She shoved back the door, stepped inside, and pulled it half-shut behind her. Jerry mouthed, 'Now what?'

'Wait,' Joseph signaled back.

The chill settled about them. Water droplets coated Jerry's jacket in a gelid frost. Far in the distance a lorry laboured up the hill, engine noise fading in the encroaching silence. A light showed faintly through the doorway of the crypt.

'What can she be doing in there?' Joseph whispered. Somewhere nearby, a branch broke beneath a shoe. They looked at each other and dived back behind their respective gravestones. A figure appeared beside the crypt, moving with a spiderlike gait, a man wearing a brown slouch hat and a tattered greatcoat. As he paused before the door, Jerry looked over at her accomplice, puzzled.

After waiting for a moment or two at the entrance, the tattered man stepped through the gap, entering the crypt. Barely able to contain her excitement, Jerry ran over. 'That's the man,' she said. 'The one who attacked me in the theatre. At least, I think it is.' Uncertainty nagged at her.

'Well, is it or not?'

'He's dressed the same, but—he's a lot taller.'

'Great,' said Joseph. 'A murderer who changes height. Why not?' He rose, exasperated. 'Why not add it to the rest? Add it to the vandalism, explosions, and poisonings. What *is* it with you, anyway? If you're so scared of the dark, what the hell are we doing in a *graveyard at night*?'

Before she could think of a reply, there was a guttural grunt followed by a squeal, and the door of the crypt was shoved open. As they ran towards it, the tattered man emerged. Peggy Harmsworth had fallen to the floor of the mausoleum and was thrashing from side to side. Joseph ran down the crypt steps towards her, only to slip over in the blood that had been smeared across the flagstones.

The tattered man threw something aside as he ran, an instrument that shone with a steel edge. Jerry closed in behind him, running hard. The figure in front moved quickly across the slick grass between the gravesites, coattails flapping behind. For an instant, the tunnel of trees and the fleeing dark figure threw her back into the searing panic of her nightmares and she stumbled, slamming her hip against a memorial slab.

By the time she had pulled herself up and resumed her pursuit, the tattered man had almost reached the main gate. Jerry ran back on to the path and limped toward the cemetery entrance, just as he flew at the lock with a kick that smashed open the small gate through which Peggy Harmsworth had entered. Then he dashed across the road, hauling himself into a small white van parked at the side of the road. Seconds later, Jerry reached the Triumph and painfully straddled it, keying the ignition.

The van pulled away down the hill with a squeal of skipping tyres. Jerry jerked out into the road, her crash helmet still locked in the rear pannier. The bitter wind tore at her skin, blasting aside rational thought. Although she'd borrowed the bike before, she'd never ridden it at high speed. She tried to keep the van in her sight, but the fog grew thicker with their descent.

Van and motorcycle shot across one junction, then another. The roads were virtually deserted this close to Christmas. For the moment no other vehicle appeared in their way. Then the van swung right so hard that it seemed it would topple over, and cut across the path of an oncoming bus.

Sounding her horn, Jerry skidded in an arc around the vehicle, mounting the pavement but holding her position behind the van. Together they raced over Dartmouth Park Road and down towards the city.

She tried to pull out ahead of the van, intending to force it over, but the blinking amber lights of open road-works warned her back. Her quarry was still picking up speed.

Jerry knew that if she jumped the lights, collision with another vehicle would be unavoidable. The only way to cut off the van would be to do it right now. She twisted the throttle, opening it wide, praying that her tyres would keep their grip on the shining road surface.

In the next moment she had drawn alongside the van. The figure within had opened his window and was waving something in his hand. As soon as she saw the shotgun, Jerry's grip on the bike throttle instinctively relaxed, and the Triumph fell back, wheels slipping as they tried to bite on wet tarmac.

They hit Kentish Town Road at seventy-seven miles per hour. An oncoming Peugeot and a Morris Minor swerved as the van burst from the fog, catching the first car by the front bumper and spinning it into the path of the other. Jerry pushed ahead as the van struggled to right itself, taking to the oncoming lane of the road as she raced towards the red and green Christmas lights of Camden.

The Triumph drew along the inside of the van, and then into the lead. As the van's radiator grille touched her rear mudguard, she knew that the driver was planning to push her off the road. The grille slammed against her back wheel as the van accelerated.

A crowd of pub-crawling revelers scattered in their path. Jerry swung the bike aside, resuming her position at the rear of the speeding vehicle. It was a stalemate.

Where the hell were the police when you actually wanted to be pulled over? They usually swarmed all over the West End at Christmas. Jerry's face and hands were dead, her fingers locked and frozen, her eyes stinging from the intensity of staring into the pulsing fog. She was surprised at how well she handled the bike, but knew she would have to stop before she killed herself, or some-one else.

The van began to slow down.

Jerry eased back as it cut through the red lights of an intersection, ploughing across Camden High Street into Delancy Street. She suddenly realized that the driver was lost. The tattered man had missed his turning somewhere and no longer recognized his surroundings.

As she tore on to the empty streets circling the railway lines above the city, she knew that the van would have to stop. Here in this corner of North London, all the roads were effectively sealed off by the tangled network of rail tracks fanning out fifty feet below them. There was no way to safety. The triangular area beyond was known to locals as the Island, hemmed in on each side by Regent's Park, the railway, and the canal systems.

The van was in trouble. Following raids, getaway cars usually turned left because they followed the traffic flow.

Her quarry was doing the same thing. They tore into the street, and Jerry knew that it was over. Ahead was a brick wall, a humpbacked pedestrian bridge, and a long drop to the railway tracks. There was everything but a road.

The van slammed its brakes on hard, to no avail. The vehicle continued to charge forward, fishtailing over tarmac as if the brakes had not even been applied. It hit the metal fencing beside the wall and uprooted two concrete posts. For a moment Jerry thought that the chickenwire might hold. Then the van tore through, the fence screaming over its roof, and slid down the embankment to the lines below.

She had just pulled the bike over and dismounted, planning to head down into the cutting, when blue lights reflected on the walls ahead, and she turned to find herself facing a pair of arriving squad cars.

As Joseph ran down into the Whitstable family crypt to attend to Peggy Harmsworth, the door was pulled shut behind him and an oppressive darkness closed over his senses.

For a moment he heard and saw nothing, nothing at all. Now he knew how Jerry must feel in the dark. There was someone else breathing right next to him. With a shrill shriek of laughter Peggy thrust out her hands, raking her fingernails across his face, spinning him away from the faint light around the entrance. His legs slipped from under him and he hit the stone floor heavily. She leapt on to his back, pulling at his hair, trying to dig her fingers into his eye sockets.

He lashed out at her throat, or where he imagined it to be, and hit stone instead. Trying to force her body away from him, he moved towards the door, but his sense of direction had been confounded.

Before he could think further she was upon him again, shouting laughter in his face, digging her nails into his skin, sinking her teeth into his shoulder, kicking and screaming and lashing him with her hair like an inmate of Bedlam.

As he fought for the door, blinded by his own blood, carrying the ranting maniac on his back, it seemed that he had left the realm of the sane to enter someone else's nightmare. He fell painfully to his knees as the mad-woman dug deeper into him, screaming and howling in an echo chamber of her own insanity.

27 / Guilty Parties

Welcome back, Miss Gates,' said May wearily. 'We had almost begun to miss you.'

Jerry wanted desperately to lie down and go to sleep. It was after midnight, and she ached like hell. A few minutes ago she had rung Gwen from the station pay phone, and the call had quickly disintegrated into a shouting match. The last thing she wanted now was an official interrogation as well as a parental one.

'Where's Joseph?' she asked, her voice hardly rising above a croak.

'Your friend is next door,' said Bryant. 'He's all right, no thanks to you. Congratulations, we don't often find you in the company of live people.'

'Can I have a cup of tea? I can't talk.'

May eyed her suspiciously for a moment, then opened the door and spoke to someone. 'You can have a shot of brandy in it,' he told her, 'only because it's Christmas. This had better be good. I was about to go home when they brought you in.'

May pulled out a chair for his partner. 'Peggy Harmsworth was attacked in her family vault in Highgate Cemetery.'

'My God, is she dead?' Bryant asked.

'No, but she's of little use to us as she is.'

'Why?'

'She appears to have taken a vacation from reality.

They took her away tied to a stretcher, raving about the power of the moon.'

'What was she doing in a vault, for heaven's sake?'

'I really have no idea, but guess what? This young lady was on hand to apprehend her murderer. In case you're not keeping score, this is the third life-threatening experience Miss Gates has managed to witness. If you ever lose your job at the Savoy, you might consider becoming one of the Four Horsemen of the Apocalypse, Miss Gates. The full gory details, please.'

Jerry tried to explain how she and Joseph had come to be there, but to do that she found herself having to backtrack to the blackmailing of Kaneto Miyagawa and the withdrawal of the Japanese consortium from the Savoy to make way for Peggy Harmsworth's theatre society. Which meant explaining everything that had happened to her, including the assault in the theatre.

May looked angrier the more he heard. Bryant nodded every once in a while, suggesting that he had guessed as much already.

'So you deliberately withheld information from us.' Bryant sighed. 'I thought you had more brains than this.'

'Mr Herrick has been quite taken aback by the events of the evening,' said May. 'The poor bloke thought he was helping you by going along with your half-baked plans. Instead he spent his evening shut inside a crypt being mauled by a madwoman. Luckily one of the door bolts was out and it couldn't swing completely shut, otherwise no one would have known he was inside. There's a guard living on the premises, and he raised the alarm.'

'You should be pleased,' said Jerry hotly. 'I caught your murderer. I saw him run out of the crypt seconds after he attacked Mrs Harmsworth.'

'You think he also murdered Max Jacob?' asked May.

'Yes.'

'And Peter, William, and Bella Whitstable?'

'Well—yes.'

'What about kidnapping Daisy Whitstable? He did that as well?'

'Probably. Ask him.'

'He's also the one who assaulted you at the theatre?'

'I suppose so.' Jerry faltered.

'You don't sound too sure.'

'Well, he's much taller than I remember. Different looking, thinner.'

'Good,' said May, draining his tea. 'I thought for a minute you'd solved the entire investigation and we could all go home.'

His sarcastic tone bothered Jerry. It seemed out of character.

'You're holding him in custody, aren't you?' she asked. 'You didn't let him get away?'

'He couldn't exactly run off,' replied May. 'Seeing as both his legs were broken. He fell out of the van as it bounced down the embankment, where it finally came to rest on his head.'

'He's not dead, is he?'

'Very.'

'Was he a member of the family?' Jerry asked nervously. 'Was he a Whitstable?'

'No, he was a gentleman from India. A window-cleaner.'

'*What?*'

'You obviously didn't read the side of Mr Denjhi's van.'

'You mean he didn't do it? But I saw him—' Jerry was aghast.

'We won't know what he did until the body has been

blood-typed and fingerprinted, and his clothes have been sent to a forensic lab. There's a bit of a queue these days. There are still several Whitstables in the line ahead of him. But there's certainly no reason to assume that he has any connection with the other murders.'

'He *has* to be the one,' said Jerry desperately. 'It said in the papers that the man who abducted the little girl was driving a white van. I saw him leave the crypt, we both did. It *couldn't* have been anyone else.'

'Did you get a good look at him?'

'No, not exactly. His head and shoulders were in shadow.'

'What I fail to understand,' said Bryant, 'is what you were hoping to achieve by following Peggy Harmsworth. All right, you thought you could get your friend compensation for losing his job. There had to be an easier way of doing that, surely? The motorcycle isn't registered in your name. Then there's a charge of reckless driving. Do you have insurance?'

'No.'

'How about a licence?'

'No.'

'Foolish of me to ask. You really think you can screw us about, don't you?'

Jerry shifted uncomfortably on her seat. 'The man was trying to kill me.'

'What is it that keeps you coming back?' asked Bryant. 'You always manage to be in the right place at the right time. Is it merely a ghoulish interest in police procedure, or were you planning to trap the killer by yourself?'

Jerry wanted to describe how she felt, but in the harsh light of the crime unit's interview room, she knew her explanation would sound foolish.

May was watching her. 'Tell me about your family, Jerry,' he said, sensing something unspoken between them.

'Family.' She shook her head, as if failing to recognize the word. 'If you met them you'd understand. Gwen's been following the whole thing in the papers. She really admires the Whitstables. My father's company even worked for them once. They represent everything my parents aspire to, and I'm supposed to be like them. The Whitstables know what's going on. Families like that always do. They're just trying to protect themselves from something they don't want to face.'

'And if the Whitstables are discredited, your parents won't admire them any more,' concluded May. 'They want to decide your career, but you won't let them.'

Jerry didn't answer. She could hear Gwen now. *Look at my daughter. She was a problem child, but she has a business head on her shoulders—she has real family spirit.*

She wanted to see the Whitstable family fall into disgrace. Then perhaps Gwen and Jack would be forced to put their faith in her, the daughter who had exposed them.

'You'll be interviewed by the Met about your involvement in the accident that killed Mr Denjhi,' Bryant told her. 'They'll decide what to do with you, not us. But we can protect you to some extent by placing you under our supervision. For the record, I happen to agree with you. I think the Whitstables are deliberately hiding knowledge of something that is causing all this to happen. Daisy's parents have already refused to let anyone interview her. Nobody will talk openly to us.'

'I could get you inside information,' said Jerry, sitting forward.

'Out of the question,' said Bryant.

'You said they won't talk to you, but they might to me.'

'Go home, Jerry. Get some sleep.' Bryant rubbed his forehead wearily. 'You'll be contacted in due course. Until then, you do nothing, understand?'

They watched as the girl was escorted from the room. 'Involving her would be taking a terrible risk,' warned May.

His partner waved the suggestion aside. 'I have a feeling she'll continue whether we sanction her or not.'

'It doesn't look like we're going to get any sleep tonight,' May warned.

Bryant wound his scarf pythonlike around his neck. There was no point in going off duty when the body of Peggy Harmsworth's attacker waited in the morgue. 'In a world like this, only the innocent can afford to sleep. Let's go and wake Oswald Finch. Nobody rests while I'm up. Tell me about Peggy Harmsworth.'

'She was taken to the Royal Free Hospital, sedated, and placed under observation. She assaulted the ambulance men and bit one of the nurses. Screaming and laughing, suffering the effects of a hallucinogenic drug, they think.'

'At least *someone*'s having a merry Christmas.'

'That's an extremely tasteless remark, Arthur. They're pumping her stomach without knowing what she's taken. That's what this case needed on top of murder and kidnap—a madwoman in a cemetery.'

'Wait a minute...' Bryant's eyes widened gleefully. 'Of course! *"Mad, I? Yes, very? But why? Mystery!"*' he cried suddenly.

'What on earth are you on about?'

'Peggy's another name for Margaret, isn't it?'

'I suppose it is. Why?'

'Don't you see? She's become Mad Margaret. An in-·
sane woman, creeping through a darkened graveyard. A
character from *Ruddigore*. It's Gilbert and Sullivan again.'

As she was escorted back along the corridor, Jerry peered
through the window of the next office and spotted
Joseph. He lay curled up on a row of seats, wrapped in a
heavy grey blanket with his huge boots sticking out of the
end. His eyes were closed, his face framed by a corona of
wild hair. He looked like Burne-Jones's painting of
Perseus, except he was covered in scratches and bruises,
had a bloody nose, and was black.

She wanted to place her arms around him and kiss the
curve of his bandaged neck, to be wrapped in his sleeping
warmth. She wanted to tell him things she had never told
any man. He would probably never want to speak to her
again. She had done nothing but cause him trouble. It felt
as if she had never given anyone reason to admire or even
like her. Perhaps it was too late.

She stayed beyond the smeared glass for a moment
more, then followed the officer out on to the freezing
street.

28 / Visited by Devils

David Balbir Denjhi, aged twenty-nine, was survived by a wife and three children, Janice Longbright noted as she pulled back a corner of her hastily compiled background file. He and his young bride had met in London, having both emigrated to England with their respective parents. David had clashed with the legal system several times, first with tax inspectors over a filed claim for company bankruptcy, then over an accusation of handling stolen goods. This had attracted the unwelcome attentions of the immigration authorities, but he'd come through the ordeal and had satisfactorily proved his right to remain in the country.

The woman seated before Longbright seemed calm and sensible. If she had been crying earlier, she gave no sign of it. Mrs Denjhi poured coffee and sat back in her chair, waiting to be asked more questions. The sergeant knew that her life had become a nightmare, culminating in the identification of her husband's body. Sirina Denjhi had spent several hours making statements to the police, and now faced another interview. Matters would not improve for her; soon she would receive the less sympathetic attention of the press.

'I must understand what happened to my husband,' said Sirina softly.

Standard interview procedure dictated that the sergeant could not reveal details of the investigation in progress, even if she felt that doing so would facilitate the discussion. Instead she concentrated on David Denjhi's background.

'Our families had known each other in India,' Sirina explained, 'and although our marriage was not arranged it was understood that one day we might wed. Our parents were business partners, you see.'

'What kind of business were they in?' asked Longbright.

'Exporting silk. At first it was very successful, but then David's father died. Our money was invested in a business that went bankrupt. We lost everything. David was a good father, a good provider. He worked hard to keep his company afloat, still dreaming that one day his children would run it. But it was not to be.' She folded her hands in her lap, looking away.

'Tell me what happened after the company collapsed.'

'David set up the window-cleaning firm. He was expanding it, taking on office contracts. His head was filled with ideas.'

'Did your husband have many friends?'

'We were his friends. His family. He had no others. People saw him in the street, at his job, but I don't suppose they really saw him. People don't, you understand? They don't notice us. We go about our work, we spend time with our families, but to most English people we're quite invisible. The hostile ones see us, of course. The others are neither angry nor happy that we're here—just disinterested. When we came to this country, we thought we had left the castes behind, but we hadn't. We simply became a new one.'

Silence settled in the room. 'We need to talk about David's disappearance,' Longbright said. 'I know you've already made a statement, but I must ask you to think harder. You say he'd been troubled...'

Sirina Denjhi withdrew a handkerchief from her sari and dabbed her nose. 'That's right. It was on Friday morning. The devil was in him. He would not go to work, and he would not tell me why. He was furious with the children. Our youngest daughter broke a saucer, and he slapped her face. He had never raised his hand in violence before. His mood grew worse and worse. Finally, just after ten in the morning, he stormed out without a word.'

'You asked him where he was going?'

'Of course, but he gave me no reply. I watched from the window as he drove off in the van.'

'Had he ever done anything like this?'

'No, never.'

'And the name Peggy Harmsworth, he'd never mentioned it to you?'

Sirina shook her head. She turned her amber eyes to the sergeant. 'You must find out why this terrible thing happened. Perhaps he was possessed. All I know is that we have been visited by devils, and there will be no rest for us until we know the truth.'

By lunchtime the blustery day had swept the sky clean of cloud, and the two detectives sat in the operations room at Mornington Crescent bathed in winter sunshine. Bryant was trying hard to stay awake, but the long hours were beginning to take their toll. They were awaiting the preliminary forensic report on David Denjhi's body.

'You haven't found any connection at all between Denjhi and the Whitstables?' Bryant asked May.

'Not on the surface, but it's conceivable the families had crossed paths in business. I'll have to go through Denjhi's company records. And I'll see if he'd ever had window-cleaning appointments at any of the Whitstable houses. God, Arthur, a window-cleaner. It doesn't make sense.' He shoved the folder away from him. 'Jerry saw him leave the crypt seconds after Mrs Harmsworth screamed, so there's no doubt about who attacked her.'

'It's in,' called Longbright, walking briskly between the typewriters with a pair of document pouches in her hand. Bryant was charmed by his glamorous sergeant, just as he had been by her mother so many years earlier. Last night, without a word of complaint, she had stayed with them through the shift in order to help clear the backlog of interviews. 'Finch wasn't going to release it without speaking to you first, but I managed to persuade him.'

'You know what that means,' said Bryant, accepting the papers. 'He must have found some positive matches. No one else knows about this yet, do they?'

'I'm afraid he's already copied in Raymond Land, Sir.'

'Bugger, there goes our head start.' Bryant yanked open the first document pouch. 'I haven't got my glasses. Could you decipher?'

May took the papers. 'We've got multiple matches. Fingerprints all over the crypt, and on the knife Denjhi threw into the grass. For some reason he decided not to use it on her. Peggy Harmsworth's blood on the crypt floor, and on Denjhi's shirt and trousers. It looks as if she banged her head in the struggle. Keys fitting the crypt found on his body. No positive matches with the other deaths, but it's early days yet. They need to check with the partials found on segments of the bomb that killed Peter Whitstable.' He pulled out another carbon.

'Definitely no match with the prints we found on the razor from the Savoy barbershop, though. So we're dealing with at least two different killers. Oh, and Finch confirms that Denjhi died at the accident site.'

'You can tell a man is dead by sticking his finger in your ear,' recalled Bryant unhelpfully. 'If you put your own finger in your ear you hear a buzz from tiny muscle movements.'

'Two or more murderers,' mused May. 'I suppose it fits in with your Victorian conspiracy theory, not that it makes a blind bit of sense. Anything new to report on that front?'

'I've got some people working on it.'

'A couple of clairvoyants and a palmist, no doubt.'

'There's no reason why you should place more faith in technical wizardry than in the supernatural.'

'Technology is about accurate prediction, which is more than can be said for your crystal-ball merchants. I know you've been seeing them again, Arthur, don't pretend that you haven't.'

Just then the overhead lights momentarily dimmed. 'So much for the reliability of science,' said Bryant with a mocking smile. 'We're not much good without electricity, are we? Suddenly we're back in the Dark Ages, telling ghost stories in front of the fire. Janice, your interview with Mrs Denjhi was very thorough, but there's still one thing I need to know. Where did he get the money?'

'I'm sorry, Sir?'

'Denjhi lost everything when his company collapsed. You can't start a new one without capital outlay. Find out where he got the cash.'

The telephone rang, and Bryant answered it. 'I just wanted to be the first to offer my congratulations to you and your colleagues,' Faraday bellowed. The junior arts minister sounded extremely cheerful. 'A job well done, I'd say. I haven't received your full report yet, of course, so if you'd—'

'I have no idea what you're talking about,' snapped Bryant, although a terrible thought was forming in his mind.

'Catching our vandal,' Faraday explained. 'The news couldn't have come at a better time. Things were getting pretty sticky with the Aussies, I can tell you.'

Suddenly the realization dawned on Bryant. Raymond Land had read the report and had immediately contacted the Home Office. Faraday seemed to have assumed that with the death of a confirmed assassin, all loose ends connected to the vandalism of the loaned Waterhouse painting were now tied up. It was essential for Land to prove that the new unit was getting results; it had been funded for an initial eight-week trial period.

Bryant knew he would be expected to back up his superior. He also knew that he could not do so without compromising everything he believed in.

'I'm sorry to disappoint you, Mr Faraday,' he said finally. 'We've confirmed the identity of the person who assaulted Mrs Harmsworth last night, but that's all.'

'How can that be? I don't understand,' said Faraday with an anguished squeak.

'Put simply, there's a murderer very much at large.'

'You mean you still don't know who he is?'

'Worse than that,' replied Bryant. 'There's more than one. And we don't know who *they* are.'

29 / Brotherhood

After a night of bad dreams, Arthur Bryant arose unrefreshed and sat on the end of his bed, trying to order his thoughts. He hated to admit it, but they had failed. Failed the public, failed themselves. He had not felt this depressed in years. The pestilence attacking the Whitstable family would try to run its course before they could discover its root. Checking the notes he had left for himself on the bedside table, he rang Jerry Gates at her home. An icy-voiced woman, presumably her mother, asked him to hold. A minute later, Jerry picked up the phone.

'Yesterday you mentioned something about your father working for the Whitstables,' said Bryant.

'That's right, he had contracts with a couple of their companies.'

'There's something you could do for me.'

'Anything. Just name it.'

'You could find out about the people he deals with. I realize this might involve a certain disloyalty to your father. I need documentation concerning deals with silk manufacturers and exporters in Calcutta and Bombay. You might talk to your father and find out if he's seen or heard anything unusual. You know the investigation almost as well as we do. You should know what to ask, and what to look for.'

'Don't worry about that. I'll get on to it right away.'

'Call me if you find anything, anything at all. Do you have the number of my direct line?'

'No.'

'Neither do I. It's written down somewhere . . .'

'I'll find you, don't worry,' she promised.

The morning had dawned cold and dull, the weather Bryant loathed the most. His appointment with Peregrine Summerfield was set for nine A.M. He would walk as far as Vauxhall Bridge, then hail a cab. It was a pity the trams had stopped running in 1952; one used to pass right by the front door of his building. He missed the hiss and crackle of the gliding cars.

That was the difference between himself and May. John had no attachment to the past, sentimental or otherwise. He was interested in moving on. He saw life as a linear progression, a series of lessons to be learned, all extraneous information to be tossed away, a continual streamlining of ideas.

Bryant collected the detritus of historical data as naturally as an anchor accumulates barnacles. He couldn't help it; the past was as fascinating as a classic beauty, infinitely fathomable and for ever out of reach. But this was one secret he was determined to lay bare. He would stake his life on the answer lying in the Whitstable family's burst of good fortune at the end of the last century. Could there really have been an event of such magnitude that it involved an entire dynasty? A moment of such far-reaching consequence that even now, nearly a hundred years later, it was reaping a revenge of misery and destruction?

As he reached the eastern edge of the park, a phrase resounded in his head. *The sons shall be visited with the sins of the fathers.* James Whitstable and his kindred Olympian spirits, the Seven Stewards of Heaven. The Inner Circle.

The Alliance of Eternal Light. They were one and the same. How the Victorians loved their secret societies, their gentlemen's clubs and hermetic orders, their table-rappings, recitals, and rituals, gatherings primarily designed to *exclude*.

Was that it? Who had James Makepeace Whitstable and his friends wanted to exclude this time? Their society of seven was no mere parlour game for the menfolk, somewhere to escape from family responsibilities. Their alliance was built *within the family itself*.

If its purpose was not to exclude, then it must be to protect.

To protect the lives of the Whitstable clan? No, these men were well respected and powerful. They would have made dangerous enemies. What else might they have wanted to protect? Their money? Wasn't that far more likely? He looked out at the Thames, a curving olive ribbon two hundred and fifteen miles long, flowing back and forth with the pulse of the moon.

The art historian was late, as usual. Summerfield was sporting the traditional English art-history uniform: an ancient tweed jacket with leather elbow patches, a brown woolly tie, baggy corduroy trousers, and battered loafers, presumably intended to identify him to civilians in the event of an art emergency. He noisily hailed Arthur across the forecourt of the Royal Academy in a shower of pipe ash, then clapped him on the back as they entered Burlington House together.

Although he had been a regular visitor in his youth, Arthur had not called at the Academy for quite a while, and was pleased to find it unchanged, Michelangelo's spectacular Carrara marble tondo of *The Madonna and Child with the Infant Saint John* occupying its traditional space. Every accepted member of the foundation submitted a piece of his or her work to the Academy as a gift, with the result that Reynolds, Gainsborough, Constable, and Turner were all represented on its walls. The Academy's summer exhibition, an event of unparalleled blandness open to all artists irrespective of nationality or training, had been dismaying critics for more than two centuries.

'Glad you could make it,' boomed Summerfield, looking about them. 'Some halfway decent pictures are hung around these walls. Y'know, this business of yours has got me hooked. The Waterhouse study is being authenticated downstairs. I told them it's genuine but they insist on checking for themselves. Tosspots.'

They descended a winding marble staircase that led to the workrooms where paintings and sculptures were unpacked and studied. Summerfield pushed open a door marked *Access By Appointment Only* and led the way across a large white studio, one wall of which consisted of opaque backlit glass, to a cluttered wooden bench, on which lay the study Bryant had discovered in Bella Whitstable's basement.

'Tell me what relevance you imagine this picture having to our investigation,' he asked, watching as the historian lowered his bulk on to a corner of the bench. 'Beyond the fact that one of the victims defaced it, I mean.'

'Ah, I think you understand why I've asked you here,' replied Summerfield. 'I wondered if you'd see it first.'

Arthur stood before the study and examined it once more. Although just two thirds of the five-foot-long picture had been blocked with colour and all but two of the figures were only roughly delineated, the formal structure of Waterhouse's finished painting could easily be discerned.

'Perhaps I should explain my thinking,' said Arthur,

picking up a paintbrush and running his thumb across the sable tip. 'At an early point in the investigation I became convinced that the answer lay in the Whitstable family's past. There was a madness of purpose that suggested a curious kind of Victorian sensibility at work. Each death has been achieved with grotesque flair, an oddness beyond anything we find in our bright, modern world. Naturally my partner doesn't agree, so I've been forced to go it alone.'

He paused to scratch his broad nose with the end of the brush. 'I only had a vague date, some time at the beginning of the 1880s, and a number, seven. Seven men in an alliance, six courtiers and an emperor gathered in a painting. I tried to imagine seven wealthy businessmen, heads of a successful trading family, forming themselves into a society that would protect their self-made fortunes from harm, a society with an acceptable public face, and perhaps less reputable private pastimes. But how would they commemorate its inception without drawing attention? What would the traditional Victorian do?'

'Commission a painting,' said Summerfield.

'Exactly. Your comment about Victorians smuggling sex on to their parlour walls in the form of mythological paintings gave me the idea. But there is a problem with the theory. When the details of this club—The Alliance of Eternal Light—finally came to light, I found that its foundation date was some time in 1881. And you say that Waterhouse produced his painting at the end of 1883. I have a two-year discrepancy in the dates...'

'I can explain that easily,' said Summerfield. 'The first oil sketch for *Emperor Honorius* was knocked out on a manky old bit of board less than a foot square in 1882, and there was probably a gestation period predating that.

So it could easily have been commissioned by your alliance. But you've got a bigger problem to think about.'

'What?'

'Well, look at it,' said Summerfield, waving at the study. 'If this really was commissioned to celebrate the founding of a new alliance, it doesn't do a very good job. Think of the subject matter. What the finished painting shows is a society out of control. Honorius's councillors can't get his attention because he's too busy pissing about with his birds. I told you before—as the supreme ruler of an empire, he was a plonker of the first order.' Summerfield sucked his whiskers, thinking. 'Suppose this bloke Whitstable chose Waterhouse for the painting, and then the artist discovered something unpleasant about his patron? Talk about having your cake and eating it! Waterhouse got to keep the commission by producing this wonderful, satisfying piece of work, and the artist got back at his patron through the insulting classical allusion contained within the picture.'

'There's no way of proving that.'

'Perhaps not, until you remember what the finished painting looked like.' Summerfield scrabbled beneath the study and produced a crumpled colour photocopy, which he proceeded to flatten out on a cleared part of the bench.

'Here,' he said, pointing at the copy. 'Remember I told you that the key character changes? In the study, the central figure is the emperor's attendant. In the end result, he's been relegated to the background. The former picture shows a group of men in repose. The allusion is greatly reduced in terms of offence. The latter shows a master surrounded by sycophants. It's as if Waterhouse was intending to have a gentle dig at his patron, as many artists did, but then—some time between 1882 and

1883—discovered that the situation was far worse than he had imagined. So he changed the finished picture.'

'James Whitstable was an educated man, by all accounts. Surely he would have understood the allusion and taken offence?'

'I think that's exactly what happened. The painting was sold to an Australian gallery soon after its completion. Waterhouse remained true to his ethical code. He produced a magnificent work of art. He simply went too far.'

'Which helps to explain why William Whitstable threw acid on the picture. The painting was an affront to his ancestor, and by extension to his entire family. It was the first time it had been exhibited in this country for a century.'

'I have another "seven" for you,' added Summerfield. 'John Waterhouse was a Royal Academy painter. The Pre-Raphaelite Brotherhood was begun by seven men. Rossetti, Millais, Holman Hunt, and four others dedicated themselves to a "childlike submission to nature." The actress Ellen Terry once told Bernard Shaw that she always visited Burne-Jones at his studio when it was foggy, because he looked so angelic painting by candlelight. Subsequently the group was joined by many other artists, and Oscar Wilde started poncing around with his sacred lily, wetting himself over the Pre-Raff sensibility because it neatly fitted in with the fact that he was horribly camp. It didn't help having a fat old queen as a spokesperson, even a brilliant one, and pretty soon everyone started taking the piss out of the Pre-Raffs.'

'Including Gilbert and Sullivan...'

'That's right. One of their productions parodied the Pre-Raphaelite Brotherhood.'

'...at the Savoy Theatre.' Arthur reached for his cap

and adjusted it on his head. 'Peregrine, I can't tell you what a help you've been.'

'Let me know how you get on,' shouted the historian. 'I want to see how this one turns out.'

But by then his friend had already left the gallery workroom.

30 / Machinery in Motion

Her eyes flicked wildly back and forth, searching the darkness for demons. The wall clock read four fifty-five A.M. She forced herself to focus on it, driving out the hallucinations. A nurse would call to check on her in five minutes. Perhaps she could find some way of communicating her pain. The muscles in her arms and legs felt like twisting bundles of hot wires. Her brain seared with hellish images. Five more minutes. It wasn't long to have to hold on.

'Mad Margaret' lay in the psychiatric ward of the Royal Free Hospital, not a stone's throw from the cemetery where she'd been attacked. Her teeth were covered with soft rubber shields to prevent her from chewing through her tongue. Restraining straps crossed her chest and pelvis, locking her into the bed. She wanted to scream, to tell them she was not mad. She feared they would take her frantic signaling as proof of insanity.

Three minutes to go. She tried counting to a hundred, remembering the names of TV programmes, anything to stay awake and aware, at least until—

Moments before the nurse entered the room to check on her patient, Peggy Harmsworth slipped into a coma, as the chemicals ravaged her nervous system with renewed force and filled her sleep with unimaginable nightmares.

* * *

Ever since the murders had been reported in the newspapers, Gwen Gates had gone out of her way to avoid any mention of them. This morning, Jerry had interrupted her father's breakfast to draw attention to the subject, only to hear Gwen hurriedly change the conversation to something less controversial. Jerry looked around the dining room, at the cut-crystal candlesticks set on the polished mahogany table, at the cherub-encrusted mirror above the marble mantelpiece, at the sheer weight and age of the household, and hated the permanence of what she saw.

Everything her parents owned was built to outlive them. Her father had told her that 'One doesn't buy furniture, one inherits it.' They were pleased to think of themselves as snobs; it meant they had standards worth preserving. Unable to have any more children after the birth of their disastrous daughter, her parents were determined to leave something of value behind.

Jerry wondered what her mother would say if she knew there was a spy in their midst. Right now, she was waiting for them to leave the house so that she could begin a search of her father's private study. She had seen Jack clipping newspaper articles, but what did he do with them? She felt sure she would find something interesting in his desk.

If the Whitstables recognized the cause of their destruction, wouldn't they take steps to prevent further deaths occurring? What could the family have done that was so terrible they were still being persecuted for it?

The slamming of the front door as her father left was the only signal she needed to begin burrowing from within. Jack's study was his private domain. The door was never locked, but it was understood that no one should enter uninvited.

The book-lined room was richly textured with inlaid wooden panels. A Victorian escritoire stood on a heavy Chinese rug near the far window. Along one wall stood a pair of Georgian side tables, one of them supporting a nondescript marble bust of Disraeli. A blue crystal ashtray was filled with butts. It was the one room in the house where Jack was permitted to smoke his cigars.

Jerry made her way over to the desk and tried the drawers. None was locked. She removed the contents from each in turn and studied them, but found nothing of interest.

When she was younger she had often wondered what her father was doing in his study all afternoon. Riffling through the bills and business correspondence, she saw now that Jack had used the place as a refuge from his wife. Suddenly the room seemed less exotic, diminished by mundane matters.

She pulled out the lowest drawer, expecting nothing more than correspondence. Instead, she found an old photograph of her mother, in her early twenties. She was standing in a garden with a cluster of anemones in one hand, smiling tightly, shading her eyes from the sun. Jerry had never seen the picture before. It was hard to believe that her mother had ever been this young.

As she studied the picture, she realized that another quality shone through it. Gwen looked happy to be alive. She radiated joy. Before the thwarted ambition, the bitterness and the recriminations, she had been attractive and carefree. Then had come a series of setbacks: the knowledge that she could have no more children; the fading of Jack's interest in her; and the contemptuous, destructive anger of her only daughter.

Suddenly Jerry was filled with remorse for the grief she had caused her family.

'My God, it's cold in here,' complained Bryant, clapping his arms around his shoulders. 'If I'd known I was going to be standing in a crypt on Christmas Eve I'd have worn a thicker vest. Did you see the crowds waiting outside the main gate?'

The detectives were attending a prayer-giving for Daisy Whitstable at St Peter's Church, Highgate. They had returned to the nearby vault where Peggy Harmsworth had been attacked, to take another look at the scene of the attack. The forensic team had finished their work, but the area was still closed off to the public. The site was attracting ghoulish observers. They pressed against the railings, pointing out the crypt to each other.

Although the outside of the family vault was overgrown with ferns, the white marble interior was clean and well tended. Eight members of the Whitstable family were buried here, as well as Peggy's husband. Each was sealed behind a small door marked with a brass plaque, and every door was fitted with a brass holder containing a single white flower. Behind them the wedged-open portal flushed staleness from the tomb with loamy morning air.

'I must say it's not the kind of behaviour you expect from a respectable middle-aged woman,' said Bryant, eyeing the vault wall.

'Who can tell these days?' replied his partner, looking around. 'Especially with this family.' A routine check had turned up a police file for Peggy Harmsworth. Four years earlier she had been convicted for possession of cocaine. Yesterday, several grams of white powder had been found in one of the brass holders within the vault. Wary of keeping drugs at home, it seemed that Peggy had been in the habit of stashing her supply in the nearby family mausoleum. Little did she know that by the 1980s, dinner-party guests would happily be racking it across their coffee tables.

'She'd arranged to meet a friend for drinks on Wednesday night,' said May, his smartly combed hair ruffling against the low ceiling. 'She stopped off to collect the drug on the way. There was an empty vial in her purse. But her supply had been doctored. Either Denjhi forced her to take the new mixture, or she couldn't wait for a taste.'

'Longbright says Forensics are getting conflicting results,' said Bryant, peering into each of the holders in turn. 'Did you see the list they've turned up so far? Atropine, meadow saffron, panther mushroom, betel-nut seed. There are other strains they haven't yet identified. Nobody seems to know what the combined effect might be. Do you think she's going to be all right?'

'I don't know. It sounds like a pretty lethal mix.'

'I've been trying to fathom out the sequence of events. See how this sounds. It begins with Max Jacob being summoned to London by his old friend and client, Peter Whitstable. Peter wants Jacob to oversee the removal of the Japanese from the Savoy deal. He's earmarked the theatre for his prestige charity, CROWET. Peter is determined to own the theatre. He resorts to subterfuge, arranging to have one of the heads of the Tasaka Corporation compromised. The number 216 is written in Jacob's diary, the number of the hotel room where the incriminating blackmail material will be held.

'Jacob is the go-between in this little blackmail plot; perhaps he's acted for Peter before in a similar capacity. He arrives at the hotel, but there's a mix-up. He's given the wrong room. And before he can sort out the situation, he is killed.'

'But the photographs still find their target,' said May.

'Indeed.' Arthur folded his scarf beneath his bottom and seated himself on a shadowed bench. 'Someone gets into the room and removes the pictures in a hurry, leaving one behind. We have Miss Gates's evidence to support that. The compromised businessman is exposed and the buyout collapses.'

'Jacob was murdered *before* the Japanese were forced to abandon the theatre deal, which rules out any idea of a revenge killing on their part.'

'True. The Bible found by Jerry in Max Jacob's room belonged to William Whitstable. Perhaps it was a gift, or the lawyer was returning it. Jacob was Jewish, so we must assume that the Bible had symbolic value only. The highlighting of all those passages to do with light and dark suggests some deeper significance.'

'I'd forgotten about that,' May admitted. He glanced down at his watch. 'The service is due to start.'

Below them, the pale city lay in gathering frosty fog. Arthur was gazing off at the horizon, his thoughts unreadable. 'We're inches away from losing everything we've ever worked for,' he said. 'It will mean the end of both our careers. The Inspectorate can appoint a full-scale inquiry into our methods. We could even face criminal charges.'

'The case will go somewhere else, and it'll get a new team. They'll have our data, but no physical experience of the investigation. In the time it takes for them to catch up, others will be dead.'

Bryant gave no reply.

'I know you have ideas you're not telling me about, Arthur. You always do.'

'You want to know what I really think?' Bryant asked, looking down at the straggling figures who had just entered through the private gate of the churchyard. 'In 1881 James Makepeace Whitstable set up the Alliance of Eternal Light. On the surface, the society was seen to carry out good works—building hostels, helping the poor, funding charities, restoring buildings. Privately, it was dedicated to something else, some secret cartel for the betterment of the Whitstable family—their fortunes certainly prospered in the years following its foundation. With that betterment came a price, which the family is now paying.' His eyes hardened. 'Until we understand the machinery that was set in motion, I don't see how we can stop it.'

The service was brief and gloomy, more of a wake than a well-wishing. The detectives were leaving the cemetery when they were accosted by Isobel Whitstable. Throughout the service Daisy's mother had held herself with quiet dignity, supported by her husband and her son. As she threw back the veil of her hat, Bryant could see the debilitating effect of the last few days in her eyes. For a moment, he thought she was going to lash out at them with her fists.

'You two,' she spat furiously, 'I hold the pair of you responsible for this.' She gestured at the gathering behind her. 'My daughter is traumatized, and you did nothing at all to prevent it. Ever since this whole nightmare began you've done *nothing*. How many of us have to die?' Tears spilled from her bulging eyes. 'What do we have to do to get protection from this—this—'

'Mrs Whitstable, every person here today has a police detail,' intervened May. 'Your houses are being watched around the clock. Until we find the information we need to make an arrest, there's nothing more we can do.'

'Well, there's something I can damned well do,' she

hissed, thrusting her livid face forward. 'I'm going to make sure your little experimental unit is closed down and this investigation is turned over to someone with an ounce of competence. You'll wish you'd taken the police pension, because believe me, both of you, this was your very last case.'

She turned on an elegant high heel and stalked from the churchyard to the waiting Bentley parked beyond.

31 / Purpose

As their last two dates had ended with Joseph being locked up in the dark, it didn't augur well for a third try. Jerry wondered if he had come to the Gates home to say good-bye. He stood in the doorway before her. 'How's your hips?' he asked.

'And good morning to you. I have a bruise the size of Belgium.'

'Well.' He looked around. 'I could stay here on the doorstep, but in this neighbourhood someone will call the police if they see a black guy hanging about.'

'I'm sorry,' she said quietly. 'Come in. I'm having a bad day.'

'Coming from you, that's one omen I'd take notice of.'

He entered the foyer, marveling at the domed ceiling above the entrance hall. 'Nice place. What days do you open it to the public?'

'Around here, we are the public. In this neighbourhood the carolers sing in descant and get a tenner for their troubles.' She was smoothing back her hair and smiling too widely. *The effort might kill me*, she thought. Still, she was very pleased to see him. 'It doesn't feel like Christmas, does it? Can I pour you a seasonal toast?'

She led the way through to a large, light kitchen adorned with outsized copper saucepans. 'My mother had all this installed, but she can barely boil an egg,' she said, removing a bottle of whisky and two tumblers from the cabinet.

'You never have a kind word for her.'

'Defence reaction. How are your war wounds?'

'I'll live.' He gingerly touched the plaster below his left eye. There were two more, one on his chin and another across his forehead. 'I feel like I had an incredibly bad dream.'

'She really had a go at you, didn't she?' Jerry passed him a glass and raised her own. 'Merry Christmas.'

'I hear you handled the bike pretty well.'

'So well that the Met are going to press charges. Listen, I think I'm going to need your help again.'

'You're out of your mind. Forget it, Jerry. You don't need me. I came by to tell you that I'm going back to San Diego.'

'You can't do that!' She turned on him angrily, betrayal on her face. 'You're the only friend I have! The only one I can trust.'

'You know, I felt sorry for you when I first met you. Poor kid, I should make an effort to be friendly—'

'I didn't realize it was an effort,' she said, bridling. 'I was right, though, about the murders and everything.'

'Okay, I admit it's been very weird since I met you, but you're just trying to stay involved to bug your parents.'

'I thought you were on my side.'

'It's not a matter of sides, Jerry.' He was losing his temper with her. 'I can see how you live. You're bored and searching for the next game, and I'm not going to play.' He sat down at the breakfast bar with his drink. 'Why did I listen to you? I'm living in a bug-infested room in Earl's Court. I've no money left. I can't find a job. I don't have a future. I don't even have the fare to get home. Give me another whisky.' He held out his empty glass.

She poured his drink, then opened the refrigerator. 'Want something to eat? There's cold pheasant, foie gras, roast veal. Us rich folk have everything.'

'That stuff'll kill you. Got any eggs?'

Jerry made them cheese omelettes. 'How are you going to get anywhere if you don't have any money?' she asked.

'I'm figuring this out as I go along,' he told her through a mouthful of toast. 'I threw my clothes into a bag and slipped out of the boardinghouse without paying the bill. Considering the amount of insect life in my room, I don't feel bad about it. The BBC could have shot a wildlife documentary on the bedroom carpet. I'll manage—I always do.'

'Maybe you could stay here while I get some money together.'

'No, I've made up my mind. I'll take a few bartender jobs, get some money together. I'm sorry, Jerry. It's been fun in a perverse, self-torturing way, but I have to figure out what *I* want now.'

She took a mouthful of omelette, petulance masking her desperation. 'Come on, you could help me and I could help you. I can't do it by myself.'

'And I can't do it for you.' He pushed back his plate and rose to leave.

'All right, but I really want to give you some money, just to tide you over. Take what you need.'

'I'm still not going to help you, Jerry.'

'So you said.'

'It's disadvantageous to my health.'

'Please, Joseph, just give me ten minutes.'

He gave her a suspicious look. 'You're not going to explain another one of your whacked theories, are you?'

'No,' she replied. 'I promise.'

Ten minutes later, he sat on the floor in her father's study while she sorted through the contents of the desk's lower drawers.

'Suppose your father comes back?'

'They won't be home until later. I found this when I was looking for Jack's contracts with the Whitstable family. I was fourteen when they were sent.'

She unfolded a sheet of white vellum and passed it across. He studied the handwriting for a moment and began to read:

> *Dear Gwen,*
>
> *You said not to use the phone. I barely know what to say to you about Geraldine. Naturally, I am horrified by what has happened. If only there was some way to undo the harm that has been caused. As her mother, you must decide what is best for all of us.*

'Christ, what did you do, murder somebody?' he asked, handing back the letter.

She passed him another. 'This is dated a few days after, also unsigned.'

> *Dear Gwen,*
>
> *Everything has been arranged as you requested. She can start on Monday. She'll be entering during mid-term, but that can't be helped. No one will ask questions. It is unsafe to visit her. I am only thinking of Geraldine's welfare. I only pray she remembers nothing of what has transpired.*

Jerry sat back, carefully smoothing the envelope. She looked up at Joseph, waiting for him to comment.

'You don't remember any of this? Who are they from? What the hell happened when you were fourteen?'

'I told you, I had a breakdown. Gwen had a Steinway piano that belonged to her mother. I took a chisel and carved my name in the top, then cut all the wires. They put me in therapy, and then when I got too violent they sent me to a special school. I was tranked up for weeks at a time. I've blocked most of what happened.'

'From the tone of these letters there's something else you've blocked. They're so incriminating, why would anyone save them? What made you hate your mother so much?'

That year had passed in a blur of pain. Jerry never spoke of it to anyone. Wayland, her therapist, was in her mother's pay, and her father avoided any kind of emotional commitment.

'Gwen was always concerned about my behaviour,' she explained. 'Once she had to cancel a lunch date because I threw up in the living room. I can't remember the first time I did it, but I was surprised how easy it was. She'd drop everything and come home. Make me soup, put me to bed. But she never stayed for long. Motherhood hadn't turned out to be as satisfying as she'd expected, so she went back to social climbing. She watched families like the Whitstables getting all the respect, and was eaten up with jealousy. She never got the social standing she felt she deserved. This isn't about money at all, it's about breeding. My mother makes the right moves, but she's still shut outside with her nose pressed against the glass. That's my fault. Just when she started receiving the right invitations, I began to behave badly.

'Soon people started turning down my mother's charity luncheons. They never knew what they might find when they got here. I took a somewhat theatrical stab at cutting my wrist in the middle of one of her little soirées. That's why she sent me to a therapist. Even then, she couldn't resist showing off. He was the most well-connected doctor in town. She could tell everyone I was being treated by Lady So-and-So's shrink.'

'You sound almost as bitter as you make your mother out to be.'

'Why not? That's where I get it from.' She hunched herself forward, dark hair falling into her eyes. 'There's something else, though. The letters prove it. I could ask Gwen, but if it's as bad as it sounds, I'm not sure I want to know.'

'What makes you think you can change anything? The past can't come back.' Joseph climbed to his feet and picked up his backpack. 'I'm leaving all my designs in storage. I won't need them now. I can't stay any longer. I need to get on the road.'

'Joseph, you can't just go.' She had really believed that he would stay with her. She had never been denied anything before.

'Jerry, how can I say this?' He smiled awkwardly at her. 'The Savoy suits you. It's not my style. There's too much of a gap between us.'

'No, there isn't,' she said, wanting to add, *Not when you're in love with someone*. 'Please, I'm scared of what might happen. I don't want to stay here alone.'

'You're not alone. Leave the investigation to the police. You could have been killed the other night.'

'Why won't you help me any more?' she asked him again, standing at the open front door.

'Because,' he said, embracing her, 'now you have a reason to help yourself.' He kissed her lightly on the cheek, then stepped out into the falling rain. 'I'll call you.'

'You won't,' she called back. 'People always say that but they never do.'

He raised his hand in salute, waving without turning back.

He's gone, she thought. *I'm on my own.* But as she closed the door on him, her sadness was replaced by a growing sense of purpose.

32 / Ensemble

The frost that had begun to fern the windows of the Mornington Crescent PCU that evening was felt inside the building as well as out; the workmen had still not managed to fix the central heating.

In the streets below, gangs of home-going secretaries sang drunken Christmas carols, undeterred by strikes and threatened blackouts. The traffic dissipated as commuters returned home to be with their families. But within the unit there would be no Christmas. All leave had been canceled. A few miserable paper chains had been strung across the operations room. Bryant's desk displayed two Christmas cards. May had dozens, but had not found time to open them.

The detectives returned from another uneasy Met briefing to find Raymond Land seated in their office with a mortified look on his slack, tired face. One glance told them that his patience, and their deadline, had both come to an end.

'Sit down, you two,' he said, waiting impatiently while Bryant extricated himself from a new Christmas scarf, a gift from his landlady that appeared more suited to Hallowe'en than yuletide.

'What can we do for you?' asked May casually. Bryant took the cue from his partner and offered his acting superior a careful smile.

'I'd like to know why you contradicted my report to Faraday.'

Bryant raised a tentative hand. 'We didn't think you'd contact the arts minister before discussing the matter with us. As it happens, we disagree with the inferences you seem to have drawn from the forensic reports.'

'Perhaps you'd like to tell me what conclusions you think I've reached?'

'All right,' said Bryant, steadily eyeing his partner. 'You told Faraday that this man Denjhi is responsible for the death of William Whitstable, whom you presume was killed in some squabble over the painting. You know there's no forensic proof connecting Denjhi to any other member of the family besides Peggy Harmsworth.'

'But it's only a matter of time. We're tearing that man's house apart, and until—'

'You've ordered that?' asked May angrily. 'You had no right.' Denjhi's widow had been through enough without having the indelicate hands of the Special Branch ripping her sofa cushions open.

'Until you can present me with some solid evidence, I have every right to supersede your orders,' said Land with a faint air of desperation. 'You may have ruled the roost at Bow Street and West End Central. Here you take orders from me until I'm replaced by a permanent officer.' He rubbed bitten fingers across a sallow brow. 'You have to understand the kind of pressure that's being exerted on us. These are calculated assassinations, for God's sake. Front page of the *Daily Mail*, page three of the *Express*. The *Mirror* had four pages on us this morning: maps, diagrams, baby pictures. If it wasn't for the prime minister's mess with the unions we'd be splashed all over the broadsheets. Isobel Whitstable is attempting to sue the unit for deliberate obstruction during the course of the investigation. She's also suing you both personally for incompetence in the wake of her daughter's trauma.'

'You know it's impossible to reconstruct the events surrounding the girl's abduction without being allowed to talk to her,' said Bryant. 'She was kept in a disused railway arch, but we've found nothing except a few silk fibres on her clothes. We can't give her mother theories that we cannot prove.'

'This morning our legal department received a letter detailing outlined lawsuits from several other members of the Whitstable family,' Land went on.

'Charging us with what?'

'Failing to protect and uphold the law, among other things.'

'Can they do that?' wondered Bryant.

'I've been asked to close the PCU down. But I'm determined to avoid that course of action. Know why? I can see that you're holding out on me. After all, I'm not an idiot.' Land filled the contradictory silence that followed by trying to appear stern. 'There's no chance of wrapping this thing up today, but I know you have something. Do you understand that you're about to lose everything you've ever worked for? The only possible way you can stay on is by giving me total access to your information. Even then, I'm not sure I can keep this within our jurisdiction any longer.'

'Oh, Raymondo, old chum, the only reason we're holding out on you is because you'd find it impossible to believe what we're uncovering.'

'Try me,' said Land. 'I'm pretty gullible.'

Bryant shot his partner a look, then proceeded to explain their findings. After he had watched the incredulous expression spread across Land's face, he sat back in his chair and waited for a reaction.

'You're saying some kind of century-old satanic ring is killing off the family?'

'Your terminology's a little contentious, but—'

'Don't get smart with me, Bryant.'

'Then I'll tell you something else,' offered Bryant. 'I think Denjhi kidnapped Daisy Whitstable and couldn't bring himself to murder her. He disobeyed his orders.'

'This is madness. A satanic circle, and the Whitstables all know about it?'

'I never said satanic. But somebody must know, certainly.'

Land slapped his hands on to the desk. 'How can I tell the H.O. about any of this?'

'Now you understand our predicament,' said May. 'We need you to keep the pressure off for just a little longer. That means retaining all the case files here in the building. Nothing more to go to the Met.'

'But what about the Whitstables?' asked Land, chewing a nail.

'You can leave them to us,' replied Bryant with a reassuring smile.

When they heard the detectives' demands, the Whitstables' reaction was predictable—total, steaming outrage.

It was May who had thought of moving them all into William Whitstable's house. The property was enormous and standing empty. It would be easy to secure from both outside and within. Also, considering the elaborate security operation that was currently in force, it would stop resources being stretched over the yuletide season and save the taxpayers a considerable amount of money.

Twenty-four members of the family had remained in

England for Christmas, despite the threat of power strikes. Of those, two were in nursing homes and one was bedridden. That left twenty-one Whitstables to be rehoused and settled without fuss or publicity. The detectives informed the family that anyone wishing to opt out of the arrangement was perfectly free to do so, but they would find police protection no longer afforded to them at any residence other than the Hampstead house.

Four of the younger family members—Christian and Deborah Whitstable and their children Justin and Flora—chose to remain at their home in Chiswick. The rest reluctantly accepted the deal, but not without letting their annoyance be heard and noted by anyone who came within earshot.

Several unmarked police vans had succeeded in discreetly moving clothes, bedding, personal effects, security equipment, and food supplies into the house. The remaining seventeen Whitstables were driven to the rear entrance and installed within its gloomy brown rooms. Shortly after this, Bryant and May risked a visit to make sure that their reluctant charges had settled in.

'No matter what they say, I don't want you to lose your temper,' cautioned May as they passed the undercover surveillance car parked in front of the main entrance. 'Try to remember that we are public servants.'

'That shouldn't be difficult,' muttered Bryant. 'They treat everyone as if they're hired help.'

May approached the brightly lit porch and rang the doorbell according to the prearranged signal. 'This attitude of yours isn't easing the situation, you know. Try to be nice.'

'What am I supposed to say?' asked Bryant. 'It's demoralizing, trying to help a bunch of arrogant ingrates who aren't prepared to give us the time of day. What is it that makes them so superior? Owning a few smelly sheep-fields and getting the Queen's Award to Industry. If we weren't doing our duty and providing a service we'd be invisible to them. We should have got rid of the class system two hundred years ago, when the Frogs had their spring clean. *Let them eat cake*. Try saying that with your head in a wicker basket.'

'Anarchist,' said May. 'You're as guilty as the rest of us. Look at the way you've been treating the workmen re-painting the office.'

'That's different,' sniffed Bryant. 'They're common as muck, for God's sake.'

'So what would you do? Machine-gun the royal family?'

'Now that you mention it, that's not a—'

'So you've finally arrived to gloat.' Berta Whitstable, a voluminous, overdressed woman in her fifties, was hold-ing the door open before them. She had elected to wear all of her most valuable jewellery rather than leave it be-hind. She looked like a lady mayoress receiving unwel-come guests. 'We're freezing to death in here. The least you can do is show us how to start the boiler. I presume you're good with your hands.'

The detectives entered. In the hall, noisy children chased each other to the foot of the stairs, thrilled to be staying up so late. Several adults sat morosely in the par-lour as if waiting to be told what to do.

'Are there going to be pheasants?' asked one pimply young man with a half-broken voice. 'We always have game birds at Christmas.'

'I don't know,' replied Bryant truthfully. 'Did you re-member to bring any?'

'Cook takes care of those things.' The boy scratched his Adam's apple, thinking. 'There *are* people coming in to cook and clean, presumably?'

'Surely there are enough of you here to handle the household chores.'

'We never cook at home. Annie does everything, but they wouldn't let us bring her because she's just a domestic.'

'Well, this will be an exciting experience for you, won't it?' said Bryant maliciously. 'You'll be able to write a book about it. *How I Survived Without Someone to Make the Beds.*'

'Arthur . . .' warned May angrily.

'You mean we have to make our own beds?' said someone else. Bryant turned to address the speaker, a young woman in a blue Chanel suit with blond hair arranged in an elaborate chignon.

'I'm afraid so—Pippa, isn't it? You'll be roughing it for a while, putting on your own pillowcases, emptying the vacuum-cleaner bag, that sort of thing. It'll be grim, but I'm sure you'll pull through. We'll bring supplies in to you, and you'll be allowed out in pairs accompanied by a guard, but only for short periods. Like being in prison, really.'

Everyone groaned. *They wanted more protection*, thought Bryant. *That's what we're going to give them.*

'Of course, I *will* be allowed to attend my exercise class, won't I?' asked Pippa. 'And I have to look after Gawain. He's my horse.' She turned to the others and smiled. 'A Christmas present from Daddy.'

'That shouldn't be a problem, providing of course that it's your turn on the roster to leave the house,' said Bryant, enjoying the sense of power. 'Unfortunately, you won't be able to telephone out, because of the risk that one of you may accidentally mention your whereabouts.'

'Just how long do you propose to keep us here?' Berta Whitstable's voice overrode questions from the others.

'Nobody's keeping you here,' replied May. 'This is for your own protection. Until we find out why this is happening, and who is causing it.'

'And just how long will that be?'

'I hope it'll be for no more than two or three days,' Bryant said. 'There will be a roll call every night and every morning. And a curfew.' More groans. It was harder to protect the outside of the house at night. There were too many trees around the building.

Once all the questions had been answered, the detectives ran through the name list, checking everyone off. Bryant looked at his notepad in puzzlement. There was one name he didn't recognize. 'Who is CH?' he asked.

There was an uneasy silence.

Several of the men awkwardly turned their attention to their children. Bryant turned to Berta Whitstable. 'Do you know?'

'That would—probably—be Charles,' she replied.

Bryant frowned. There had been no Charles Whitstable marked on the genealogical table. 'I don't understand. I thought everyone was accounted for.'

'Your family tree shows only the Whitstables living in this country. Charles is based overseas.'

'Where?'

'In India. Calcutta, to be exact.'

'Are you absolutely sure about this?' asked May.

'Of course I am,' said Berta. 'I should know. He is my son.'

'Do you have a number where he can be reached?'

'Berta!' called one of the men. 'You have no right to

bring Charles into this. It's better to leave him where he is.'

Bryant's interest was piqued. 'I think perhaps we should discuss this in more detail,' he said, placing a hand on Berta Whitstable's broad back and guiding her out of the room.

33 / Into Darkness

The Imperial overlooked the Thames, and was newly furnished to appear old. The restaurant's floor-to-ceiling windows ensured that the rooms were airier and lighter than anything on the menu, and its waiters had been especially selected for their arrogance. The place had instant appeal for the kind of inherited-wealth forty-somethings who salted their meals before tasting them, and who referred to dessert as pudding. The seventies were not a good time to eat out in England, unless you liked coq au vin, trout with almonds, and half a grapefruit served as a starter.

Gwen regularly dined at The Imperial without her husband. Jerry was surprised to find the restaurant so busy on Christmas Eve. She had donned a dark suit and blouse for the occasion. It was Gwen's favourite outfit, purchased for a party that Jerry had spitefully failed to attend.

Jerry spotted her mother sitting at a crimson-clothed table, morosely studying the centrepiece. Gwen looked thinner in the face, as if some private burden had begun to take its toll. She smiled wanly at Jerry's approach.

'Mother.' Gwen accepted a light kiss on each cool cheek. She liked to be called that.

'So.' She studied her daughter as she unfolded a napkin into her lap. 'I thought we should at least spend part of the holiday season together. Your father sends his apologies. He's having one of his migraines.' They both knew this meant Jack had drunk too much at his company dinner the previous evening. He always spent Christmas Eve sleeping it off in preparation for a major onslaught on his liver.

Now's as good a time as any, Jerry thought. 'Mother, there's something I want to discuss with you.'

'It's Christmas Eve, Geraldine. I'm too weary for another declaration of independence. Don't tell me you want to study with the Maharishi or travel to Tibet in a camper van. Let's just try to enjoy one another's company tonight. Perhaps this nice waiter could get you something to drink. I'll have another dry martini.'

Jerry picked up a fork and pretended to study it. For a while they sat in silence. 'I'm tired of working in the hotel,' she said finally. 'I want a job with some responsibility. I've proved to myself that I can do it, and I think I have some ability.' She decided not to mention that she hadn't turned up for work in days. 'I want to join Dad's company.'

Gwen was in mid martini and looked as if she'd swallowed the olive. This wasn't at all what she had been anticipating.

'I don't expect to be paid much at first. I'll have a lot to learn, but I'm willing to try.'

'Well—I don't know what to say,' said her mother, nonplussed. 'You've always been so set against the idea. All those lectures you gave Jack about capitalist pigs. This is the last thing I expected to hear from you.'

'If you don't think it's a good idea—'

'No, it's not that,' Gwen said hastily. 'If this is a genuine change of heart then I don't see why we can't organize something. Are you sure about this? You know what it would involve.'

They had told her often enough. It would mean being apprenticed in one of her father's boring businesses, courses in bookkeeping, accountancy, or brokerage if she preferred. It would mean being controlled.

She had to allay any remaining suspicions her mother harboured. During the course of the meal Jerry attempted to explain her change of heart, describing her hopes for the future. By the time she had finished, Gwen was finding it so difficult to contain her delight that she looked as if she might spontaneously combust at the table.

'Well, I think this is something to celebrate,' she said, ordering a very decent bottle of Bollinger. 'Would you like to tell your father, or do you want to leave it to me?'

'Why don't we both tell him?' said Jerry, raising her glass with a smile.

'This really is excellent news,' said Jack, making a miraculous recovery from his headache. 'You don't know how much this means to us, Geraldine; to see you taking your future into your own hands. You'll grow up overnight. I think you'll soon discover that you've made the right choice. I never had a son...' Her father broke off to blow his nose, then fumbled about with another bottle of champagne.

'We always wanted the best for you,' Gwen insisted, filling the glasses. 'This will bring us closer together as a family.' Her mother's eagerness to employ her as a reentry point into decent social circles was palpable. She was like some horrible stage mother, using her offspring to wedge herself into the life she never had. Jerry felt no malice toward her father, only sadness. Jack had always done as he was told. She tasted a raw bitterness, and felt her hatred for Gwen deepening.

Most of all, though, she felt the thrill of control. 'So, what's the next move?' she asked, looking from one pleased parent to the other.

'I think I can arrange some kind of apprenticeship for you,' said her father. 'You'll get a chance to see what opportunities are available, and which company you're best suited for. Did you have anything particular in mind?'

'I thought perhaps there might be an opening with Charles Whitstable. I don't suppose he'd remember me. After all, it was a long time ago.'

Jack was silent for a moment. 'Of course he'll remember you,' he said at last. 'He used to bounce you on his knee. He treated you like a daughter. One of my best clients.'

Jerry vaguely remembered an overstuffed Chelsea apartment, but little else. She had been accessorized to so many of her father's colleagues. What was important was the link...

'Of course, that was before he went to India. But I believe he's back now.'

'Then could you talk to him?'

Jack looked over at Gwen as if requesting permission. 'We could catch him while he's here.'

Jack left the room to make a phone call, despite the fact that there was a telephone beside his armchair in the lounge. Gwen sat there patting Jerry's hands and smiling at her, stumped for further conversation.

No one had thought to probe the reason for her change of heart. She hoped they would not decide to do so.

After a few minutes, Jack returned to the room. 'Couldn't have been easier,' he said cheerfully. 'There's no point in wasting any time. You've some catching up to do. I've arranged drinks for you tomorrow morning.'

'On Christmas Day?'

'Just a seasonal snifter before lunch. I happen to know Charles is on the lookout for new blood. He's terribly influential, and he's still the chairman of the Worshipful Company of Watchmakers. Sounded jolly pleased to hear from me.'

John May's Muswell Hill apartment could not have been less like his partner's. There was nothing in his surroundings to remind him of his past. The walls of the flat were bare and bright. Various pieces of gadgetry sat in nests of wiring: a fax machine, a state-of-the-art hi-fi with huge speakers, unkempt stacks of books and LPs, magazines, and an alarming pile of washing up, despite the presence of a dishwasher.

He had returned home late that evening, depressed by Land's attitude but thankful that they had managed to buy themselves a little more time. He was coming down with a cold. He'd probably caught it from Bryant, who managed to pass on the usual winter diseases without undue suffering himself, like Typhoid Mary. As the day went on his throat had grown sore and his head had begun to throb—he could tell that he had contracted this year's mutant flu germ, and Longbright had finally sent him home, assuring him that she could easily finish handling the Whitstables' security demands.

It annoyed him that, far from feeling tired, he was nervy, irritable, and wide awake. He had specifically blocked the Whitstables' more petulant requests in order to reduce distractions during the investigation, but now that they had been assembled en masse he knew that they would be far harder to ignore. Several of them were still ringing to protest vigorously, complain, and demand items from the PCU unit, despite the fact that they had been specifically requested not to tie up the division's phone lines.

The fact that they were under voluntary containment seemed to have escaped them; one of the Whitstable children had demanded that her pet rabbits be brought to the house, otherwise she would tell Daddy to have a word with the Home Office. It had been that kind of day.

May stirred himself a hot lemon drink and poured a shot of brandy into it, looking out from the kitchen window across the misty panorama of London. The fourth-floor apartment was situated at the top of a hill, and commanded spectacular views of the city by day.

Now the streets below were silent and deserted. Cars were garaged. Home lights blazed. It was the one night of the year when families could be relied upon to spend time together. The city death toll would be up tomorrow. It always rose on Christmas Day. Surprising how many heart attacks occurred after lunch and the queen's speech, when rows between husbands and wives came to a head.

May thought of Jane, his own wife, and wondered how long she would be away this time. He thought of his daughter's disastrous marriage, and what he could possibly do to help her. And he wondered if it was selfishness that kept him working when he should have been with them.

He had not heard from Bryant for several hours. The case was taking its toll on them both. An astonishing amount of paperwork had built up in the office and had yet to be cleared. The PCU differed from other experimental units previously tested by the Met, insofar as routine procedural elements could be farmed out to auxiliary teams, leaving the senior investigating officers free to concentrate on other aspects of the investigation.

Hundreds of hours of interviews, forensic tests, fibre separations, evidence collections, blood and tissue typing, witness documentation, and many other daily activities were handled by groups attached to West End Central. This kind of specialization upset the Metropolitan force members who got stuck with door-to-doors and foot patrols. Something would have to give....

The sudden buzz of the telephone made May wonder if his colleague was calling to check on his health. Instead, he found himself speaking to Alison Hatfield at the Goldsmiths' Hall.

'I'm sorry to disturb you at such a late hour on Christmas Eve, Mr May, but your sergeant told me it would be all right to call,' she explained.

'Not to worry,' he said. 'Merry Christmas. I'm afraid I've rather lost track of the time.'

'I'm not a big fan of Christmas, to be honest. All that eating. My flatmate's a nurse and she's working round the clock, so I'm enjoying the peace and quiet at home. I've turned up some information I think you'll be very interested in. I mean, it looks important. Would it be possible for you to visit the hall?'

'I could be there in half an hour,' said May, brightening. At least it would take his mind off his cold. 'Could you wait for me in the main entrance?'

'No problem. I'll bring a thermos of tea and brandy. At least we can toast the compliments of the season.'

'What a very sensible woman you are, Miss Hatfield.' After he had replaced the receiver, he called the unit, but Bryant had still not returned from Whitstable Central, as the older detective called it. May knew he shouldn't be venturing out into the chill night, but felt sure that when the case broke, it would be through the findings of someone like Miss Hatfield, and not because of a fibre match.

Twenty minutes later he reached the main entrance to the Goldsmiths' Hall. Alison was waiting for him. Once again she was dressed in heavy warm clothes that seemed too old for her, as if the sombre surroundings were trying to drain away her youthfulness.

'I hope I haven't dragged you away from anything,' she apologized, shaking his hand.

'I'm glad you called,' May assured her.

'Everyone's gone for the holidays. The chambers are all locked up. I have the run of the building.'

They walked across to the Watchmakers' Hall through a deserted avenue of mirror glass and ancient stone. 'Yesterday I received a call from a Mr Leo Marks,' said Alison. 'He wanted to know the whereabouts of certain documents pertaining to the guild.'

May remembered asking the lawyer to check out the financial history of the Watchmakers. It sounded as if he was finally following up the request.

'I've been with the guild for six years,' said Alison, 'and I still have no way of locating the older files that have accumulated here. This area suffered terribly during the Blitz. There must have been hundreds of stored documents. They were moved out for safety, but everything was done in such a hurry that no alphabetizing system was used. When the files were returned after the war, there was no one left who remembered how the temporary storage system worked.'

They passed through the building to the basement goods lift, and May pulled back the heavy trellis, mindful of catching his coat between the oil-smeared bars.

'I told Mr Marks that it would be difficult to locate what he was looking for, as my records are incomplete.' Alison closed the trellis and pressed the brass wall stud behind her. With a shudder, the lift began its descent.

'What exactly was he after?'

'Oh, details of overseas payments made to religious charities, all sorts of things. I thought I'd come down here and have a look around for them. At least that way I'd be able to say I tried. I didn't have much luck, but I found something else I thought you should see.'

The dampness filled their nostrils as the lift thumped to a halt. Alison passed the detective a torch, and they entered the dim corridor ahead. On either side of them, furry black watermarks stained the walls.

'Didn't you say there's another floor beneath this?' May could feel the distant rumbling of the drains through the soles of his shoes.

'Yes, and there are probably lots of files still down there, but it's not safe. There are things beneath these old buildings that no one will ever find. You know the Billingsgate Fish Market in Lower Thames Street? The City Corporation wants to close it down, but there's two hundred years of permafrost inside it that the strongest steel can't cut through. The river maintains a natural ice age in the basement. So heaven only knows what's beneath us here.' She stopped before a brown-painted door at the far end of the corridor. May could see another dark hall stretching off in both directions.

'What's that way?' he asked.

'I have no idea, and I'm not sure anyone else has.' She shivered and opened the door, her breath dispelling in the torchlight. 'It's always freezing, even in summer.' She tried a brass light switch on the wall, and a filthy low-voltage bulb glowed above them. The room was filled with mildewed cardboard boxes. As Alison disturbed one, hundreds of small brown beetles scattered across the floor.

'I had the caretaker locate the emergency lighting circuit for me before he went off duty,' she said. 'God knows what it runs from. Over here.'

She pulled open a box and shone her torch over its contents. The beam picked up the familiar circled flame symbol of the alliance. She pulled out part of a heavy leather-bound file and handed it to him, wiping off a filmy web. 'I didn't think I should remove these without you being here, in case it counted as disturbing the evidence or something.' Gingerly reaching into the carton, she removed a second file.

'What are these?' he asked, puzzled.

'I think one of them's part of the original trading contract for the alliance. It looks like there are some pages missing, but I'll try and find them for you. The other is someone's notes, but the handwriting's illegible. It's of the same era, so I thought it might be useful.'

'How much more is there?' asked May, pointing to the boxes.

'I don't think there's anything else quite as old. The files below this were printed in the mid-1950s. It must have come from another box. To be honest, I don't much fancy digging any deeper, in case I disturb the rats.'

'Don't worry, I think you've found something important.' He flipped to the back of the document. The last page read: *This agreement witnessed and signed on December 28th in the Year of Our Lord 1881, at the Savoy Hotel, London, England.*

There followed seven signatures. The top one belonged to James Makepeace Whitstable.

'Can we go up now?' asked Alison. She was shaking with cold.

May stopped reading. 'Of course, how thoughtless of me. You must be frozen.'

When they reached the comparative warmth of the

entrance hall, he gripped her hand fondly. 'This is the second time you've been a great help to me,' he said. 'When this is over I would most enjoy taking you out to dinner.'

Alison laughed. 'I'd like that. But I warn you, I'm a healthy eater.'

He felt suddenly sorry for her, spending Christmas alone. 'Do you need a lift anywhere?'

'Thanks, I have my little car.'

'You're welcome to come over to the unit,' he offered. 'We won't be celebrating much, but we'll always give you a welcome.'

'That's very kind of you.' She smiled shyly. 'I'd like that very much.' Turning up her collar, she took her leave, walking briskly off into the rain.

On his way back to the car, May sneezed so hard that the document beneath his arm nearly disappeared into the gutter. His head felt terrible, but at least he had a further lead. As soon as he reached home, he rang Bryant at his flat in Battersea.

'Do you know what time it is, calling here?' said Alma Sorrowbridge. She sounded tipsy. 'He hasn't come back yet. He promised to spend Christmas Eve with me. I cooked him a casserole. I opened a bottle of sherry.' It sounded as if she'd done more than just open it. 'He never even rang to apologize.'

'You know his work has to take precedence, Alma.'

'I know, married to the job and all that. He's told me a hundred times.'

'Do you have any idea what he has planned for Christmas Day?' May asked.

'Yes, I do,' said the landlady disapprovingly. 'He's going over to see that crazy godless woman, the one with the bright clothes and the funny earrings.'

Only one acquaintance of Bryant's fitted that description: the leader of the Camden Town Coven. 'You mean Maggie Armitage?' he said.

'That's the one. The nutcase.'

'Perhaps you could have him call me before he goes there. I'm sorry about your Christmas, Alma,' he added. 'None of us are having much of a festive season.'

As rain rolled against the lounge windows, May blew into a handkerchief and opened the first of the files. The pages smelled musty and corrupt, as if they had become tained by the words printed within. *No more false leads*, he pleaded silently. *Take me into the darkness*. He began to read.

34 / Assailant

I've *had enough of this*, thought Pippa Whitstable angrily. She had been supposed to spend Christmas Eve with Nigel at the RAC Club. Instead, she was being forced to play nursemaid to a bunch of appalling, brattish children. She barely knew any of them. The only time the family met was at weddings and funerals. Now they were being made to live under the same roof, and the police saw the whole thing as a big joke.

She reset the grip in her blond ponytail and sat on the edge of the makeshift bed. It had just passed midnight, too late to call Nigel now; he would already have left for the club.

She could go there and meet him, just turn up. It would be the perfect Christmas surprise. She'd heard he was buying her something very special. God, she'd dropped enough hints about the new Mercedes. Would he be cheap and pretend he hadn't noticed, palm her off with some pretty Aspreys bauble?

Thank God she had brought her basic black with her. The problem was how to get out of the house without any of the family seeing. At least she had her own room here, even if it hadn't been aired in centuries and was the size of a rabbit hutch. She wondered how many were still in the front parlour. She could manage the stairs without them seeing her, but the police guard would be waiting on the porch. Even if they could be persuaded to let her pass, they'd insist on telling her mother, who was always prepared to close off any promising avenues of pleasure she might wish to explore. It was a shame she'd not been old enough to experience the Summer of Love, her one great chance to tune in and drop out. Debutantes weren't allowed to have that kind of fun.

The bedroom window looked more promising. Pippa slipped off the catch and pushed open the frame as quietly as possible. At least the rain had eased to a light drizzle. She was on the first floor, a drop of about fifteen feet. Too far to jump. It was then that she noticed the drainpipe. It had handles, ornate little grips for climbing. Thank God for the Victorians! She quickly changed into her black frock and pumps, placed her purse and makeup in a tiny black bag, and wound up the strap to her collapsible umbrella. Very carefully, she stepped out of the window and on to the first grip, testing its weight.

Solid as a rock. She smiled to herself in the darkness. Moments later she stepped down on to the lawn.

Wiping her dirty hands on the wet leaves of a bush, she looked around for the best way out of the garden. The far end led off into woods. Not a good idea in these shoes, she decided. But the left-hand fence backed against an alleyway, which was accessible via a wooden side gate. She wrenched open the latch and slipped through, careful to leave it slightly ajar so that she could reenter later.

This was perfect. It didn't matter how long they were stuck in the house now; she had found herself an escape route. It would be easy to get a cab from Hampstead High Street, but which direction was that? The alley stretched off in pools of rain-sparkling light.

He must have seen her open the bedroom window from a hiding place in the garden, because she had only just turned from the gate when he grabbed her, pressing an icy hand across her mouth and dragging her away from the overhead streetlight. Her first sweeping fit of panic passed as she realized how small her attacker was. He had caught her by surprise and managed to knock her off balance, but now she uprighted herself and dug her heels hard against the ground. *You've really picked the wrong victim this time, you bastard,* she thought, prepared to take him. It would teach him to mess with a taekwon-do student.

She could feel his ribs against her spine and threw her elbows back as hard as she could. Bones cracked and shifted; the arm around her shoulder was released. Opening her mouth to admit the fingers pressing against her lips, she bit down hard.

She broke free and began to run as her assailant threw himself at her legs and crashlanded on the flagstoned walkway with her. His fingers snaked through her hair, slamming her head against the wet stone. A blinding pain cut across her right frontal lobe, spurring her to twist him away. When she finally managed to catch sight of him, she was surprised to see the face of a sick old man. He was bald and brown, with lank clumps of long hair above his ears. His eyes were sunken, and almost opaque with cataracts. Most striking of all was his clenched expression, a look of agony and pitiful confusion. As he raised himself on one leg she brought up her fist and punched the tortured face before her, sending him over.

She didn't expect him to rise again, and did not see the kukri knife in his left hand. He looked down as he thrust it forward, almost as if he was ashamed of trying to take her life.

35 / Darkness Descending

Christmas Day, eleven fifty-five A.M. Jerry looked out at the Scrabble board of frosted white fields of Hertfordshire and speculated about her meeting with Charles Whitstable. According to her father, when news reached him of the Whitstable murders, Charles left unfinished business overseas to return to England, only to be waylaid by urgent financial meetings. Still, he could hold the key to his family's decimation.

Jack's keenness to set her working in the family business negated any guilt she felt about deceiving her parents. She was determined to be present at the conclusion of the investigation, and she would uncover the meaning of her mother's correspondence. A part of her life would be closed so that a new part could open.

Jack's black Mercedes pulled up outside the gates, its exhaust purling clouds into the chill morning air. A young Indian boy appeared from the gate-lodge and spoke to Jack in clipped public-school English. He showed every sign of recognizing him.

A veil of wind-blasted trees parted as they turned into the drive to reveal the Georgian grandeur of Charles Whitstable's estate. Her father turned and smiled reassuringly. 'Quite a place, isn't it?'

'It's beautiful. Have you been here before?'

'No, but Charles often mentioned it.'

'How did you meet him?'

'We got talking at a lodge dinner years ago, and I helped him with some cotton imports. Of course he's from a guild, and there's no finer recommendation than that. But Charles is rarely here these days. He came back because this trouble with his family is adversely affecting his stock. He's having to reassure his shareholders.'

'It sounds like he's got his hands full. You're sure he wants to see me?'

'I heard he was keen to find someone he could train up as an assistant. He's not prepared to trust the job to an outsider. He'll even consider a woman.' Jack winked. 'It's not just a man's world any more. Your change of heart has come at the perfect time.'

This is the lion's den, she thought, *and they're happily putting me in it.* Her father turned off the engine and fidgeted with his tie. He had every reason to be nervous. Their meeting was as much for his benefit as her own.

The front door was opened by an attractive young Indian maid. She showed them into the breakfast room, where she said Mr Whitstable would presently join them, and silently withdrew.

They seated themselves within a cluttered treasure trove of Victoriana. The wallpaper featured rose sprigs tied with satin ribbon. Ebonized cane chairs were set about an oak gate-leg table. On a green velvet runner stood bronze animals, penwork chests in black and gold, elaborate rosewood boxes, and sentimental figurines of children and dogs. The atmosphere was smothering, the room unaired.

Neither of them spoke. A slow-ticking grandfather clock provided the only sound. After several minutes, Charles Whitstable entered.

He was tall, six feet three inches at least, imposingly broad-chested, in his late thirties. His conservative black suit and slicked dark hair provided an image somewhere between city stockbroker and lord of the manor, and he bore a natural air of authority.

'Geraldine. You've grown since I last saw you.' His handshake was firm and cold. Jerry smiled back and met his eye. This was the man who had once thought of her as a daughter? It was like meeting a stranger. He was deeply tanned, almost as if he was wearing stage makeup. There was an absolute stillness in his face that quickly became unnerving. Charles approached her father and welcomed him. 'Jack, I'm sorry we've seen so little of each other. I've been meeting with investors, trying to calm their nerves. Liverpool is not to be recommended in the winter.'

He seated himself in one of the cane chairs. 'Well, young lady, you've blazed quite a trail since we last met.' For a moment, Jerry feared her real motive in coming here had been discovered. 'Let's see—you dropped out of school and embarrassed your parents. You made yourself ill, took a spell in care, indulged yourself at the expense of those who clothed and fed you. You've been acting like a child for long enough.' Charles pressed a brass buzzer on his desk. 'You'll soon be eighteen, but why should I assume you're ready to start behaving like a responsible adult?'

The maid appeared in the doorway, and Charles gestured to her. Jerry shifted uncomfortably on her chair.

'I appreciate your honesty, Mr Whitstable. I know only what I read about your family in the papers, so you have the advantage over me. My parents have long wanted to find me employment in family business.' She couldn't resist a glance at Jack. 'Father thinks that I can be of use to you, and I'm willing to learn.'

'You have no plans for university, Geraldine. You

haven't had a guild apprenticeship. What makes you assume you could handle our kind of managerial training?'

'Enterprise is served by individuality, not conformity. That rather makes me a Whitstable in spirit, if not in name.' She had cribbed that part from the CROWET brochure.

Charles Whitstable rose and walked to the floor-length windows that overlooked the estate's misty grounds. 'I need someone I can trust. There aren't many younger members of our family left. Too few children.'

'I understand. You need someone with new ideas.'

'Exactly.' Charles turned from the window. 'Jack, I think you can leave the two of us to chat for a while.'

'I should stay with Jerry,' said her father, half rising in his seat. In that fleeting moment, she saw the discomfort in his eyes. He was afraid of Charles. But why?

'That won't be necessary. Come on, Jack, it's Christmas Day. You should be with your wife. Jerry can stay for dinner and keep me company.'

'But there's no public transport today . . .' Jack began.

'Then she can stay over. I'll have one of the rooms aired. You can collect her in the morning.'

Even though they had yet to discuss her terms of employment, Jerry knew that she had been accepted into the poisoned embrace of the Whitstable family.

Maggie Armitage lit a joss stick and set it in the nosehole of an African spirit head. 'That's better,' she said. 'Get rid of the smell of damp in here.' They were standing in her front room above the World's End pub, opposite Camden Town Tube station. The streets outside were as bright and empty as an abandoned film set. The windows of the flat were misted with condensation. Water dripped steadily through a black patch on the ceiling. A few faded postwar paper chains had been strung between the corners in a desultory attempt to usher in some Christmas cheer.

Maggie was only a little over five feet tall, but what the white witch lacked in height she made up for in vivacity. All problems, national, local, or personal, were dealt with in the same brisk, friendly manner. For all the complexity of her personal belief system she was a practical woman, and it was this streak of sound sense that had kept the Coven of St James the Elder alive at a time when so many other branches were shutting up shop.

With their ranks now swollen to include a number of part-time honorary members, meetings took place in the flat every Monday evening, and were concluded rather more raucously in the pub downstairs. Much of the coven's work was of a mundane nature—inter-coven correspondence was dealt with, and a mimeographed newsletter was produced. Public queries had to be answered, a forum for the discussion of world events was chaired, and new excuses were invented for avoiding eviction notices.

'You've managed to hang on to this place, then.' Bryant warily eyed the saturated ceiling.

'The landlord's been trying to sling us out for years, but his heart isn't in it any more,' said Maggie. 'Especially since Doris put an evil enchantment on his car.'

'I thought you didn't do that sort of thing.'

'Well,' she confided, 'we don't as a rule, but he was being a real pain in the arse.'

'Did it work?'

'I think so. Whenever he comes around to collect the rent he's always half an hour late and his hands are covered in oil. Would you like one of my special Christmas cups of tea?'

'I don't know,' said Bryant, narrowing his eyes at her. 'Is it full of strange herbs and aromatic spices?'

'No, Earl Grey with a shot of brandy.'

'Oh, that's all right then.' He shifted a stack of magazines and seated himself. 'Where's everyone else?'

'We finished early with just a few madrigals because Maureen's cooking her family Christmas dinner, which she's against in principle, being a practising pagan. The others have gone downstairs to the pub. They're busy arguing about the origins of Yggdrasil, the cosmic axis. Things can get quite heated.'

'I'm afraid I'm not familiar—" Bryant began.

'Well, you should be!' said Maggie, pouring a generous measure of Calvados into his cup. 'It's why we put presents under the Christmas tree. Yggdrasil is the eternal tree of Northern belief, the great natural core that links our world to heaven and hell. Decking the tree is an act which symbolically brings us the gifts of wisdom. And strangely enough, it has something to do with your investigation.'

Bryant couldn't wait to hear this one. Maggie crossed the room, nimbly skirting a pair of buckets collecting rainwater, and removed a large volume from one of the overflowing bookcases. 'I've been delving into your dilemma, and I believe I've come up with something.' She set the book down on the table before her. 'This is an album of Christmas beliefs, printed in Scandinavia at the end of the nineteenth century. After our last meeting I started thinking about your Mr Whitstable and his Stewards of Heaven. I couldn't see what had inspired him to form this kind of society, although it didn't surprise me one bit that he had.'

'It didn't?'

'Oh, no. You have to imagine the Victorian empire-builders as they were. Champions of industry, taming the savages, spreading the word. How grand they must have thought themselves! How godlike! People like James Whitstable saw themselves as superior human beings, educated, enlightened, and powerful. They wanted to separate themselves from the rabble, to have their worth acknowledged by their peers. And they sought methods of spiritual improvement. Sometimes, however, they got sidetracked into bad habits. These days one tends to dismiss the Victorian age as a time of mindless imperialism. It comes as rather a shock to recall that the youthful Queen Victoria envisaged a new era of democracy, tolerance, and freedom for all. Things turned out differently due to the rigours of the class system, and because men like Whitstable put themselves above the common herd. Power is about access, and private societies are designed to exclude.'

She opened the book at its mark and revealed a pair of graceful watercolour drawings. One was a traditional evocation of Saint Nicholas with his reindeer. The other was a representation of the god Odin, astride an eight-legged creature with horns. Both looked very similar. The distance between these two mythical icons was far less than Bryant had realized.

'I felt it was significant that Whitstable saw himself as Och, the Bringer of Light. The group photograph reminded me of something, but I couldn't think what it was. Then I remembered. The room in which the seven men were standing was decorated for Christmas. You could see holly lining the mantelpiece. Now, Christmas is a unique festival, originally celebrating not the birth of Christ but the rebirth of light following winter's shortest, darkest day. Do you want a mince pie?' She shook a tin at Bryant that sounded as if it contained rocks. 'Midwinter has always been regarded as a time of terrible danger. To primitive man, it must have seemed that the nights would continue to lengthen until darkness reigned continuously. The people of Britain sought to ward off this all-consuming darkness with rites and ceremonies, and have continued to do so for over five thousand years. What a relief it must have been for them to find the days lengthening again! What an excuse for a party! You probably know that the festival of Christmas celebrates this turning point; the triumph of light over darkness, and thus the victory of good over evil, Satan held at bay for another year. People whinge about Christmas becoming too commercial, but before heavenly choirs of angels made it so bland and solemn it was a marvelously rowdy pagan celebration.'

'And this has something to do with James Makepeace Whitstable?'

'Sorry, I thought I'd made myself clear. Let's assume that the photograph of the Alliance of Eternal Light was taken at the end of December. The Winter Solstice is the twenty-first or twenty-second of December. You see?'

'Not at all,' admitted Bryant.

'Look at the pictures,' said Maggie patiently. 'Saint Nicholas is a cleaned-up Christian version of the fearsome one-eyed pagan god Odin, the original "Old Nick." Odin's horse, Sleipnir, becomes Rudolph the reindeer. When was the first murder committed?'

'The sixth of December.'

'The feast day of Saint Nicholas. The first day of the battle between light and darkness. A battle that can't end until the light starts to lengthen once more, after the twenty-second of December.' She closed the book and handed it to him. 'I'm afraid your murders aren't over yet.'

'But it's Christmas Day. The days have already started to lengthen again.'

'Have they?' asked Maggie. 'With the terrible weather we've been having in the past few weeks, we're well below the seasonal average for hours of daylight. Instead, we've had more and more darkness. What about all the power cuts? The government isn't giving in. They're forecasting three hours of darkness every evening, and they reckon it will get worse. Perhaps the sacrifices aren't working.'

'I can't afford to believe that the world is descending into darkness because a secret society has failed to restore the daylight, Maggie. Next you'll be trying to make me believe that there's a chamber full of cloaked figures somewhere clutching knives at a sacrificial altar.' Bryant scratched at his unshaven chin, confused. 'You're assuming that Whitstable's alliance is still active, but we've found no evidence of that. Why would they act now, after waiting so long?'

'Perhaps it's some kind of anniversary.'

'No, the big one would surely be one hundred years. That's not due yet. And you're suggesting the alliance wages some kind of occult war by actually murdering people; if that were the case, they would surely be going after their true foes, the enemies of day and light. These deaths are occurring *within* their guild, not outside it. That means they're attacking their own people, their own blood. Why would they deliberately hurt themselves?'

'I agree with you,' said Maggie reluctantly. 'It doesn't make sense. But a lot can happen in nearly a hundred years. The system has inverted itself somehow. Perhaps it's not stoppable.'

'It's killing them one by one, Maggie. If they knew the danger of such a society, don't you think the Whitstables would try to expose it?'

'Perhaps they daren't confide in the police. Perhaps they're too scared of what might happen.'

Bryant thought of the uneasy silence that surrounded the mention of Charles Whitstable's name. 'Perhaps they know they can do nothing to halt it,' he said uneasily.

36 / Internecine

Laden with the volumes on pagan winter rituals that Maggie Armitage had lent him, Bryant drove back from Camden Town to his Battersea apartment. He arrived to find his partner furiously pacing the floor.

'Where the bloody hell have you been?' May snapped. 'We've been trying to page you for hours, but there's been no response.'

'That's odd,' said Bryant, pushing past him to remove a bottle of wine from the refrigerator. 'My bleeper's in the tie drawer of my wardrobe. You should have been able to hear it from in here.' He searched for a corkscrew. 'I promise I'll try to get used to new technology before one of us dies.'

'Arthur, there's been another attack.'

'What are you talking about? I rang in first thing this morning and everything was fine.'

'That's because they didn't discover Pippa Whitstable was missing until they got around to searching her bedroom. The Met constable on guard forgot to conduct a morning roll call.'

'Pippa . . .' Bryant's cheerful demeanour evaporated.

'She sneaked out last night and was stabbed in the alley beside the house.' May ran a hand through his chestnut mane, exasperated. 'She'll live, but she's not much use as a witness. Says her attacker was a small Indian man, and that they "all look the same" to her.'

'She's been around too many white people. There's madness at work here. It's like an epidemic—the more we seek to contain it, the more virulent each outbreak becomes.'

'We need to do something fast.' May was studying him, concerned. 'Have you eaten anything today?'

Bryant shook his head. 'It's been the last thing on my mind.'

They located the casserole his landlady had prepared the night before. 'Where is Alma?' Bryant asked, suspiciously eyeing the steaming bowl as he unwound his scarf.

'She gave up waiting for you and went to stay with her sister in Tooting.' May ladled chunks of stewed beef into bowls. 'Tell me what happened with the spiritualist.'

'Maggie's not a spiritualist, John. The fields are only vaguely related. It's like calling your dentist an optician. She's managed to establish the source of my occult connection.'

'Whitstable's secret alliance?'

'Yes, and you won't like it. Someone in the family has failed to carry out the ritual that should ensure the renewal of light to the world.'

'*What?*' May carried a laden tray into the dining room. 'This is the twentieth century, not the nineteenth. Are you telling me these are sacrificial murders?'

'I'm not sure about that,' replied Bryant, peering into his bowl and sniffing. 'Why would James Whitstable deliberately sacrifice the future generations of his family? I'm still missing something.'

'Part of your brain, by the sound of it,' muttered May, seating himself at the table. 'I hate to disappoint you, but the Whitstable alliance was formed for a more mundane purpose.'

'Which is?'

'We must go back to the unit. I locked the trading contract in my desk. It's safe there until I can arrange to have it properly analysed.' The forensic department operated beyond the official jurisdiction of the PCU, and was running shifts with a skeleton staff through the Christmas break.

'I suppose we've missed the queen's speech,' said Bryant gloomily, filling their glasses.

'I don't understand you,' said May. 'You're a republican, and yet you want to hear the queen.'

'She's a good woman who happens to be surrounded by idiots. Every outmoded hierarchy is the same,' said Bryant. 'Look at the Whitstables. They still trade on the respect of their ancestors, but that respect was created by fear. There's nothing noble about power won in that fashion. And apart from that, they're horrible people. How's the casserole?'

May prodded an indeterminate piece of vegetable matter with his fork. 'If your landlady cooks like this because she cares about you,' he said with a grimace, 'I dread to think what she'd make if you fell out.'

They arrived at the Mornington Crescent unit to find their office door wide open. The workmen had downed tools for the Christmas holiday. Water was pouring in through the unsealed frames. The office reeked of turpentine. Although all leave had been suspended in the division, the rest of the staff had been granted lunch breaks so that they could at least share a quick Christmas meal with their families.

May unlocked his desk and removed the sealed envelope containing the Whitstables' signatory contract.

'This document was drawn up to protect and further the family's business interests,' he said, spreading the damp pages carefully across his blotter. 'The Whitstables had little in common with their hardworking Northern brothers, who were running mills and forging communication links across the country. They were too old, too finely bred to be industrialists. They were entrepreneurs, opening markets via powerful Foreign Office connections, and made regular party payments to ensure favourable trade conditions.' He tapped the pages with his forefinger. 'It's all here, couched in suitably euphemistic English. James Makepeace Whitstable set up the alliance to protect his family by preventing their assets from falling into the wrong hands.

'These seven men declared their financial goals in writing. They had investments in iron, steel, and the railways, goldsmiths' and jewellers' concerns, and of course the Watchmakers. Remember you said that the Whitstables were the Victorian empire in microcosm? The terms of this contract suggest they were something more: a right-wing organization aimed at the furtherance of a dynasty. Look at this.' He singled out one of the handwritten clauses. ' "*In a situation of unfair competitive practice, the Alliance is fully prepared to disaffect said competitor with the utmost vigour.*" I wonder if they were prepared to kill in order to safeguard the supremacy of the company.'

Bryant sat and examined the document page by page. Finally he looked up at May. 'Have you been able to verify any of this?'

'I called Leo Marks. I thought he'd be bound to have other documents on file somewhere, but he says he's never heard of them. Legally binding contracts more than fifty years old are stored in a shared vault, and take time to locate. His office is closed until the third of January. Janice checked with the Savoy to see if they kept guests' registration records, and how far they go back. She asked them to run through the last two weeks of December 1881. The hotel's ledgers are stored in immaculate condition. They were able to verify that Mr James Whitstable and friends—he paid for the rooms of the other six—stayed there for just one night. But it wasn't on December the twenty-first of 1881. It was on the twenty-eighth.'

Bryant's face fell. 'You mean they missed the winter solstice by a whole week?'

'I'm afraid so. Your theory is wrong, Arthur. Your dates have to be purely coincidental.'

'According to Maggie's books, the day of each death matches points in the supposed battle between day and eternal night. The culmination of the fight occurs at the end of December. I'd have written it off as coincidence myself if I hadn't seen the photograph of the Stewards of Heaven signing their contract at the Savoy. The whole business is filled with strange associations. Have you noticed how the lights always seem to flicker just before there's a murder?'

'Oh, that's ridiculous!' May exploded. 'You can't tell me they've put a spell on their descendants!'

'Perhaps not, but I think the contract bound them spiritually as well as legally. The others *had* to sign. They didn't dare not to.'

'You're sure all the dates match up?'

'So far.'

'You'd better see if there are any further events in the mystical calendar that we should be aware of.'

Bryant stared at the pages, his thoughts far away. May

knew the look. It meant there was something on his partner's mind that he had failed to mention.

Bryant opened his mouth to speak, then closed it again.

'All right,' May said finally. 'What is it?'

'I've been thinking. Why did he pick the Savoy? The hotel had only been built two years before. Why sign the document there? Why not have it certified in legal chambers?'

'No doubt the Savoy was the smart new place to be seen taking one's business partners.'

'I suppose if they were clandestinely signing the document, privacy would have been desirable. But I can't help wondering if there was an association with the hotel that gave James Whitstable a reason for signing up his alliance partners there.'

'We could go through their records, but I feel like we're heading off track.'

'Look at the contract,' said Bryant. 'It's handwritten, filled with grammatical mistakes and anomalies, as if put together on the spur of the moment.' He fanned the pages wide before him. 'There are three different hands at work here. It was too much for one person to write by himself in an evening. Whitstable coerced his partners into creating a blueprint for their financial future. I think the contract was just one part of a broader ritual.'

'Arthur, we've spent long enough rooting about in the past. We need someone who's alive today.'

'I agree,' rejoined his partner. 'But until the Met comes up with a single shred of incriminating evidence, our only chance of finding a motive lies in understanding the family's ancestry. Find the motive and we trace the culprit.'

'And your motive is human sacrifice for the return of

the daylight?' May shook his head. 'These aren't the Dark Ages. Greed, jealousy, revenge—those are the only enduring reasons for murder. Human nature stays the same. This agreement was signed in late-Victorian Britain, an age of enlightenment. Advocating the murder of the family it was designed to protect makes no sense, can't you see that?'

'All I can see,' said Bryant stubbornly, 'is your refusal to acknowledge the debt we all owe to the past.'

'You can't bend the facts to fit your theories. Whitstable did not form his alliance on the day of the solstice. How much more proof do you need?'

'I could have sworn I was right about that. Everything pointed to a supernatural ceremony.'

'Are you absolutely sure? Look at your own interests. You love all this mumbo-jumbo about pagan worship. Does it honestly belong in the investigation? I have a theory of my own, but I'm not trying to force it into place.'

'And what is it, might I ask?'

'A team of hired assassins carrying out instructions from someone in the family who bears an old grudge. The way everything's meticulously planned, it's as if it's being computed.'

'Now whose personal interests are coming through?' Bryant exclaimed. 'Look out there.' He pointed to the window. 'The days are *still dark*.'

'Raymond Land's been telling people you're suffering from mental stress,' said May, 'that you're intractable, bloody-minded. I told him not to be so damned rude. But unless you start working with me instead of developing these crazy notions by yourself, I'll start thinking he's right.' He stalked from the office and slammed the door.

Bryant sat back and pressed his eyes shut. What was happening to the Whitstables was also happening to them.

The investigation had lost its way in internecine fighting. He would develop a practical appliance for May's theory, but that meant first discounting his own. He began to compile a date list of events in the pagan winter battle of light and dark. The articles in Maggie's books had been assembled from unreliable sources. Eventually, though, he was able to create a list of the most important dates.

Bryant looked down on the lights of Camden, shining bright on to bare wet streets. If only he could step back to that winter's night long ago, if only he could see what *they* saw. . . .

He needed fresh air. As he slipped into his overcoat, his attention was drawn by the ragged patch beneath the window. Lost in thought, he examined the striated section of wall where the workmen had peeled away layers of paint, revealing their own inchoate glimpses of the past.

37 / Whispering

May knew he shouldn't have asked if there were any problems. Everyone in the room had a hand raised.

The Whitstable family had just set a new record for living together, and the strain of so many difficult people having to share with each other was beginning to manifest itself in a form of upmarket cabin fever. Pippa's mother had collapsed upon hearing that her daughter had been attacked, and now remained under medical supervision in one of the bedrooms.

As everyone was talking at once, May called for quiet by blowing the sports whistle he had strung around his neck, and pointed at Isobel Whitstable. 'You have a question?'

'Being cooped up like this is making me sick. The food is frightful, and we're having to share bathrooms. How much longer do we have to stay here?' There was an immediate hubbub of assent.

'Until the danger to all of you has passed,' replied May. 'You saw what happened when Pippa ventured outside.'

The noise level rose sharply, and he was forced to shout. 'It's come to my attention that some of you have been trying to speak to the press about your treatment here.' The family had been giving bitter, sarcastic interviews about their treatment at the hands of the incompetent police. Several secret phone calls had been logged by the security team. 'I'm afraid we're going to have to stop that.'

This was followed by a barrage of angry demands.

'It sounds like you're frightened of the papers putting their own investigators on the case,' said Edith Whitstable, who was still being guarded by her twin grandsons. 'We want whoever's doing this run to earth. It's irrelevant who catches him, just so long as someone does before there's another death.' Everyone seemed to agree on that point.

'I feel the same way as you,' said May, 'but some of the journalists are showing a lack of responsibility in their hunt for a new angle. They might inadvertently reveal something to your enemies.'

Before May could field any further questions, Sergeant Longbright entered the room. 'Alison Hatfield is on the telephone for you. Do you want to take it?'

May looked over at the unruly assembly of mothers, fathers, sons, grandmothers, daughters, and babies, all arguing across each other. 'I'll call her back. No, on second thoughts, let me take it.'

The hallway outside was relatively quiet. He lifted the handset. 'Alison, how are you?'

'I'm fine. I hope I haven't disturbed you, but you did say to call if anything—'

'You did the right thing. What's on your mind?'

'I was going through the basement papers I brought home with me, and found some correspondence between James Makepeace Whitstable and one of the other members of the alliance. It's mostly shipping arrangements, but he makes reference to the night of the signing, and states that a full account of the event was subsequently written up. He doesn't say what in, unfortunately.'

'You think he kept minutes?'

'That's what I wondered. All papers and personal effects pertaining to the guild eventually revert to the hall, many of them through bequests and donations. I was thinking of going to the office later. Do you want me to look for it while I'm there?'

'Yes, if you don't mind. I mean, it is a public holiday. You should be enjoying yourself.'

'Oh, this *is* my way of enjoying myself. I can hardly hear you . . .' By the sound of it, tempers were flaring in the lounge.

'I have to go,' said May. 'Please, Alison, call me if you find anything.'

One of the Whitstable children was tugging at his trouser leg. 'Come on, Mister Policeman,' he said with a grin. 'The mummies are trying to hit each other.' Clenching his teeth and his fists, May strode back into the tantrum therapy centre formerly known as the front parlour.

Alison Hatfield had fidgeted about in her apartment, unable to settle, before deciding to return to the lift in the foyer of the Watchmakers' Company. It was exciting to know that the police were relying on her assistance. She was looking forward to seeing John May again. There was something intriguing and rather sad about him.

The basement file rooms had been closed for so many years that those in charge of maintaining their order had now retired. She pulled the trellis door shut and as the lift descended she thought about the boxes stored beneath her.

The Victorians were great note-takers, letter-writers, and diarists. It was likely that their documents were kept here, within the guild, and had simply been forgotten. Dead files were rarely examined, and mundane artefacts like balance sheets fell beyond the scope of interested historians.

Her breath clouded across the beam of her pocket torch as she opened the lift door. The corridor ahead was in darkness. She had not asked for the emergency lighting to be turned on again, for fear of arousing suspicion.

Any further documentary proof would lie in the room she had begun to explore with May. As she reached the door, she was surprised to find it partially open. She distinctly remembered locking it. She pushed it wide and shone her torch inside.

Someone had definitely been down here. Chairs and boxes had been moved. Frowning, she crossed the floor and shone her torch into the first carton. This morning it had contained three tied packets of correspondence; now there were only two. Her shoes slipped on sheets of paper. She looked down to find that a number of letters had been dropped or tossed aside. She lifted the sheets and held them to the light.

Apart from the caretaker, no one else knew she had been sifting through the documents. Who had been here?

Her thoughts were interrupted by a light scuffling sound in the corridor outside. She scanned the torch beam across to the door, but saw nothing. She knew about the rats that came up from the river; she didn't want to consider how many might have bred in the ancient cellars. She was about to resume her search when a feeling of unease prickled at the back of her neck.

Alison was a practical woman, not given to easy fears, but she suddenly knew she was not alone. She lowered the torch beam to the floor and quietly made her way back across the room. As she did so, she sensed another human body.

The darkness in the corridor was palpable. A slight breeze brushed her face. She began to walk slowly towards the goods lift, keeping the torchlight trained at her shoes.

There was someone within feet of her, of that she was sure. She stared at the beam. A chill cloud was dissipating in the cone of light, the remnants of someone's shallow breath. She took another step toward the lift, and another. The metal door stood less than three yards from her. Far below, the river drains faintly pounded, rushing through darkness.

A scrape behind her as someone or something divorced itself from the wall. Unable to contain her panic for another moment, she ran to the lift with her arm outstretched, grabbing the brass handle and twisting it back, slamming the trellis open and forcing herself inside.

As she pulled it shut she saw the bulky shape of a running man. A hand thrust itself through the diamond-shaped gap in the bars, grabbing at her sweater. She screamed as she jabbed at it with the torch, but the fingers, groping for a purchase, seized her flesh and pulled. The torch case was lightweight and plastic, and the batteries fell out as she thrashed at the invading limb.

She hammered the floor buttons, and the lift jerked into life, slowly rising. The fist remained locked around her arm, gripping tightly. Her attacker was being raised from the floor, and had braced himself against the lowering ceiling. Far above, the lift mechanism began to whine as it strained to raise the cage.

It was a stalemate: the lift could ascend no further, but her attacker could not recall it. Bending her knees abruptly, Allison lifted her legs from the floor. The move caught her assailant by surprise as the deadweight hit his arm. With a sickly crack his hand lost purchase on her sweater and the lift suddenly shot up.

She slammed to the back of the lift, staying there until she reached the ground floor. The foyer was deserted. If he knew where the basement staircase was, he could be here in seconds. The porter wasn't due back until tomorrow. Until then, the main door keys were in her purse, inside her desk. She had planned to double-lock the entrance upon leaving.

Her heels clicked rapidly across the marble floor, echoing in the dark stairways above. She was scared to look back. She could feel her heart bellowing in her chest. Behind her, the staircase door slammed open. She knew better than to waste another moment in the building. Without detouring to collect her coat or purse she ran from the entrance.

The city streets were utterly deserted. This was Boxing Day, and there was not a soul to be seen.

Her car was parked in the darkened narrow street behind the Goldsmiths' Hall. There was no point in heading back there without her keys. She ran along the empty pavement in the direction of St Paul's Cathedral.

Behind her, a dark man dressed in an ankle-length raincoat emerged from the hall. She increased her speed, searching for traffic as she crossed the road. Behind, the figure gained speed, his unbuttoned coat beating about him, his damaged arm clearly causing him pain as he closed the gap between them with long loping strides.

Boots hammered behind her as she lurched across the road ahead. The churchyard of St Paul's was always kept open. She ran through the gates in the direction of the main entrance. There was bound to be someone at the door.

As she fled up the steps of the cathedral he lunged out at her, but she had reached the doorway, and offered a prayer of thanks as she slipped inside.

One of the wardens was switching off the lights.

She halted, trying to catch her breath. 'Father... there's a man...'

A young, bespectacled ecclesiast with thinning hair looked at her quizzically, unsure of the problem facing him.

She tried again, aware of the figure looming behind her. 'Someone is following me...'

The warden looked beyond her to the waiting figure. 'The service has finished. We're closing for the night,' he began.

'But this is a church,' Alison screamed suddenly. 'You're not supposed to close!'

'I'm sorry, but you two will have to sort out your differences outside.'

He thought they were having a lovers' tiff! She looked around to see the raincoated figure striding quickly towards her.

The warden stepped forward, shaking his head and raising his hands in front of him, refusing her entry. Ducking beneath his arm, she ran into the nave, expecting to find other clergymen ready to help her. There was no one in sight. Surely they didn't entrust the safety of an entire building to one man?

Scuffling footsteps made Alison turn in fright. Her pursuer had been apprehended by the warden, who was ineffectually attempting to hold him outside. Suddenly the raincoated figure struck the warden hard in the face with the flat of his good hand, knocking him down on to the tiled floor. The sound of the assault reverberated through the cathedral in a dull boom.

He had stepped around the unconscious form and was moving fast towards her.

A narrow opening in the right transept appeared in

her vision. She took it without thinking and found herself in the steep stairway that led to the Whispering Gallery. She glanced back, only to find him right behind her.

There was nowhere else to go.

Up she ran, her heart hammering painfully, the hot blade of a stitch forming in her side. As he reached out again she kicked back with her spiked heel, connecting hard with his chest.

She reached the gallery entrance. The chill stone balustrade curved away on either side. She intended to follow the path around, knowing that she would be able to see if he changed direction.

The vast dome rose above them to create a giddying sense of space, its monochromatic paintings fearful and austere. St Paul's was a gruesomely Christian church, a monument to the idea that redemption invoked awe, not comfort.

He was panting hard as he came through the door. There was no time to put any distance between them. She stopped and looked back, but the dim exit sign above his head cast a shadow over his face.

'What do you want from me?' she called out.

No reply came. He was breathing heavily, balancing lightly on the balls of his feet. He seemed disconnected from the pursuit, as though he hardly realized what he was doing.

'I didn't find out anything.' She took a step back as he slowly approached. 'I swear I was only trying to help. I can't do you any harm—please, I don't want to end up like the others.'

The longer she talked, the more she felt she had a chance of being saved. But how? It was obvious that they were alone in the eerie vastness of the cathedral. There was no holy sanctuary for her here, only harsh judgement. He was beside her now. The touch of his hand was soft and almost reassuring.

'Sorry, Lady. It's not my fault.'

His voice was little more than an exhalation of air with the trace of an Eastern accent. Alison was so surprised that he had actually spoken that she failed to move as he suddenly seized her, his thick fingers snaking across her opening mouth. He was a powerful man, and effortlessly lifted her off the floor. She saw the bitter irony of facing death surrounded by the very history she had spent her life loving and trying to understand.

She looked up into his brown eyes. There was no malice in them, just commitment to duty.

'So very sorry,' he whispered again in a tone of genuine regret. With a grunt, he hoisted her twisting body over the balcony and released it. With thrashing limbs and a throat stretched taut by the power of her scream, she plunged a full hundred feet to the floor below.

Her last sight was of the unforgiving cathedral spinning above her, as the echo of her fall refracted back and forth between the tombs of sleeping saints.

38 / Illumination

Beneath the white traverse arches of the green-house were orchidaceous clusters of crimson and scarlet flowers: bougainvillea and beloperone, callistemon and strelitzea, surrounded by fan and sago palms, some of them over eight feet tall.

'This was my great-grandfather James Makepeace Whitstable's house, and these are the plants that he himself tended. Until recently they were like our family, deeply rooted, tough, surviving. Now they might outlive us all.'

Charles had brought her here after dinner, the perfect place to sprawl in armchairs beneath the glass roof. During the course of the afternoon there had been endless questions about her upbringing and complex explanations of how the guild ran its businesses. He was a decisive man, a Mason, a figure of restless intensity, and had inexplicably chosen to admit her into his world. He had spoken about the supervision of Anglo-Indian exports, and it sounded incredibly, unbearably dull.

Beyond the greenhouse a lurid sunset flooded the sky in a vermilion wash, mirrored in shimmering fields of frost. Charles had humanized himself by changing into blue jeans and a heavy green cotton sweater. During the course of the afternoon he had not smiled once. A number of times he had started at noises in the endless dark woods beyond the house. He appeared to be under a great amount of strain. Now, as he sat warming a brandy in his hands, he seemed on the verge of imparting a confidence.

'I imagine it's been pretty dull for you today,' he began, studying his glass. 'Christmas and all that, you'd probably rather be with your friends, someone of your own age. I'm not used to having young people around. Our family was always old and big and inescapable.'

'I just thought there would be others here.'

'Normally there would be, but this year my visit is under extraordinary circumstances. My childhood memories are filled with decrepit relatives tottering about these rooms. As a kid I was always being scolded for disturbing my sleeping elders.' He leaned back against the headrest, recalling his upbringing in the vast dusty house above them. 'Our family—a blessing and a curse. Until recently we were only fighting to stay alive in business. Now look at us. What a sorry state we're in. I suppose you've been following it all in the papers.'

He looked across at her, his grey eyes eerily luminescent in the setting sun. He tasted his brandy and set it down. 'You have a very strong-willed mother, Geraldine. I assume you're aware of her ambitions.'

'What makes you say that?'

Charles studied his glass. 'It's Gwen who wants you to work for us.'

'She had nothing to do with me coming here.'

'I wondered if you had her ambitions.' He gave a rare smile. 'But no, you're different. I can sense a certain antipathy toward your parents. I know you're acting under your own volition. You must understand something about us, Geraldine.' He gave a thin smile, no lips, no teeth. 'The only way to effect an entry into the Whitstable family is to operate in its interests. The family always protects itself. Even if it means curtailing its own freedom.'

He drained his glass. 'It's hard to explain one's behaviour under threat. Mr Heath will continue to hold out against the unions, and that will be just the beginning. The world is waiting to move into London to pick its riches. There are dark times ahead, and only the strong will survive. Once we were the giants, the whip-wielders. Now we're nothing compared to the mighty modern conglomerates. They are the new imperialists, not us. British Associated Tobacco is opening markets in the Far East. Coca-Cola is buying real estate.' He pulled open a drawer in the small oak chest at his side and withdrew an engraved gold pocket watch, passing it over for inspection.

'This is the sort of thing our guild used to make. Who wants it now? Who can afford it? Once, craftsmanship was as necessary as breathing. Now it's a curiosity, quaint and redundant. In order to stay alive, we've been forced to diversify.' He poured fresh brandies for both of them as she studied the watch. 'It was James Makepeace Whitstable who put the family and the guild back on the right track.'

'How did he do that?' asked Jerry, carefully sipping her liqueur. She wanted to remember everything clearly.

'James was a gifted businessman, a man of great charity and honesty, a practising Christian. When he rose to assume his position at the head of the family, he knew it would take more than mere financial expertise to clear our debts and spread our business. Nearly a century ago, on twenty-eight December 1881, he gathered together the most trusted men in his guild. That night, they formed an alliance to protect their craftsmen.

'James wanted to devise a formula that would keep the

company in the right hands, not just then but for generations to come. The future held great promise. The empire was at its zenith. The chances for expansion were
limitless. James was a visionary. He saw that, just as
quickly as it had grown, the British empire could wane.
The Americans were establishing trade routes at an extraordinary pace. The Japanese had begun to conduct
commerce with outsiders. Consumerism had begun.
Gilbert and Sullivan wrote *The Mikado* to cash in on the
fact that London had a fancy for anything from Japan.
Liberty's in Regent Street was decorated like a Japanese
pagoda. Ethnic purchasing fads were already in place.
People were looking for the next big thing. What hope
was there for an ancient London guild with so many keen
rivals on the horizon? Rivals who didn't care about craftsmanship or tradition.

'After that night at the Savoy, our business continued
to prosper. And just as our rivals grew strong enough to
challenge us, they always disappeared. Their trade figures
would get this close to ours,' he held his thumb and forefinger half an inch apart, 'and they'd go out of business.'

'Didn't James tell anyone else in the family what his
alliance was doing or how it worked? Didn't people
wonder?'

'Nobody minded so long as the company grew. The
Watchmakers' Company was happy to let the Alliance of
Eternal Light take care of the problem. James Whitstable
swore his partners to secrecy.'

'What happened to the alliance when the original
members died?'

'It died with them. Eventually everyone forgot about
it. By the time I took over, the guild's administration was
a shambles. The old skills had been lost. I was forced to
start the administration afresh. I fired many of the old

overseas staff and formed new business strategies for each territory. In England, the Whitstables still own all of the controlling stock. You'd be surprised how many staff members are direct descendants of the seven original alliance members.'

Jerry wondered if they were the same people who had eventually become victims. She knew so much more about the Whitstables now, but still the answer remained elusive. She needed to know how one man's recipe for economic recovery could result in a massacre nearly a century later.

Charles Whitstable raised his glass. 'You're entering an extraordinary family, Jerry,' he said. 'It'll take great bravery to be one of us.'

'Why do you say that?'

In the indigo gloom, only his eyes retained the light. 'Because James Makepeace Whitstable's plan for salvation is fast destroying us,' he said, almost amused by the paradox.

'Can I ask you something?' she ventured. 'You don't have to answer.'

'It's done me good to talk tonight. I owe you an honest answer.'

'Do you know how James Whitstable's system worked?'

It was only now that she realized how oppressively dark it had become. 'I am a direct descendant,' came the reply. 'Of course I know.'

'But you saw him. You even spoke to him,' said Bryant, exasperated. 'You must have some idea of what he looked like.'

The young warden grimaced apologetically. His head

was bandaged where his nose had been broken, and his nostrils were packed with cotton wool, so that it was hard to understand what he was saying. He looked from the detective to the female sergeant walking at his side, hoping to find some sympathy. Dawn was approaching, and the nave of St Paul's was bitterly cold. Because of the murder, today's services had been suspended for the first time since the war.

'As you can see, this part of the cathedral's entrance hall is poorly illuminated,' the battered warden explained. 'Most of the main overhead lights were shut down last night. They're normally lowered after the money box has been emptied.'

'What money box?' asked Bryant.

'We like visitors to leave a donation.'

'So we have to pay to get into heaven now?' Bryant was feeling blasphemous, bad-tempered, and cold, and furious with the warden for failing to help prevent Alison Hatfield's miserable death. The thought of having to tell John what had happened appalled him.

'The man was standing beneath an arch. I thought he was wearing a bandage. It fell off when he hit me, and I saw it was a turban. His face was in shadow. Obviously, we don't get many Indians in here. I thought she was having an argument with her boyfriend. Couples often sit in the courtyard.'

'In the dead of winter? On Boxing Day? She didn't have a boyfriend. Did this man speak to her at all?'

'It all happened so quickly. I told them they couldn't come in, and he ran at me.'

Bryant rubbed his hands on his trousers, trying to improve his circulation. 'Is there any detail at all you remember about him?'

'All I can think of is his callousness. He must have followed her in here knowing that he was going to kill her. As if he was just doing his job.'

'If everyone had been doing that, Alison Hatfield might still be alive,' said Bryant. 'She came here expecting to find sanctuary.' He turned on his heel and strode angrily from the cathedral.

He leaned on the Embankment railing, his scarf pulled tightly about his neck and shoulders, watching the low mist eddying across the whorled, shining surface of the Thames. A police launch chugged past, struggling against the ebb tide. *That's what we're doing*, he thought, *fighting the flow. Trying to hold off a caul of darkness that grows thicker by the minute.*

Now no one was safe. Alison Hatfield had died for a specific, identifiable reason. According to May, she'd been searching for a diary, unaware that perhaps someone else was also looking for it. Her death had come as the cruellest blow of all. She had wanted to help them, and they had encouraged her to venture into the dark alone. He would never rest until he had found her killer. He owed her that much.

Right now, a hastily assembled forensic crew was removing every one of the boxes from the storeroom below Goldsmiths' Hall. Bryant was sure they would find no diary. Somebody had beaten Alison to the discovery. Could a colleague have overheard her on the telephone? The building had been closed for the holiday season. She had made a special trip to open it up, so it was unlikely that anyone else would have been there. Tomlins probably had his own set of keys, but he didn't fit the description of her killer.

Seagulls circled above, dropping sharply from the still-dark sky like snapped-shut parasols. Bryant slipped his hands into his overcoat sleeves and waited, and watched, and thought hard.

Death in a cathedral. Murder most foul within a holy shrine. What did he know about the place? He tried to remember what he had read.

In the eighteenth century, St Paul's had been unpopular and unfashionable. Whores had paraded in its grounds, using the nave as a shortcut. Many had thought the place as pagan as it was Christian. And how the hell did the songwriter Ivor Novello ever get a memorial plaque in the crypt along with Lord Nelson? This was no good; just when he needed it most his mind was cluttered with nonsense, pieces of quiz-show trivia.

The chill air was biting hard at his bones. As slivers of light grew between the clouds, he forced himself to clear his mind of ephemeral detail and think clearly.

So many ideas had been put forward, and all of them wrong. So many dead ends. The Common Market conference. The Nazi symbol. The sacred flame. Cut through them. Look beyond.

Was it revenge or simple monetary gain? Why were all their suspects Indian? May's theory: a number of assassins involved, each murder logged and computed from the start. Could it be that John was right after all, and that Alison's death was a panicky mistake?

There was something else that bothered him.

The business with the dates. The winter solstice had passed on December twenty-second. The document forming the Alliance of Eternal Light had been signed at the Savoy on the twenty-eighth. If James Makepeace Whitstable was genuinely concerned with the symbolic act of bringing light to the world, he would have gathered his men a full week earlier.

Dawn broke across the City of London.

Suddenly the Embankment lights began to flick off. Pearls of luminescence, familiar and friendly, looped in hazy necklaces along the riverline, were disappearing, one string after another.

Bryant watched as row after row vanished into the night, all the way down the South Bank promenade, past Coin Street and Gabriel's Wharf, past the Oxo Building and the Anchor pub, past Spice Wharf and St Katharine's Dock and Tower Bridge, to the distant lights of Greenwich.

'Oh, my God.'

His mouth slowly opened as he realized the answer. 'How incredibly, irredeemably stupid of me,' he said aloud. 'How could I ever have been so blind?'

He jumped back from the railing, tucked his scarf across his midriff, and set off as quickly as his frozen limbs would allow.

39 / The Rain Gauge

Jerry's tongue felt thick and dry from last night's brandy. It was the first time in years that she had slept without a night-light. Slowly she raised her head and examined the room. She saw dark walls of densely woven brocade, a ceramic washstand and jug, a mahogany dressing table and wardrobe. She rose from the high brass bed and drew back the curtains.

Grey sheets of rain obscured the fields below. A flock of miserable sheep stood huddled beneath a line of dripping beeches. Her watch read nine fifteen. She wondered if her host had risen yet.

Why had Charles chosen to unburden himself to her? Did he find her attractive? He had refused to elaborate on his closing remark about James Makepeace Whitstable. Perhaps he had no intention of confiding in his new apprentice.

After she had washed and dressed, she explored the house. The sound of rain could be heard throughout the upper floors. She smelled old wood burnished with lavender polish, damp and time and emptiness. The rooms were kept in such immaculate condition that they reminded her of Joseph Herrick's stage sets. They needed a boisterous family to bring them to life.

A broad central staircase led downstairs to the breakfast room where Charles Whitstable, casually attired in a sweater and cords, was already seated with a newspaper.

The look on his face when he rose to greet his guest suggested further bad news.

'Please,' said Charles, gesturing at the heated tureens on the table, 'help yourself to breakfast. My mother told me there was another attack on the family.'

'What's happened?' she asked.

'Pippa Whitstable is in hospital. She's only a little older than you.'

'I'm sorry,' Jerry said, not sure what to make of his reaction. 'Are you closely related?'

'Distant cousins. We've met once or twice. I thought we were all supposed to be under police surveillance. They're not saying who attacked her.'

'Have you tried calling the police for information?'

'The line is permanently engaged. I don't suppose there's anything I can do to help. The family resents my interference. They think my great-grandfather caused this. They know I administrate the alliance's business system. But I want to find a way to help them.'

'Do you think you'll have to return to England permanently?' she asked, seating herself before eggs and coffee.

'Perhaps. Whether they like it or not, the family needs me. And I need to think about taking a wife. With so many of us dying, it's time we produced a few heirs. Taking over the family's affairs took up all my time. Everyone had been relying on the alliance to bail them out whenever there was a crisis, but now the system has turned against them. I cleared away their outdated ideas, but all I've succeeded in doing is earning their enmity. They think I'm cheating them. They can't see that the Whitstable "empire" is no more. The land they owned is being auctioned off. Soon there won't be anything left but the houses they live in. I'm streamlining the group, investing in technology they can't understand, and this way we may just survive. But to listen to them, you'd think I was diverting their dwindling capital into a drug-running operation.' He drained the cup and checked his watch. 'That's why it's important to bring in people with new ideas. I called your father and asked him to join us for lunch. Can you stay on until tomorrow? There's more I'd like to discuss. Besides, you're charming company, and you brighten this old house no end.'

She sat back and studied him carefully. She had never met anyone like him before. Charles was mature and urbane. He treated her like a woman and seemed prepared to give her responsibilities. Her mission of subversion had taken on an interesting new aspect.

'Do you think the police will ever catch anyone?'

'The deaths will end as suddenly as they began, and no one will ever be able to say why.'

'How can you be so sure?'

'Because the same thing has been happening to our overseas rivals throughout the century. Of course, the attacks were never this densely concentrated before, and they took place on another continent, so investigations were never concluded. British justice doesn't concern itself with the deaths of a few Indian businessmen. But now that the tables are turned on the British, there's hell to pay.'

'What's India like?' she asked, watching as he finished his breakfast.

'Vibrant. Shocking. A sinkpit and a paradise.' His eyes maintained their serene quiescence. 'In India, the cycle of life is fast and full of fury. The rites of birth and death are closer together. We English seal away our emotions. Our grief, and much of our joy, remains private. Their feelings are more exposed, and it makes them strong. I admire their survival in the midst of so much damage and confusion. My relatives could learn a thing or two from them.'

If she performed well in her new career, he would probably take her with him. But wasn't her request for a job just a ploy? She had to remember that she had no real intention of taking him up on the offer, even if it represented an escape from the house in Chelsea. The thought of returning there depressed her. She was alarmed to discover how much she liked Charles.

'I have to make a lot of long-distance calls this morning,' he said, rising. 'Why don't you take a look around the estate? We'll reconvene just before lunch.'

'I'll be just as happy sitting in the library. Do you have any documentation on the companies that I can read?'

'Now that's the kind of initiative I like,' he said, smiling for the first time that morning. 'I'll see what I can find for you.' As he passed, he squeezed her shoulder affectionately, and she found herself sharing his pleasure.

To be left alone in the library was a mark of how far she had gained his trust. The room couldn't have exuded more masculinity if it had been lined with dead stags. There were so many pipe racks and gun-racks and lewd Indian carvings that it reminded her of Peggy Harmsworth's house in Highgate. She was happy to leave huntsmanship to the gentry. Still, the library's stock was surprisingly varied, and contained many first editions. For the rest of the morning she read everything she could find about the Whitstables, but judging from the curious gaps in the bookshelves, any incriminating material had been carefully removed.

It wasn't until she had worked out how to operate the

rolling stepladder that she discovered a top shelf filled with obscure Victorian volumes. While several editions proved individually interesting, they provided her with no collective insight to the mysteries of James Makepeace Whitstable and his Stewards of Heaven. Seating herself in one of the deep leather armchairs within a bay window overlooking the frozen fields, she began to read.

Just before one, a bell sounded in the hall. 'No doubt that will be your father,' said Charles, who had come to look in on her. 'Don't get up—finish what you're reading. I'll have him wait in the parlour until you're ready.'

The shift in authority was clearly meant to be noted. Now that she was being accepted into the family business, she enjoyed the protection of Charles. Her father would meekly wait outside while she finished reading her book. The thought gave her little satisfaction. Poor Gwen and Jack. They had offered her up as a sacrifice to their ambition, only to find themselves excluded again.

Lunchtime with Charles and her father was punctuated throughout with awkward pauses. After the meal Jack was virtually dismissed and told to return to London. Charles would see to it that Jerry was returned safe and sound first thing on Monday morning.

For the rest of the day she and Charles worked side by side in the grand study, as he explained his long-term plans for the guild. She saw that the work was not as dull as it had first appeared. Indeed, she could envisage certain circumstances under which it would be a pleasure to remain beside him all day.

Their meal together that evening had the intimate quality of a candlelit dinner, even if it took place beneath electric light.

* * *

John May sat at his desk and fought to keep the horror of Alison's death from his mind.

But there would be time enough later for grief. The best thing to do was find a way to avenge her. May was a logical man. He sought patterns in chaos. Now he thought about the chart of deaths Arthur had logged to date. Could the attacks be following a sequence, even if they conformed to no easily identifiable pattern? *More than one murderer.* How could that be? The latest death had thrown him. It wasn't taken into consideration on the chart, and it was a different modus operandi. Once again, the murderer had been seen but not apprehended.

If someone was working out a sequence for the murders, how would he choose his dates? Then there was the deadline: 28 December. There wasn't much time left. He spread the details out before him, each death, each attack on a separate piece of paper.

No particular numerological significance. Could the dates have been chosen haphazardly? Suppose they were scientifically random, like a Turing code? Turing had successfully cracked cryptographic messages created on a typewriter attached to a print wheel, and had suggested that computers would be capable of human thought only if a random element, such as a roulette wheel, was introduced. But why would anyone go to the trouble of doing that?

There had to be a logic at work. The deaths were irregularly spaced, but there had to be a pattern. By what coordinates, though?

December the sixth to the twenty-eighth. Why not the first of the month to the last? That would be more logical. Why not a correspondence to the lunar cycle?

The new random element is easier to explain, he thought. *Panic has set in, and that's dangerous for everyone.*

Across the desk, a weather chart in Bryant's folded newspaper caught his eye.

Wettest December since the war.

May turned the paper around and studied the article more carefully. The murder dates corresponded with those when individual records had been broken for the most rainfall in a twenty-four-hour period.

He withdrew a chewed pencil stub from beneath his shirt and drew two lines on a sheet of paper. Along both lines he marked days six to twenty-eight. On the first line he added a mark whenever a death had occurred. On the second, he marked the record rainfall highs.

The spacing was the same. The rain highs were precisely ten hours before each of the deaths, except for the unpremediated attacks on Alison Hatfield and Pippa Whitstable.

What on earth was he supposed to do with information like this?

Whatever it was, he needed to start thinking fast; it had just begun to rain again.

40 / Automaton

'For God's sake, Arthur, you've been missing all day. Can't you come back in the morning?' May had returned home to find his partner standing on his doorstep, looking like a rain-battered scarecrow.

'Don't ever complain about me not wearing my bleeper again, because I've been trying yours for the past four hours.' Only Bryant's eyes and ears were poking out above his scarf. The top of his head was an odd shade of greyish blue. 'A car pulled up a few minutes ago and some kindly Samaritan asked me if I needed a bed for the night. I had to see him off with a stick. Where on earth have you been?'

'I've been walking and thinking,' said May, finding his keys and opening the main door.

'Well done, you. Come up with anything?' He trudged wetly behind May up to his apartment, his shoes squelching on the stairs.

'The deaths are tied in with the monthly rainfall figures.'

'Excuse me, I'm going deaf,' said Bryant, unwinding his scarf and chafing his ears as he entered the room. 'For a minute I thought you said the deaths were tied in with the rain. They always used to say the butler did it. Now you're telling me it's the weatherman?'

'I'll explain after you tell me what you're here for.' May was used to working through the night with his partner, but Arthur had never waited on the doorstep for him before.

'While we're exchanging information, I know why James Makepeace Whitstable formed his alliance on the twenty-eighth of December. I know what he formed it for, and I know why people are dying. You'd better put the kettle on. This is going to take some time.'

While May made tea, Bryant turned up the central-heating thermostat, then located a bottle of brandy. 'It's funny how things just hit you. I was standing at the railings on the Embankment this morning—'

'God, where have you *been* all day?'

'Working it out. You know how I am.'

'You must have been freezing,' said May, setting down a tray.

'Got my thermals on.' Bryant tapped his leg. 'I needed the wind coming in off the river to clear my thoughts. It certainly shifted some phlegm, I can tell you. Anyway, it was dawn and suddenly the lights went out, all the way along the Embankment. That was it. I made the connection. It was Gilbert and Sullivan, you see.'

'No, I don't see.'

'James Whitstable had called his men to town to discuss an idea he'd had. Think of his position. These were trusted friends, guildsmen born and bred, people he'd known all his life. He wanted to justify their loyalty, to protect and strengthen the Watchmakers. He thought he could do it by providing the guild with a group of like-minded individuals dedicated to keeping the bright light of private enterprise burning, no matter what. He would see that British craftsmanship remained unchallenged by foreign rivals as it went out into the world. The Victorians were building for immortality. James

Whitstable wanted to ensure that the Watchmakers lasted for ever.'

'Arthur, I fail to see where this is leading—'

'The aims of the alliance are stated in the signatory contract. We know that James Whitstable summoned his men and booked them into the Savoy at noon on the twenty-eighth of December 1881. The group took a light lunch in the hotel restaurant, and Whitstable arranged another reservation at ten-thirty that evening. This is also clearly documented. What had Whitstable planned for the rest of the day? Well, we know they spent the main part of the evening in his suite, drawing up the charter and signing it. But what of the afternoon? There were plenty of red-blooded pursuits to take their fancy. Remember, this was a time of great licentiousness in the West End.'

'Whitstable ran reform charities. Surely he would have frowned on anything too risqué?'

'The Victorians weren't quite so naive as we like to think. Prostitution was rampant, despite various efforts to clean up the streets. During the day, society whores promenaded through Rotten Row. At night, Leicester Square was host to all kinds of delights. Three years after the alliance was formed, the Empire Variety Theatre was built there and became such a traffic-stopping spot for prostitutes that a plasterboard barrier was erected to shield them from the nonpaying public.

'No, on this occasion James Whitstable had something else in mind. I was sure I knew what it was, and my theory was backed up when I reexamined the documents Alison Hatfield obtained for you. There, among all those loose bits of paper, was part of a ticket.'

He raised an oblong section of green paper in his hand. 'This was James Whitstable's ticket for a trip next door to the Savoy Theatre, which had just been completed. Whitstable was a keen patron of the arts, remember. Gilbert and Sullivan were presenting their production of *Patience* there. It had been running at the Opera Comique since the twenty-third of April and transferred to the Savoy on—let me see—' He flicked through his dog-eared black notebook. 'October the tenth. The Prince of Wales attended, and Oscar Wilde. Of course, it would have been hard to keep Wilde away. *Patience* parodied him and the whole of the Aesthetic Movement, as well as the Pre-Raphaelites.'

'And this was where James Whitstable took his partners.' May shrugged. 'So what?'

'Don't you think it strange? This particular opera was a topical joke. Its references weren't entirely understood by cosmopolitan audiences even then. We know from the Savoy records that most of Whitstable's colleagues had journeyed up from the country. Such esoteric entertainment would hardly have suited their tastes. No, James didn't want them to attend just so they could enjoy the show.'

'This had better have some point to it, Arthur.'

Bryant savoured his brandy-tea and smiled. 'There are moments in history that change our way of looking at the world, don't you think?' He always enjoyed knowing more about a case than his partner. He paused for another sip, relishing the moment. 'Some are obvious events that we all agree on. Kings fall, battles are lost or won. Sarajevo, twenty-eight June 1914. London, three September 1939. Dallas, twenty-two November 1963. Other changes are of a subtler degree, and some go quite unnoticed.

'On the night of twenty-eight December 1881, James

Whitstable and his partners witnessed an extraordinary symbolic moment. For the first time ever, a public building was completely lit with the new electric light. Darkness was thrown from the corners of the night. In this case, by over twelve hundred electric lamps. They'd tried to do it once before, on the tenth of October the same year. On that occasion, the entire company of the Savoy Theatre came on stage and sang three choruses of "God Save the Queen" in a dramatic new arrangement by Sullivan, but then—fiasco. The steam engine driving the generator in a vacant lot near the theatre couldn't provide enough electricity, and the stage remained gas lit.

'But at the matinee on December the twenty-eighth, they finally got it right. Richard D'Oyly Carte, ever the grand showman, walked onto the stage and ordered the gas lighting to be turned off. He followed with a lecture on the safety of electricity. This was news to the audience; many of them had thought electricity was fatal. Then he took a piece of muslin and wrapped it around a lit lamp, which he proceeded to smash with a hammer. When he held up the unburnt muslin, proving that there was no danger to the public, the audience went wild.

'Gas light was unclear, yellowish, smelly, and hot. The new electric illumination was here to stay. Imagine, John! To these men—businessmen, craftsmen—it must have seemed that the myths and mysteries of the shadowy past had truly been swept away by the cold, bright light of scientific reason. There couldn't have been a more appropriate symbol for them to adopt.'

'You think it was coincidence, or did James Whitstable know about this?'

'Oh, he knew all right. He used the performance as a display to show them they were doing the right thing by signing with him. What an extraordinary start for a grand new era! No wonder James had spoken of the winter solstice, the championing of light over darkness. Why, Victoria herself became queen on Midsummer's Day! It was the beginning of a bright new Britain. The end of myth and magic, the end of superstitions that could only survive in a nation of shadows. We know the alliance flourished. The original members passed away and their fortunes were handed down to their eldest sons. The money and the power stayed within the inner circle of the family. I'm not sure what happened after that.'

'This is where I can help,' said May, pleased that he could finally contribute something. 'Whoever obstructed the expansion of the guild always ended up withdrawing their objections, or vanishing altogether. One by one all their rivals disappeared. I'd say they were most likely beaten or killed for getting in the way of progress. It's in the company's overseas records, if you know what to look for. Not so many cases in this country, where investigation might have led back to the alliance, but a lot of skulduggery overseas. Whitstable and his gang took, and they didn't give much back. And they made sure that they retained control beyond their own deaths. Their fortune was passed down to each generation on one condition: that at some future time, the heirs might be asked to secure the continuing good fortune of the company by performing a simple, unspecified task, something they would be notified about when the time arose.'

'You mean the fathers made their sons killers?'

'Oh, nobody high-ranking got blood on their hands, but yes, I think the winning formula—a formula that was way ahead of its time, I might add—was granted with a burden of responsibility.'

'It's a strong motive.'

'Death by proxy. A series of murders that would

ensure the continued survival of the guild's financial empire, carried out by the descendants of the alliance's staff. I just spoke to Longbright. An hour ago she received a telex from the Bombay police confirming something about the window-cleaner, David Denjhi. His father and grandfather had both worked for a company owned by the Whitstable family. Specifically, they were in the employ of Charles Whitstable.'

'But how would the alliance know when someone was dangerous enough to require removal? And if they're still picking victims, why are they killing members of their own family?'

'The Watchmakers were craftsmen. I think Whitstable got his inner circle to come up with some kind of system for automatically fingering their enemies. But somewhere along the line the system screwed up. And now, nearly a century later, nobody knows how to stop it.'

'Raymond Land is never going to believe this.'

'At least it beats your supernatural explanations.'

'That depends who you find more objectionable, capitalists or satanists. Where do we go from here?'

'To James Whitstable's most direct descendant,' said May. 'We overlooked Charles Whitstable because of his position; how easily we still protect those in power. Berta Whitstable is a very unconvincing liar. The more she insisted her son knew nothing, the more I wondered if he could help us. If anyone knows about the alliance's device, Charles will.'

'Suppose he was at the guild when Alison called me about the diary? He could have arranged for someone to reach the basement before her. It's only a short distance from Goldsmiths' Hall to St Paul's Cathedral.' Bryant's brow furrowed. 'You mentioned the alliance's *device*. I presume you mean that they came up with some kind of formula for removing rivals that they've stuck to ever since.'

'No, Arthur, I mean a device. They were craftsmen, remember? I think we're looking for some kind of automaton.'

41 / Tiger, Tiger

At five twenty-seven the following morning, the elegant Chiswick home of Christian and Deborah Whitstable lay in darkness, and would remain so until an alarm rang in one hour and three minutes. Only a small porch light, operating on a time switch, stayed alight. The two officers May had insisted on appointing to secure the house were about to come off duty, and waited together in the front garden for the day shift to replace them.

Christian Whitstable had been badly disturbed by his sister Isobel's trauma. Little Daisy had remained mute since her rescue. Her mother's health had declined so alarmingly that she had been admitted to a private hospital in Fulham. And he'd heard that Pippa's mother was not doing much better, either.

Despite the danger, Christian had opted out of the police-protection scheme, preferring to spend Christmas at home. There had been too much reliance on the authorities, and what had they done but consistently let them down?

He and Deborah had argued bitterly over the decision. Having seen what had happened to her niece's child, Deborah was keen to place her own children in the safekeeping of the police, but her husband had refused to join the rest of the clan huddled together in William Whitstable's gloomy house. He believed in being the master of his fate, and extended that philosophy to his children, even if they were not yet old enough to appreciate the concept.

Deborah had complained that her husband's misplaced sense of machismo was putting their children in harm's way.

'Nonsense,' Christian had retorted over their cold turkey supper the previous evening. 'We have the police guarding us day and night. There are always two of them outside, in plain view where the children can see them. And even if, God forbid, someone managed to slip inside the house, we'd be able to summon help before anything untoward happened. There's only one door at the front and one at the back. They'd never be able to escape without capture.'

'I suppose you're right.' Deborah had sighed, knowing that she could never win an argument with a Whitstable. She had taken to sleeping with a carving knife beneath the bed. If she had little faith in her husband, she certainly had none in their guards. One of the night officers, PC Graham Watson, looked around seventeen years old, and was as thin as a stick. He spent his time sitting on the porch disconsolately picking his nose and reading Ian Fleming novels until the shift was over.

Now he was standing by the garden gate, looking up into the black sky, adjusting the strap of his helmet and hoping that the shift change would arrive before the rain began again. He looked around for his partner, who had gone to carry out a final check at the rear of the house, and had not yet returned.

Behind him, somewhere on the right-hand side of the overgrown front garden, the bushes rustled heavily, water shaking from the leaves.

'Dez?' His portly partner for the night shift, PC Derek

Brownlow, was not the most zealous of officers, and was in the habit of sneaking into the garden's potting shed with a Mars Bar and a copy of *Health & Efficiency*. Now it sounded as if he had lost his way.

'Dez, what are you doing in there?' Watson pulled the pocket torch free of his rain mac. The porch light had just snapped off, throwing the garden into darkness. He had been meaning to tell Mr Whitstable that he should reset his timer.

He shone his torch into the bushes and walked slowly along the path, watching raindrops glitter in the fractured pool of light. Ahead, the shrubbery shook violently once more.

'Dez?' he called softly. 'If that's you, I'll bloody kill you. Come on out, you're making me nervous.'

Deborah Whitstable hadn't been able to sleep properly since Daisy had been found. No such trouble afflicted her husband. He was lying on his back, snoring lightly. The bedroom door was ajar, and a cool draught was blowing into the room. She hadn't noticed it when she went to bed. It was always colder at this time, before the thermostat kicked in to heat the boiler and warm the children as they sleepily descended to the breakfast room.

She slipped silently from the bed and padded across to the window, moving aside the curtain. No sign of the policeman who was supposed to be guarding them, she noted, but the porch light had turned itself off, so she wouldn't be able to see him standing there anyway.

There was a definite draught coming into the room, as if someone had left a door open. She stopped to pull on her dressing gown, then walked out into the hall. Immediately she noted the smell, musty and brackish. Had she remembered to empty the kitchen bin? She switched on a light and peered over the balustrade, down into the hall. It looked as if something had been thrown across the grey slate floor tiles. Then she realized that a batch of newspapers had been torn and scattered over the floor. It looked as if mud had been trodden in. The papers had been neatly piled when they had gone to bed. Who had knocked over the stack and rummaged through it so carelessly?

She was still trying to puzzle out the mystery when she heard the terrible breathing. Deep and rasping, asthmatic and obscene. And she saw the door to the children's room moving back, widening slowly.

Her first thought was to run back to her bedroom and wake her husband. She considered calling to him, but knowing what a heavy sleeper he was, Christian would not hear her. It was when she saw what stood in the doorway that she attempted to scream.

Eight feet away from her, in the entrance to the room where Justin and Flora were fast asleep, was a fully grown male Bengal tiger.

It was insanity to think of such a creature standing in a suburban London house. But there it was, watching Deborah with ancient yellow eyes, its tail restlessly swinging, rhythmically thumping against the door jamb.

The beast was over six feet long, and its shoulders rose higher than the door knob behind it. It was old and distraught, confused by its unfamiliar surroundings. Long white hair hung from its sunken cheeks. Its fur was a deep orange-brown, beautifully marked with dark ochre transverse stripes. Its underparts were a dirty cream, its large splayed paws covered in mud and hooked with vicious black claws.

As the creature raised its enormous head and dilated

its nostrils, picking up her scent, it began to pad towards her, and she saw its ribs sticking painfully out beneath its hide. She had read somewhere that old or disabled tigers would eat human flesh if they were hungry and considered their prey to be weaker than themselves. The animal moving in her direction looked half mad from starvation.

As Deborah's shrill scream filled the air, the tiger loped forward and threw up its forepaws in a half-hearted leap, smashing her to the floor. Within seconds she heard shouts from her son and daughter, and even the sound of Christian attempting to rouse himself, but the body of the beast was crushing the life from her, its fetid breath blasting over her as it batted her head with its claws.

The creature opened its jaws to reveal rows of tall brown teeth, and stinking saliva poured on to her face as it reached down to clamp its mouth around her head and bite down hard, cracking bone and flesh, tearing sinew and skin from its thrashing, defenceless prey.

As Christian stepped into the hall in his pyjamas, his eyes widening in disbelief, the tiger dropped the victim it was lifting by the head. Attracted by the sound of the children screaming behind him, it turned its attention towards a more tender meal.

42 / Proposition

Arthur Bryant stood beneath the indigo stained-glass saints in the hallway, furling a dripping umbrella and slowly unraveling his wet Christmas scarf. What the hell was he doing here, Jerry wondered? If the detective made a display of recognizing her, her cover would be wrecked. Worse, he might decide to explain how they knew each other. She hastily slipped back against the wall, away from his line of vision.

Luckily, when Jerry next looked she saw that Bryant was now standing with his back to the parlour door. She watched him speaking to Charles Whitstable. Moving closer to the doorway, she strained to hear what they were saying.

'...understood that you were summoned back to England by your mother just last week, is that right?'

'No, not exactly,' Charles admitted. 'I'd spoken to Berta before that. Naturally she was alarmed by what was happening, but she said there was little to be gained by my returning home, particularly as some members of the family have grievances about how I run things.'

'Then what made you come back?'

'I was concerned that the current adverse publicity should not affect the faith of our investors. And I'd received a summons from a business colleague who wanted me to help him with a problem.'

'What kind of problem?'

'He was trying to locate a document that belonged to my great-grandfather.'

'Mr Whitstable, I need to know what you were asked to find for him.'

'It's no secret.' Charles shrugged, unfazed by the demand. 'Apparently James Makepeace Whitstable kept a personal chronicle covering certain key events of his life. It's possible it may shed some light on recent events. I was concerned about my mother's safety in London, so I decided to make the trip and check on her at the same time.'

'Did you have any luck finding this "chronicle"?'

'I'm afraid I was no help whatsoever. I barely had time to look. There were too many other problems weighing on my mind. Late on Christmas Day I received a call to say that I needn't worry about finding it any more. He didn't sound very pleased, I must say. Lawyers never are when you interfere with their plans.'

'It was Leo Marks who summoned you?'

'That's right.'

'I need to make a call to London,' said the detective, pointing to the hall telephone. 'May I?'

'Of course.'

Arthur Bryant was furious with himself for being so easily misdirected. Of course the law firm would be privy to the secrets of their oldest and most valued clients. If Max Jacob had known about the alliance's philosophy, it explained why he had been carrying William Whitstable's annotated Bible with him. The pages of the volume were marked according to William's doctrine of light and darkness. He was a continuing part of the alliance.

May had foolishly dismissed Leo Marks from his mind after noting the youth and inexperience of the junior partner, ignoring the fact that the lawyer was acting on behalf of his ailing father. Marks had probably searched the guild for the diary, but it seemed unlikely that he would have murdered Alison Hatfield. He may, however, have unwittingly caused her death.

But once the diary was in the possession of Leo and his father, what had they intended to do with it? If it revealed the cause of the Whitstable family's gradual destruction, surely they'd have wanted to protect the lives of their clients by turning it over to the police?

Bryant wished he understood the thought processes of lawyers. He had to make sure that Leo Marks was brought quickly and safely into custody. Tomorrow was twenty-eight December, and who knew what the anniversary would signify this time?

After the detective had departed, Charles came looking for Jerry.

'Who was that?' Jerry asked casually, rearranging a stack of books on the table before her.

'Another policeman. He made a phone call to London and left in a hurry. Judging by the look on his face, I'd say he'd received more bad news.'

She wondered what Arthur had discovered now. She'd been right to go her own way. The police would never discover the truth. If she could only get Charles to confide in her. Last night he had seemed upon the point of opening his heart and unburdening himself. She just needed more time with him.

'I promised to get you back to London this morning,' he was saying, 'so that's what we should do. I have to attend to some financial matters in the City, and then I must look in on my mother.'

Make another date, she thought. *Make him want you and he'll tell you everything. Don't let him slip away.* 'I still have to go back to work tomorrow, but I'm free tonight,' she said.

He came around to her side of the table and stood a little too close, looking down, smiling slightly. 'Then let's meet later. I have an apartment in Mayfair. My cooking's no great shakes, but there's an excellent Indian restaurant nearby. I promise we won't talk about business. You can tell me all about yourself.'

'Fine,' Jerry replied. 'And you can tell me all about your family.'

John May had not been able to sleep. The continuing rain bothered him. The weather was becoming ever more inclement. He decided to rise and head for the PCU. He arrived in Mornington Crescent at six forty-five, just in time to intercept a second report call from the Chiswick residence of Christian and Deborah Whitstable.

Thumbing back through the incoming night reports he found that the first radio call, at five past six, had reported that two of the family were dead, cause unknown, and two were alive. Raymond Land had been the only senior official still on duty, and had responded to the alert.

By the time May reached the crime scene, the entire house was surrounded with vehicles. He noted three ambulances, a fire engine, dozens of press photographers, an armoured truck, several squad cars, and a mob of onlookers. So much for keeping a low profile, he thought as he approached the overcrowded garden.

'We managed to corner him, Sir,' said one of the security officers. 'It took three tranquillizer darts to bring him down.' At first May assumed that they were talking about a human murderer, but before he could ask any further questions the unconscious orange-furred beast was carried out by guards on a long tarpaulin.

As the white-coated attendants reached the garden gate they were caught in a firestorm of flashbulbs.

'May, in here,' cried Land, shoving his way through a sea of blue uniforms. He looked as if he was about to be sick.

'For God's sake don't let the press see in through these windows, man,' shouted May as they reached the stairs. 'If they can get into the trees opposite with a long-distance lens they'll be able to shoot all of this.'

The officer he was addressing pulled the tall curtains closed, and turned on a battery of free-standing spotlights. An animal smell of rancid offal filled the building, mixed with the pungent odour that rose from the droppings left in the hall. May stepped over the forensic markers and walked on to the landing where Deborah Whitstable had met her death.

Broad arcs of blood had smeared and splattered the walls, and lay coagulating in black pools on the stair carpet. There were further splashes and bloody handprints on the white-painted banisters. Mercifully, the bodies had already been photographed and removed.

'How on earth did such an animal ever get in here?' May asked, amazed.

'We've been trying to piece together the sequence of events,' said Land. 'As far as we can tell, something first went amiss shortly before five-thirty, while the guards were waiting to be relieved of their shift. One of them was at the rear of the house. The other was beaten unconscious. The front door was opened with his passkey, and the tiger was admitted. A bloody *tiger*, John. What kind of people are we dealing with here?'

'There had to be a large van or truck parked in the area, and it must have been brought close to the house. We'd better start checking with the neighbours.'

'That shouldn't be difficult. They're all standing at the front fence in their dressing gowns.'

'What happened once the tiger was shut inside?'

'It would seem that the family were all still asleep. The veterinary surgeon we called in from the London Zoo reckons the creature had been systematically starved and conditioned to attack.'

'Have there been any reports of such an animal going missing?'

'It won't take long to find out that information. It scented the humans in the house and came up the stairs to here.' Land pointed to the claw marks on the surrounding woodwork. 'It must have woken Deborah first, because she came out on to the landing in her dressing gown. That's where it attacked her.' He indicated a blackened corner of the passage.

'Then it turned its attention to the little boy. When the police arrived, they found the husband barricaded into the children's bedroom with the daughter. He'd been whacked in the shoulder and chest by its paws, but was unhurt. The creature finished off Deborah, and dragged the boy down the hall by his head. Maybe it was saving him for later.'

Land lowered his voice further. 'This is completely insane, John. Can you imagine the headlines we'll get?' May noted that his superior's first concern was the intervention of the press, not the plight of the butchered family.

'It's not insane,' he replied. 'It's clever. They knew that whoever went in to kill the family would have trouble getting out again, so they chose a murderer whom nobody in their right mind would get in the way of. Someone—some*thing*—unable to confess when he was inevitably captured.'

He looked out of the window at the crowds gathering below. 'Everything's accelerating, cause and effect, faster and faster. Don't you sense that?'

'Then bloody well find a way to stop it,' said Land, angrily heading for the stairs.

Just before noon, John May arrived by police helicopter in Norwich, descending through the rain squalls to the offices of Jacob and Marks. He found the building sealed off and a team of officers ransacking each of the suites in turn, searching stacks of brief boxes for incriminating evidence. Leo Marks had been detained at the local station before being moved to Mornington Crescent PCU for questioning.

'What exactly are we looking for, Sir?' asked one of the officers.

'According to Bryant it'll be in a ledger,' replied May, 'a handwritten document, or just several sheets of loose paper. It's over ninety years old, so it may have been sealed in something like a plastic folder.'

'You mean like this?' PC Bimsley was holding up a clear plastic bag filled with loose cream-coloured pages of hammered vellum.

'Bimsley, I can't believe it. For the second time in your dismal career you've actually done something useful.' May took the bag and opened it, carefully unrolling the top page of the manuscript. It was entitled *The Alliance of Eternal Light: A Proposition for Inducing the Financial Longevity of the Worshipful Company of Watchmakers of Great Britain.* 'Where did you find this?'

'It was in the safe behind his desk, Sir. Do you think it'll help the investigation?' asked Bimsley.

'I'm hoping it'll end it,' replied May.

43 / Mechanism

Leo Marks was as jumpy as a cornered cat. 'I keep telling you—I was acting on my father's orders,' the lawyer was saying. 'I rang Miss Hatfield at the guild and asked her to help me locate specific documents pertaining to the family's financial accounting system. It was simply what my father had asked me to do.'

'Then you went there yourself to look for them?' asked May.

'Yes—she was having no luck. I think she was too busy trying to help you.'

'What time was this, exactly?'

'I've already told you.'

'So you did,' said May. 'Tell me again.'

'It was just after noon on Boxing Day. My girlfriend waited in the car while I went in. She was furious with me for having to come into work. You can check with her.' *That places the lawyer's visit before the trip Alison made,* thought May. *Alison went there in the evening.*

'What I don't understand is how you managed to locate the very thing that Miss Hatfield was unable to find.'

'That's the point, I couldn't have found it without her help. She'd cleared away half of the cartons in the basement. And I had a better idea of where to look. My father had suggested trying certain box files. He was too ill to go to London himself.'

'I'm sorry to hear he's in the hospital. Don't you think

it odd that Miss Hatfield should be murdered immediately following your visit to the guild?'

'No—I mean, yes—I don't know.' Leo dropped his head into his hands and massaged his temples. 'I know how it looks, but I didn't touch her. I didn't even see her.'

'Let me get this right.' May rose and approached the young lawyer. 'Miss Hatfield tried to locate a long-forgotten document for you, and was killed for her troubles. You, on the other hand, actually found what you were looking for, and managed to stroll out of the building with it. Doesn't that strike you as odd?'

'No, it's just—'

'Why the hell not?' shouted May. 'Why should she be murdered and you be allowed to walk away?'

'Because she had more reason to be killed,' retorted the lawyer. 'She was an outsider, interfering in other people's business.'

'Why didn't you bring the document to us? You must have realized that it was connected with Miss Hatfield's death.'

'Because,' Marks answered softly, 'my father was under strict instruction never to reveal its contents to anyone outside the family, whatever the circumstances.'

'Who gave him such instructions?'

'*His* father. And he got them from James Makepeace Whitstable,' he replied, 'in 1883.'

May placed an arm around his partner's shoulder. 'Come on,' he said, 'I need some air. Let's get out of here.'

They could see their breath in the corridor. 'Why is it so cold in this building?' asked Bryant as they reached their outer office. 'My blood's stopped moving.'

'We're still trying to clear airlocks from the heating

system,' Sergeant Longbright explained. 'I've had to let most of the staff go home. It should be fixed by next weekend.'

'I may be dead by then. Has there been any change in Peggy Harmsworth's condition?'

'The doctor says if her present status doesn't change soon, she'll suffer brain damage. They can only administer limited medication because of the impairment caused by the drugs in her system.' The sergeant hadn't slept for two days. There were four pencils in her hair and five half-drunk cups of coffee lining her desk. She was typing with gloves on, and, for the first time in living memory, wasn't wearing eyeliner.

'Where's Raymond?'

'He's over at the safe house. The family were demanding to see someone immediately, otherwise they're going to leave the building and report their grievances to the Home Office and then the press. Neither of you were available.'

'Thank God for that,' said Bryant. 'Don't they realize how much safer they are staying together? Didn't they ever watch old horror films? It's the ones that go off to the cellar with a torch that get a sabre through the windpipe.'

'Get your stuff and let's go,' said May.

Bryant could hear people shouting beyond their office window. The noise level was extraordinary. He crossed the room and looked out. 'Just look at this lot, howling for blood.' He snapped the blinds shut and collected his bag from his desk.

The Peculiar Crimes Unit was under siege. By eleven A.M. journalists had surrounded the building and had begun calling up to the first-floor windows. They were furious that Raymond Land had failed to set a press conference following the deaths of Deborah and Justin

Whitstable, and had remained outside, demanding that the superintendent appear before them with an explanation. Land had, however, managed to slip from the rear of the building without doing so. It was now half past five, and there was no sign of the mob dispersing.

'You'd better use the rear stairs,' said Longbright. 'I'll find you if things get worse.'

'How could they get any worse?' asked May. 'We've nothing to hold Marks here on. He has a watertight alibi for the night of Alison's murder. We can't even hold him for removing the diary without permission, because it was supposed to be in his father's custody in the first place. Has Jerry Gates come in?'

'I haven't seen her for days,' admitted Longbright. 'Mr Bryant, are you all right?' The detective was steadying himself against the wall. He looked as if he was about to pass out. Thunder rumbled ominously overhead.

'It's this blasted cold. I'll be all right when I get something to eat. I need carbohydrates. Potatoes. Gravy.'

They caught a cab to the north side of Fitzroy Square, where Gog and Magog was just opening its doors for the evening. Named after the statues of the two giants that had adorned the Guildhall until it was bombed during the Second World War, the restaurant offered a selection of Victorian and Edwardian delicacies that the uninitiated found alarming.

Bryant brought his partner here only on birthdays and in times of great upheaval. May knew that they should be feeling guilty, stopping to eat while mayhem was occurring around them, but sometimes more could be achieved across a restaurant table than in an interview room.

'"Nature has burst the bonds of art,"' said Bryant,

removing his wet coat. 'You remember who said that, John?'

'It was the night we confronted William Whitstable outside his house. You reckoned you'd heard the phrase somewhere before.'

'That's right, I had. This morning, I remembered where.'

Although they ate here infrequently, their host greeted them like old friends and showed them to a table beneath the moulting head of a wall-mounted elk.

'It's Gilbert and Sullivan, of course,' said Bryant. 'But I couldn't recall from which opera. Then I remembered that the poet Bunthorne sings the line in *Patience*. Taken with the marked Bible, it confirms—'

'That William Whitstable knew about the alliance as well.'

'Precisely. Perhaps all of the victims did. I think the Whitstable family is divided into those who know about the survival of the alliance and those who don't. God, how they like to keep their secrets. Now we begin to see the real reason why William damaged the painting on that rainy Monday afternoon at the National Gallery.' Bryant raised his hands, framing an image. 'Imagine this. After a severe fire the Savoy Theatre is put up for sale, and to everyone's horror an offer from the Japanese is accepted over the British bid. Government help remains unforthcoming. The prime minister has his hands too full with the unions to care about keeping a theatre in British hands. Peter Whitstable concocts a strategy with the family lawyer: they'll take charge of the Savoy by arranging to have the Japanese compromised and removed. The Whitstables want the theatre because of its symbolic place in their family history.

'Their secret system can no longer be trusted to take

care of business rivals—for some mysterious reason it isn't working properly any more, and hasn't been for some years. The family is having to fight its own business battles. Peter and his lawyer must take control of the situation. They discuss their plan with William, but he disapproves of their illegal tactics. The Japanese have shown nothing but good intentions. The Whitstables, on the other hand, are about to behave like common crooks, swindling them out of the deal.

'Does William tell Peter and Max that he'll have nothing to do with it, that family ideals are being betrayed? No, in typically excessive Whitstable fashion William makes a public statement by destroying the painting that commemorates everything that the alliance once stood for.'

'Then William couldn't have known that his brother was simply planning to continue the practices of his ancestor.'

'There's the irony.' Bryant accepted a menu. 'Peter and the lawyer knew exactly what James Makepeace Whitstable had been up to, but it seems that William genuinely had no idea. If only we could talk to them now.'

'We don't need to. We have a firsthand account of the event from the old man himself.' May tapped the side of his briefcase.

'You have the diary with you?'

'It's not a diary, just a brief chronicle of the alliance and its aims, something James must have read out to his future partners. But he's added his own notes at the end.'

'Let me see it,' pleaded Bryant.

'In a minute. Food first.'

Their waiter listed the specials without explanation of their contents, it being assumed that if you ate here, you knew what you were in for. 'We have spring, Crécy, or julienne soup,' he offered, '*chaud-froid* pigeons with asparagus, forequarter of mutton with stewed celery, thimbles, and—'

'What have you got for dessert?' asked Bryant, rudely interrupting him in mid-flow.

'Anchovy cheese, Aldershot pudding with raspberry water, rice meringue, cabinet pudding, and gooseberry jelly.'

Bryant sat back, delighted. Like the Victorians they emulated, the restaurant kept an ostentatious table. This was the first time the detective had thought about something other than the Whitstable family in weeks.

May opened his briefcase and withdrew the yellowed pages of the account. 'To be honest, I was having trouble reading it,' he admitted. 'It's written in such convoluted gobbledygook I thought it would be better to let you translate.'

Bryant wasn't sure whether to take this as a compliment or an insult. He accepted the document and carefully opened it, attempting to read the title as he searched for his spectacles. 'A proposition for inducing financial longevity, eh? Sounds dodgy.' Each page was covered in finely wrought black ink. After this followed a separate document, also handwritten. The heavy italicization of the letters made deciphering difficult. While May tasted the wine, his partner read on. After a while, he banged his fist on the table so hard that a pair of waiters resting at the rear of the restaurant jumped to attention.

'So that's it!' he cried. 'I knew it had to be something of the sort.'

'What is it?' asked May, not unreasonably.

'Much as I hate to say so, you were right. Why else would James Whitstable have invited craftsmen to be the founding members of the alliance, and not financial experts? He suggested the building of a mechanical device. Listen to this: *"For if our lawyers can create a scheme for life annuity such that the overall dividend augments upon the demise of each subscriber, why not a form of mechanical tontine? These are modern times, and such an automated auguring device could be created wherein the subscribers and beneficiaries of the Worshipful Company of Watchmakers might be provided for long after their deaths, by the simple expedient of the creation of a device to inhibit the encroachment of our rivals."* Dear God, no wonder this country's in a state if it was based on language like this!'

Bryant took a sip of wine and leaned forward, laying the pages before him. 'So James Whitstable sees the finances of the guild failing. Foreign rivals are producing cheaper wares in direct competition to the guild's own exports. He must act quickly, or their empire will be undermined and nothing will be left for their heirs. He is taken with the germ of an idea, and invites to London the men who may be persuaded to help him carry out his plan.

'On the afternoon of twenty-eight December 1881, he lunches with his group, filling the craftsmen's susceptible heads with talk of light and dark, preserving the strength and sanctity of the guild, and God knows what else. No doubt these loyal, hardworking men are easy to entice. They're probably amazed to be in London at all—and to be taking lunch at the Savoy!

'After the meal, he trots them to the theatre next door—to witness a display which he has already been informed will take place. Suddenly they see that everything he says is true; James Makepeace Whitstable has predicted the future, when light will triumph over darkness for all time. They're given proof that a bright new age is about to begin. Who could fail to be impressed?

'Whitstable then leads them, awe-filled, back to his

suite, and draws up a charter which they sign. He presents each of them with a commemorative gold pocket watch manufactured by the Watchmakers' Guild, inscribed with the sacred flame. He wraps up his speech in supernatural mumbo-jumbo, invoking the curse of the Stewards of Heaven. Then he swears them all to secrecy, and looks to them for a solution to his problems.

'And his work pays off. The craftsmen put their heads together, and come up with a tracking device that will calculate the guild's accumulation of profit according to the information fed into it. The machine will also identify the owners of shares.'

'You mean to tell me that the Alliance invented a primitive form of computer?'

'No, because their system isn't binary. Unfortunately, they were craftsmen before they were mathematicians. But you're on the right track. I'm only halfway through. Let me read the rest.'

'Your pigeon's getting cold, or hot, or something,' May pointed out.

But he had lost Bryant to the pages. Once in a while the detective would release a 'Hmmm' or an 'Aha!' Finally he looked up, realized that his meal was still sitting before him, and began to eat voraciously. Neither spoke until the plates were cleared.

'Well,' declared Bryant, wiping his mouth with a napkin, 'it's made of brass.'

'Is that it?' cried May. 'Isn't there anything else?'

Bryant set down his napkin and checked the pages again. 'It took them two years to build and calibrate the device.'

'My God, how big is this thing?'

'I don't know, it doesn't say. But it's mechanical, and it

runs on electricity. Is it possible that it could still be running? I mean, there's no such thing as a perpetual motion engine.'

'Does it mention how it works?'

'Only that it relays information to an outside source, where "the necessary steps" are taken.'

'Some help. What about its location?'

'Again no clue, presumably for the sake of security. There is one man who might know. We must talk to Leo Marks's father. I'll find out which hospital he's in. If the old man was supposed to be the keeper of this account,' Bryant wondered, 'why did he have to send his son looking for it?'

'Alison Hatfield told me all the valuable guild papers were shifted to the vaults during the war for safekeeping. No doubt Marks assumed that it was the safest place for them. Later, when the attacks on the Whitstables started occurring, the family closed ranks, and Marks Senior realized that he was failing to honour his promise by leaving the document with the back files at the guild. I wonder how many of the Whitstables knew what was in that document?'

'Even if they had heard tales of such a mechanical tontine, I doubt any of them believed it was real. And they'd never admit it if they did.'

'The older generation certainly must have noticed their unfailing good fortune and wondered. The guild even made money in the year of the General Strike. I bet the family did some paper-burning when they heard that William Whitstable had been murdered.' May rose from the table. 'If they'd been less worried about their dwindling finances and a bit more concerned about each other, perhaps we'd have been able to halt the bloodshed at the start. Don't go anywhere. I have to make a phone call.'

Bryant sat back with a sigh. He knew that they would end up visiting the hospital tonight, and saw his chances of enjoying a leisurely dessert retreating along with the possibility of a decent night's sleep.

44 / Loyalty

In the taxi on the way to the Wentworth Clinic in Gloucester Terrace, Bryant read the remaining section of the chronicle, which bore the personal imprimatur of the family patriarch, James Makepeace Whitstable.

28 December 1881, evening

> *Shortly after the performance, we returned to our rooms. One look into the eyes of my colleagues told me that our sojourn to the newly illuminated theatre had convinced them of the veracity of my design. These honest artisans had seen the future, and would now agree to my request. They had each been granted the Grand Order of the Heavenly Stewardship, though doubtless they knew little of what it meant. Would they still be willing to participate in the building of the device when they realized it was to end the lives of others?*
>
> *We began to assemble a little after eight. I had given notice to the chambermaids that under no circumstances were we to be disturbed tonight. I had drawn the heavy green curtains shut and had lowered the lights, removing both of the copper lamps from the table, the better to impress upon the assembly the utter seriousness of our venture.*
>
> *Radford was the first, creeping into the room apologetically, his club foot sounding hard against the floor. He was*

closely followed by Lamb, then Chambers, then Suffling. As I had requested, each bore the satin sash of his Stewardship, and now I requested that they don their colours. Radford—Hagith—timidly asked something which had clearly been pressing on him. If, tonight, we would agree the terms under which our mechanism could be constructed, what need was there for our collective presence as the Stewards of Heaven?

——I'm glad you asked that, I said, directing him to be seated opposite me, for you may recall our discussions on the role of faith and occultism in the coming scientific age. Their attention held, my Stewards took their places around the octagonal baize table.

——The system that will preserve our fortunes and remove our enemies for ever will succeed because it is Scientific, I explained, studying each face in turn. So far you have been presented with little more than an engineering proposal, namely the construction of a device that will tabulate our expenditure and calculate the damage inflicted by the enemies of the Company. You agree, Lamb, that such a device is within the realms of possibility?

——Most certainly, Mr Whitstable, he agreed, although certain problems arise.

——Namely? I enquired.

His fingers tugged at his cravat as he attempted to frame his reply.

——Keeping it hidden, he said finally. How shall we protect such a piece of equipment and maintain it finely tuned?

——You shall have no need to worry on that account, I assured him. The tontine will provide us with advice. But how can we carry out its instructions? Will Science remove our adversaries? No. For this, we require loyalty beyond the call of normal duty. We are an organization ahead of our time, gentlemen. One day all business will be conducted in

such a manner. But let us be the first. Even now, Guildsmen are working to solve the problem of removing our enemies. For without their help, the seeds of destruction are built into our system. Suppose one of our own was apprehended in the process of vanquishing a hated rival? Should he attempt to explain his actions, why, we are done for. And if any one of you were to carry out the deed, how might you feel after? Even the most righteous cause carries a burden of guilt when the death of another is required. The solution lies in India. Gentlemen, I do not ask you to go against God. It is why I have enlisted those who are Heathens. They will be our loyal assassins.

I rose from my place at the head of the table with six pairs of eyes following my every move, and warmed myself against the blazing hearth. Tonight the loyalty of my most trusted men was being put to the test, and I was sure that they would follow me. I had not counted on Radford, of course.

I'll be d-mned before I have a part of this——cried Radford suddenly, leaping up.

——It is against my will that you leave our circle now, I replied.

——You have no power to stop me, he exclaimed, turning to the others for approval, but I could see that they were with me. It was time to provide Radford with a demonstration of the faith I command. As my foolish employee tugged at the door (from which I had removed the key) I donned the scarlet robe of Och and began to recite the profane phrases that have been bequeathed for my voice alone. It was a strange sight: Radford tearing at the paneling of the door in desperate panic as the others sat on either flank, mute and immobile, siding with their mentor.

As I raised my hands and completed the summoning gestures of Bethor and Ophiel, the air in the room grew stifling, and the lamp-wicks lowered as though the atmosphere could no longer support their flames.

Just then, Rajeev, my faithful servant, stepped forward from the next room, and awaited my orders.

Radford turned and saw him, and slammed his back against the door in shock. He tried to call out but Rajeev, at my sign, slipped a red silk cord around his throat. As Radford fell to the floor the servant followed him, clinging tight no matter how briskly he tried to brush him aside. When he could no longer draw breath and lay still on the rug, his arms at his sides, Rajeev removed the cord from his swollen throat and silently departed from the room. Lamb drew back the curtains and opened a window. The draught raised the lamps to normal.

Radford was left with little sign of misadventure upon his lifeless body. His death that night was marked by the doctors as asphyxiation due to an excess of drink, and diminished by the hotel for the sake of their reputation.

Still shaking, the others turned back from witnessing this demonstration of loyalty and concentrated their minds upon the formulation of the alliance's founding document.

We had no further trouble that night.

Bryant slipped the yellowed pages back into their folder. 'It's all here, laid out by James Makepeace Whitstable himself.'

May wiped the window and peered out. 'We're here,' he said.

The clinic had ended its visiting hours for the night. The Wentworth was an expensive private recuperation home for heart patients, and enjoyed the patronage of financially upholstered clients from across the country. As the taxi pulled up before the entrance, Bryant glanced at his battered Timex. He had purchased it after seeing a commercial in which the timepiece was tied around the leg of a galloping horse. Unfortunately, his operated as if the horse had sat on it.

'If Leo Marks's father doesn't want to tell us, we can't force the information out of him,' he said, digging around for change to pay the driver. 'Three pounds?' he complained. 'Are you descended from highwaymen, by any chance?'

'We can tell him that we have his son in custody,' replied May. 'Come on.'

'You're not getting a tip,' warned Bryant.

'Don't worry, mate,' said the driver, snatching his money from the detective's proffered hand. 'I've read about you in the papers. You haven't got any to offer.'

In the marble foyer of the clinic, a smart black-suited receptionist sat reading beneath a low light. 'Look at this place,' marveled Bryant. 'We should have been lawyers. Everyone hates you while you're alive, but at least you have a great time when you're sick.'

'I called earlier,' said May, a trifle too loudly. 'We're here to see Mr Marks.'

The receptionist raised her telephone receiver and whispered into the mouthpiece. Moments later, a young woman in a discreet uniform appeared at the bottom of the stairway.

'Mr Marks is out of danger now, and quite awake,' the nurse said, walking with them to the first floor. 'He was asking for a whisky an hour ago, so he's obviously on the mend. You're his second visitors tonight.'

'Who else was here?' asked May.

'An Indian gentleman, I didn't catch his name. I think he's still with Mr Marks at the moment.' May's sense of unease caught alight. Grabbing his partner's arm, he broke into a run.

'Which way?' he called to the nurse.

'End of the corridor and right,' she replied, flustered. 'Third door on the left. There's no rush—'

They reached the end of the corridor, their shoes squealing on the freshly polished floor. The hallway ahead was in virtual darkness, but they could already see that the door to Marks's room was wide open.

Their patient lay halfway out of bed, the drip feed severed from his arm, his mouth opening and closing like a fish out of its bowl, his left hand helplessly grasping the air.

His right wrist had been nicked, and blood was blossoming across the starched white bedspread.

'We were just in time,' said Bryant. 'Mr Marks, we know about the tontine device. You must tell us where it is. We have to stop it.'

'Tell Charles,' the old man mouthed. 'Tell Charles, the river. He must look to the Guild at the river.'

'Of course,' whispered Bryant. 'Where else could it be?'

45 / Seventy-Seven Clocks

On the way back to London, Jerry considered her position. Her new career was supposed to provide her father with a colleague and her mother with a better social circle. Neither of them had imagined that she might prove desirable to Charles Whitstable in another way.

Arriving home, she saw that Jack had told Gwen the bad news: Charles Whitstable had decided to apprentice their daughter without including her parents in the social upgrade. Unable to bear the awkward silence, she left the house. She reached another decision: to leave the Savoy. Now that her parents had been reduced to a state of confusion and disappointment, there was no point in staying on. Perhaps it would give them pause to think about what they wanted: from her, and from each other.

She decided to stay away from the PCU, too. Normally she would have headed there hoping to find someone to talk to, only to end up helping Sergeant Longbright with the photocopying. So much for the glamour of police work. From tonight there would be a new beginning.

Now she stood in the narrow road below Curzon Street ringing the polished brass bell marked C. WHITSTABLE ESQ.

She looked up at the darkened windows, but there seemed to be no one in. Surely Charles couldn't have forgotten their arrangement? Tugging her short black dress around her thighs, she sat down on the step to wait.

Shortly before nine P.M. the two detectives appeared in Mornington Crescent at a virtual sprint. 'Janice,' called Bryant, searching the offices as he passed, 'we need Charles Whitstable. What have you done with him?'

'He's still in the detention room on the second floor,' replied the sergeant. 'Raymond wanted to let him go—'

'I gave strict instructions not to let him out of the building.'

'I know, and I didn't allow him to leave.'

'You're worth your weight in diamonds, do you know that?' he shouted back, and they were gone. Sergeant Longbright smiled to herself and touched her hair into place. Like most policewomen, she wasn't used to being complimented.

Charles Whitstable had one of Bryant's nasty scarves tied over his shirt collar and his jacket pulled tight around him. The detention room was freezing. 'Get me out of here,' he said angrily as the detectives admitted themselves. 'I have an engagement to attend. Your uniformed clowns interrupted a very important investors' meeting. It didn't help having the police strong-arm their way in to demand an interview.'

'I'm afraid they were acting on Detective Superintendent Land's orders, Sir,' explained May.

'Your superior is a very frightened man. He seems to think that our family has set out to deliberately destroy his career.'

'Leo Marks's father was attacked in his hospital bed a little over an hour ago,' said May. 'He won't be doing the polka for a while, but he'll live.'

'Congratulations,' replied Charles, unperturbed by the news, 'you finally managed to save someone's life. Do you have any idea who did it? At least you have proof that it wasn't me.'

'I think you have a pretty good idea who it was.' Bryant circled behind Charles and leaned on his chair. 'I should have asked myself exactly what you were doing in India.'

'Look, I know my rights. You can't detain me here without good reason. Do I have to call my lawyer?'

'No,' replied Bryant. 'What you have to do is remain nearby for the next twenty-four hours while I wait to hear back from the Calcutta police. Then we'll have this interview again.' He tapped his partner on the shoulder, beckoning him from the room.

'Janice, we'll be out for a while. What time do you come off duty?'

'Tonight I don't,' she replied with a sigh. 'We haven't any cover at the moment. Do you want me to come with you?'

Bryant looked her up and down. 'Make a muscle,' he said.

Longbright crooked her arm.

'Huh,' grunted the detective. 'Sparrows' kneecaps. You're safer here. Where can I find a pickaxe?'

'Will a sledgehammer do?' She remembered seeing the tool bag that the workmen had left in Bryant's office.

'I suppose so.'

Overhead, the neon striplights fuzzed and momentarily dimmed. Bryant gave his partner a meaningful look.

'For God's sake stop doing that,' said May. 'You're starting to give me the willies.'

* * *

424   CHRISTOPHER FOWLER

They climbed into Bryant's battered Mini and headed into the rain-shrouded city. May was driving so that his partner could continue talking. When Bryant conversed and drove simultaneously, he had a tendency to dislodge the illuminated bollards that stood in the centre of the road.

'When Alison was showing me around the basement of the hall,' said May, 'I asked her about the rushing noise beneath our feet. She explained about the river drainage, and said part of the floor below had been cemented up at the beginning of the century because of problems with flooding. James Makepeace Whitstable had the rooms partitioned off down there for a very good reason. He diverted the river around them so that no one would attempt to break through the wall, no matter how curious they became. I think if we open up that wall, we'll find our doomsday machine. Of course, if I'm wrong we'll probably drown.'

As they unfolded themselves from the miniature car, May looked up at the cheerless edifice of the Worshipful Company of Watchmakers. He was convinced that Charles had full knowledge of the guild's inner circle. The difficulty lay in forcing his hand.

'How are we going to get in at this time of night?' he asked Bryant, who was removing the tool kit from the rear seat and attempting to untangle his scarf from the safety belt.

'One good thing about having Charles Whitstable brought in when we had nothing to hold him on—I had his keys lifted from his jacket. I didn't want to ask him for them in case he tried to warn someone.'

Two locks had to be unfastened before the door could be opened, following which they had to key off an alarm system in a cupboard at the foot of the main staircase.

May located a battery of light switches and brightened the hall, but they would have to rely on torches, brought along to cope with the unreliable illumination afforded by the basement's emergency system.

The lift jarred to a halt. 'We're still on the first level below ground,' said May, puzzled. 'Alison said there was another floor under this.'

'Perhaps you have to take the stairs.'

'I remember now.' He pulled open the trellis. 'The electrics operate on a separate system. We'll walk down.' The fire door at the end of the hall had obviously not been opened for years. May was unable to budge it, and it took several blows from the sledgehammer to release the locking bar. As they pushed it back, their torch beams sent hordes of brown rats scurrying into darkness. The walls were wet with condensation.

'Be careful on these steps,' called May. 'The cement's softened up in places.'

'It smells like something died down here.'

Ahead, the stairway twisted. Bryant stepped gingerly downwards, and nearly fell when his heel pressed down on the bulky body of a dead rat. Turning the torch to his shoe, he saw tiny bleached maggots swarming about the rodent's head in a diseased halo. The sound of rushing water could be plainly heard now. They reached the foot of the stairway, and shone their torches into the dark hole of the corridor ahead.

'Who's going first, then?'

'I suppose I will,' offered May.

'Thank God for that,' said Bryant, much relieved.

Their shoes splashed in shallow puddles as they followed the passageway. The walls were marked with furred spears of mold. Two sets of irregular markings showed where doorways had been sealed up with cinderblocks and cement. 'It can't be either of those,' said May. 'The brick-work's too modern.'

'The 1930s, at least,' agreed Bryant. 'What about this one at the end?' They had reached another, larger sealed doorway. The entrance was almost twice as high as the previous ones they had passed, and had been closed off with standard-sized house bricks. The paintwork covering them matched the walls.

'This has to be it,' said May, crouching to study the cementwork.

'The best way to find out is by dismantling the wall.' Bryant ran his fingers over the mildewed surface. 'It shouldn't take much. The bricks are soft. Too much water vapour in the air. Give them a bash with your hammer.'

May gave the sledgehammer a practice swing. 'I hope you're right about this.' The first blow gouged a shallow path through the rotten mortar. May kept the hammer swinging, concentrating on one part of the wall. His partner stood off to one side, listening as the sound of water continued to grow. The next blow dislodged a pair of bricks.

May lowered the hammer and shone his torch inside. 'Oh, you're going to love this.'

Before his partner could see, May continued to swing the hammer until the hole was large enough to climb through. Then he stepped back. 'You figured out where it was,' he said. 'You should be the first to go inside.'

'Er, thank you,' said Bryant uncertainly, stepping over the low brick wall and ducking his head. The floor of the room was covered with six inches of icy water. Something in the dark was slowly ticking with a heavy steel ring, like a giant grandfather clock. Bryant pressed his back against the inner wall and raised his torch.

The light from the torch beam reflected a dull gleam

of curved brass. The device was between twenty and twenty-five feet high, circular in construction, resting on a base of four cylindrical brass pipes. Its appearance reminded Bryant of an astrologer's instrument, an astrolabe, consisting of skeletal globes laced within one another, so that each could move independently of the rest.

At the centre was the most mechanically complex part of the instrument, a partially enclosed steel dome housing a series of cogs and ratchets that allowed the movement of the various metal bands comprising each globe. As they watched, one of the inner bands shifted fractionally, providing a subtle alteration in the composition of the whole.

Immediately there was a buzz and a tiny blue flicker of electrical light at the centre of the device, as if a new connection had been made.

As Bryant approached, he could see that each of the brass strips on the outer globe was calibrated with finely engraved measurements. Then he noticed that all of the curving bands were marked, one with minutes and hours of the day, another with the days of the year, and another with the years of the century. Others were inscribed with monetary equations for accruing interest, and financial configurations covering every possible eventuality. At the end of every arm was a tiny enamel-faced clock, set in an engraved gold bracket.

'Look at all the clocks,' said May. 'There must be dozens of them.'

'One for every heir and rival in the Whitstable empire,' added Bryant in awe, looking at the names attached to them. He tallied them quickly. 'Seventy-seven in all.'

'James Makepeace Whitstable gave his stewards commemorative gold watches. All of the victims had

Victorian gold timepieces. Even Daisy had a gold christening clock.'

Bryant knew that they were looking at the cold, damaged heart of the Whitstable empire, a manufactured embodiment of everything that had grown flawed and had failed in imperialist England.

The pair stood mesmerised by the vast, imperceptibly turning machine, their torch beams bouncing from one section to another. The room was silent but for the steady steel tick from the centre, and behind that, the fainter ticking of dozens of smaller clocks.

'It's like an orrery,' said Bryant, awed. 'You know, one of those mechanical models of the solar system.'

'It's beautiful,' agreed his partner, slowly stepping back against the wall. As he did so, he brushed against the warm flesh of another living creature. His shout of fear filled the room, echoing as the metal bands of the astrolabe acted like tuning forks, reinforcing his cry to an unbearable din.

46 / The Engineer

You already apologized for being late,' Jerry said. 'You don't have to make any rash promises about the future.'

'They aren't rash promises, I assure you,' said Charles, refilling her wine glass. True to his vow, he had arranged for the delivery of an Indian meal. The choice of nationality was fitting, for the apartment was filled with Indian carvings and tapestries. Ancient terracotta figures of Harappan women stood beside finely carved friezes of tigers and elephants. 'I would love to show you India. My work there has only just begun. For a major industrial country, they export very little. It's a situation we're trying to help remedy. When I have time, I travel to the great plains beyond the cities, where the night skies are the deepest blue-black, so vast and dark that you think you'll never see the dawn again.'

'It sounds beautiful,' she said, suppressing a shiver.

'Not as beautiful as you. You're a woman now.' He reached forward and kissed her lightly. She tasted wine and spice on his lips. This was the moment she had been expecting. Everything in her life had taken on a contradictory quality, as though only part of it was real, and part hallucination. She was scared of becoming intimate with Charles, knowing that she might be forced to betray him.

'What's the matter?' His face was still close to hers but he was looking at her oddly. She realized how tense her body had grown. When she failed to reply, he detached himself from her.

'Jerry, it's okay. Nothing will happen that you don't want, I promise.'

'I'm scared.' Finally the words emerged. She had not been able to speak them to Joseph, but was determined to say it now. 'I haven't done this before.'

'I'm sorry. I didn't realize.' He gently took her hand in his. 'I thought . . . well . . .'

'I've wanted to, but something . . .' She rubbed her hand across her forehead, trying to clear her thoughts. 'It's like the dark. I can't—I panic.'

'That's right; the dark scares you, doesn't it? But that's just a psychosomatic problem. It can be easily cured.'

'No, it can't.' Jerry shook her head. She had spent too many therapy sessions discussing the problem.

'A phobia is a learned emotional response,' he replied, releasing her hand. 'It's an extension of the fear that's produced at a time of emotional development. I know how you're feeling, but it's okay.' His pale still eyes were fixed on her, never moving. She saw the lamplight glinting on wet windowpanes, the softly lit carvings beside the fireplace. He was showing his faith in her.

He ran the tips of his fingers gently over her face. 'Just relax and close your eyes. Think of times when you were happy, when you were young.' She heard Charles's voice softly seesawing in the distance, like the droning of bees in June. His tone was low and mellifluous. She felt calmer now, and clearer. She could see inside herself.

She saw glimpses of a past she had long expelled from her mind. Bad behaviour at school. A teacher's face, close, shouting. Gwen, furious, screaming. Something broken, blue china, water on a yellow rug, tears. Guests around a dinner table, staring at her. Wigmore Street in the rain. Alighting from a cab. Waiting in the therapist's surgery.

She opened her eyes and found him holding the blindfold.

Suddenly alert, she sat up, moving her feet from the couch.

The room was shifting beneath her. Disoriented, she put out a hand to steady herself. She rose and slipped on her shoes.

'Wait, Geraldine, don't leave—'

But she had already managed to slip her arm into her coat sleeve, and was running from the room.

'Sir, I fear you scared me far more than I scared you.'

The face illuminated in the torchlight was old and Asian, thin and worn from a life of hard toil. Sparse grey hair straggled across a scarred bald dome. The man who stood before them was wearing a blue boiler suit, and looked like a maintenance engineer.

'If you would care to step through to my office . . .' The old man gestured to a small recessed door in the rear of the wall. Startled beyond speech, Bryant silently complied with his request.

The antechamber beyond the room housing the astrolabe was fitted with an overhead light. A cheap desk and chair, filing cabinets, a stack of untended paperwork, a typewriter, a litter bin, a tea mug, a wall calendar with faded views of Norway.

Then Bryant noticed that the calendar was over forty years out of date, and that the paperwork was thick with mildew.

'You must excuse me, Sirs,' the little Indian man said, clearing the paperwork to the back of the desk. 'I have never had visitors before. My name is Mr Malcolm Rand, and it is my duty to tend to the equipment you see in the next room.'

'How long have you been here?' asked May.

'At the guild, most of my life, Sir, since I graduated from my apprenticeship. I took over the tending of the machinery in 1957 from my father's brother, God rest his soul.'

'How do you get in here? You do go outside, don't you?'

'Of course, Sir. I have seen you several times before, for I am also the head of the maintenance staff here at the guildhall. I visit the equipment twice a day, once in the morning and once before I leave at night, to ensure that it is well oiled and able to continue functioning correctly.'

Now May remembered seeing Rand beside the staircase on his first visit to the Watchmakers. 'Does anyone else know about this?' he asked.

'No, Sir, and nobody must know. It is written into the rules of my employment. You are not supposed to be down here. I could lose my job.'

'I'll see to it that you don't lose your job,' promised May. 'Have there been other custodians here before you?'

'Most certainly. It is our duty to ensure that the equipment is never damaged.'

'But it is already, man. Do you know what it does?'

'Of course, Sir,' Rand quietly replied. 'It is the great Imperial Financial Machine. When it calculates that the profits and shares from the Watchmakers' Company have been spread unwisely, or are falling into the wrong hands, it pinpoints the guilty party. When the financial loss reaches a certain level, the machine ascertains the culprit and transmits the person's fiscal details to the appropriate authority in the outside world.'

'Where to, though?' asked Bryant. 'How does it do it?'

'The machine is electrically connected to the telephone system, Sir. I do not know where the messages go. Is there something wrong?'

'Do you know what happens after the machine transmits each message?' asked May.

The custodian shook his head uncertainly, puzzled by the air of tension in the room.

'It arranges the deaths of people in companies it has named.'

'No, no. How is that possible?' answered the shocked custodian. 'It cannot be true.'

'I'm afraid it is, old chap,' said Bryant. 'And I think Mr Charles Whitstable will be able to tell us all about it.'

The detectives looked back toward the ticking astrolabe.

47 / Chandler's Wobble

Rand had turned on a dim overhead bulb, and the brass machine beneath it shone darkly, a monstrously beautiful engine of death, the shadow of its metal limbs revolving elliptically below the swinging light. The clocks glittered, ticking faintly.

'The mechanism rotates imperceptibly, marking off the calibrations as it moves. The marks correspond to the members of the family and their business associates,' explained Rand. 'Details of new companies entering the field are given to me by the lawyers, and I adjust and update the names accordingly.'

He indicated several taped pieces of paper on the brass arms of the interior globes. 'I would like to bring someone down here to etch the new names properly into the brass, as the original names have been, but it is against the rules of my employment.' He pressed one of the peeling labels back in place with his thumb. Rand took great pride in his work, even if he failed to understand the lethal nature of it.

'If it's targeting the wrong people, something must have changed the settings,' mused Bryant, wading around the astrolabe. 'Have there been any roadworks carried out near the building recently?'

'Oh, yes,' said Rand, 'very many. The city is changing fast. There is much building since the war. Last month developers demolished the old bank next door, and everything kept shaking. I thought it was an earthquake, but they don't have them in this country.'

'Then that's it.' Bryant ducked beneath the outer globe and carefully stood up inside the revolving mechanism. 'What setting is this inner circle supposed to be on?' he asked Rand. 'Do you know offhand?'

'Let me get my chart.' He returned with a clipboard and yards of perforated paper, running his finger along a timetable line. 'At the inner core, 162337.918. The number is located beside the bar nearest your left hand, right at the end.'

Bryant dug out his reading glasses and checked the number. 'It reads 162338.984. It's out by just one notch, but the gears have magnified the error. The whole thing's turned in on itself. A bad case of Chandler's Wobble.'

'What's that?' asked May.

'It's the movement in the earth's axis of rotation. It causes the latitude to vary. That's what's happened here. The vibrations from the demolition have thrown the calibrations out. It's made them incorrect by a single notch. The effect has been augmented through the device. The clocks no longer correspond, so the tontine is selecting the wrong people.'

'I knew the blockage in the river drain was a problem,' said Rand. 'Every time it rains, the room gets a foot of water, and it takes hours to go down again. I wondered if it could cause a mechanical malfunction. This is an electrical device. It could be quite dangerous.'

'It's not that,' said Bryant. 'I'll bet vibrations preceded each rainfall because the demolition crew was working to beat the rain. That's why the calibrations matched the water levels.'

'Come on out from there, Arthur,' called May. 'We have to find a way to turn this thing off.'

'How on earth do we do that? Where does the electricity supply run from?'

'We are not on the main circuit,' answered Rand. 'The supply here comes from an independent generator. The running costs are billed to the Watchmakers.'

Bryant was still inside the device when one of the outer rings clicked another notch, causing an electric spark to crackle in the central housing of the machine. 'The wiring duct goes straight down into the floor,' he said. 'We need to get this shut down before the twenty-eighth.'

'What's the time now?'

'Somewhere approaching midnight.'

'Can't you be more accurate, Arthur?'

'Not really, no. I'm wearing a Timex.'

May checked Rand's wristwatch. 'According to this one, we have about twelve minutes left in which to do something.'

'Obviously the damned thing needs to be unplugged.'

'It is not that simple.' Rand sloshed through the water toward them. 'There are a great many wires.'

'Then we'll have to jam it,' May, picking up the sledgehammer he had leaned against the wall. 'Arthur, you've finally got your chance to do some damage to the British aristocracy. Have a bash about with this.'

He passed the hammer through to Bryant, who hefted it like a cricket bat, gauging its weight. 'Not bad.' He swung it against one of the inner brass rings with a re-verberating thump. 'The Victorians really built this thing to last,' he said admiringly.

It took six healthy strokes to dislodge a single section of one of the globes. As the metal band buckled and dropped, it jammed against the outer arms, seizing the rotational segments of the sphere firmly in place. One of the outer sections tried to move, but was prevented from doing so. The ticking suddenly stopped.

'I'd get out of there, Arthur. There's no telling what it might do when the pressure builds up.' Even as May spoke, there was an agonized rasp of metal and the structure shuddered, attempting to shift once more, like tectonic plates pushing towards an earthquake. This time, however, the globe succeeded in moving a single notch. As Bryant clambered between the jammed sections, propping the sledgehammer between the rings, there was a loud click and the central mechanism emitted a series of cracking electrical sparks. Two of the clocks crashed to the floor.

'It's sending out orders,' cried Rand. 'That sound was the electrical connection being made.'

'How many orders?' asked Bryant, trying to untangle his scarf from the machine.

'I don't know,' said Rand. 'Two, ten, twenty, it's hard to say.'

'Isn't there any way of checking, anything that we could—could somebody help me out of this damned contraption?' Bryant was wrenching at his scarf, which had become threaded between the inner and outer globes. May ran over and tried to pull him free.

'I know, wait a moment.' Rand splashed back to his room, peered around the corner, and returned. 'This transmission did not go overseas.'

'How can you be sure?' asked May.

'Each signal is annotated according to its destination. This one has a London telephone code.'

'John, it's sending out another blasted death command.' Bryant gave up wrestling with the scarf, looped it free of his neck and abandoned it to the astrolabe. A horizontal arm of the inner globe attempted to move forward, but was restrained by the scarf. There was a sulphurous pop and sizzle as something shorted out in the central housing.

Bryant was just stepping free of the sphere when the cable-filled central core blew its ancient ceramic fuses and burst into flame. A second explosion followed as the electrical cables touched water.

All three men started as a low voltage shot around their ankles.

'The river will put out the fire,' said Rand, pushing them back in the direction of his office. 'I have never seen it this high before. You must hurry, you have no time to waste if you wish to stop the command from being fulfilled.'

'We have to find out where the signals went,' said Bryant.

'Sometimes they go all around the world,' said Rand. 'Not just to India, or to people who owe debts to the guild, but to those who have gained from it in the past.'

'It's too late to stop the weapon being primed, but we can get to the targets first,' said May as they climbed the stairs. 'Luckily the whole family is still under one roof.'

'No, it's not. Christian Whitstable and his daughter are recuperating in the Royal Free Hospital,' Bryant pointed out.

'And Peggy Harmsworth's still being cared for there too. I'll go there; you take the house. I can drop you off on the way.' The time was now twelve seventeen A.M.

'Arthur, do you have your bleeper?' asked May.

Bryant patted his pockets. 'Er, no, I must have dropped it.'

'What do you do, sell them? We have to call out every unit we can rouse. I have no intention of going into this without backup.'

Weary and wet, covered in spiderwebs and brick dust, the pair returned to the main hall. At the reception desk, May placed a call to Sergeant Longbright.

'We need everyone you can get hold of,' he explained. 'Tell Raymond Land what I've just told you. You'll have to explain that there's no way of knowing how many assassinations we're dealing with. I'm sure he'll be thrilled to hear that. And I need you to bring in Charles Whitstable.'

'But we already let him go.'

'This time you can arrest him.' He replaced the receiver. 'Let's get going,' he told Bryant.

'I've been trying to puzzle something out,' said Bryant as he turned the Mini back towards King's Cross.

'I'd rather you concentrated on your driving,' said May.

'You must agree that Rand is only guilty of crime by association. He's merely carrying out the duties he was employed to undertake.'

'I suppose so,' agreed May.

'Then who on earth killed Alison Hatfield? She's the only victim who couldn't possibly have been targeted by the astrolabe. As Leo Marks pointed out, she was an outsider.'

'I think you'll find there are other custodians who know about the system, apart from Mr Rand,' said May. 'And I don't suppose they're all so agreeably disposed. Maybe they realized she was interfering in the guild's business, and arranged to have her punished.'

'There has to be at least one other overseer,' said Bryant. 'Whoever was appointed the task of eliminating Christian and Deborah Whitstable must have had help getting that damned tiger into their house. There are others around. Their ancestor seems like a man who would have covered every option. I'm willing to bet we've had spies following us since the day this began. I woke one in the cellar of Bella Whitstable's house. Jerry Gates was warned off by another at the Savoy Theatre. They're probably just paid help. The machine telegraphs assassins. Replacing the Savoy barber in order to kill the Major took careful planning. And getting close enough to William Whitstable to slip him the bomb took great skill. If their deaths hadn't been filled with such baroque flourishes we may never have come to pin the blame on James Makepeace Whitstable.'

'You think James Whitstable planned the details of his rivals' deaths?'

'Certainly,' said Bryant, stamping experimentally on his accelerator. 'That's why no modern methods of execution were employed. The murders were designed to strike fear into competitors.'

'It makes you wonder how James Whitstable's conscience could have allowed him to set this up.' May looked through the windscreen and blanched. 'Mind that bus, Arthur.'

'I suppose he thought he was more Christian than the rest,' replied his partner. 'Think of the times in which he lived. He honestly believed that his family was more worthy of preservation than others.'

'Er, do you want me to drive?'

The little car swerved across into the next lane to avoid a pair of cyclists riding abreast, then accelerated through amber lights.

'He behaved no differently from our missionaries,' continued Bryant, 'smashing up the religious artefacts of one civilization to replace them with our own idols. I'm sure half of England still thinks that their religion is better than anyone else's.'

'I hate to ask,' said May, 'but can't you go any faster?'

'We're doing over sixty and running the reds, which isn't bad for Gray's Inn Road in the pouring rain, considering I've only got one windscreen wiper and bald tyres and I can't see out of the rearview mirror.'

The little Mini cut across the five-way intersection at King's Cross, causing a truck to slew sideways across the road, shedding its load as it ploughed into the safety barrier.

They had just reached Chalk Farm Tube station when they noticed the rain-haloed streetlights flickering further up Haverstock Hill. A moment later the lights went out, and the entire roadway ahead was plunged into darkness.

'We were warned this would happen,' said May. 'The Electricity Board is conserving energy because of the strikes. They've started pulling the plugs on whole areas of London.'

'Oh, that's wonderful,' snapped Bryant. 'We've gone full circle. They've got the night on their side at last.'

48 / Bringing Back the Day

'Y ou bitch, you knew all along.'
'Geraldine, whatever else you may think, I am still your mother, and you have no right—*no right at all*—to talk to me that way.'

They were facing each other across the parlour like a pair of evenly matched actresses in a stage melodrama. Gwen was even poised with a whisky in one hand. God only knew where Jack was, presumably sulking in his study, still smarting from his daughter's success with Charles Whitstable.

Jerry was operating on pure adrenaline. With the past suddenly clear to her, it seemed that her life had been building to this moment. 'You always knew,' she seethed.

'This is quite uncalled for.' Gwen threw back the Scotch and reached for the decanter with an unsteady hand. 'I don't know why you're behaving like this.'

'I was convinced I was ill, abnormal, incurable, and all the time it wasn't me at all.' Jerry took a step forward. She feared she might rush at her mother if she moved any closer. 'He said he wanted a daughter. You farmed me out to him. I remember it all now, so you don't have to pretend any more. I used to arrive with you at his apartment. It was you who took me, not Jack. You left me there. That's when he started the hypnotherapy, gently putting me to sleep. Did he ever tell you what he did?'

'Geraldine, you have to believe me, I was horrified when I found out—'

'I remember his hands crawling all over me. He used a blindfold, did he tell you that part? He said it was a game.' She was hysterical now, shouting at the top of her voice.

'He never—had intercourse—with you.'

'He would have if you hadn't found out when you did.'

'I arrived early one afternoon to collect you. The door was open, so I walked in. Charles had—his hands were inside your skirt. You were asleep, you couldn't possibly have known what was going on. I think he'd given you Valium, just a little pill. I started hitting him, screaming at him. He admitted he'd done it several times before. He blindfolded you because he was ashamed of his actions. He couldn't look at you, but he couldn't stop himself. He promised you wouldn't remember anything.'

'All I remember was being touched in the dark. All the bullshit you fed me about my nyctophobia! It wasn't fear of darkness.' No wonder she had barricaded herself from Nicholas, and fled from Joseph's room. No wonder she had frozen at Charles's touch.

'I just wanted what was best for you,' said her mother. 'We had your welfare to consider. If I had gone to the police, the scandal would have made all our lives hell.'

'So you helped him to cover it up. Then you let me go back there, even though you knew the truth. How could you do that? Knowing what he'd wanted to do?'

'You have no idea what he was like.' The tremor in Gwen's voice was a declaration of damage. '*No idea*. He knew my position with Jack and he used it.' She refilled her glass with unsteady hands. 'He's a very forceful man. I threatened to go to the police, but he persuaded me not to. He said he would help your father's business. I refused to let him see you again. He said he couldn't help himself. What could I do? He was highly thought of; he knew *royalty*. He would have lost everything if the scandal had come out. I felt so ashamed.'

She wiped her eye with the back of her hand, pacing back to the drinks cabinet. 'When your father and I met, Jack was a different man. Full of energy, exciting to be with. Then he lost interest in me. He lost his drive, his ambition.'

'You knocked it out of him.'

'He said he no longer saw the point of wanting to improve our social standing. He was offered a directorship with one of the finest guild companies in Britain and he turned it down! I turned to Charles for help, and then his foolish, weak mistake cost us everything. After finding him with you, I thought I had the upper hand. I didn't, of course. He just carried on, talking his way around me. I found myself doing anything I could just to keep him quiet, to keep him from harming us.'

'Jack must really despise you,' Jerry said viciously. 'No wonder he keeps your letters in his desk drawer.'

'What letters?' Gwen threw her glass back on the cabinet counter with a crack. Whisky splashed on the floor.

'The notes you and Charles sent each other. When he couldn't call the house. Jack found them, and he saved them. It's his proof, you see. It's how he keeps his hatred of you alive.'

Gwen was crying now, smearing her lipstick with the heel of her hand. 'I just wanted the best for us all. I should have made you my priority. But it was my life, too.'

'And now you have nothing.'

Jerry turned from the room and closed the door as

her mother sank into the corner chair with her face in her hands.

The Royal Free Hospital was one of the few buildings in North London with any electricity that night, and shone like a fog-smeared beacon as they approached it. The hospital's emergency generators had taken over, and the patients and nurses could be seen at the windows moving through a sickly half light.

Two squad cars had already arrived in the visitor's car park before them. Both were empty. May slipped into the Mini's driving seat.

'If everything's all right here,' Bryant called, walking backwards towards the main entrance to the hospital, 'I'll join you up at the house.'

'Good luck.' May started to reverse the Mini out of the forecourt. Bryant was about to enter the main foyer of the hospital when his partner reappeared.

'What's the matter?' asked Bryant, startled.

'On second thoughts, we'll do this together,' May said. 'I don't want anything happening to you.' He alighted from the car with his head tilted, straining to listen. 'Can you hear something funny?'

'Don't let your imagination run away with you.' Bryant was about to head inside when he heard the noise himself. Someone was banging on the glass above them. As they looked up there was a loud crack, like the shot from a gun.

Spears of glass showered down as the body fell, its scream mingling with shouts of horror from the room behind the burst window, six floors up.

The figure in white hospital garb hit the ground headfirst as the detectives jumped aside. The sound of flesh and bone impacting on concrete was like no other on earth. The victim lay before them, the body arched into a position that could only be possible if its spine had been fractured.

Almost at once, the police began to arrive at ground level. One junior constable turned white and vomited. Sergeant Longbright came running across the foyer.

'He bluffed his way into the room, Sir,' she told Bryant, trying to catch her breath. 'He was wearing a doctor's coat and walked right past the night nurse. We arrived just after, and that constable there,' she pointed to the one being sick, 'walked into the room to find him strangling the life out of the patient with a length of wire. We were just in time.'

'What do you mean?' asked Bryant, looking over at the corpse.

'Peggy Harmsworth started to come out of the coma a couple of hours ago. She's going to be all right. That's the man who tried to kill her.'

'My God,' said Bryant. 'If the first thing she saw when she woke up was someone throttling her, it's surprising she didn't go right back into a coma. What happened then?'

'He ran at the window before anyone could stop him, went through head first. Why would he do that?'

'Just obeying orders, Janice,' said Bryant, patting her on the shoulder. 'Let's get to Christian Whitstable and his daughter.' He made for the hospital entrance, dragging May in his wake. 'There are more like him on the way. We have no idea how many.'

In the corridors of the fifth floor, dim emergency lights dragged at their shadows. The hall ahead was deserted and silent. Longbright slowed to a walk. 'I don't understand,' she began, alarmed. 'I left a detail of men to guard Peggy's room. They were here just a few minutes ago.'

'Which is Christian Whitstable's ward?'

'He and his daughter are in a separate room, the last door on the left.'

Bryant, May, and Longbright approached as swiftly and quietly as they could manage. Bryant was the first to arrive. The door was wide open. In the half light he saw Christian Whitstable, up and out of bed, warning him back. As he walked further into the room, he saw the reason why.

'He has my daughter,' said Christian, never moving his eyes from the white-coated figure in a paper face mask, standing against the far wall of the room. Two other officers stood impotently nearby. Flora Whitstable was held close against the masked figure's leg, a rubber-gloved hand fastened across her mouth, a scalpel shining at her pale throat.

'All right, nobody move an inch,' said Bryant quietly, holding up his hands. 'He has nothing to lose. He must fulfill his obligation or die.'

The killer had no interest in his victim. Like his accomplice, he was performing a task against his will; paying off a debt of honour that demanded the ultimate payment of a taken life.

How many of these assassins had struggled with their consciences? It explained why Daisy Whitstable had been spared. What a terrible dilemma her killer must have faced. Unable to comprehend why such a young life had been targeted for termination, he must have known that sparing the girl would place his own life in danger.

Did the man standing before Bryant have any idea of the complex forces that had brought him to this spot tonight? Was he prepared to complete his task with a clear conscience, like Bella Whitstable's murderer? Or was he suffering the uncomprehending agony of being here?

'I know you don't want to harm the girl,' said Bryant gently. 'We know all about the duty you've been instructed to perform. If you let her go, I promise to help you.'

The killer took a step towards them. The hand tightened, the blade touched Flora's neck. Bryant could hear the assassin moaning softly behind his face mask.

'Listen to me,' Bryant said, standing motionless. 'You were supposed to finish the job after the tiger failed to do so. Neither of these two must be allowed to live. Am I right? Just nod once if I'm right. I won't come any closer.' He raised his hands in a gesture of peace. 'Please, just nod your head. Show us that you understand.'

Reluctantly, the assassin gave a slight nod.

'Put down the knife,' said Bryant. 'Your orders are no longer valid. There's been a mistake. You don't have to do this now. I know the burden you're under, and I want to relieve you of it. I believe you are a man of honour. Terrible things are happening around us. You don't have to do this any more; I beg you, let us help.'

As they watched, the eyes above the mask glossed and spilled, and the man began to tremble, the pressure of the moment racking his body, tearing at his soul. Flora darted forward as the knife clattered to the floor. Longbright stepped in with the other officers and took control.

'Give the black bastard what's coming to him,' said Christian Whitstable, wrecking the moment.

Before anyone could move, the tormented assassin fell to the floor with a terrible guttural wail, overcome with shame.

* * *

'We have to get to the safe house before we lose any more.' Bryant hitched his raincoat about him. They had returned to the hospital forecourt, which had been sectioned off with makeshift barriers. The lights were still out in the streets, and the rain was falling in soaking waves. This was no time to think of himself. Without knowing how many assassins were on their way to the Hampstead house, everyone was in danger.

May looked back at the hospital as he climbed into the Mini.

'Let's bring back the daylight,' he said.

49 / Under Siege

As the headlights of the rusty yellow Mini caught the lettering on the Mulberry Avenue street sign, they found that the route to the Whitstable house had been cordoned off with miles of yellow plastic tape. Police cars blocked the road ahead.

'I asked them to be discreet about this,' grunted Bryant. 'Pull over here. We won't get any closer.' As they walked towards the house, Raymond Land came running forward.

'What the bloody hell is going on?' he demanded. The rain was falling in a thick soaking drizzle. Land looked as if he'd recently fallen in a pond. 'You *two cannot* place the whole division on alert without my authority. Your damned sergeant should have known better than to take such an order. What if there's another emergency tonight?'

Thank God for the courageous and wonderful Longbright, thought Bryant. 'Then we'll pull someone out of here,' he suggested. Behind him, May sneezed. 'I'd stay away from us, Raymond, our colds are getting worse.'

'We spent part of this evening standing in filthy, freezing water,' May explained.

'I'm not interested in the state of your health,' said Land sarcastically. 'Could someone give me an update on the situation?'

'We're reaching the end of a long, bizarre journey—'

'Then what the hell are we all doing here? Your sergeant gave me some cock-eyed story—'

'There are still a few loose ends to clear up.'

'Like what, might I ask?'

'A squad of assassins is on its way here to wipe out the remaining Whitstables. This could turn into the Alamo.'

'What are you talking about? How many "assassins"?'

'I couldn't tell you. I don't know how many members of the family they've been instructed to finish off, either, but if they can arrange to slip a starving Bengal tiger into a suburban house I think we should be ready to expect the worst, don't you?'

The detectives stepped past their astonished superior and walked towards the house.

'Well, I'm surprised you two have the nerve to show your faces in here again,' said a sour-faced Berta Whitstable, examining the detectives by the light of her raised hurricane lamp. Even at this time of night she was dressed in expensive, garish clothes. She looked like Joan Crawford playing Rochester's first wife. 'I wouldn't be surprised if you were somehow responsible for killing us off.'

'I can assure you it's nothing to do with me,' said Bryant, removing his wet trilby and placing it on the hat stand. Candles had been placed in saucers and ashtrays throughout the hall. The flickering yellow gloom had reversed the century, returning the building to its true status as a Victorian mansion. 'Gather the family together please.'

'Who the hell do you think you are, Mr Bryant?' Berta's eyes narrowed in fury. 'You can't just keep ordering us about. This is still William Whitstable's house, and you are trespassing on—'

'Just fuck off and get the family, will you?' said Bryant

wearily. 'Pardon my French. It's late, and the night is far from over.'

Berta stormed off up the stairs, calling for the others in an injured, tremulous voice.

'How many officers do we have altogether?' May asked Land.

'Eight,' he replied. 'Nine counting me.'

'Is that all?'

'Four are at the hospital with your sergeant,' the detective superintendent explained. 'I think you'll find that the rest are Met boys making a protest at the way you two have been conducting this case.'

'God, why did they have to pick tonight, of all nights?' cried May. 'Have we got all of the windows covered?'

'As far as it's possible to cover them,' said Land.

'At least we've managed to get the men well armed. There are dense woods behind the property. No way of stopping a sniper in there, I'm afraid.'

'You see?' Bryant told his partner. 'If William Whitstable had lived in a council house this wouldn't be a problem.'

He looked up to see a crowd of arguing, angry-faced relatives heading down the stairs towards him bearing torches and lanterns. 'My God, it looks like they're getting ready to go and set fire to Frankenstein's castle. Right, let's get everyone into the dining room.'

As usual everyone was talking at once, but this time fear showed beneath the anger and confusion. The dining room was illuminated by a large crystal chandelier filled with fresh candles. Shadows bounced crazily about the ceiling. Bryant half expected to see Edgar Allan Poe taking notes in a corner.

Bryant turned to the gathered family as his partner seated the last of the older children.

'You might not realize it, but this house is under siege,' he began. 'We have good reason to believe that as-sassins will try to attack one or more of you during the night.' Better to frighten them into behaving themselves, he thought. 'I want you to keep away from the doors and windows, and stay as near to the centre of the house as possible. We'll protect the outside of the building as best as we can, but we can't guarantee you one hundred per-cent safety. After this night, however, we can promise that you will have nothing more to fear.'

'You mean you've finally pulled your finger out and managed to catch someone,' snorted Isobel Whitstable. 'Perhaps you'd like to tell us who the culprit is.'

'Now is not the time,' said May, pulling his old friend to one side. 'We're duty-bound to protect them.' He led Bryant away as the Whitstables began hurling insults af-ter him. One of the children threw a plastic beaker at his head. 'You're a pair of hopeless old failures,' the boy jeered.

'I can't believe they're being so rude,' said May.

'They're going through a nightmare,' said Bryant. 'They don't even know if they'll be alive in the morning.' He turned to one of the officers standing inside the front porch. 'Have you seen anyone around? Any sign of dis-turbance at all?'

'Nothing yet, Sir.'

'The sight of you lot has probably put them off.' He scratched his chin thoughtfully. 'On the other hand, the people we're after are more loyal and diligent than the men who employed them. They'll be determined to carry out their instructions if they can. It's the only way they can ensure their own safety.'

'You sound as if you know more of what we're dealing with than you're prepared to tell us,' complained May.

'John, I've done some reading from Maggie Armitage's books about Indian cults. These chaps can put themselves into states of heightened awareness. Look, there's no point in you getting any wetter. Why don't you oversee operations inside the house? I can take the perimeter.'

'I suppose it's better than leaving you to get into a fight with them,' sighed May. 'Just be careful.'

Outside, rain drummed through the trees in the woodland beyond, crackling like a forest fire. Land was seated in the front patrol car making a call. Around the house, disconsolate soaked policemen stood in pairs, unsure what they were watching for.

It's going to be a long night, thought Bryant.

Inside the house, things were just as bad. May was having great difficulty holding the family together in one room. The children had a habit of ducking out the moment his back was turned, the men's moods ranged from threatening to abusive, and the women were bitterly contradicting one another.

'I have to use the bathroom,' announced Berta Whitstable, rising from her armchair and pushing her way through the door in a jangle of jewellery. 'I really can't believe we're prisoners in our own property. *Private* property.'

As she reached the foot of the stairs, however, she hesitated. Several of the candles on the landing had blown out, and the first floor was virtually in darkness. As she climbed, she found herself listening for sounds from above. The ill-dressed detective had shut the lounge door behind her, and she could no longer hear the familiar hubbub of the family arguing.

Somewhere overhead, rain was falling on a skylight. What a relief it was to be away from her relatives for a moment. She had forgotten how appallingly self-interested they were when gathered all together. She wondered where Charles was. His place was with the family. He had promised to come. Why wasn't he here?

At the top of the stairs she leaned forward and peered down the darkened hall. The bathroom was right at the end, and only one candle had remained alight. No wonder—there was a chill draught coming in, and now she felt several tiny spots of rain on the back of her neck. Someone had stupidly left a skylight open. Berta walked on down the hallway, the wet air wafting eerily around her shoulders.

She reached the bathroom and saw that the door was half open. The candles on the sink had blown out, but she could see a box of matches beside them. She was reaching out for it when a cold hand grabbed hers. She found herself facing a wide-eyed man who slipped his hand across her mouth and pulled her to him as he slammed the door shut.

'They can't come down the street because they'll see the police cars,' said PC Bimsley. 'If I had to assassinate someone, I'd climb up one of the beech trees in the wood and shoot them through the windows. With a bow and arrow, so it would make no noise.'

'That wouldn't work,' Bryant countered. 'These men are given specific targets. From outside the house, you can't tell individuals apart.'

They were standing by the dustbins at the end of the garden, shining their torches into the woods. Rain filled their beams like glittering steel needles. Bryant checked his watch. Two forty-five A.M. His boots were full of icy water.

'How long have you been in the police, Mr Bryant?' asked the young PC.

'Longer than you've been alive,' said the detective with unconcealed pride.

'That must make you the oldest team on the force.'

'Not if we keep lying about our ages.'

'I bet you've worked on some really exciting cases in your time.'

The detective's eyes caught his. 'There's been the odd trunk murder I wouldn't have missed for the world.'

'Mr Bryant, if you were a criminal, how would you go about getting inside the house?'

'Me?' He thought for a moment. 'First of all I'd wait until the initial activity had died down, say around about now. This is the danger time. Everyone's getting tired, and the family are starting to feel a little safer again. They're lowering their guard. Some of them have probably left the room, because they won't be told what to do by a stupid policeman. Security's a bit looser now. The other officers are thinking we've got it wrong, that nothing's going to happen after all. That's when I'd make my move. I'd come in disguise, as someone in a position of trust. Say, a copper.'

'One of the ones guarding the house?'

With one thought between them, they started to run back through the flooded garden just as the first shot was fired.

50 / Glorious Sacrifice

One of the constables was holding him down on the grass when they arrived. The young Asian man was wearing a standard police-issue navy-blue raincoat and cap, and had been stationed alone at the side of the house.

PC Bimsley, clearly elated by his newfound respect as a useful member of the force, had spotted the bogus officer reaching into his jacket as he crouched beside the parlour window, studying the family through the curtains.

'It was his shoes, Sir,' said Bimsley, panting. 'Black plimsolls.'

'Well done, Bimsley,' said Land. 'You can take your foot off his throat now.' Together he and Bryant helped the silent figure to his feet, and the detective superintendent pulled him close to get a good look.

'Look at his eyes, Raymond.'

'My God.' Land took a sharp step back. Their captive's eyes had an opaque, filmy appearance, as if they had been boiled dry.

'The poor bugger's blind, and he still turned up to fulfill his duty,' said Bryant. 'When you take him to the van, be careful with him, Bimsley. He may try to harm himself.'

The constable tried to move his prisoner, but the man refused to budge. Suddenly it was as if a plug had been disconnected, for the assassin dropped silently to his knees and fell forward onto his face in the grass.

'He's in a trance state.' Bryant was fascinated. 'It's a complex Eastern ritual based on a combination of scientific and occult principles involving hypnosis, local medicines, and invocations. I've read a lot about it, but never actually seen it in action.'

'Christ Almighty, Bryant, this isn't Open University,' fumed Land. 'We'll have to take your word for it. I'm a pragmatic man. I like my explanations clear-cut. *This*—' He pressed the toe of his boot against the prostrate prisoner's shoulder, disgusted. 'This doesn't fit in anywhere. There are no rules in this kind of situation. How the hell are we supposed to know when we've caught them all? Take him away, Bimsley, for God's sake.'

'Sir, there's a call for you in the car,' said Sergeant Longbright, who had just arrived from the hospital. Bryant walked briskly around to her vehicle, slid into the passenger seat, and pulled the handset free. 'Bryant.'

'Sir, this is Mr Rand at the guild.'

'Has the tontine device burned itself out?'

'Yes, Sir. The damage is shameful. After all these years...' The old Indian sounded disappointed that the astrolabe had been shut down. Even though he was merely a maintenance engineer, Rand possessed the true spirit of the guild craftsmen. 'I have been trying to decode the final set of transmissions. The calls went to North London, seven of them in all. I think I can get the addresses of the recipients.'

'Give them to an officer after you've finished talking to me,' said Bryant. 'What about the targets?'

'That's why I called you, Sir. It's all of them.'

'What do you mean? The whole Whitstable family?'

'That's right, Sir, every single one.'

Bryant thought fast. The machine's final command had fallen on the alliance's anniversary. In its attempt to clear away its enemies in one broad sweep, the misaligned device had targeted the wrong group.

'Thanks for the warning, Mr Rand. There's something I wanted to ask you earlier.' It had bothered him when he'd first seen Rand's office, but the question had been pushed from his mind by more urgent matters. 'When you need supplies for the maintenance room, who approves the orders?'

'Mr Tomlins, Sir. I report only to him.'

Bryant had been convinced of the guild secretary's involvement at some level. Tomlins had tried to obstruct the investigation right from the start.

'Do you have a way of contacting him at home?'

As Rand was giving him the address, Bryant kept the front of the house in view through the rain-smeared windscreen of the car. There was a sudden flash of movement as someone darted between the bushes. Leaving Rand holding on the line, Bryant ducked out of the vehicle and began to run back to the house.

'You there, look out!'

The constable turned in time to deflect the blow but could not avoid it altogether. He slipped backwards and fell into the grass, his attacker landing squarely on top of him. Before Bryant could reach the fighting pair, Longbright ran forward. She swiped the assassin a hefty blow across the back of the head with her torch.

'Duracell batteries,' she said, rolling the inert body off the squashed constable. 'Very dependable.'

'Seven assassins,' said Bryant, fighting to regain his breath. 'Of course, it has to be seven. The Stewards.'

'Don't put this man anywhere near the other one,' he told the sergeant. 'You'd better call for another secure van. We're going to need it.' He left them and walked off along the side of the house, shining his torch into the bushes. The rain was growing heavier once more, and the beam's visibility was reducing to a tunnel of grey mist. Bryant wanted to check that May was all right inside the house. There were still five more assassins to be located.

At first, he assumed that the figure walking briskly towards him across the lawn was another officer. Then his torch picked up a streak of steel in the figure's left hand, and he realized that he had located the third assassin. This one was bull-necked, younger, fresher.

He looked back at the side of the house, but the remaining officers had moved to the front where they were presumably helping Sergeant Longbright with her prisoner.

Bryant had no weapon on him of any kind. He was alone.

He felt a cold prickling behind his knees and at the back of his neck as he realized the recklessness of the situation in which he had placed himself. He had done the exact thing he had warned others against. The assassin was almost upon him as the detective backed up against the brickwork and shone the torch at his assailant's eyes. For a moment the man faltered, blinded.

Bryant rolled away from the wall and ran up on to the lawn.

The wetness of the grass had greased the slope. His foot slipped beneath him and over he went, painfully on to his knees and then his back, helplessly spread before his attacker. The assassin stood over him, swaying slightly in the rain. Then he dropped forward, the knife raised at his waist. Bryant felt the cold hand of death seize his heart.

Suddenly there were two of them, one clinging to the

back of the other. Longbright had seized her chance and was attempting to haul the assassin over on the garden steps. 'Run, Mr Bryant!' she shouted as their protagonist's left arm flew up and his blade slashed the air, striking at Longbright's chest.

The sergeant cried out as Bryant staggered to his feet and called for help. Officers were pouring into the rain-swept garden. Two of them pulled Longbright free, grab-bing the assailant by his wrists and forcing him to release the knife, which spiraled harmlessly into the turf. Bryant caught Longbright as she slipped back, the front of her sou'wester slashed apart. He tore open the raincoat and examined the wound. The flesh of her chest had been cut, but not deeply. The heavy material had absorbed the brunt of the attack.

'Thank God I wear an upholstered brassiere,' she told him breathlessly, somewhat amazed by her escape.

'You're going to have a small, intriguing scar,' he said, tousling the sergeant's wet hair. 'Aren't you glad I made you wrap up warm?'

Shocked by her brush with death, Longbright looked back at the anguished young Asian twisting in his cap-tors' arms.

'There are four more on the loose,' Bryant said ur-gently. 'I think one's already inside. Look at the roof.'

As Bryant loped off in the direction of the front door, Longbright looked up and saw the smashed glass of the skylight lying on the tiles.

Land was returning to the patrol car when he rounded the end of the garden wall and walked directly into an eld-erly Indian gentleman. His shout of surprise alerted the men in the car, who ran to his help just as the killer lashed out at the soft flesh of his throat. The superintendent stumbled against the wall, gasping for breath as his attacker surrendered. 'I did not want to do this! shouted the old man. 'I am paying the debt for my son!' The officers led him away.

As Bryant pushed open the front door of the house, Susan Whitstable hit him on the head with an omelette pan. 'I'm frightfully sorry,' she said, not sounding sorry at all. 'I thought you were one of them. Why are you making so much noise outside? The children are trying to sleep.'

'Where's my partner?' asked Bryant, rubbing his skull and shoving past her to the foot of the stairs.

'We have enough trouble keeping track of our own people without having to find your staff for you,' Susan said, walking back to the dining room still clutching the pan. As Bryant began to climb the stairs, his torch beam faltered.

'Oh no, not again.' He felt sure that somewhere up above, the spirit of James Makepeace Whitstable was watching over the house, enjoying their battle to hold back the darkness. Upon reaching the landing he found himself without any light. From somewhere further along the hallway came the sound of scuffling. Then a hand shot out and pushed him back against the wall.

'He's got Berta Whitstable tied up in there,' whispered May. 'I think he's arming some kind of explosive device. I saw him detaching a large wired object from his belt.'

'I wondered if they would resort to something like that,' hissed Bryant. 'Nothing short of an explosion would get rid of this lot. The orders came in to remove all of the remaining Whitstables tonight. What can we do?'

'Go back downstairs and start getting everyone out of the house as quietly as possible. Send one of the armed officers up. No more than one, though. I need the element of surprise, but I daren't tackle him alone. Berta's still in there, and he could trigger the device.'

Bryant ran down the stairs and opened the living room door. Everyone was seated around one of the girls, who was reading aloud. *How typical of the Whitstables to set up a reading circle when their lives are under threat*, he thought. Gathering a pair of officers, he sent one upstairs to May, and had the other assist him.

'I want your attention,' said Bryant, stepping into the centre of the circle. '*Everybody*, please.' Several Whitstables craned their heads to one side, gesturing for him to move.

'We're reading *A Christmas Carol*,' said one of Susan Whitstable's daughters. 'We always do at Christmas. It's nearly the end and you're spoiling it.'

'Scrooge beats Tiny Tim to death with his crutch,' said Bryant maliciously. 'Now, I want you all to move outside as quickly and as quietly as possible.'

There was a chorus of protest. 'But it's *pouring*!'

'Have the girls got time to go and change?' asked Susan, indicating her offspring with the omelette pan.

'Everyone must go right now, in the clothes you're wearing.'

'I'm wearing a Cecil Gee sweater,' complained Nigel Whitstable. 'If the colours run I'm sending you the bill.'

'If you're not all out of this room in twenty seconds, I'll have you dragged out,' Bryant warned, hoisting two of the smaller children to their feet. 'You shouldn't be listening to Dickens at your age, you're too impressionable.'

'Daddy says we can do whatever we please because you're public servants!' said Berta's granddaughter, Delilah Whitstable. The others started to file out, complaining as they went.

'He does, does he?' Bryant looked for her father as he

lifted the child into his arms. 'I must remember to see if his road tax has expired.'

Outside, in the dark, in sliding sheets of rain, Longbright stood alone, watching the trees for movement. She wiped her torch against her sodden trousers. When she raised the beam, she saw the assassin walking towards her from the end of the garden. Tall, middle-aged, and sickly, he was nevertheless dangerous. In his left hand was a long-handled weeding fork, presumably all he could find in the gardener's shed.

She walked towards him, wary but unafraid.

He came to an unsteady halt and peered at her. The rain had plastered his hair flat, giving him a skeletal appearance.

'You are Whitstable?' he asked awkwardly.

'No, I'm a police officer, and you must put down your weapon.'

He seemed so pathetic that she almost felt sorry for him. Lumbering at her, he raised the red metal fork, but long before it could connect she clouted him with the house brick in her hand, stone cracking against bone. Knocked from his feet, he fell into the weeds, raised himself on one arm, then dropped.

Longbright tossed the brick aside and walked away. Usually, she kept one in her immense handbag, but tonight she had left the bag back at the unit.

Upstairs, May and the constable had been discovered. The assassin was standing in the bathroom doorway, unsure of his next move. Behind him Berta lay whimpering on the tiled floor with a towel knotting her ankles and a flannel stuffed in her mouth. In front of her was a heavy six-inch-thick steel disc, joined to an electronic detonator. After appraising the situation and recognizing the conditions of a stalemate, the assassin knelt and calmly continued setting the detonator.

'We have to get him to hand her over,' May whispered to the constable. 'He's going to set the thing off without worrying about himself.' During his career in the force, May had never encountered the most dangerous kind of assassin: a fanatic prepared for glorious sacrifice, unconcerned for his own survival. At this point in the twentieth century, such people were still a rarity. 'Can you pick him off from here?'

'I can't be certain, sir. He's too close to the woman.'

'Then hold your fire. Wait here for a minute.' May slowly crept forward, his eye fixed on the detonator.

'Your orders were wrong!' he called suddenly, making the assassin start and Berta Whitstable flinch. 'You're not supposed to hurt these people. I know that's what you've been told to do, but the command has been canceled. Please, don't move.' Knowing he could not dissuade, May spoke to divert. He directed the armed officer to edge towards the assassin, who looked up only briefly before returning his attention to the bomb.

'Stay there and keep me covered,' May told the officer, lowering himself slowly to the ground with a grunt. 'And to think my mother told me I'd be happier in a desk job.'

He began to move forward, one foot shifting quietly in front of the other. The assassin finished twisting the wire caps of the detonator shut. He turned a switch, set the box down and took a step back, bracing his wasted body for the worst. Behind him, Berta spat out the flannel and began to scream.

Judging by the size of the casing, the bomb blast would be too big to contain by simply throwing himself on it. May looked at the floor, judging the positions of assassin and captive. Towels had been dragged from the rail above the radiator; several had fallen on the floor. It was all he needed to see.

The assassin was still staring at him, waiting for the safety countdown to end, when May threw his torso forward. Moving with a speed that surprised them all, he slid into the bathroom with as much force as he could muster, slapping the steel disc across the floor. It skittered over the polished bathroom tiles like a hockey puck and thudded into the towels which had fallen against the far wall.

Berta released a howl of fear as the armed officer darted in and brought his knee up hard into the assassin's stomach, punching the breath from him. The man landed hard on the floor as May twisted the bomb's safety timer back.

'Some help up here, please,' he shouted, untying Berta's ankles and pushing her from the room, out of harm's way. As officers thundered up the staircase and prepared to take their prisoner, May leant against the wall to regain his breath, and realized how very, very tired he had suddenly become.

Behind him, still connected, the bomb's countdown readout zeroed itself, jumped back to OVERRIDE: MINS: 5:00, and began to flicker downwards once more.

'Take him downstairs quickly,' May told his men as he passed them on the stairs. 'There's still one assassin loose, in or around the house. Nobody's safe until he can be found.'

51 / The Finger of Blame

'Can we go in yet?' complained Nigel Whitstable. The colours in his sweater were starting to blur together. Several of the younger ones had started to cry. 'This is an absolute bloody outrage.' Nigel looked around, as if noticing the police cars for the first time. 'It would help if you were to explain what you're hoping to achieve with all this ... ridiculous fuss.'

Bryant and Sergeant Longbright were busy trying to settle as many of the children as possible in the cars. Most were treating the evening as an adventure, and had to be slapped away from the dashboard instrumentation.

May led Charles Whitstable's sobbing mother out to join the group as the remaining police gathered around to help the family. Berta looked fragile and rather pathetic in the rain. As Bryant backed out of the last car he realized that everyone was staring at him, waiting to be told what to do next.

In this brief instant, for the first time, he almost felt sorry for them. Huddled together in the downpour with no coats or jackets, frozen, sopping wet, confused and utterly miserable, the Whitstables looked a hopeless lot. Whatever else happened he would always remember them like this, the bedraggled dynastic dregs, suspicious of everyone, capable of complaint but little else, waiting for someone stronger to direct them.

The moment was broken by Nigel Whitstable, who

had come to the boil again. 'When the papers get hold of this,' he cried, poking Land in the chest with a bony forefinger, 'you'll be about as popular as the Gestapo. You're finished, all of you! And especially those two pathetic has-beens you call detectives!'

Bryant had had enough. He stepped forward and called for silence.

Behind him the neighbours were watching, standing in doorways with their arms folded, or peering from around their curtains. When everyone had finally stopped complaining, the detective began to speak.

'You asked me earlier to tell you the cause of all this. You wanted me to point the finger of blame. I'll tell you now, if you haven't already realized.' He drew himself to his full unimpressive height and studied the faces before him. 'It's *you*. The Whitstables. The company. The alliance. The family. The empire. You did this to yourselves.'

There was an immediate uproar. Finally, Berta made herself heard above the furious chatter.

'What on earth are you talking about, you silly little man?' she cried. 'We would *never* knowingly harm ourselves. We know how to protect our own people.'

'That, Madam, is precisely what caused the problem in the first place,' retorted Bryant, growing heated. 'If you want to accuse anyone, accuse James Makepeace Whitstable. If your ancestor hadn't been so determined to keep your money from the hands of upstarts by killing them off, and if you hadn't been prepared to pass on his secret from father to son, mother to daughter, then you wouldn't have accidentally turned this destruction upon yourself.' He strode angrily before them. 'My God, instead of helping to cast out the dark and keep the fire of free enterprise alight—that precious symbol of the burning flame none of you professed to have any knowledge of—you've all become party to a new darkness. It's been descending on you all this time, and not one of you noticed. All to preserve the values of your guild. Purity. Decency. The new bright light.' He pointed at each in turn, unable to control the fury he and May had fought to keep in check since hearing of Alison Hatfield's death.

'You're supposed to be the apex of civilization, but you're just the opposite. The only thing at which you all excel is lying—to us, yourselves, and each other. And now that we've managed to save the rest of you, you'll undoubtedly show your gratitude by having us thrown off the force. Well, go ahead, do your worst. Our job is ended here.'

He turned his back on them and stalked away, leaving the bewildered group gaping after him.

'Sir,' called PC Bimsley, 'I just saw someone run in through the front door. He's going upstairs.'

'It can't be one of us,' said May. 'Everyone's outside now. Looks like you've found our last man—you'd better go after him.'

'Yes, *Sir*!' said Bimsley, sprinting off toward the house, going for the hat trick.

Just then, the entire upper floor of William Whitstable's house exploded with a deafening roar that bounced off the houses and echoed across the city. The night sky billowed out in a boiling wave, causing their ears to sting. The surrounding trees were filled with the zing of scattering glass. Small pieces of blazing timber fell on the gathered assembly. The air was filled with an acrid stink as flames executed exuberant flourishes in the upper windows.

As the horrified Whitstables picked themselves up off the wet pavement, May climbed to his feet and ran back into the garden, searching for PC Bimsley. The constable was looking up at the roaring building with a dazed expression on his face.

'I wouldn't bother going in after him now, Bimsley,' May said consolingly. 'By the way, your jacket's on fire.'

Behind them, the top floor of the house burned brightly on, a pyrogenic beacon that ignited the stars and stole the sombre blackness from the night.

52 / Inundation

Thank God we managed to get everyone out in time,' said May later, as they were heading back towards the PCU's offices in the Mini. At this hour of the morning it was safe for Bryant to drive, providing you weren't a cat or a pigeon. 'I thought you were a bit hard on them. Did it ever occur to you that it might be just as difficult for them to be who they are?'

'If they don't like it, they can opt out,' replied Bryant. 'It doesn't work the other way around. The poor can't choose to be rich.' He stared thoughtfully out at the deserted streets of Camden Town.

'Jerry Gates has been accepted as one of them now. Did you hear Charles Whitstable offered her a job? It will be interesting to see what she decides to do after this.' May blew his nose. 'Do you think I've caught pneumonia?'

'It's possible,' said Bryant, never one to look on the bright side. 'There's a distinct chance that I may die in my sleep tonight. I can't take the pace any more. I've got fallen arches, varicose veins, and now my valves feel bunged up. I don't know how I got to middle age without passing through a misspent youth.'

'I know what you mean. We haven't done this much running about since that business with the Deptford Demon four years ago.'

'Wait a minute, we can't go home yet,' said Bryant,

slapping the wheel. 'We have to pick up Tomlins and bring him in to the station.'

'It's ten past five, for heaven's sake. Let someone else do it.'

'We daren't do that, John. We can't risk losing him. Somebody on the inside has to relate the full story to Land before he submits his report. Nobody else knows about the astrolabe. Radio Longbright and tell her where we're going.'

He turned the Mini around and headed for the Maida Vale address that Rand had given them.

The house they sought was pale and pebble-dashed, a bay-windowed thirties villa, far below the social standard of the Whitstables' homes. On the fifth buzz, a middle-aged woman in a quilted dressing gown opened the door and attempted to stifle a yawn. Bryant and May identified themselves, and asked to see her husband.

'I'm afraid you've missed him.' She waved a hand in the direction of the garage adjoining the house. 'He got a phone call, said he had to go out, that it was to do with work. I didn't understand what he meant. I mean he's not a doctor, he doesn't get house calls.'

'How long ago was this?'

'About half an hour.'

'Did he say where he was going?' asked Bryant.

'I've no idea.' She rubbed her pale cheeks, trying to remember. 'Wait, he said he was seeing someone called Rand.'

The city was still deserted at five forty-two A.M., as the yellow Mini slid to a halt outside the entrance hall to the

Worshipful Company of Watchmakers. The front doors of the guild had remained closed since the night of Alison Hatfield's death.

'I don't want to alert him in case he does a runner,' said May. 'How are we going to get in?'

Bryant smiled and dug into his overcoat. 'I still have Charles Whitstable's keys,' he reminded May. 'We'll have to bring in poor old Rand as well, you know. I bet Tomlins will try to swing the blame on him.'

'You want me to call for backup?' asked May, looking about.

'After what we've been through tonight, I think we can handle the two of them.'

They alighted from the car and walked to the door. Bryant unlocked it as quietly as possible and stepped inside. The foyer was dark and empty, and answered their footsteps with muted echoes. Switching on their torches, they made directly for the staircase at the rear of the building. Using the lift would only draw attention to their approach.

'I'm starting to feel like a mole, all this burrowing around by torchlight,' said Bryant, gingerly descending to the lower landing. 'Can you hear something?'

From the darkness below them came the sound of an angry, ranting voice. They increased their pace, descending through the mire of the lower floor. Rand's office was deserted. They tried the room that housed the astrolabe. The emergency-lighting circuit evidently ran from a generator, for the bulb above the huge brass globe was still lit.

They found Tomlins standing over the little Indian with the sledgehammer in his hands. Rand's twisted, terrified figure on the floor suggested that he may already have been struck.

Tomlins started at their arrival, his dismayed, disapproving face turned to them.

'Get back,' the guild secretary warned. 'This has to be ended properly.' He turned to the prostrate figure beneath him and swung the hammer once more, slamming it into Rand's back. 'I should crush his skull for what he's done,' he explained dispassionately.

'What has he done?' asked May, stepping closer.

'He's destroyed everything. Betrayed his sacred trust. To the alliance, to the guild, and to the family.'

'He didn't know what the machine was capable of doing.'

'Well, it can't do anything now, can it?' He raised the sledgehammer again. 'All the work, all the years of loyalty and hardship and *duty*, all for nothing.'

As the weapon began its descent May grabbed Tomlins's forearm, forcing the hammer back. With a terrified moan, the supervisor scrambled painfully across the floor, heading for the safety of his office. As the two men grappled with the hammer, Bryant tried to pull Tomlins down from behind.

The guild secretary was stronger than either of them had expected. He pushed Bryant away with one hand and threw himself backwards, slamming May hard against the wall once, then a second time. Bryant heard his partner's skull thump hard on the bricks and watched as he fell into the water. Tomlins turned on Bryant, his teeth bared in fury, and swung the sledgehammer, the weight of its iron head carrying the momentum of the swing.

Bryant jumped back and realized that he was pressed against the edge of the astrolabe. Stumbling, he found himself inside its structure, the brass rings protecting him from his enraged attacker.

The hammer swooped again and smashed against one

of the globe's support poles. The machine clanged sonorously as the blow reverberated through the rings. Bryant's torch was shocked from his hand. He fell back against the defunct central housing. Another blow hit the poles and they buckled. The entire structure was creaking and starting to turn. Bryant tried to raise himself up in the water, but found the brass arms of the inner 'planet' descending on him. In another moment the astrolabe had twisted from its stand to seal him inside.

'You're not going to get away,' called Bryant, gasping for breath as one of the brass bars was brought to rest on his chest. 'It's over. Your rivals are still alive. The tontine was faulty. It reset all the clocks and killed the family instead. It failed you.'

Tomlins did not reply. Instead, he walked away from the shattered globe to the far side of the room and began to swing the hammer at the seal of the drain door behind him. Instantly, Bryant realized the danger of his predicament.

Bryant's mind was racing. The old Indian, Rand, had possessed no knowledge of the astrolabe's assassins, so there had to be an overseer. Someone was needed to organize the details, to take care of payments and arrangements, to help with the cover-ups. Bryant had considered Charles Whitstable most likely to be the remaining link in the chain of command.

But Charles had been handling business in India. It had to be someone in daily contact with the guild. Tomlins had most certainly watched Alison Hatfield getting closer to the terrible truth. Finally he'd been forced to remove her. But there was more Bryant had to know.

'If you were aware of the astrolabe's existence, you must have seen that it was inaccurate,' he shouted, trying to slide his body from the grip of the brass arm as a black-eyed rat swam past, inches from his face.

Tomlins lowered the sledgehammer for a moment and wiped the sweat from his forehead. 'Who's to say it was inaccurate?' he said. 'It was designed to protect the Watchmakers' investments. The Whitstable family does little more than leech from the guild. Let them all die, and return the money to the system's administrators.' He swung the hammer at the wall again, and this time the lock cracked, releasing a fine spray of filthy water around its edges.

'If anyone deserves to benefit, it's the craftsmen,' cried Bryant. 'Without them there would be no guild in the first place.'

'Three generations of my family have worked for the Watchmakers,' said Tomlins, grunting as the sledgehammer dented the door. 'All of them were paid a pittance for guarding someone else's fortune, and all were sworn to secrecy. Where did it get us?'

'So the money was coming in to you,' said Bryant weakly. Realizing that the astrolabe had failed, Tomlins had discovered an advantage over his employers. Bryant tried to free himself from the pressing weight of the metal exoskeleton, but was unable to budge any further. His partner had not moved since he was hurt. He prayed May hadn't drowned while unconscious.

'It was until you interfered,' Tomlins replied.

His next swipe burst the drainage hatch wide. A black fountain rained across the chamber. Bryant knew that Tomlins would easily be able to flood the room, and no-one would ever find their bodies. He would be able to claim his share of the tontine after all.

Icy drainage water poured into the shallow depression within the area of the globe, raising the level around the trapped detective. The temperature fell sharply as the vault became filled with the stench of the sewer.

The bitter water swirled itself around Bryant's trapped body as he strained against the imprisoning brasswork. May had fallen with his head propped up against the fallen bricks, so the rising river was still clear of his nose and mouth. Only Longbright knew where they were, and she had no cause to be alarmed. On the contrary, she would be expecting both of them to take a few hours' rest before reporting in to Land.

To perish in such an ignominious fashion as this was terrible. To die below the streets of the city he loved, within its very heart. Bryant wished he was at home, surrounded by his records, his books, and his memories. It seemed such a grotesque, undignified way for life to leave him.

He twisted his head to watch as Tomlins swung insanely at the wall. In his impatience to fill the room, he was trying to open up the entire drain. Each blow carried the frustration of a blunted life. The wall was cracked in several places, and had begun to bow outwards.

Tomlins, blinded by his bitter zeal, driven by a lifetime wasted in subservience, once more charged the bricks with his sledgehammer. Suddenly the concrete membrane bulged and split wide in a tsunami of water and brick. Tomlins was lifted from his feet and hurled backwards as the deluge burst over him, slamming him against the fallen astrolabe.

As the unleashed river rocked his metal prison, Bryant seized the moment, shoving against the brass bar across his chest. He could summon little strength. The freezing water was rapidly dulling his senses. He hammered against the bars again, and was astonished to find the cage rising of its own accord.

'You're pleased to see me this time, are you?' asked Jerry Gates, holding out her hand. Amazed, unable to catch enough breath to reply, Bryant reached out and allowed himself to be hauled to his feet. 'John!' he gasped, pointing to the figure floating facedown in the rising water.

Jerry steadied him and set off to help his partner.

Bryant pushed himself free of the mechanical rings and began wading across the room to help her. Through the hole in the wall he watched as the black torrent rushed past. The stench rising from its foul waters was unbearable. The river of darkness thundered on beyond the shattered wall, denied access to the world above.

He had waded halfway across the room when a pair of wet arms seized him around the neck and pulled him back beneath the surface of the vile torrent.

Tomlins's hands sought purchase on his throat, but as Bryant struggled to twist free, one of them pushed down on the top of his head. The detective forced his eyes to remain shut in the pulsing effluent, knowing that the poison content of the river would kill him if absorbed for too long. Now both hands were locked firmly over his skull, holding him under.

A dull booming sounded in his ears as the deluge thundered through the steel cage, twisting it back and forth. Red flares of light exploded against his eyelids. His lungs were filled with fire.

And then the hands went limp, and Bryant's head bobbed up above the surface of the river, suddenly released. Tomlins had rolled back in the water. His upper arm had become trapped in the shifting blades of the astrolabe, pulling him beneath the surface.

Bryant fought free as the structure groaned and shifted once more. As soon as he was unsnagged, he allowed the current to carry him across the room. Jerry was wading over in his direction. He could not tell if John May was alive or dead.

He looked back in time to see Tomlins's arm lift from its mooring as his body swirled towards the opening in the wall, where it was sucked back into the fast-flowing river, to be swept off into the pounding Stygian darkness.

The three of them sat beside one another in the back of the patrol car, soaked and shocked, wrapped in blankets, as an officer drove them to the nearest hospital clinic.

'Do you mind if I open a window, Sir?' asked the driver. 'I can't breathe.'

'Are you insinuating that we smell?' asked Bryant weakly.

'Well, you did get dipped in sh—er, the sewer, Sir.'

'Oh, all right.'

May turned to Jerry. She looked as if she was having a wonderful time. 'Why did you follow us back to the guild?' he asked.

'I went to the unit to find Sergeant Longbright, and they told me where she was. I was there in the car when you radioed in your destination. The main door to the building was open, and there was an incredible noise coming from the back of the hall. I just followed it down.'

'But what possessed you to come here?'

'Thought I'd return Mr Bryant's bleeper,' she answered, pulling the bulky box from her sodden coat. 'He'd dropped it again.'

'Why on earth didn't you wait and give it to him another day?' demanded May, amazed. 'He never uses the bloody thing.'

'I had to return it immediately,' said Jerry. 'His apartment keys are taped to the back.'

May's mouth fell open.

'That's the point,' said Bryant, taking the bleeper and turning it over to reveal a pair of labeled Yale keys sellotaped in place. 'I thought I wouldn't lose it if I needed it to get into my apartment.'

'Do you mean to say that I owe my life to—to—'

'That's right,' said Jerry, pleased with herself. 'If it wasn't for your partner's annoying little habits, you'd have drowned.'

The patrol car sped on across the bridge, towards a lightening sky.

53 / Captain of Industry

For once, Charles Whitstable was at a loss for words. He was still wearing the previous day's clothes, and had not slept.

'We just want to know how you did it,' said May, hunching forward on his chair. The workmen had made a surprise return to Mornington Crescent, and there were tools all over the floor. There was also, inexplicably, a large hole in the ceiling.

'I'm not sure what you'll even be charged with,' added Bryant, 'but it'll certainly be as an accomplice to murder. Try to explain what happened. Then we'll decide what you need to put in your official statement.'

Charles lifted his head from his hands and attempted to smooth his hair back in place. 'All right,' he said, resigning himself to the first in a series of trials. 'When I went to Calcutta, I found the guild's group of companies still operating under archaic conditions. There had been no technological advances, no updating of the infrastructure. The offices were staffed by the grandsons of the original owners. Bureaucracy was rampant, even by Calcutta's standards. Nothing had changed from James Whitstable's time.

'Back in London, Peter and Bella were moaning about profits dropping. They were all complaining, even the damned lawyers, and no one had the balls to come and sort out the mess. Everything was left to me. I soon noticed that certain "obligations" transmitted from London were being honoured by staff members. Every once in a while, someone would disappear for a few days on "company business," financed by money orders transferred through the lawyers' office in Norwich. That staff member would then reappear and continue working without a word of what had transpired. Apparently, this had been going on for years.

'I noticed a pattern in the type of people chosen for this clandestine work. They were always the sons and grandsons of men who had been granted a great favour by the guild at some point in the past.'

'What sort of favour?'

'The usual sort of thing—a cash advance for a newly-wed, an executive post for a son—a favour that demanded repayment at some unspecified point in the future,' explained Charles. 'Employees of even the most distant branches of the Watchmakers could, in extreme circumstances, be granted special deals in the form of large low-interest loans. In return, a brown-paper package was delivered to the home of the borrower, to be kept within the family and opened at a time specified by the company.

'When the time came, instructions were to be carried through to the last letter. The debt was canceled once the rival was out of action. There could be no defaulting on repayment. At least, that was how the system had worked in the past. I arrived to find dissent. People had begun to refuse to honour these "obligations." They'd been held to promises by their fathers, their grandfathers, but couldn't see why they should perform favours for the English any more. Victoria's reign might have gone, but it was a damned long time dying. Our employees had been kept in place with threats and superstitions, but they no longer feared the power of the alliance. India now had its independence, after all.'

Charles Whitstable looked as embarrassed as a captain of industry could ever be seen to be. 'Well, I couldn't completely abolish the system. But the Calcutta police were becoming suspicious. I had to take control. I had the family's best interests at heart. The machine provided the competitors of those marked for removal because it was regularly updated in London by Tomlins. I had no idea that the system had begun to backfire, or that it would kill my own family. James Makepeace Whitstable used everyone—his craftsmen, his lawyers, the heirs of his most loyal members of staff. That was the simple beauty of his scheme. All the dirty work was done overseas, thereby keeping his own hands clean. James never dreamed that one day it would all come home.'

'That was why the assassins used such old-fashioned methods of execution,' May realized. 'They were working to a tried and trusted formula. When Max Jacob's killer used cottonmouth snake venom, it was probably the closest he could get to a native Indian reptile.'

'What an apt Victorian process,' snorted Bryant. 'Butcher your rivals, dupe the locals, and improve your own fortune. If anyone gets caught it's only an invisible foreigner, a third-class citizen, and who'll believe him against the word of a white man? So men like poor Denjhi had their lives destroyed by the debts of their forefathers. His conscience prevented him from killing Daisy Whitstable, so he was used again. But he beat the system a second time. Instead of lethally poisoning Peggy Harmsworth, he diluted the concoction, hoping to spare her life without failing to honour his debt.' Bryant rose and refastened his shapeless brown cardigan. 'You have the deaths of your own family on your conscience. It'll be interesting to see if we can make you pay in the court-room.'

54 / Mother & Daughter Revisited

Gwen Gates stared at the glowing end of her cigarette and smiled ruefully. The room was flooded in cold sunshine as panels of light reflected from the wet pavements outside. She wore no makeup and was wrapped in a heavy white towelling robe. Jerry had rarely seen her mother like this, in what Gwen would regard as an unfinished state.

The hour was still early. Jack had gone to thrash a ball about at the Highgate Golf Club. Gwen had heard Jerry moving about and had come down, almost as if she had sensed something was different about today. She looked up at her daughter now, and for a moment Jerry felt a flicker of sympathy. It had been a shock to discover that Gwen's desire to improve her social standing had outweighed her love for her only daughter, but it was as if something Jerry had always suspected had now proved to be true.

The knowledge produced little satisfaction, only the bitter taste of betrayal. Her love had been weighed as a commodity, quantified and traded off for something more rewarding. And yet, there was still the faintest trace of a bond between them.

'If it's any consolation, I'm ashamed for not speaking

up and stopping you going back to Charles Whitstable's house.'

'You just wanted me to work for him and be accepted by the Whitstable family,' Jerry replied, folding the flap of the nylon backpack over and clipping it shut. 'You'd convinced yourself I wouldn't remember what had happened. Even if I'd taken up Charles's offer, he would never have given you the things you wanted. If and when he gets out of jail, that's assuming he even goes, he'll carry on with his business quite happily without me or you. All of them will. The Whitstables will carry on long after all the press and television coverage, after all the scandals and investigations. The Whitstables don't need anyone else. Poor Gwen, let down by yet another man. First Jack, then Charles Whitstable.'

'You're a very cruel girl.'

'I'm not a girl any more, Mother. You must have been able to see that nothing would ever change for us. What were you hoping for? Did you think you would get Jack's respect back? That's long gone. What do you want any more privileges for, anyway? It's not as if they would have made us different people.' She checked the spines of a few paperbacks and added them to the bag. There were some books she had to take with her wherever she went.

'I thought it would be nice if you could marry well.' Gwen's voice was soft and tired.

'If I really wanted what the upper classes have, I'd have to be as dishonest as them.'

'I never meant to be dishonest with you, Jerry.' Gwen seemed to find the taste of the cigarette disagreeable, and ground it out. 'I simply wasn't honest with myself. You have no idea what it was like being so close to them, and so far away. To tiptoe around the edges of their lives, always within sight of something better. I wanted to have what they had, for you as well as me. It didn't seem fair.'

'Well, it's not what I want.' Jerry picked up the bag and walked to the door. 'That's why I have to go. I want to make my own changes. You're right, the Whitstables aren't fair. They keep what's theirs by building barriers. The whole rotten country's founded on them. It's a nation of boxes and walls. Mostly walls.'

'You're being naive if you think you can change anything. Nothing changed for me.' Concern shadowed Gwen's face. For whom, Jerry couldn't tell. 'You have no idea of the things that went on.'

'Perhaps not,' said Jerry. 'You never talked about—'

'What could I have said? How could I have described the contemptuous looks on those damned faces?' She checked herself. 'Half the family hasn't talked to me for years. Oh, they'll give cold smiles when you're around, and cut me dead behind your back. All the clever little cruelties, the endless subtle indignities. Because of you, and the way you behaved. The trouble you caused.'

'I'm sorry, Gwen. I didn't know.'

'Well,' she said bitterly, 'there's a lot you still don't know. People are monstrous. When you're protected by money, there are a thousand ways to hurt someone.' She clearly had no intention of allowing her daughter to feel sorry for her, and changed the subject. 'What are your plans? Where are you going to go now?'

'I'm not sure. I'll try to find some places where there aren't so many restrictions.'

'That'll be a lot harder than you think. God, you've some learning to do.'

'Then I'll learn.'

Jerry's career at the Savoy had ended. She had been forced to give it up after realizing that it was Nicholas who had collected the photographs for Peter Whitstable. May had uncovered that particular detail during his interviews. The management had subsequently caught her slapping Nicholas around the face. The satisfaction of her stinging palm still stayed.

Her mother was pacing in front of the lounge door, as if frightened to see it opened. 'You barely know this boy Jacob.'

'His name's Joseph. He wants to travel for a while, and so do I.'

'You're not planning on getting married, are you?' Gwen asked cautiously.

'Of course not. It's the seventies. Nobody needs to get married any more. We're just friends.'

'Well, I don't suppose there's anything I can say that will make you change your mind.' Gwen searched for a fresh cigarette, something to occupy her hands.

Joseph Herrick had talked about touring Europe, and Jerry had jumped at the chance. His Christmas, unlike hers, had been a quiet one.

'Say good-bye to Dad for me. Don't let him worry.'

'I think he'll be rather pleased for you. Especially if he sees it as a defeat for me.'

'Oh, Mother. What are you going to do?'

Gwen glanced up at the clock. 'I'm supposed to be chairing one of my charities in an hour. I have a feeling it's arthritis.'

'Then you'd better get ready,' Jerry said, smiling.

Gwen lit her cigarette and looked out of the sun-smeared window. 'I don't know. I may go for a walk instead.'

'The park should be nice.'

'I was thinking more of Harrods.'

She turned back to Jerry, her eyes narrowing. 'Tell

me,' she asked, 'what's the point of having children if they only leave?'

'Because of the love,' Jerry replied. 'I always wanted to be able to love you.'

'Yes,' Gwen agreed, taking a step toward her, then thinking better of it. 'It may surprise you, Geraldine, but there is love.'

'I'll let you know where I am,' Jerry promised. As she looked back at her mother from the door, standing squarely in the centre of the hallway, her hands by her sides, her feet bare, she saw how fragile Gwen's life had been, and how much emptier it would be now.

'I'm going to come back,' she said.

'I'd like that very much, Jerry. I wish—'

'What?'

'I wish I could go away somewhere. Start learning again.' She gave a rueful half smile.

'You can learn right here,' Jerry said. 'You don't need to go anywhere.'

'That's simple for you to say. Everything's easy to the young.'

'At least you could try, Mother.'

'Mother.' Gwen turned the word over, as if hearing it for the first time and trying it for size. Finally, she raised the palm of her right hand in farewell, coolly watching as Jerry walked to the end of the road. But even as Jerry turned the corner, she knew that Gwen would be standing at the door long after she had passed from sight.

55 / Turning On the Lights

Tower Bridge was the gateway to London, the first bridge a ship encountered upon its passage into the Thames. Its Gothic turrets are merely stone clad over steel, and have guarded the river for barely a hundred years, yet it has become as definitive a representation of the city as the Tower of London itself. Below the bridge, smelt, dace, roach, and perch have been known to swim with flounders and elvers through the thick brackish water of the Thames. The riverbank here was once a thick slope of orange sand known as Tower Beach. From the 1930s to the 1950s, families swam and played on it as if day-tripping to the Brighton seashore.

On a Friday evening at the end of January, as a sulphurous sunset jaundiced the roof of the southern turret, two middle-aged gentlemen surveyed the river scene. Above them rose the tower's massive pressurized-water pistons. The bridge had recently been repainted a rich blue, the colour of a summer sky. It was deserted as the two men crossed it on the west side, their hands thrust deep into their pockets.

John May paused to lean on the wooden handrail and look down over the edge. Arthur Bryant had summoned up another vile scarf from his infinite collection of depressing knitwear and was even now peering over its folds like a perished frog. The top of May's head was still swathed in bandages, lending him an Oriental air.

'I don't know what the bare-breasted woman on roller skates was supposed to be doing,' he said, puzzled. 'And why on earth was she wearing a centurion's helmet?'

'That was Britannia,' Bryant explained. 'I told you, it was a very modern interpretation. Still, it was nice to see the Savoyards again.'

'Yes,' agreed May, 'they weren't bad for a group of people who are obviously deranged. I'm afraid it's not my cup of tea, all that theatrical stuff. It's just not real enough. Good tunes, though, I must say.'

The Savoy Theatre had finally reopened its doors to a brand-new production of *Patience*. Bryant had dragged along his reluctant partner on the first night that they had been provided with a corresponding respite from their duties.

'Actually, I think I might have dozed off in the second half,' May admitted.

'I know. I heard you. So did everybody else. You should have your sinuses seen to. Look, John.' He stopped in the centre of the bridge and looked back at St Paul's. 'It's nice to see that the cathedral still stands high above the other buildings.'

'That's just because they haven't given planning permission to build office blocks around it,' said May unsportingly.

'I love this skyline. It's less spectacular than other cities, but when I think of the men and women who fire-watched for the domes and spires through the war, the mere fact that it still survives at all amazes me.'

'You're a dreadful sentimentalist, Arthur. Look at the crumbling tower blocks and the empty docklands buildings.'

'I know they're there, and I can't do anything to change them. I suppose they'll all get pulled down and replaced.

Soon there will be nothing left of the city I played in as a kid.'

'Perhaps the next batch of politicians will improve our lot. I hear this Mrs Thatcher is a rising star. It would be good to have a woman prime minister. She'd be more inclined to kindness, one feels. She could end inequality in the city.' May withdrew a cigar and lit it. He was allowed one at the end of a case. 'You know what Tower Bridge reminds me of? The Shepherd's Market diamond robbery, our second case.'

'Good Lord, you're right,' exclaimed Bryant. 'Remember Sidney Dobson, the deaf explosives expert? The mastermind behind Mayfair's finest safecracking ring. His old dad ran the Smithfield black-market sausage syndicate during the war. To think that Sidney would have got away with the diamonds if he'd taken London Bridge instead of this one.'

'That's right. I almost felt sorry for him, stuck in a lorry full of pigs while they opened the bridge for a barge full of illegal bananas.'

'He was very decent about it. The last of the gentlemen crooks. Had a nasty three-legged cat called Wilfred. I visited him in prison, you know.'

'That was nice of you.'

'Not really,' conceded Bryant. 'His sister-in-law sold me a car with no brakes. I was trying to find out if he'd heard from her. Sidney told me she'd emigrated to New Zealand, but on the way back from the prison I passed her at a bus stop.'

'What happened?'

'Nothing. I couldn't slow the damn vehicle down. I think she heard me yelling. I suppose men like Sidney are into property scams now. That seems a rather sleazy, backdoor style of crime. The old ways felt more honest.'

'That's enough, Arthur,' said May, raising his hand. 'Looking back is morbid and unhealthy. I think I prefer you cantankerous. Anyway, there are all kinds of interesting crimes now.'

'Did I tell you? I got a postcard from Jerry Gates. She's on her way to India with some chap. She'd do well to stay away from the Calcutta offices of the Whitstables' shipping company. Mind you, there's no one left at the addresses Charles Whitstable gave us.'

'Raymond Land says he's going to refute the possibility of the entire case with tested scientific evidence.'

'We saw the device with our own eyes. How can they refute that?'

'There's no concrete proof left, Arthur. Even Land doesn't believe it, and he was there.'

A variety of lurid theories had allowed the tabloids to speculate in all kinds of colourful, alarming ways. Yet, despite this and other damning publicity resulting from the investigation, the fickle press had decided to champion the Peculiar Crimes Unit. After all, it had provided them with gruesome entertainment for weeks. Although the official hearing had yet to take place, there was now at least hope for the unit's future.

Charles Whitstable's fate still lay in the hands of the British magistrates' court. May had to admit that James Makepeace Whitstable's system was ingenious. It was impossible to estimate how many families had been bullied into accepting his sabotage orders. Many would still be keeping their secret packages for years to come—just in case the cycle renewed itself and the system returned one day.

The most capricious casualty of the investigation had passed from her life barely mourned. May had been one of the few people to attend the funeral of Alison Hatfield. He had forced himself to stop thinking of an alternative future where she was still alive. He knew that her memory would be better served by destroying every branch of the organization that had ultimately caused her death. Sadly, this would never be entirely possible. Too many companies carried the seal of government approval. They would continue to prosper, aided by powerful financial protection.

His thoughts were broken by the ghastly sound of Bryant chuckling to himself. 'What's so funny?' May asked, leaning back against the painted balustrade.

'I was just thinking about the Whitstables,' said Bryant, his breath clouding the air. 'How W.S. Gilbert would have loved to write about them.'

'Oh? Why?'

'He adored paradoxes. He lampooned every institution in the land by putting lawyers and ministers in topsy-turvy situations. Without realizing it, the Whitstables managed to create a paradox worthy of Gilbert himself. The astrolabe, you see.'

'Talk to me while we walk. My ears are getting brittle.'

'The astrolabe destroyed the children of the aristocrats who set it in motion. And its instruments of death were the poor, the very people the system was designed to keep out.' Bryant sighed and continued walking. 'Of course, the paradox still exists. We live in a land of upper and lower orders. For every man willing to help those less fortunate than himself, there are ten others ready to exploit him.' Bryant waved his moth-eaten gloves about. 'Thanks to families like the Whitstables, the circle may one day turn again from light to darkness.'

They were standing at the southern end of the bridge,

looking back along the river. Above the battered slate roof of Charing Cross station, the clouds shone with a soft citrine light.

'I don't think London will ever be completely dark again,' said May. 'Look.'

'It's rather a shame,' replied Bryant. 'What must it have been like in the world that existed before twenty-eight December, 1881? There once was such a thing as absolute darkness. And there was something else perhaps, a collective warmth, a hidden strength. Men and women bound together by superstition and folklore. Families were connected by myths and fantasies. I think something was lost the day they turned on the lights. Something indefinable and very important.'

'You find comfort in darkness. I prefer the world brightly lit; there's so much more to see.'

'That's why we complement each other.' Bryant looked down into the swirling brown waters, at clouds of mud blossoming in the wake of a passing tug. 'Look at the river. I miss her so much, John. Never a day goes by when I don't think of her.'

'All this time, you never mentioned Nathalie.' May had not thought of Bryant's radiant French fiancée in an age. He didn't like to recall how she had died so many years ago, slipping and drowning in the fast-flowing waters below them.

'I couldn't save her, so I must always remind myself of the service I owe others. Why else do you think we return daily to the bridges of London? She brings us here. I have to see her face.'

'Oh Arthur, what's done is done. We must acknowledge the past, but we have to keep moving on, for ever forward. There's no other way.'

'I know. Nothing reduces the power of those left behind. That's their legacy.'

Unsure how best to reply, May patted his friend on
the back and set him off in the direction of the city lights.
Their shadows lengthened across the opalescent pavement, where specks of flint danced like reflecting stars.

About the Author

CHRISTOPHER FOWLER is the acclaimed author of twelve previous novels, including the Bryant & May novels *Full Dark House* and *The Water Room*. He lives in London, where he is at work on his next novel featuring Arthur Bryant and John May, *Ten Second Staircase*. Visit him on the web at www.christopherfowler.co.uk.

"Invulnerable, genial, and crafty," raved the *Los Angeles Times* of the superb—and utterly unique—sleuthing duo of Bryant and May. Now the odd couple of London's Peculiar Crimes Unit return in a tantalizing new mystery guaranteed to keep you reading late into the night.

Read on for a special early look into Christopher Fowler's **Ten Second Staircase**, coming soon in hardcover from Bantam Books. And don't miss any of the Bryant and May mysteries—look for them at your favorite bookseller's!

Ten Second Staircase

A Bryant & May Mystery

CHRISTOPHER FOWLER

On sale Summer 2006

Ten Second Staircase
on sale Summer 2006

Small Provocations

I hope you're not going to be rude and upset everyone again.'

Detective Sergeant Janice Longbright examined her boss for signs of disarray. She scraped some egg from his creased green tie with a crimson nail, then grudgingly granted her approval.

Arthur Bryant took a deep breath and folded his notes back into his jacket. 'I see nothing wrong with speaking my mind. After all, it is a special occasion.' He fixed his DS with a beady, unforgiving eye. 'I rarely get invited to make speeches. People always think I'm going to be insulting. I've never upset anyone before.'

'Perhaps I could remind you of the Mayor's banquet at Mansion House? You told the assembly he had herpes.'

'I said he had a hairpiece. It was a misquote.'

'Well, just remember how overwrought you can get at these events. Did you remember to take your blue pills?' Longbright suspected he had forgotten them because the tablet box was still poking out of his top pocket. 'The doctor warned you it would be easy to muddle them up—'

'I don't need a nurse, thank you. I'll take them afterwards. I haven't quite drifted into senility yet.' Unlike most men, Bryant did not look smarter in a suit. His outfit was several decades out of date and too long in the leg.

His shirt collar was far wider than his neck, and the white nimbus of his hair floated up around his prominent ears as though he had been conducting experiments in electricity. Overall, he looked like a soon-to-be-pulped Tussaud's waxwork.

Peering out though a gap in the curtains at the sea of gold-trimmed navy blazers, Sergeant Longbright saw that the auditorium was now entirely filled with pupils. 'It's a very well-heeled audience, Arthur,' she reported back. 'Boys only, that can't be very healthy. All between the ages of fifteen and seventeen. I don't imagine they'll be much interested in crime prevention. You'll have to find a way of reaching them.'

'Teenagers are suspicious of anyone over twenty,' Bryant admitted, brushing tobacco strands from his lapel, 'so how will they feel about me? I thought there were going to be more adults here. Teenagers can smell lies, you know. Their warning flags unfurl at the slightest provocation. A hint of condescension and they bob up like meerkats. Contrary to popular belief, they're more naturally astute than so-called grown-ups. The whole of one's adult like is a gradual process of dulling the sense, Janice. Look how young we all were when we started at the PCU, little more than children ourselves. But we were firing on all synapses, awake to the world.'

Longbright brushed his shoulders with maternal propriety. 'Raymond Land says the sensitive are incapable of action. He reckons we need more thick-skinned recruits.'

'Which is why our acting chief would be better employed in parking control, or some public service which you could train a moderately attentive bottle-nosed dolphin to perform.' Bryant had little patience with those who frowned on his abstract methods. Critics offered him nothing. They made the most senior detective of

London's Peculiar Crimes Unit as irritable as a wasp in a bottle and as stubborn as a doorstop.

"The school magazine is out there waiting to take your picture. They've seen you on TV, don't forget. You're a bit of a celebrity these days. Show me how you look.' Longbright jerked his tie a little straighter and pulled his sleeves to length. 'Good enough, I suppose, I need photographic evidence of you in a suit, even though it's thirty years old. Make sure you stick to Raymond's brief and talk about the specifics of crime prevention. Don't forget the CAPO initiative—we have to reach them while they're in the highest risk category.' Seventeen-year-olds were more likely to become victims of street crime than any other population segment. Their complex pattern of allegiance to different urban tribes was more confusing than French court etiquette—territorial invasion, lack of respect, the wrong clothes, the wrong ethnicity, attitudes exaggerated by hormones, chemisty, geography and simple bad timing.

'My notes are a little more abstract than Raymond might wish,' Bryant warned.

Longbright threw him a hopeless look. 'I thought he vetted your script.'

'I meant to run it by him last night, but I'd promised to drive Alma to her sister's in Tooting. She fell off her doorstep while she was red-leading it, and needed a bread poultice for her knee.'

'Surely the head of the department ranks above your landlady.'

'Not in terms of intelligence, I assure you.'

'You should have shown Raymond what you're planning to say, Arthur. You know how concerned he is about the media attention we've been receiving.'

The PCU had recently been the subject of a television

documentary, and not all of the press articles following in its wake had been complimentary.

'I couldn't stick to Raymond's guidelines on the history of crime-fighting because I don't want to talk down to my audience. They're supposed to be smart kids, the top five percent of the education system. I don't want them to get fidgety.'

'Just fix them with the angry stare of yours. Go on—everyone's waiting for you.'

The elderly detective took an unsteady step forward, then balked. He could feel a cold wall of expectancy emanating from the crowded auditorium. The hum of audience conversation parried his determination, stranding him at the edge of the stage.

'What's the matter now?' demanded Longbright, exasperated.

'No one in our family was good with the young,' Bryant wavered. 'When I was little, my father tried to light a cigarette while holding me and a pint of bitter, and burned the top of my head. All of our childhood problems were sorted out with a clout round the ear. It's a wonder I can name the kings of England.'

'Don't view them as youngsters, Arthur, they're at the age when they think they know everything, so talk to them as if they do. The head teacher has already introduced you. They'll start slow handclapping if you don't get out there.' It occurred to her that because Bryant had attended a lowly state school in Whitechapel, he might actually be intimidated by appearing before an exclusive group of private pupils from upper-middle-class homes.

Bryant dragged out his dogeared notes and smoothed them nervously. 'I thought at least John could have been here to support me.'

'You know he had a hospital appointment, now stop

making a fuss.' She placed a broad hand in the small of his back and firmly propelled him onto the stage.

Bryant stepped unsteadily into the spotlight, encouraged by a line of welcoming teachers. Having recently achieved a level of public fame for his capture of the Water Room killer, he knew it was time for him to enjoy his moment of recognition, but today he felt exposed and vulnerable.

The detective wiped his watery blue eyes and surveyed the hall of pale varnished oak from the podium. Absurdly youthful faces lifted to study him, and he saw the great age gulf that lay between lectern and audience. How could he ever expect to reach them? He remembered the war; they would have trouble remembering the nineteen-eighties. The sea of blue and gold, the expensive haircuts, the low susurrus of well-educated voices, teachers standing at the end of every third row like benign prison guards. It was surprisingly intimidating.

Most of the students had broken off their conversation to acknowledge his arrival, but some were still chatting. He fired a rattling cough in the microphone, a magnified explosion that echoed into a squeal of feedback. Now they ceased talking and looked up in a single battalion, assessing him.

He could feel the surf of confidence radiating from these bored young men, and knew he would have to work for their attention. The boys of St Crispins were not here to offer him respect; he was in the employ, and they would choose to listen, or ignore him. For one terrifying second, the power of the young was made palpable. Bryant was an outsider, an interloper. He rustled his notes and began to speak.

'My name is Arthur Bryant,' he told them unsteadily, 'and together with my partner John May, I run a small detective division known as the Peculiar Crimes Units.' He settled his gaze in the centre of the audience, focussing on the most insolent and jaded faces. 'Time moves fast. When the unit was first founded, much detection work was still based on Victorian principles. Anything else was untried and experimental. We were one of several divisions created in a new spirit of innovation. Because we're mainly academics, we don't use traditional law enforcement methods. We are not a part of the Met; they are hard-working, sensible men and women who handle the daily fallout of poverty and hardship. The PCU doesn't deal with life's failures. The criminals we hunt have already proven successful.' His attention locked on a group of four boys who seemed on the verge of tuning out his lecture. He found himself departing from the script in order to speak directly to them. He raised his voice.

'Let's take an example. Say one of you lads in the middle there gets burgled at home. The police handle cases in order of priority, just like doctors. They send a beat constable or a mobile uniformed officer around to ask you for details of the break-in and a list of what's missing. They are not trained as investigative detectives, so you have to wait for a specialist to take fingerprints, which they'll try to match with those of a registered felon. If no one is discovered, your loss is merely noted and set against the chance of the future recovery of your goods— a possibility that shrinks with each passing hour. The system only works for its best exemplars. But at the Peculiar Crimes Unit, we adopt a radically different approach.' As he still seemed to have their attention, Bryant decided to forge ahead with his explication.

'We ask ourselves a fundamental question: What is a crime? How far does its moral dimension extend? Is it simply an act that works against the common good? If you are starving and steal from a rich man's larder, should you be punished less than if you were not hungry? All crime is driven by some kind of need. Once, those needs were simple—food, shelter, warmth, the basic assurances of survival. But as soon as our needs are taken care of, new crimes appear within society. As we become more sophisticated, so do the reasons for our misdeeds. Now that we are warm and fed, we covet something more complex: power. Spending power, power over others, the power to be noticed. And sometimes that power can be achieved by violating the accepted laws of the land. So criminal sophistication requires sophisticated methods of detection. That's where specialist units like the Peculiar Crimes Unit come in. Think of internet fraud, and you'll find it is being matched by equally subtle methods of detection that require as much knowledge as the criminal's. I'm sure you boys know far more about the internet than your parents, but does that place you at less of a risk?'

He's off to a decent start, thought Longbright from the wings. *A bit all over the place, but no doubt he'll draw it all together and make his point.*

'Fraud, robbery, assault and murder are all cause-and-effect crimes requiring carefully targeted treatment. But all modern lawlessness carries the seeds of a strange paradox within it, for just as ancient crimes appear in cunning new versions, other appear entirely unmotivated. One thinks of vandalism. Some will have you believe it was invented in the postwar period, but not so. Acts of vandalism have been recorded in every sophisticated civilization; the defacing of statues was quite common in ancient Rome. Now, though, we are reaching a new peak of motiveless transgression. Criminality has once more assumed the kind of dark edge that existed in London during the eighteenth century. London was always the home of mob rule. The public voiced their opinions about whether it was right for a man to hang just as much as the judge. The joyous assembly would jeer or cheer a prisoner's final speech at Tyburn's triple tree. They would choose to condemn a wrongdoer or venerate him. Pamphlets filled with prints and poems would be produced in a criminal's honour. He would achieve lasting fame as a noble champion, his exploits retold as brave deeds, and there was nothing that governments could do to prevent it. Criminals became celebrities because they were seen to be fighting the old order, kicking back at an oppressive system.' Bryant eyed his audience like a pirate frightening cabin boys with tales of dancing skeletons. 'Often, thieves' necks would fail to break when they were dropped from the Tyburn gallows, and the crowd would cut down a half-hanged man to set him free, because they felt he had paid for his crimes. They rioted against the practice of passing bodies over to the anatomists, and pelted bungling hangmen with bricks. If a murderer conducted himself nobly as he ascended the gallows stairs, he would become more respected than his accusers. But time has robbed us of these gracious renegades. Last week, less than a quarter of a mile from here, in Smithfield, a schoolboy was stabbed through the heart for his mobile phone. An elderly man on a tube platform in Holborn was kicked to death for bumping into someone. These criminals are not to be venerated.'

A murmur of recollection rippled through the auditorium.

'Statistics show that the nature of English crime is reverting to its oldest habits. In a country where so many desire status and wealth, petty annoyances can spark disproportionately violent behaviour. We become frustrated because we feel powerless, invisible, unheard. We crave celebrity, but that's not easy to come by, so we settle for notoriety. Envy and bitterness drive a new breed of law-breakers, replacing the old motives of poverty and the need for escape. But how do you solve crimes which no longer have traditional motives?'

He's warming the audience up nicely, and he's still got their attention, decided Longbright, feeling for a chair at the side of the stage. *Let's hope he remembers to talk about Raymond's initiatives and can get all the way through without saying anything offensive.* She knew how volatile her boss could be, but now was the time for Bryant to exercise restraint. For once, the fortunes of the Peculiar Crimes Unit were on the rise. Indeed, they had been ever since a remarkable murder in a quiet North London street had placed them all in the public eye. Arthur's partner, John May, had appeared on a late-night programme discussing the importance of the case with several bad-tempered social commentators, a number of articles in *The Guardian* and *The Times* had examined the case in detail, government funding for the coming year had miraculously appeared, and mercifully no one outside the unit knew the reality of the case's conclusion; if they did, Longbright doubted that any of them would have survived with their careers intact. Arthur Bryant's decision to break the law in order to close the investigation had been so contentious that Longbright had turned down the BBC's offer to feature her in their film, in case she accidentally let slip the truth.

Basking in the glow of the publicity, Bryant had been asked to deliver a lecture to St. Crispin's Boys School, the exclusive private academy founded by a devout Christian group in 1653 in St John Street, Clerkenwell, and had shyly accepted.

Longbright turned her attention back to the stage.

'What we have here is a fundamental alteration in the definition of morality,' Bryant argued. 'What does it now mean to have a moral conscience? Do we need to develop different values from those of our parents? Most of you think you can distinguish right from wrong, but morality requires information to feed it, so you build your own internal moral system from the intelligence you receive, probably the hardest thing anyone ever has to do, judging by the number of times the system fails.

'In London's rural suburbs, not far from here, middle-class Thames Valley towns like Weybridge and Henley are awash with a new kind of malicious cruelty. Here the system appears to be failing. The criminals are not suffering inner-city deprivation, nor are they gang members protecting their turf through internecine wars based on divisions in ethnicity. They are wealthy white males facing futures filled with opportunities. So why are they turning to unprovoked violence and murder? Part of a generation has somehow become unmoored from its foundations, and no one knows how to draw it back from the harmful shallows. You all face complex pressures, problems that gentlemen of my advanced age are scarcely able to imagine. From the day you were born, someone has been targetting you as a potential market. Your attention has become fragmented. You are offered no solitude, no peace, no time for reflection. You are forced to create your own methods of escape. Some choose alcohol and narcotics, other form social cliques that combat the status quo. All of you in this hall are in danger. Many people of my age would suggest that you desire to break the law not because you've had a hard time growing up, but because you haven't. You've been spoiled with everything you ever wanted, but you still want more.'

He's forgotten the script, Longbright worried, *and he's stabbing his finger at them. At this rate he'll have them throwing things at him.* Some of the pupils were fidgeting in annoyance. They were clearly uncomfortable with the hectoring tenor of Bryant's sermon. The old detective hadn't given a lecture in years, and had forgotten the importance of keeping the audience on his side. *Keep it light in tone but heavy on factual data,* Land had warned, *be positive but don't say anything controversial. Remember, their parents are fee-paying voters with a lot of clout.*

Bryant's raised voice brought her back to attention. 'Well, I don't believe that,' he was saying. 'Children today have a far more complicated time growing up that I ever did. At the Peculiar Crimes Unit, we have the time and capability to see beyond stock answers and standard procedures. We claw our way to the roots of the crime, and by understanding its cause, we hope to provide solutions.'

As the audience half-heartedly pattered their hands, Longbright rose and made her way from the stage, back to the stand at the rear of the hall, where she accepted a polystyrene cop of coffee. Only the question-and-answer session was left now. Longbright had tried to talk her superior out of holding one, bearing in mind his capacity for argument, but half a dozen teenagers had already raised their hands. There was a palpable attitude of aggression and defiance in the pupils' body language.

'You say it's a question of morals,' said a pale, elongated boy with expensively layered blonde hair.

'Stand up and give your surname,' barked the teacher at the end of the row.

The boy unfolded himself from his seat with difficulty and faced the audience. 'Sorry, Sir. Gosling.' He turned to Bryant. 'Are you saying we're the ones who commit crimes because we lack a moral code?'

'Of course not,' Bryant replied. 'I'm just saying that it's understandable you're confused. You know that sneakers are made in Korea for starvation wages, so you buy a pair from a company promising to make their product locally for a fair price. They you discover that the company you chose destroyed ancient farmland to build their factory. How do you feel about your purchase now? You've been lied to, so why shouldn't you commit a victimless crime and steal them? You're given horrible role models, your divorced parents are having sex with people you hate and have given up caring what you do, you're expected to take an interest in the lifestyles of singers who'll make more money than you will ever see, so its no wonder you start taking drugs and behaving like animals.'

The hall erupted. Longbright covered her face with her hands. Bryant had never been much of a diplomat.

A small lad with a pustular complexion rose sharply. 'Parfitt. You just don't like the fact that we're young, and still have a chance to change the world your contemporaries wrecked for us.'

A heavyset boy with shiny red cheeks, cropped black hair and bat ears jumped angrily to attention. 'That's right, we're the ones—'

'Surname!' barked his master, leaning angrily forward.

'Jezzard—you always blame the young, but we're the ones who'll have to correct the mistakes of the older generation.'

'My dear boy, don't you see that you no longer possess the means for changing the world?' replied Bryant, adopting a tone of infuriating airiness. 'You've been disempowered, old chap. It's all over. The things you desire have become entirely unattainable, and you take revenge for that by being furious with your seniors all the time.'

Another boy, slender and dark, with feral eyes and narrow teeth, launched to his feet. 'You're accusing us when you know nothing about us, Mr Bryant—nothing!'

'*Name!*' squealed the teacher on the row.

'Billings. It's not us who's the problem, it's you. Everyone knows the police are corrupt racists—'

Now several more pupils stood up together, all speaking at once. Their teachers continued to demand that they identify themselves, but were ignored. Sides were swiftly being taken. Bryant had managed to divide the hall into factions. He threw up his hands in protest as the pupils barracked him.

'You condescend to us because you don't have a clue—'

'You victimize those who can't protect themselves—'

'Why is it that young people never want to take responsibility for their actions?' protested Bryant, as students popped up from their chairs in every section of the hall.

'Just because you messed up your own society—'

'Why should we be blamed for your greed when—'

'We're just starting out,' shouted Parfitt, 'and you're trying to make us sound as cynical as you!'

'I am not cynical, I simply know better,' Bryant insisted, trying to be heard, 'and I can tell from experience exactly how many of you will fall by the wayside and die before you progress to adulthood, because the cyclical nature of your short lives is as immutable as that of a dragonfly.'

There were so many things wrong with this last sentence that the Detective Sergeant could not bear to reflect on it, and could only watch the response helplessly. The lanky boy, Gosling, was the first to kick back his chair and leave. His friends swiftly followed suit. The distant authority of the teachers collapsed into panicked attempts at censorship as chairs fell across the centre of the audience, causing a clangorous ripple that quickly spread throughout the hall.

Longbright had been worried that Raymond Land might get to hear of the debacle. Now she was more concerned about getting Bryant out alive.